Stitches

"Stop it," she hissed. Her lips disappeared and her eyes became slits. She waited a beat. "Just stop it. I am sick of you putting yourself in second place. Stop being a wallflower and the perfect woman your mother raised you to be. That model went out the window in the '60s. Gloria Steinhem saw to that." She picked up the magazine and showed it to me, the picture of Arthur and me in this very room, then threw it hard back on the table. "This is not your life anymore." The sound penetrated my ears like a slap.

I had never been the recipient of her well-reported and well-deserved tirades, reflected in the media to great reviews. As the mayor of San Diego, Renee Murphy said what she needed to say, but only when it mattered.

"Look." Renee took another deep breath, pressed her lips together, placed her hands on her hips and cocked her head. "Arthur was a nice guy. He was wonderful and you had a good life. I get that. But you walked two paces behind him, and everything you did you did for him and his career. That was your job. I get that, too. But that's over now, and everything you've done and all the connections you have through that experience put you in a position to take the reins and do something really positive. Make something of it."

Who was I, if not Arthur's wife?

$$\times \quad \times \quad \times$$

HERITAGE
ART PARK SERIES

BOOK 1

Stitches

A NOVEL

KATHY WEYER

Chapter One

F I HAD A FAIRY GODMOTHER, I WOULD CLAP MY HANDS THREE TIMES AND ask to get back to my normal life of volunteering, gossipy lunches, philanthropic committee meetings, social events, and even something as mundane as nightly drinks before dinner while I worked on a piece of needlework and chatted with my husband and best friend, Arthur Francis Conrad.

He is no longer.

These days my new bestie was a certain Grey Goose I kept in the freezer. I wandered the halls of my perfect, designer *Architectural Digest*-photographed house. My slippers scuffed the thick carpet while I cradled a cold glass across my chest, moving through the house as though I were a sickly ghost. I stood in the quiet rooms as memories flooded back. I felt his presence, smelled him, heard him, loved him. One by one, I shut each door, as though closing off parts of myself.

I knew I should be productive and strong. See people. Raise money. Make the day count. Do something. But I couldn't.

My anchor was gone.

$$\times \quad \times \quad \times$$

Two weeks after the funeral, Mother's silver Lexus glided up the curved drive and beeped politely—two short riffs that made my back sprout an iron rod. Shoulders back, tits out, chin up. Pavlov would be proud.

Our (my) housekeeper Choyou slipped through the swinging door from the kitchen, hands wrung in front of her, a towel looped through the apron strings around her waist. Her silver-streaked long dark hair sprouted around her face; her eyes began to stream as she gave a firm nod at the door. She had joined us shortly after we were married, long enough to know my frailties.

This was my first public outing. Maybe that accounted for the nerves, or maybe it was the prospect of being cooped up with my mother for an hour in the car.

I pulled a wide-brimmed hat over my untidy, undone hair and dragged myself out the front door. My bones actually ached.

"Jennifer, where are the pearls?" Mother asked as I plopped with a severe lack of grace onto the cool leather seat. At the last word, puhls, she dropped her voice an octave, a sure sign she was annoyed.

"Oh," I put my hands up to my neck. "I must have forgotten them."

"They go perfectly with that gray dress. It's why I bought them, so you could look presentable. And you have no earrings." Again with the dropped octave, reminding me of when I brought home that C in algebra.

If I had a heart, it would have dropped.

Don't I get points for taking a shower?

My eyes stung—again. She slipped the gearshift with a soft whoosh. I pulled the Jackie-O sunglasses from my purse and slid them on. "I know." My voice came out a whisper. I cleared my throat.

"Speak up, dear. You must present yourself well, especially now. It would be helpful if you made an effort." She wiggled in her seat as though attempting to get a better grip.

"I'm sorry. I'm just so damn tired."

"Jennifer, this event is important. Buck up." We started to glide down the curved driveway. The new car smell, soft chamber music whispering out of the top-of-the-line speakers, and the unmistakable scent of my mother, a sickly-sweet rose scent, custom made for her by her own *parfumier* in Paris, wrapped me in an unwelcome world. I noted with particular distaste the bejeweled Christmas tree pin she sported on her red and green tartan jacket.

Ugh.

Patricia Buford Palmer was a fixture in this town: an eighty-five-year-old woman that could easily have been mistaken to have come directly from Park Avenue, an impression she never bothered to correct, but in reality hailed from the hills of Tennessee. Tall, impeccably dressed, white hair fashioned into a wavy halo around her tan face, posture-perfect and extremely formal, she was a woman of perfection, and tended to know that she was right and everyone else was, well, wrong. No one could possibly reach her high standards. God knows I tried, and so did my sister Maggie, but I fear Maggie has been more successful than I.

Valiantly, I thought, I attempted to engage: "I remember talking about this project when it first came up, back when life felt normal, like . . . a century ago."

"Don't say, 'like' dear, it is common. Now." She shifted her tall taut frame in her seat as she prepared to enter the freeway. Her voice grated on my last nerve. Every letter was sounded quietly and perfectly; her enunciation, an affect she grew into while ridding herself of the accent from Signal Hill was exceptionally clear, as though she were speaking with a child in a high pitch that sometimes cracked. "You haven't been out in quite a long time. People are going to be uncomfortable. Just be your normal gracious self and you will be fine."

Fifty-eight years old and she's still telling me what to do. My best friend and pseudo-sister Renee Murphy and I dubbed her Mother Superior years ago.

I girded myself to face the world.

We entered Historic Park, a community of six Victorian houses among what felt like acres of pristine lawns and landscaping. I hadn't been to this historical area for years. I concentrated on keeping my head down and my ankles steady as we walked toward the crowd gathered in the tent. This was Renee's day.

A weak sun tried to do its duty, obliterated by puffy clouds that floated by as though they too didn't want to be a part of this day. A slight breeze waffled the large canvas tent roof that sounded like the thwap of sails in the wind.

We, the cream of the crop, the best of the best, the exclusive club of high-minded philanthropic do-gooders (and I had been one of them) gathered on the manicured lawn of the historical site that had recently been used as bed and breakfast businesses, but now were being turned into studios and shops for local artists. My Ferragamos sunk into the soft grass and I wondered why I hadn't been smart enough to wear more sensible shoes.

Thwap, thwap . . .

I am flawed. Badly. How the hell did I get here? I don't belong with these well-heeled, perfect people, but have been among them for years.

Renee Murphy, the honorable mayor of San Diego and my best friend, appeared at my side within five minutes, wearing a Christmas green pantsuit in homage to the holidays. She put an arm around my shoulders and said, "You look good. Strong." I wanted to warn her about my shoulder blade: it felt as sharp and as big as an ax, as though it might cut her if she got too close. Everything about my body felt dry and angular; my bones might snap with a soft gust of wind.

"I don't feel it. Mother Superior is driving me nuts."

Renee snorted and leaned in. "So, what else is new? Listen. We talked about this and I need you to lead the charge. You can find an artist to sponsor and get him or her going in one of the houses. Or take one yourself. But I need your help." She stopped and looked over my shoulder. "By the time the project is ready, you will be, too." She waved to someone behind me while still talking. Renee had no time for niceties. She jumped in and said whatever tickled her mind. I loved her for that. But not today.

"I'll think about it."

Her eyes came back to me. "You did promise once upon a time, but don't feel any pressure from *me*. Can you meet me here tomorrow afternoon? You should tour the houses."

"Yes, but don't try to trick me into anything. I'm not up for a challenge right now."

"Who, me?" She crossed her eyes for a second and grinned, then put on her mayoral face, much as she did in school, the class clown straightening up when the teacher had had enough.

"Mrs. Anderson. So nice to see you," she said, addressing a woman behind me. I pulled my heels from the grass and pivoted to see the legendary socialite, looking every inch the Dowager Duchess in a lavender dress that whipped softly at her thin legs in the breeze. She carried a beautiful dark wooden cane topped with a silver fox. A large amethyst brooch clutched her collar. Snow-white hair scattered around her face in wispy tendrils that had escaped from a bun at the top of her head. Her pale skin, the color of an antique ivory cameo, folded inward along dimple lines and left soft divots where laugh lines once were. She smiled, which, despite myself, made my day just a bit brighter. Iris was, truth be told, someone you just couldn't dislike. She had no detractors, and therefore was on Mother's acceptable list. Few were.

"Your Honor," Iris said as she took Renee's hand and bowed slightly. Renee laughed.

"Iris, you are something else."

Iris winked at Renee, leaned toward me on her cane with both hands and said, "My dear, I am so pleased to see you," in a voice that spoke volumes about her upbringing: a hint of east coast proper, a drop of southern drawl. She put her blue-veined, cool hand over mine. The large amethyst on her ring finger fell to the side by sheer weight. "You have been missed." My eyes began to burn again. I became a bobble head.

Fuck.

Renee nodded to someone on her left. "Showtime," she sung. "Excuse me." She nodded to Iris and said, "Madam," with a grin. We watched as she plodded across the lawn, arms flailing like oars to push her forward. I turned to Iris just as someone blew into the microphone and asked us to come forward.

As the others passed us heading toward the makeshift stage, Iris leaned toward me. "You know," she said. "I was very fond of your husband. We worked together on a few issues and I found him very likable. More importantly, though," she leaned in toward me, and touched my hand, "he found *you* very likable. He spoke of you in loving terms. You are a lucky girl." She pulled back and nodded to me. I saw a twinkle in her blue eyes as we connected. Before I could respond, a young woman I had not seen before came to escort her to a seat near the riser. She was weird looking, with green hair and tattoos, and a piercing through her eyebrow.

I kept sinking into the soft green grass.

About fifty invitees, hand-picked to help spread the word, get involved and make this thing happen, gathered around the makeshift stage to hear Renee as she described the project.

Renee explained each house would be dedicated to a specific art by experienced artisans: painting, jewelry making, pottery, watercolor, blown glass; the list of possibilities was endless. The artisans would not only be producing and selling their art on the premises but would teach as well; a true art community for new creatives to learn from the experienced.

I watched from the back of the tent as the attendees exchanged glances, elbowed each other and grinned, agreeing that this was, in fact, a worthwhile project in which to invest their money and their valuable time.

I stood alone; a good girl listening to a catechism lecture. I quit smoking cigarettes twenty years ago, but I wanted one badly now.

Don't do it. You'll get cancer. Arthur's voice rang in my ear.

Dear God. When Arthur lost the ability to speak, I naively, perhaps romantically, thought we began to communicate telepathically. When he was alive I'd answer him out loud, but now I questioned my mental health. I ignored the voice and started to pay attention, to be "in the moment" as my former yoga instructor taught me. With great effort I concentrated on the people around me.

"Hello, Jen, how are you?" This from a woman in my old exercise class I hardly knew.

"We will miss him." A tall man wearing a bow tie and tortoise shell glasses. I did not recognize him right away but knew I should have.

"He was a great guy." From a total stranger.

"What are your plans now?"

"I am so sorry for your loss."

"How are you coping?"

"What are you doing here? Isn't it a little soon?" My sister Maggie slithered to my side. Her perfectly formed and waxed eyebrows relayed deep concern, but I knew the face and the words, perfectly in keeping with social concern, was in reality a secret slap for not following proper mourning etiquette. Before I could respond with some degree of snark, Renee appeared like an angel and spirited her away before I burst into tears.

Enough already. I can't keep having the same conversations with people I hardly recognize. All our good friends had been by and done things to help me through the process, but now that it was over I had hardly heard from any of them. These people were strangers. I had already had this conversation hundreds of times, draining me of all goodwill and diluting the message. They were all the same. I knew emotionally there was nothing they could say, and appreciated the effort, but still. They all repeated how much he will be missed. It was always about Arthur. I was just the plus-one.

Without him, I am nothing.

A horrible woman with gray hair who wore sensible oxford shoes and a prim lace-collared dress invaded my space. She spoke in a heavy New England accent about something unintelligible while she spat little pieces of lemon cake in my direction and poked me in the shoulder. I focused on the one coarse dark hair that jumped on her left upper lip as she spoke. It seemed to have its own tiny little muscle. I heard her voice and appreciated the effort, but I just didn't connect. I wondered why, in my somewhat delirious state, the woman couldn't fork over twenty bucks to have that thing yanked out.

Maybe this was a bad idea.

The rising volume of voices under the tent overwhelmed me, and I wanted to put my hands over my ears like a child having a tantrum.

Thwap thwap.

My little world was closing in on me. I saw Mother speak with someone and point her chin to me (*never point your finger when a perfectly good chin will do*), which made my stomach turn over. The sounds uttered by all these

7

people talking and nobody listening made me want to scream, if only to shut them up. I heard snippets of disjointed words that didn't string together properly. I grew more anxious as my own heartbeat raced in my ears, and nothing made sense. I had to escape, or I would go mad.

"You look like you're about to jump out of your skin." Renee's familiar voice came from behind me and brought me out of myself and my ungracious, ungrateful thoughts. She looked at the calendar on her phone. "Meet me here tomorrow at three. We'll go through the houses and maybe I can get you to pick one to fund for an artist." I nodded and she plugged it into the highly scheduled calendar on her phone.

The odor of sweet roses reached me even before her voice did. "Stand up straight, dear, and smile pleasantly. People are watching." She spoke quietly and through her almost-closed teeth. By sheer training my body reacted: back straight, shoulders back, chin up. Renee rolled her eyes, touched Mother's forearm, and left.

"Our presence is no longer required. It is time to go." The order was in.

We said our good-byes. Or, rather, Mother said our good-byes and I nodded mutely like an adolescent with acne and a stammer, my heels stuck to the soft earth.

We slid into her car and headed north. The tangerine, purple and golden sunset radiated over the Pacific Ocean on our left as we headed toward Rancho Santa Fe and my large, lonely, perfect, Arthur-less house.

"You are heading the fundraising committee for the art park," she announced. No niceties led up to the announcement—not unusual between us. Short and to the point. That explains the conversation and pointing in my direction. I had been volunteered.

"Me? Why?"

She smacked her lips, another signal something irked her. I had seen it throughout my entire life; it made me itchy, and I wondered what I had done this time. "Because you need to get back into the world, and if I don't push you, you never will. You'll simply waste away in self-pity all alone in that house." I knew Mother didn't approve of our house. She thought it *déclassé*, a sign of conspicuous consumption, the nouveau riche.

One does not show off.

But was she right? Would I just fade away like an old Hollywood star?

She pulled up the driveway. "And don't forget to visit your father, especially if you're not going to church."

"Yes, ma'am." I crawled out of the car and into my bleak house.

With nothing better to do, I took my new bestie and a cut crystal glass with me to bed and proceeded to lose the next two days from my life.

Chapter Two

RENEE'S PERSONAL CELL RANG. SHE RUSHED TO FIND IT AT THE BOTTOM of her bag and smiled when she saw the chief of police calling. If it had been about business, he would have used the city phone.

"Hi," a deep, husky masculine voice came over the phone.

"Hi, yourself." Renee smiled into the phone.

"What's new in your world?"

Might as well tell him. "I'm worried about a friend, Jen Conrad. She was supposed to meet me today and never showed. Her housekeeper tells me she's home, so she's not dead."

"Tell me about her. I knew Arthur and have met her, but don't know much about her." She could hear him settling in and heard him take a swig of the bottle of Heineken she knew he held in his hand. She could visualize him in his uniform sitting back, relaxing after a full day, his silver hair and mustache, his tan face, and his perfectly trim and muscled arms. It sent a thrill down her back. Then she frowned. Ron was the chief of police, and he worked for her. They were friends. Keep it business.

"Jen? She's an angel. We grew up together, me from the wrong side of the tracks and she with the proverbial silver spoon. Raised to be the perfect debutante, which she didn't do, and marry well, which she did. If I didn't know her as well as I do, I'd swear she was one of those socialite models. She does everything perfectly. Her husband Arthur? About to run for D.A., and she had put everything in place to support that. She ruled on every major board and committee in this town and led the group of philanthropist wives who, frankly, only participated to be seen. Her sister is one of those. Maggie Putnam is as mean as they come, dressed up as Pollyanna. Jen has had a difficult time with her family. Mom is Patricia Palmer."

"*The* Patricia Palmer?"

"The one and only. Can you imagine being her child? But Jen keeps the peace at all costs. She doesn't participate in the cattiness that is the social circle she runs around in. She takes it all in but doesn't give any shit back. I've never seen her lose control, which makes me crazy. She just recently became a widow and I think is beginning to realize she's been spoiled rotten. She's never had to work a day in her life and has been supported first by her parents and then by Arthur. She's now alone and I think is feeling a little useless."

"Are you jealous?"

Renee, caught off guard, chuckled a bit. "Sometimes, to be honest. I've had to hardscrabble it for years alone. I've clawed my way up the road and left a few bodies by the wayside. She has no idea what that is. On the other hand, I don't know what a personal life is. Never had one."

Silence.

"Speaking of which, I'm thinking of resigning."

Renee remained silent.

"You there?" His voice lowered an octave.

"Yes. Really? Why?"

"Because I'm tired. Because it's time. Because these new bucks coming up are too hard to handle. They're so entitled and don't know what it is to be a peace officer; they've watched too much TV and become disillusioned with paperwork and regulations."

"Oh."

She could hear him smile into the phone.

"And because I want a personal life."

Renee gripped the phone tighter. "Really."

"Really."

Silence. "What do you think?" He said after a quiet moment.

Renee took in a deep breath and went for broke. "I think it's one of the best ideas I've heard in a long time."

"Then you'll have my resignation shortly."

"Oh. OK."

Renee hung up, went into her bedroom and changed into sweats and running shoes and dashed out the door for a jog.

She hadn't run in years, but she smiled through her pain.

Harry's Bar was a mainstay for downtown professionals; a watering hole to see and be seen. The staff knew their clientele and treated them well. Harking back to the glam of the fifties, the decor hadn't changed much; red leather booths, massive oak bar, starched waiters, and the odor of brandy and good cigars had melded into the furnishings over the years. It's the place where deals were made over a handshake and a Bourbon & Branch, a promotion celebrated, rivals talked, and announcements made. Spouses often invaded Harry's before going to the theater.

Maggie Putnam pulled out her cell, cleared her throat and dialed. Her voice lowered, she cooed into the phone. "I'm at Harry's, if you can get away, why don't you join me for a drink? I want to see you."

A hesitation. "I don't think that's such a good idea."

"I've been thinking about you. Please? For old time's sake?"

"All right, but just for a drink. I'm not messing things up again."

"Wonderful," she closed the phone and ordered another martini.

Ten minutes later, a small, trim, middle-aged man with receding hair sat across from her and signaled to the bar he wanted what she was having. The CFO of Conrad and Putnam Law Firm sat across from Maggie and waited.

"I understand there's an audit coming up to award Arthur's wife with whatever she's due from the firm. I doubt she's aware of it, so there's no hurry to expedite the process, but I want you to make sure the audit takes a long time, and then when it is finally finished, I want you to delay the funding as long as you can." Maggie lifted her glass and took a small sip, which left an imprint of her perfect lips on the clear glass.

"Why would I do that?"

"Need to know basis, James, need to know basis."

"Maggie, I can't do that. I'd lose my job." He ran his fingers around his collar and nodded to the waiter as his drink appeared on the charger plate in front of him.

"You'll lose your marriage and your job if you don't." Maggie pierced the olive in her glass and popped it in her mouth.

"And how is that?" Beads of sweat appeared on his forehead.

"Remember that little rendezvous we had at the Hotel Del last year?"

"A big mistake, we both agreed."

"Not really," Maggie laughed, and handed over a flash drive. "On this is a recording of every second of that afternoon, including some comments about your wife that she may not appreciate. It goes to her if you don't follow my instructions to the letter." She popped another olive. "And . . . I will see to it you lose your job."

"My God. You'd really do that to me?" His face softened. A smarmy grin spread across his face. "No, you won't. It implicates you, too."

She leaned forward and lowered her voice. "You bet I would, to get what I want, and if you watch that video, my face is never seen. Remember I wore that red wig you liked so much, the costume? No one would ever dream it was me."

His face turned white. "And what exactly is it you want?"

"Just what I asked for. Delay the funding to my sister as long as you can."

"But why?"

"That's my business." Maggie folded her napkin on the table and stood up. "I want a firm commitment. Now. Otherwise, that video will go viral," she said as she leaned in to ostensibly give a kiss on the cheek. "And the answer is . . ."

"Yes, with reservations."

"Your reservations mean nothing to me."

Chapter Three

THE DAY I REJOINED THE LIVING STARTED BADLY.

My nerves colliding in my brain caused an electrical firestorm; the intrusive sound of the doorbell ringing over and over invaded. My feet pushed off the mattress to levitate my body and twist in midair, landing on my front, smashing my breasts into the mattress, then levitate again onto my back, in the process twisting myself in the sheets and forcing me to dive under pillows to escape the sounds I knew would kill me if I allowed it to go on. I smelled like rotting fish, my stomach burned, and my head was on fire.

I kicked my feet and, trapped in five-thousand-count Egyptian cotton, pulled and pushed and moaned like a cat on the prowl, but the shackles wouldn't release. I shoved and thrashed and rolled, desperate to escape.

Finally free, my legs felt like overblown balloons, but I made it downstairs with the mission to make it stop. I jerked the door open, breathing fire, ready to knock someone's head in.

The Honorable Renee Murphy stood on my front stoop. She looked me up and down. "Holy shit." Her mouth turned into a grim line. "Okay, that's it. Come with me." She took my arm in a firm grasp, kicked the door closed with a loud slam and threw my left arm over her shoulder and held her right arm around my waist. "Let's get you put back together again, Humpty. Choyou?" she yelled over her shoulder. "Coffee. Lots of it. And toast." My ears rang from the timber of her voice.

Choyou? Why didn't she answer the goddam door?

"When did you last brush your teeth? Jesus." We struggled up the stairs to my room. When she let me go, I lifted my knee to crawl back into bed.

I heard a voice from across a continent. "Oh, no, my pretty." She pulled me away from the bed and into the bathroom. She took off her watch, rolled up her sleeve, reached into the marble shower and turned on the water jets. "Get in," and pointed to the steaming waterfall.

So I did, $400 silk pajamas and all.

"Well, that's one way to do it." I could barely hear her.

Hot water invaded the soft fabric and turned it to paste against my body. I smelled my own filth. My hair hung down in itchy hanks and stuck to my cheeks. I stood still, wet and miserable, my feet suctioned to the marble floor. My head pounded and my throat burned, and I wanted to puke.

"No? Okay, let's try this."

Instantly ice-cold water pounded from jets coming at me from the left, right, back, and top of the marble shower, attacking through the silk like a thousand fire ants. I screamed, my mouth open so wide my jaws hurt. My voice echoed off the marble walls and wounded my ears, sounding like an animal being sacrificed. I reached out to adjust the faucets, but she beat me to it. I screamed at her, clawed at her fingers to let go.

"Would you like some warmer water?"

"YES. GOD!" There was nowhere to hide.

"Okay then. You with me?"

"MAKE IT STOP."

"Now that I have your attention, finish up in here and come downstairs." She adjusted the water to a more comfortable temperature. "Here's the soap. Use it." Like a child, I sniffed my anguish back up my nose and took the bar of French soap from her.

"And for God's sake, brush your teeth."

When I entered the bedroom draped in a towel, the sheets had been changed, the floor had been vacuumed, the windows were opened, and a set of sweats sat atop the bed. When I ambled closer, I found what Arthur called my hooker underwear sitting on top, a bright red set I had bought years ago. The tags were still on the tiny thong and demi-bra that showed more than they covered. I didn't have the energy to go dig out a more appropriate set, so I ripped the tags off and put them on, cursing Renee. She had a strange sense of humor, that one, and I didn't appreciate the silliness.

The smell of fresh coffee and cinnamon led me downstairs to my living room, following imagined steamy curlicues seen in the cartoons. Renee perched on the edge of the couch and leafed through a magazine.

"Feel better?" she asked, addressing the page that seemed to be fascinating, then looked up at me. She had the October issue of *Architectural Digest* on her lap, with this very room on the cover, a smiling Arthur on the couch, me on the arm with my hand on his yellow-cashmere-sweatered shoulder. The picture of prosperity and health and a way of life that's gone now.

"Not really." I smiled to show her I didn't mean it. But I did.

"What are you doing?" she dropped the heavy, thick magazine on the coffee table, the cracking sound of the magazine hitting wood made me jump. My nerves were unraveling.

"I don't know." I started to cry and felt like an idiot.

She hesitated a beat, then, "You're drinking too much."

I jerked my head up. "What?"

"Jen, vodka isn't going to bring him back, and—trust me—it's not going to bring meaning to your life. I know you. I know what you're thinking."

"No you don't. You couldn't possibly. Not unless you've been through it." My face and fingers prickled, and my back began to itch. How dare she? I wanted to get up and leave, but my legs wouldn't support me.

"Oh, don't beat that drum with me, my friend. I know all your secrets, remember?"

Not all of them.

"I've known you for the past fifty years." She took a deep breath. "Let's talk about your options."

She held up one finger and put on her don't-fuck-with-me-tone. "One, you can develop your social circle and do the philanthropic work you and Arthur started. You can be the next Iris Anderson. She's ninety-something now, and somebody has to take her place as the city's power hostess." She rolled her eyes at that one. "You're in the perfect position to do it. Two," she held up two fingers. "You can get a job. Three. You can volunteer everywhere. Four. You can travel. Five. You can start a non-profit. Six. You can start a new business of your own, take one of the houses in Historic Park that we are turning into the new art park and run with it. There. You have six options, and I bet you can think of more." I noticed she was breathing hard and raspy, like she was nervous—or pissed.

"I can't." I put my head in my hands. The art park. God. That was such a gargantuan project I couldn't put my head around it. Too much.

"Then, how about, seven, you can drink all day and wallow in self pity." I popped my head up to see my friend, head cocked to the side. Her lips reminded me of my third-grade teacher who thought I cheated on my grammar test. Renee stood up for me then, too.

I hiccupped and sank lower into the green damask chair.

"No. It's impossible. I can't. Find someone qualified."

"Stop it," She hissed. Her lips became very thin and her eyes were slits. "I am sick of you putting yourself in second place. Stop being a wallflower and the perfect woman your mother raised you to be. That model went out the window in the '60s. Gloria Steinem saw to that." She picked up the magazine and showed it to me, then threw it hard back on the table. "This is not your life anymore." The words penetrated my ears like a slap.

I had never been the recipient of her well-reported and well-deserved tirades, shown in the media to great reviews. As the mayor of San Diego, she said what she needed to say, but only when it mattered.

"Look." Renee took another deep breath, pressed her lips together, placed her hands on either side of her hips and cocked her head. "Arthur was a nice guy. He was wonderful. You had a good life. I get that. But you walked two paces behind him, and everything you did you did for him and his career. That was your job. I get that, too. But that's over now, and everything you've done and all the connections you have through that experience have now put you in a position to take the reins and do something really positive. Make something of it."

How dare she.

How dare she belittle my life and everything I did. She had no idea how much effort went into everything I did: the scheduling, the entertaining, the invitations, finding the perfect flowers, perfect dresses, perfect furniture, perfect timing.

I need to tell Arthur about this; this is outrageous.

Nana Buford's voice reeled in my head, as though her ghost were with me. *The truth is that he would have been fine without you and all the perfection. You were just icing on the cake. He had a brilliant legal mind that outwitted most of his opponents in court. He was destined to become D.A. He was revered for his mind, his compassion and his maneuverings in the courtroom. It had nothing to do with you.*

And he's gone. You're on your own, Buttercup.

"You know this is not the way to live. Arthur would be so pissed. This is not you. I know you're in pain, but there are other ways to dull it." She stood and walked over to the fireplace, then turned around to face me. "Work. Do something to funnel all your energies into. The art park is almost ready to go. We're in the final phase and we will start to lease out soon. You said you would sponsor an artist for two years. It's time. God knows you have the money to do it. Make the commitment. Now."

"Now?" I croaked.

"Now. You stood me up yesterday and I'm not letting you out of this." Damn. She's right. I was supposed to meet her at the art park . . . "You've never reneged on a commitment before, and you need something to do. It's a step."

I have always fulfilled my commitments, and I wanted to end this conversation. "All right." I mumbled. The good girl.

"Excellent. I have a city council meeting in half an hour. I have to go." She looked at her watch. "In fact, after the meeting my afternoon is free." She nodded the way she did when her mind was made up. "Let's try this again. Meet me at Historic Park, I mean the art park, at 4:30."

I nodded.

She looked down at me. "You're going to be okay, you know."

I nodded again.

"Plus, bonus points, you smell better."

She went into the foyer and raised her voice. "Choyou, see that she gets to Historic Park by 4:30. That's your job. After that, she's on her own."

"Yes, Missy."

"And thank you for calling me. You did the right thing."

Traitor.

Chapter Four

MY LIFE WAS OVER, BUT RENEE WAS RIGHT; I HAD TO GO ON. CHOYOU, my paid right hand, solid housemaster, conscience and mirror, pulled a warm quiche from the oven and placed it on the granite island counter, the one I had spent six months deciding on as though it were the most important decision of my life.

I plopped myself on the bar stool and placed my head in my hands, my head pounding.

"What is Heritage Arts?" Choyou asked quietly as she slid a cold plate of *Niçoise* salad in front of me along with two aspirin and a glass of water. I suspect she thought I would be angry about her betrayal. I was.

I took the aspirin. Her brows were drawn together, and tears flooded her eyes, which wasn't unusual. Choyou cried at card tricks. Arthur found it amusing. I found it annoying.

My mouth didn't want to work, but I put a few words together. "You know Heritage Park? The six historical houses that have been used as bed and breakfasts in Old Town?" She nodded as I took a nibble of a cracker. "It's registered as a historical site on city property, and as mayor, Renee has formed a committee that decided to turn it into an art park."

"Art park?"

I took a deep breath. This was exhausting. "They want to lease the houses to local artists to create, show and teach their art. It will be a community center to bring in tourist money and taxes while keeping it a historical site. I think it's a good idea, and the houses now are almost ready to show and lease out." My energy reserves runneth low. *Why am I always explaining things to people?*

"You are going to take one?"

"God, no. I'm not an artist. Just looking today, maybe find an artist to sponsor." I slid an olive into my mouth. The briny taste woke up my mouth and sent a mild shock down my throat.

She looked at me through thin slits. "You artist." She pointed her finger at me and gave a firm nod. She turned and started to wash up at the sink. My mouth dropped a little and I was shocked into silence. She had always been deferential to 'Missy Conrad.' The bowing and scraping, the quiet respect. How much of my everyday life was changing. She even called Renee on me, for God's sake.

Because of my husband and his high profile, I was the woman behind the man, the well-dressed, highly-connected woman who made people jump and things happen. I had made a name for myself, yes, I reflected, but it was precisely because of Arthur I was there in the first place.

With him gone, things had changed.

I picked at the quiche and salad, the national joke of Southern California cuisine, and then pulled myself upstairs to my office. I felt an obligation to take a first step to do something productive. Before I left, I turned and thanked Choyou—for more than lunch, and I was sure she knew that. She nodded sagely and went back to work.

Lois Hamilton of Hamilton and Taylor (*the* decorators to hire) took it upon herself to provide a place of serenity: a Zen atmosphere, complete with an arrangement of bamboo sticks in the corner, some beige pillows, and a dribbling water fountain that frankly only made me need to pee more often. The muted colors were intended to relax me and "enhance the creative process." I found them boring and anything but inspiring. She apparently came to the conclusion I had been under a great deal of pressure, and at the time I could see how she got that impression. In those days, my calendar was crammed.

My job was to help Arthur rise in the business and political world, and to keep him focused. I hosted dinner parties, headed fundraising committees, made polite chitchat with people I wanted to turn a hose on, and kept order in his chaotic world. I attended at least one big social event a week and was on countless committees. He wanted to be District Attorney, with an eye toward Attorney General. I stood behind him.

All for Arthur. All successful, resulting in more contacts, more business, and more exposure. Our parties were well received, and we were well liked, in demand, even.

Then my job was to pretend he wasn't dying.

The past two years had wiped me off the social landscape. There was a time when every day was packed with meetings, lunches, appointments, and duties. Now? Pristine, scrubbed, bleached white squares. Even my standing mani-pedi appointment was gone. I had had a few phone calls, but even fewer visitors.

I just turned fifty-eight. My slate was blank.

What the hell was I going to do with my life?

At this moment, taking a house at the art park was not an option. The prospect wasn't even appealing, a huge mountain in front of me I wasn't sure I wanted to climb. But I'll go this afternoon, just to please Renee.

No. I cannot divert myself from the business of my grief. I should stay home and actively mourn, not create something. It seemed disrespectful, like my husband's death hadn't affected me, a blip on the radar screen: *Oh well.*

No. Unacceptable.

But what else was I going to do?

I realized I had not ever made a major decision. Arthur and I discussed the pros and cons of major things in our life and we came to a conclusion together. Things came easily to us. We were a team.

I called a few friends but couldn't find anyone to talk to. Everyone was so damn busy keeping busy they don't have time just to talk. I had been erased.

I switched on the computer to email some friends and make arrangements to meet—anything. I found an email from Dave Putnam, Maggie's husband and Arthur's law partner:

Jen,

Since Arthur's death, we have kept his assistant Lupe on, keeping her busy out of loyalty. But the truth is Arthur's death had a huge impact on the firm, and we are going to have to lay some people off. We have to tighten our belts. I am sure you understand and hope that you can reach out to Lupe and help her find employment.

The audit will start soon to determine the value of the firm so that you can receive Arthur's portion of the partnership before I become a sole proprietor.

This is hard on all of us, and adjustments have to be made.

Dave

So the firm was cutting back, and it made sense. Arthur was half the firm doing more than half the work, plus he was the rainmaker. This email seemed harsh, businesslike, annoying.

I had never interfered in the firm's business, but the news, my mood, and my need to move forward gave me the impetus to step out of character. I shot back an email:

Dave,

As a favor to me, if not to Arthur, please keep Lupe on the payroll for a year, including all benefits, from her termination date as severance pay. When the accounts are settled, take it out of my buyout, including whatever employer expenses you incur on her behalf. I know Arthur would want her taken care of. She was his rock and he completely depended on her. Conrad and Putnam would not be what it is without her. Thank you.

Jen

If he's going to be all business, then I can, too. I sat back in my chair, knowing I had done the right thing.

Hooray for me.

I shuffled down the long hallway into our all-white bedroom. At the time the decorator and I agreed it was chic and elegant. Now it just looked sterile, unwelcoming. Arthur laughed when he saw it. "A ghost could get lost in here," he had said, pat me on the ass, and went in to take a shower. I had added some color since then to soften it up, but it turned out he was right.

I flopped across the bed, discouraged and depressed, closed my eyes and drifted off.

"Hi, Babe." Arthur's voice came to me. I lifted my head, actually expecting to see him for a split second. I dropped my head back down and started to cry. Again. That voice, that tone, just for me, gone.

Chapter Five

RENEE MURPHY WAS MY BEST FRIEND IN THE WORLD. WE MET IN kindergarten; me from the upper middle-class neighborhood of an up-and-coming young lawyer and a housewife, she from the other side of the tracks. Her mother cleaned houses and sometimes painted addresses on curbs. They lived in the basement of a church until one day her mom just didn't come home.

She moved in, but she never felt a real part of the family, and I think that was mutual. She must have felt like a permanent houseguest.

Renee never lost faith that her mother was coming back for her. Never happened.

I was closer to Renee than my own sister, with whom Renee enjoyed a mutual disdain. She thought Maggie stuck up and plastic, Maggie thought her lower than a bug. After a few skirmishes between them in which I stayed silent, they avoided each other, and I chose Renee. We had gone to college together at Boston U where Renee got sucked into political science courses in the midst of the Watergate affair, her passion for justice and her outrage at the abuse of power drove her to extremes. She went on to Duke to become a lawyer, I finished up my Masters' Degree in art history. We kept in touch with letters and long-distance phone calls.

When she returned to San Diego with a law degree, I had Arthur and she had a career laid out in front of her. Renee became sucked into politics and seemed to have the interest and the mojo to understand movements of people running for political office that I just didn't get. She seemed to interpret their motivations cleanly and understood who the good guys were, wanting to do good work, and the bad guys just trying to get their fifteen minutes. She was one of the good guys and took no shit from anyone. That was her professional life.

But she had fallen into a trap.

In her personal life, Renee had met and fallen in love with one of her professors—a married man who never led her astray. He told her early on he would never leave his wife, and if she wanted a family and children she better look elsewhere. When she moved back to San Diego, they both understood it was over.

She missed him desperately, but she recognized the end, and she was going to have to move on. He was offered a position as president of a university in San Diego, and, after discussing it with his family, he called Renee and asked if she would have a problem with it.

He moved his family and he and Renee picked up where they left off. They met every Wednesday night at her place and sometimes they got away for a weekend, but not much more than that. He brought her gifts now and then and told her how valuable she was. He truly loved her but would not leave his wife and growing family.

I didn't get it. As a newlywed, I was offended, and it caused some strain and not a little judgment on my part; we got over it fairly quickly when I realized it wasn't going to change.

She was happy, as she explained, because she was able to keep to herself and develop her life. On the downside, she was never able to develop a relationship with anyone and in fact mourned the very real issue that she could not celebrate with him when his children graduated or when he was presented with a new grandchild. On many occasions he was a no-show on Wednesdays because of birthdays, accidents, or births, reinforcing his position in her life. But he always called and explained and made up for it, meeting her for an innocent lunch soon after.

Despite that, Renee was happy with her life. In fact, she never wanted children as much as I did. The happy homemaker was not her future, and we both knew it. She was able to develop her career, make an impact, and live her life the way she wanted.

Twenty-seven years after they started, he broke it off. He was retiring and wanted some peace. He now had grandchildren and felt it was time. She had long ago acknowledged that this would come at some point, but she was devastated.

I had helped her through a major secret love affair that fell apart, then a debilitating depression that lasted weeks. She had helped me through the summer of 1969 and all the residual pain, and I had not explained a thing. And she was still with me.

Three o'clock. Time to get my ass together and down to Historic Park to meet Renee.

My hair had grown out. A foot of silvery gray sprouted from my scalp; a line of faded auburn delineated the processed from the natural. My appearance had been of no importance to me for the past two years and I wondered if my hairdresser was still in business. A hat hid the offensive gray at the funeral. Today it was bundled in back, no auburn to be seen, which made me look twenty years older but I felt fifty. I put on a camel-colored cashmere sweater I had made years ago over designer jeans. I forgot my jewelry but remembered sensible shoes.

The sun was out on this bright but cool December afternoon. While the rest of the country was typically knee-deep in snow, we enjoyed sunshine and a slight breeze just cool enough for a sweater. As I drove south, I realized how much I missed being out in the world. It felt good to navigate the car wherever I wanted to go, watching the sun reflect on the water on the Pacific.

I'm not supposed to be enjoying anything. I'm in mourning.

Historic Park had been in disrepair for some time, and Renee had been the force for change. I could hear renovation efforts underway as soon as I parked. Hammering and sawing and the whine of sanders reverberated in the wind. I caught a whiff of sawdust and paint.

As I ambled my way up the curved cobblestone, I admired the healthy shrubbery and small trees and the large, expertly manicured lawn that looked like velvet. The houses, set in a U-shape, were separated by large, even gray cobblestones. An ancient coral tree at least sixty feet tall stood sentry at the roundabout, encircled by a waist-high black iron fence. I sat under the tree on one of the iron benches, put my hands under my thighs and took several deep breaths. I felt my lungs begin to expand and iron out the wrinkles of grief and sorrow. The smell of good soil and grass with a hint of ocean air mixed with sawdust on this winter day lifted my spirits a little. Here in living color: life, progress, and nature. It was going on with or without me.

A blue butterfly with golden spots fluttered down onto the bench beside me. "Hello, beautiful," I said. "Come here often?"

Renee, with her trademark helmet hair, patent leather flats and polyester off-the-rack pantsuit, trundled up the walk to me. She carried a huge ring of keys and her cell phone.

"Come on, Gigi, let's pick out a house." The old nickname hadn't been used in years. She had teased me about being such a good girl for so long, it became the initials, then the name Gigi.

God, that was a long time ago.

"The contractor's doing a good job," she said as she pushed her sunglasses on top of her head and eyed each of the six houses. "The paint is perfect, and I see the windows are in. Excellent." She jangled the keys and started toward the first house. "Every house has been researched and retrofitted to conform to the original design. The lattice work had been duplicated perfectly from the original drawings . . ." She stopped in front of a house and exclaimed, "Look at the dentils!" and pointed to the roof.

What the hell is a dentil?

"The molding that goes around the house with rectangle holes in it." Renee read my mind. "See it? Such detail!" She looked back to me with a smile that I had not seen often in the fifty years I knew her. "The contractor is all over this."

I attempted to be funny. "The contractor, hunh?" I smiled back. "What, is he cute?"

She cocked her head at me. "Don't be absurd."

I changed the subject. Sometimes Renee could be more of a snob than I. "How is this going to work?"

We had talked about this ad nauseum before Arthur became ill, but my memory was fuzzy. Renee sighed. "If you choose to sponsor an artist, we can arrange an interview and decide how to proceed. If you want to lease a house yourself, just do it." She started to walk down the path. "I can see you here in one of these houses running a needlework shop."

A well-executed offhand comment. She deliberately continued to look at the houses rather than look at me. Her chin pointed up; her hand provided additional sunshade for her eyes. I knew instinctively it was a setup. She wanted me to take a house and run it myself. The left side of my head tingled; a phenomenon Nana Buford had told me was a sure sign my angels were trying to get my attention.

"Oh, Renee, you give me too much credit. I can't run a shop."

Besides, as my mother would say, women like us don't run shops, we patronize them.

Renee stopped, turned to me and pushed her sunglasses down her nose, the classic Audrey Hepburn move we'd practiced in my bedroom in junior high.

"Bullshit. You started Arthur and Dave's firm. You did it all, I know you did. Your sister was no help. Even though she was married to Dave, she let you do all the work. You did the books, the marketing, the court filings . . ."

"But that was just . . ."

". . . just what? Conrad and Putnam turned out to be the largest and most prestigious law firm in the county, and you started it." She sighed. "Jen, you don't give yourself enough credit. You have no idea how much power you have. Now come on. Let's look at prospects." She grabbed my elbow and dragged me into the first house.

"This one I see as an oil painter's paradise. Look at the light coming in. It would make a great studio." She turned to me. "It was the shurriff's house," she said with a laugh.

Small and intimate, the house would make a wonderful studio and gallery, I thought. The rooms upstairs could be used for art classes or individual studios.

"Wow," was all I could say.

I felt my body come to life, the synapses in my brain began to fire and I could feel the blood run through. My imagination started to sprout like seedlings popping. I hadn't experienced it in a while, and it was like a window opening to sunlight on whitewashed floors. Renee and I were in sync. We had the same visions.

We moved next door to the second house where we found an exquisitely carved dark wood bar that spanned the entire wall. "Coffee bar," we said in unison.

Renee crossed her arms on her chest. "This house belonged to Hiram Miller."

"The famous Miller's Pub?"

"Yup. First tavern downtown on Market Street, built in 1893. He imported this bar from Ireland and installed it in the tavern. When the city started renovation downtown, the Historical Society rescued it from destruction and brought it here to what had been his house. It's two hundred years old."

I wondered how many drinks had been served at this plank of wood. How many people sidled up to this particular bar?

"The stories . . ." I mumbled.

"I know, right? People who appreciate the ambience and history buffs would love it. Maybe more literary types. This dark living room might make sort of a beatnik-type book and coffee spot. Who knows?"

"Wow. Where did that come from?" This was not the straight laced, less-than-imaginative Renee I knew.

She harrumphed and clomped through the back door where a large bricked-in patio could hold small tables and the manicured lawn would prove *the* spot for parties. The gargantuan kitchen had been tiled in pristine white squares with modern appliances faced to look Victorian. "Caterers," we said, and giggled. It felt good to be with Renee, who understood me so well.

I'm feeling disloyal and brought myself down to earth.

We went on to the next house and stood looking up at the burnt sienna, three storied, gable-topped house. "Look up—see the widow's walk?"

"How appropriate," I said. Renee ignored me.

Pink hydrangeas fronted the porch. Asparagus fern sprouted around them, forming a soft lacy effect. Renee cocked her head toward the door. "Let's go." She fumbled with the jailer's key ring and finally we entered into the empty house. Sunlight streamed down the hall directly in front of us from what looked to be the kitchen in the back. A dark, heavily–bannistered staircase rose on the left. I saw what must have been the parlor through a large doorway to the right.

Mesmerized, I closed my eyes and absorbed the feel and smell of this house. I felt a calmness, as though I had been here before.

"I thought this one might get you," Renee grinned like the know-it-all she was. "This was the mayor's house, used for entertaining and public functions." She opened a door on the left with a multi-faceted crystal doorknob. "Here's the perfect spot for an office." A bright room with whitewashed wainscoting and floors welcomed me. I suspect it was the maid's room.

"Look," she said, and pulled me across the hall and into the parlor. Renee's shoes made clomping sounds on the original wood floors, and my own shoes squeaked loudly, confirming the fact that this space was, after years of use, empty, but ready for a new life.

The parlor was even larger than the living room in my own house, which was not inconsiderate. An ornate mantelpiece with a beveled mirror hung over the fireplace that took up most of the far wall.

"This was the room where formal recitals and receptions were held. There is enough room for a grand piano and several dozen chairs. Jenny Lind was rumored to have performed here." She turned in a circle in the middle of the room, arms out. "Have some bookshelves made for merchandise and you have a room to knit, do needlepoint, and demonstrate. Put in some comfy furniture and have gatherings." Her arms flew, pointing to various areas around the room. "Yarn and canvas and needles, oh my," she sung. "Isn't it perfect? Come with me. There's more."

I followed her, turning around once to take in the parlor again, into the dining room. It, too, had a fireplace, and would seat probably twenty people for dinner, as was the custom in Victorian days. "More space for inventory. Or classes. Or whatever."

I had a reputation for having gatherings that overwhelmed, and it was a secret pleasure of mine to outdo even myself. For a split second I wanted to have a dinner party right here with blazing candles and a voluptuous, over-the-top centerpiece, a Victorian celebration.

My dining room furniture would fit in here perfectly and I warmed with envy I hadn't felt since I was a young bride with my folding card table that held wedding gifts I was too nervous to use. That dining room was perfection, and I wanted it.

But my entertaining days were over, weren't they?

If I chose to take the house, I'd use this room for needlepoint. Kits and accessories on the walls, displays on a real dining room table, tapestry yarn spilling out of glass goblets . . .

I saw it. A division of labor: knitting in the parlor, needlepoint in the dining room, and production in the kitchen. We'd have steamers, blockers, and sewing machines.

But no. I can't. My legs were giving way. I started to shake.

Between Renee's excitement, my body coming to life, the alcohol that still ran through my veins, and the excitement of a possible new venture, I had had enough for one day, and it hit me like the proverbial brick wall.

Renee took one look at me and then her watch. "The sun's officially over the yardarm. We're going across the street for dinner and a margarita." She slammed and bolted the door, that huge key ring jangling fiercely. We followed the pathway and crossed the street to what had been repeatedly voted as the best Mexican restaurant in town. Hot flashes grabbed me and shortened by breath, which made me unsteady and dizzy. And mad. Would this never end? Will I ever feel normal again? I shook badly and wasn't sure I could walk much further.

The restaurant was festooned with bright, cheery holiday decorations. I wanted to gag.

Can't we just skip the merriment this year?

The hostess bowed and scraped as Her Honor was ushered to a table immediately on the purple and yellow, bright pink and turquoise accented patio. I followed with my head down and resisted the urge to apologize to

KATHY WEYER

those clearly waiting in line. We sat in the cool air with heaters overhead; the sensation was a pleasant one.

Our waiter plopped down two cold waters, and I downed mine quickly through a straw as Renee ordered margaritas. "You're not really having a problem with alcohol?" she asked when he left, her eyebrows raised. I shook my head. I pushed my glass away and said, "No. A momentary aberration. You caught me at the one time I let myself go too far, and I am grateful." I smiled at her.

"Good. You were a flippin' mess, but I'm pronouncing you responsible. If you don't want yours, I'll have it. So. What do you think?" she asked while she smiled and waved at someone over my shoulder.

"About what?"

She slumped, and I laughed.

"Renee, what would I do with that huge house?"

I knew exactly what I would do with that huge house.

I felt a pull and the beginnings of excitement about a new project and shoved it down as I dipped a tortilla chip into salsa and jammed it into my mouth. The saltiness of the chips and sharp taste of the salsa gave me a jolt and brought me back to reality.

There is no way, and now is not the time, for me to start something exciting. I'm in mourning.

Renee leaned forward on her elbows. "I told you, a needlework shop. There is nothing around here. This is a tourist area, so you'll have the benefit of being a draw for the locals *and* the tourists will go ape over something other than statues and figurines serving as souvenirs." She rolled her eyes. "Not that that's a bad thing," she added and looked around for eavesdroppers. "Look," she said and squared herself in her chair. "You can do this, and you should do this. You're an excellent needle worker. Hell, just look at all the things in your house and the gifts you've made. I know for a fact your creations have been requested for raffle items, and they have gone for big bucks. You are not entering into this without some experience."

I shook my head, not because I was saying no, but because I just didn't know what to do. I saw it: the yarn, the furniture, the customers, the dining room, the front porch. I saw it. I just didn't know if I could do it.

33

"Okay, then, go back to plan A and sponsor a house for an artist." She glared at me, expecting some kind of answer.

"Which would mean somebody else can take the house and muck it up. It deserves more than the usual retail treatment. It's a house with personality that deserves to be honored and treated well." I couldn't help but speak the truth as I knew it. My words came out too sharp and I placed my finger over my lips, knowing I had shown my hand.

Renee grinned. "I knew it. You're hooked."

"No. I can't. I'm not qualified. I have no energy, and no interest."

"Bullshit. You just don't want to enjoy yourself. You think you don't deserve it."

Direct hit.

The waiter stood behind Renee with his tray holding two margaritas. Hearing Renee's comment, he hesitated, and I smiled at him. The good girl, making other people feel comfortable. He placed them before us and bowed, backing away.

Poor guy.

We licked the salt from the rims and indulged. I felt better and leaned back in my chair, allowing the tequila to do its magic. I consciously dropped my shoulders and my arms and leaned back in the white plastic patio chair.

"Tell me what's going on in your life," I said.

Renee's face flushed, something I hadn't seen in quite some time.

"Between us?"

"Of course."

"Ron Walker's retiring."

"The police chief?" I took another chip. "What . . ."

She cocked her head and looked at me as though I was the dumbest woman on the planet, which I was. She had told me two years ago she was attracted to him, but he worked for her, which meant hands off.

"Oh. Right. He's retiring? Why?"

"Because he says he wants a personal life."

"You mean . . ." My eyebrows shot up.

"I think so. He called me on my cell and asked what I thought."

"And you said . . ."

"I told him," she took a sip, "I thought it was the best idea I'd heard in a long time."

"What was his reaction?" I began to smile and warm up.

"He laughed, hung up, and I got his resignation/retirement letter on my desk the next morning." I hadn't seen her smile like that for a while.

I couldn't help but feel happy for her, and a little depressed. I was all alone. Just when Arthur left me, Renee was stepping into a real relationship.

Chapter Six

CARL HENSHAW WALKED FROM HIS CUBICLE INTO DAVE PUTNAM'S OFFICE at Conrad and Putnam, LLC at 10:00 on Wednesday morning. The carpet still smelled new, and the dark woods and pale green walls hadn't yet had a scratch put on them from the recent, very expensive redecorating job. It looked exactly like what it was, an expensive law firm. The only decoration honoring the season was a large green wreath over the marble receptionist desk.

"You wanted to see me?"

"Yes, come in. Close the door." Dave closed a file and adjusted himself in his chair. His corner office was large, with an entire wall of law books, a huge mahogany desk with two leather chairs facing it, and a small round conference table piled with case files.

Carl hesitated a few seconds, closed the door, and slowly lowered himself into a chair. He took in his boss's appearance, looking for clues. Dave's face seemed paler than usual, his normal *joie de vivre* had gone. His silver hair appeared mussed. Carl thought he saw the beginnings of bags under his eyes.

"Relax. This is personal." Dave leaned back, his chair creaked as he shifted and focused on Carl.

"All right."

Dave took a deep breath. "With Arthur gone, the firm has to be rebuilt. It's as if we have to start over. His expertise in criminal matters is what made this firm. I have no problem admitting that, but he really shined as the rainmaker; his personality and connections brought in a ton of business. We didn't need to hire a marketing guy because he was a natural; his charisma and legal mind and reputation brought people in. I am the researcher, advisor, and sounding board, and he the face of the firm. Without him..." Dave brushed his hand over his face. "I really thought he'd make it." He shook his head. "But it is what it is."

Carl waited, his eyes intent on Dave.

"Arthur's illness and death has affected me personally. He was my best friend as well as my law partner and my brother-in-law. He was family." He sighed heavily and leaned back in his chair.

"As you know, the plan was for Arthur and me to retire at the same time and leave the firm to my son and you as partners, to pick up where we left off. It seemed as though you both were interested, and it would have been a good plan. This is not news to you." Dave turned and placed his hands on the desk, fingers spread far apart. His platinum wedding ring gleamed in the light from the desk lamp. "But now, with both Arthur and Eric gone, we have to put a new succession plan in place." He looked up at Carl. "Since Eric died, his sister is now in line to inherit the firm. She will take the bar exam in a few months. She'll do well, I know, but what I don't know is if Tricia has the killer instinct that Arthur and I had, or that you and Eric would have had." He stood up and put his hands in his pockets and looked out over his view of San Diego Bay. "I'm worried about the future of this firm, both in the short- and the long-term. Arthur taught me we're not immortal." He turned back to Carl. "What if something happens to me before Trisha takes over?"

Carl nodded. "A logical concern."

"In the short term, cases are down, and we aren't as busy as we once were. Our biggest priority now is the fact that our CFO just quit—no notice, no explanation. We cannot exist without a CFO, especially now that an audit has to be done after Arthur's death so his widow can get her share. But after that, we are going to have to lay some people off."

"Who? Me?"

"No. I can't run this place by myself. But your first official role is to find a replacement for Richardson; someone who knows legal accounting and can do an audit and file all the forms."

"I think I know just the guy. I'll call him."

"I'll want to approve whoever you bring in. Bring in three different people for me to interview."

"I thought this was my job." Carl stared Dave down. "If you want me to take this on, I'm going to want to run with it."

Dave sighed. "I'll still want to meet with them and work with you on final approval."

Dave nodded.

". . . and one more thing: if you're going to be part of this family, you're going to have a huge part to play in this firm." He stopped. "You *are* going to be part of this family, correct?"

Carl nodded. "I believe so, eventually. Tricia and I haven't talked about it, but I believe that's where we're headed. She still needs to pass the bar before I'll ask her to commit to me, but, yes, I believe eventually that will happen."

"I'd like it to be sooner rather than later."

"Why?"

"Because when Tricia does pass the bar and comes on board, she'll want a plum position here, but she won't have the experience under her belt. That's where you come in. I love my daughter, but I don't know if she's a leader. I want you in position to partner with her when I retire, and if you're my son-in-law it makes sense. She'll need time to get up to speed. You have proven yourself here. I want you to be as good as Arthur and continue to bring in the clients. Tricia can run the place with you, just as you would have with Eric."

"Understood. But what happens if she says no?"

Dave shrugged. "Then you're out of a job, Tricia steps in, and I don't retire." He took his hands out of his pockets, pushed his silver hair back, and sat back down. "Look, I'd hate to see all your years of hard work here go down the drain. If you marry her, I'd know I'd have double the coverage, you'd be real partners, and I could retire someday without a care. If there's no marriage, she inherits it completely without you, and I have a lot of work to do."

Carl hesitated. "I've been approached by McLean and Oliphant to come in as partner."

"Then we make you partner. But I want some kind of commitment from you that this is going to happen, or Tricia inherits the firm in its entirety."

"Managing partner." Carl stated rather than asked.

"*Managing* partner when Tricia joins the firm. *Junior* partner now."

"Done."

"Make it happen, son."

Carl turned on the thick carpet and left Dave's office. He texted the message:

All systems go.

✕ ✕ ✕

Tricia Putnam readied herself for landing in St. Louis. She took a deep breath, dropped a mini bottle of bourbon into her backpack, and pulled the headphone buds from her ears that blasted her favorite heavy metal music. She put her earphones in her pocket and began to delete contacts from her contact list, appointments from her calendar, and music from her collection.

It was time for a new life, and she wanted no reminders. She had a job to do.

Graduating from Harvard Law was something she had done to please her parents. It had been expected, and she was not in a position to deny her parents' wishes, especially after her brother Eric's death.

All she wanted to do was please them. They had suffered enough.

But now it was different, and she was the only one who could fix what had gone wrong.

As always, her parents had provided her with a first-class ticket, which allowed her to use the member club facilities, a private club with showers and any amenity she could possibly want. She headed directly for the club at the top of the escalator.

The receptionist buzzed her in and, when she saw Tricia, demanded to see some identification. When she was satisfied, she sniffed and pushed a button that allowed Tricia to go into the inner sanctum.

Tricia rushed through to the lounge area, where she found a private shower area, locked the door and stared at herself in the mirror.

Time to morph.

A sob caught in her throat, but she pulled herself together and poured the little bottle of bourbon down her throat, stripped, got rid of all the jewelry except for the leather bracelet, and stepped into the shower.

She applied a special formula to her hair and shampooed; the water ran bright pink down the drain. She scrubbed her face with a washcloth that came back black with heavy eyeliner and orange lipstick.

The tattoo on her thigh she could do nothing about. Thank God she didn't have one that would show. She shaved, rinsed, and stepped out.

What she saw was striking—her naturally dark hair was still there, and it was curly. She had lost weight but had covered that with the bulky costume she had adopted for the past two years.

A red wool skirt and bright white silk blouse was uppermost in her bag, along with new underwear, stockings and tartan plaid shoes that cost over a grand.

"What a waste . . ." She mumbled as she put them on and faced herself, once again, in the mirror. Her hair was drying into a soft halo around her face, and her freckles showed. She brushed her teeth and put on some moisturizer.

She opened up a box of makeup she had assembled earlier—everything she would need—and began to apply it conservatively. Her hands shook as she tried to delicately hide the purple under her eyes and plump up the worry lines between her brows.

She put on the diamond pendant her father had given her for her twenty-first birthday. She had never worn it. The diamond watch went on and the pearl earrings her grandmother sent her slid into the pierced ears and she frowned at the conservative look. She spritzed some perfume she picked up in Boston ("a present for my mother," she had said the astonished cashier at the airport shop) and moved over to the mess in the corner.

A brand new, name brand purse sat in the suitcase, all pre-loaded. She crammed her discards into the backpack along with all the trash and pushed the thing into the trash bin. She wheeled her almost-empty suitcase back into the lounge, a bit wobbly on the heels. She wandered out to the bar area. "Would you mind checking if my flight is on time?" she asked the concierge and gave him the envelope with her boarding pass.

"It would be my pleasure." Tricia noted she would not have gotten that response if this guy had seen her walk in. She smiled at him, and he smiled back.

She sat primly on a lounge chair and opened up her phone.

"May I buy you a drink?" Tricia looked up at a nice-looking man, late thirties, she guessed, and smiled. Might as well test out the merchandise.

She hesitated. He put his hand out, "Paul Miller."

"Tricia...Smith."

"Well, Tricia. . .Smith, what will it be?"

Shoving aside her preference for a beer, she said, "A glass of white wine, Sauvignon Blanc, if they have it." Mother's lessons weren't wasted after all.

He loped away, and she quickly wrote a message to her friend Carl, who would meet her at the airport.

> In St. Louis. Conversion complete.
> Ready to do this?

He wrote back immediately.

> Absolutely. I do have some news
> and I think things are moving on the
> right track.

> Good. Flight should be on time but
> check for yourself. You know how I hate
> to have you wait.

> For you, I'd wait forever.

> Charmer.

She was interrupted by a hand cradling a cold glass of wine, clicked off her phone and leaned back.

"Where are you headed?" Paul asked.

"San Diego. You?"

"Denver. I live there, just now going back after a long trip down the Amazon."

"Really. Fascinating. What were you doing there?"

"I'm a doctor. I was doing some research on tribal medicines. It was incredibly life-changing." They chatted for a bit while sipping.

"Miss Putnam? Your flight is ready to board now at gate B45" the concierge whispered and handed her boarding pass back. "May I be of assistance?"

"No, but thank you." Tricia rose from the chair, gathered up her purse and slung it over her shoulder, offered her hand, "Well, goodbye, Paul, and thank you for the wine," she said with what she hoped was a warm smile.

"You are most welcome, Miss… Smith." She nodded and tried to elegantly sashay out the door. Busted.

She landed in San Diego and went straight out the sliding doors into the cool December evening. Carl waited by his black BMW, trunk open and ready for her luggage.

She floated into his arms and snuggled into his neck.

"How's my girl?" He asked into her ear.

"Shaky."

She could feel him nodding in agreement.

"I told your parents I was taking you to dinner before I got you home. Besides, they're at an event anyway. Hungry?"

"Starved."

"This it for luggage?"

"Nothing left." She shrugged. "My books and personal possessions were shipped ahead, but what I'd need to wear is already in that huge closet at home."

Carl laughed. "Got it." They went to Mr. A's, a high-end top of the line restaurant overlooking the airport and the bay.

"So, what's the news?" Tricia asked as she worked on a bourbon, neat.

He looked through his horned-rim glasses, took a sip of his drink, and said, "Richardson just resigned."

"What??? The CFO? We need him." She slumped back in the posh chair.

He shook his head. "I admit it kind of blows, but maybe now we can replace him with someone who can. . ."

"Maybe. . ."

"And I know just the guy," he smiled. "Ray Chandler. He's a forensic accountant, but your dad doesn't have to know that. He can be an interim CFO if Dave doesn't like him, but we need someone now."

"What happened to Richardson?"

"Your dad made it so difficult for him, he had no choice. Rich used words like 'constructive termination,' so I'd bet there's going to be a lawsuit that will have to be settled."

"Ya *think*?" Tricia said with not a little sarcasm, plopped her glass on the table. "Jesus. What else?"

He shrugged. "Not much really. I'm just keeping an eye on things."

"Thank God you are there."

"And you will be shortly, too."

"Don't remind me. I don't like corporate law. But it has to be done."

"If we are right and there is more, we can do what needs to be done, save the firm, and you can reconstruct it any way you want. We'll inherit the firm, but he wants me first chair. Dave said so last week."

Tricia snorted. "You!?" She looked up at him sharply. "I didn't mean it."

"I know. It sucks he chose me first but look at it this way: I am licensed, and it seems safe; it's not about the fact that you're a woman. I'll take care of it, I promise."

"I know you will." She reached over and squeezed his hand.

On the way home, he told her to open the glove box. A blue velvet box was in there with a beautiful ring, one she had seen before, and she put it on her finger with no ceremony.

"Are you sure?"

"Absolutely."

"Okay, then, Phase One in place."

Chapter Seven

RAY CHANDLER WAS A TYPICAL ACCOUNTANT: FOCUSED, EFFICIENT, AND quiet. He specialized in forensic accounting, looking for errors and criminal endeavors. He had his own firm serving several law firms looking for criminal activities, money laundering, tax schemes, pyramid schemes, and had been making very good money doing it, all from his home.

Carl wasn't sure he could grab him and take him away from the entrepreneurial business he ran out of his house, but he was going to try.

He and Tricia had talked this over many times and were now re-hashing this in Carl's dining room. This was the first step in a huge project to back up their plan, and they wanted it just right. But they realized Richardson leaving actually made it easier.

"You're sure we can trust him." Tricia said for the millionth time.

"Yes. Yes yes yes," Carl said and grabbed her by her forearms. "Trust me."

A knock reverberated through the house. Carl opened the door to find a small, bespectacled, trim man, slightly bald, with puffs of blond hair and a clean-shaven face standing, holding an old-fashioned briefcase in one hand and a six-pack of beer in the other.

Introductions were made, and they ate their sandwiches and drank their beer renewing acquaintances and telling a few stories of college days.

Tricia liked him right away. They swore him to secrecy and began their story, their suspicions, and their fear that they may be right.

Chapter Eight

AFTER DINNER WITH RENEE, I HEADED FOR HOME EXHAUSTED AND depressed.

Renee was a woman that men respected and followed. She was bold, strong, and self-assured, and she had made her mark. Her term as mayor would be up soon, and she could do anything—anything at all. The world was her oyster, as they say to the young. She wouldn't fail at whatever she attempted in her second chapter. She was not even sixty yet—the new forty.

She couldn't have picked a better guy than Ron Walker to share her life with. He was smart, dependable, honest, and handsome. Plus, he was funny. Everything a girl would want.

Everything I no longer had.

My identity happened to be connected to someone else's achievements: Arthur's sidekick, the second banana, the straight guy.

And I had been okay with that.

The idea of Renee being someone else's Second Hand Rose was absurd.

Had I wasted my life? No, of course not. But what do I have to show for the past fifty-eight years? Maybe if we had had children I might feel differently, but as it was, there was no mark I would leave on the world.

I approached the bar out of sheer habit. My hand hovered over the vodka decanter. As much as it pulled me, I opted for tonic water.

Choyou had gone for the day, and the silence suffocated me. I selected some Vivaldi and listened to the opening bars as I placed my drink on the end table and dropped into the green wingback chair with a sigh. I pulled out some knitting from the wicker basket beside me and looped a few stitches, replaying my conversation with Renee. What she said about the multitudes of creative handwork I had done was true. I took inventory of my surroundings in a new light.

Needlepoint pillows of animals taken from Victorian paintings lived on the couches and chairs, the inspiration to offer this room as a model of an English drawing room: heavy, dark furniture, pots of ferns and flowers, velvet drapes, and priceless antiques. Crewelwork pieces of Jacobean designs were on display, as well as a needlepoint fire screen of a typical English coat of arms. The masterpiece was a rug-sized tapestry hung on the wall, stitched over years of keeping busy while Arthur worked, watched sports, and, most especially, during the pre-dinner cocktail hour he insisted we have every evening.

I think that's when I missed him most: that hour before dinner when we were just there, alone together, chatting. I looked over at his chair. Choyou had placed the monarch butterfly pillow, another of my creations, on the seat. This chair was taken.

I sipped my drink and heard the grandfather clock tick in the hallway. My ears picked up every sound, the fabric in my sleeve crinkled as I placed the glass onto the coaster. I cleared my throat and the sound echoed through the living room.

God. I am so alone.

This was my house, my sanctuary, embossed with my own creations. All these beautiful things had been made with love and enthusiasm.

So what? I could make beautiful objects with my hands. Isn't that a little flimsy as far as accomplishments?

I can throw a damn near perfect dinner party. Again, not enough.

I coordinate volunteer efforts, arrange lunches, and deal with caterers and printers for events and fundraisers.

Big. Fucking. Deal.

Why not start a needlework shop?

Because it's not what we do. Others work. Others have shops, and people like me support them. We do not put ourselves at the mercy of others or worry about inventory or accounts payable.

I knew what a balance sheet looked like, I knew that you had to bring in more than you spent, and I knew that you had to risk it all, which scared the hell out of me. That's all I knew about running a business. But was it enough? If I were to put aside my own ingrained idea of what I should be or do, could I do it?

The house at the art park spoke to me, and I knew I belonged there one way or another. As I saw it, I had three choices: find an artist to take the house and support him or her financially to practice and teach a craft, find and sponsor someone to specifically lease the place as a needlework shop, or run it myself.

Or I could renege on the whole thing and go back to wilting away.

What would Mother say? Would Arthur be behind this? (Of course he would.) Can I do this? Should I do this?

My phone rang. I sidled into the family room and looked at the caller I.D. Mother. Shit.

"Good evening, dear. How are you?"

"I'm fine . . ." *What could she possibly want?*

"Have you spoken with your sister?"

Maggie and I don't hang out over the phone chatting. "No. Why?"

"I have some news for you, then. Tricia was engaged last night to that nice Carl."

"How wonderful. She's home?"

"She arrived last night. In time for the holidays." I knew Mother shook her head on the other end, dismayed at my lack of family interaction. Mother Superior shakes her head at her disappointment of a daughter.

I hadn't known, so deep in my own world. How selfish could I be? Dave and Maggie's daughter Tricia had recently graduated Harvard Law a semester early, flew home, and became engaged completely out of my orbit. Damn. A big moment, and I missed it.

"Now. About the art park. The fundraiser will be at your house, a formal affair after the holidays. I have contacted the caterers as well as Renee to coordinate the date. The next step is to make the announcement and have Warwick's do the invitations."

"My house?" *And you didn't clear it with me first. Just pointed your finger and made it so. But then again, I'm the chairman and haven't done a thing. Damn.*

"Of course. You are the committee chairwoman. This will give you your entrance into society again, and your house will be cleared of all the Christmas decorations and nonsense. Opening your doors will announce you are back in circulation. Don't worry, your sister and I will take care of everything."

Of course they would. And why would she assume I would be decorating? Oh, of course, because she would.

A silly thing like my husband's death shouldn't preclude me from putting up jingle bells.

"Fine. Just let me know when and I'll be ready. Good-bye, Mother." I was done with this.

"Good-bye, dear."

I never made a note, and I didn't bother to tell her I had not done any decorating, which seemed inappropriate and, frankly, too depressing.

I had no desire to entertain, but it seemed to be Mother's *raison d'être.* How in the hell was I going to summon up the energy to do this? Damn it. Once again, I accepted Mother's plan for my life. When would I grow a backbone where she was concerned?

Maggie was already in on this, probably making plans as we speak. Apparently I was heading the fundraising committee, but they would do it all. For a party in my house.

I inspected every room and found them perfectly acceptable for an event of the magnitude Mother expected. God knows I had done it before, successfully, I might add.

I tamped down my feelings of inferiority and being put upon. I did not tell Mother I had just been to the art park or was contemplating (more like resisting) becoming an active member of the art park nor did I tell her I wasn't interested in hosting the benefit.

One doesn't tell Patricia Palmer. She asks, you do. Maggie doesn't see it, or doesn't object, because she's the same way.

Damn.

I went to bed in a fit of pique.

$$\times \quad \times \quad \times$$

The next afternoon my cell rang. I heard my niece's distinctive voice, chirpy and happy, at the other end. "Aunt Jen? I'm home!"

"I heard. Mimi told me. When can I see you?" My heart lifted.

"Are you free now? I think I can escape Mother's clutches for a bit."

I laughed. Maggie had apparently already started in about the wedding. My sister is, if nothing else, efficient.

"Sure. I'll have Choyou put the kettle on."

I went into the kitchen. Choyou opened a glass container that held her special lemon cookies—Tricia's favorite. She had ears everywhere, and I had gotten used to her prescience, like Radar O'Reilly. "You're way ahead of me," I said as she gingerly and lovingly placed the cookies on the plate that we always used for Tricia and Eric's secret birthday cake. If Maggie knew I had provided a sugar cake for them she'd be apoplectic. Maggie didn't believe in sugar, and I indulged the twins, risking the wrath of Margaret Palmer Putnam.

"Missy Tricia home," Choyou said, and she smiled brightly. I believe she loved Tricia just as much as I. Her hands clasped over her chest and her eyes filled.

"Let's have some champagne, too," I said. "Tricia's engaged!"

Choyou's eyes opened wide and a tear fell down her dark cheek. "To be married?"

"Yes, to be married." I smiled.

"Mr. Carl?"

I nodded. "Good old Carl."

She put her hands to her face and cried. "So happy," she said. I rolled my eyes, pat her on the shoulder and scooted upstairs to shower and change. On my way out, I stopped at the wall safe, unlocked it, and pulled out a letter-sized envelope addressed to Tricia in Arthur's handwriting.

Tricia had always been an enigma to me. Arthur understood her. They shared secret jokes and seemed to have a connection I didn't. But I adored her as well as her twin Eric, and we had them over often when they were young. They loved spending time with Choyou, who showed them mysterious Asian arts and kept them mesmerized with stories from her childhood.

I felt a pang when I remembered my early barren childbearing years. My heart broke when Maggie told us they were expecting a baby. Our Catholic upbringing said it was God's will. I knew better.

When Maggie announced she was pregnant with not one but two babies, I filled what few empty spaces I had in my calendar with things I had no interest in to avoid watching her grow into impending motherhood. Arthur never said a word.

The hardest part was giving her a baby shower, which I was obligated to do as her sister. The good girl.

I smiled and giggled at the onesies, the rattles, the diapers, and the receiving blankets while I inwardly seethed and cried and threw a tantrum. My nerves were so shot I claimed a urinary tract infection and kept going into the bathroom to breathe. I avoided going to the hospital when she delivered the twins by claiming a virus. I knew stepping foot onto a maternity ward would crack me wide open and I was terrified I'd spill everything.

But when we were expected that very first day they came home receiving visitors, I held the twins for the first time and knew I would be a big part of their lives and got over it fairly quickly. Tricia's tiny fingers wrapped around my index finger and I was a goner.

They stole our hearts. Arthur loved Tricia and understood her, and she and I became close because of that connection, but she and Arthur were closer. Eric tolerated us. He was a shy mama's boy and stuck close to his parents. Tricia was the explorer.

How I hated myself for not giving them a cousin.

Twenty minutes later, I found Tricia and Choyou hugging fiercely when I descended the curved stairs. Choyou was crying again.

I led Tricia into the living room where we found a presentation of tea, champagne, and lemon cookies on the coffee table draped in a white lace tablecloth to make it extra special.

"Let's see it," I said as Tricia held out her left hand. What I saw took my breath away. A square diamond surrounded by baguettes in a platinum setting looked antique, even art deco. "It was his mother's," she whispered. "I love it. It sort of reminds me of Zelda Fitzgerald." She cocked her head, and I agreed. Tricia and I had read all of F. Scott Fitzgerald's books and stories and became entranced with his biography, falling in love with his wife, the flawed Zelda.

I poured champagne and asked Choyou to come in with another glass. "You mean a great deal to Tricia, and I know you love her, too. Come, join us."

She started to cry again, gulped her champagne and left, sobbing. Tricia rolled her eyes. "Some things never change."

"We've certainly been a pair the past month," I said, and grimaced at the stab of pain I felt. I had forgotten my grief for a moment.

"I'm so sorry I missed the funeral."

"And I'm sorry I missed graduation," I said. "So we're even."

"Not even close." She smiled sadly. "I miss him. He was as much a father to me as Dad."

She saw my eyes brim over and quickly said, "I saw the funniest thing. I stopped in at the Waterford this morning to get one of their fabulous pastries, and there were about a dozen women sitting around a table wearing red hats and purple outfits. They seemed to be having a good time. What's up with that?"

"Ah. The Red Hat Society is a group of women over fifty who have retired or have in some way made it."

She sipped from her flute. "Why aren't you a member?"

"One has to be invited, and anyway, I've not accomplished anything on my own to warrant admission."

Tricia's eyebrows went up. "What? You're kidding, right?"

I picked up my tea and leaned back. "So, tell me about your plans."

"I have to pass the bar exam. That's my first priority, and Carl agrees." She took a cookie and groaned with pleasure.

"Is he still with the firm?"

She nodded. "Dad has made him a junior partner. The original plan was for him and Eric to take over the firm when Dad retires, but now that

Eric's gone, I apparently slide into his spot." She took a sip of her tea and looked away.

Her twin Eric died four years ago in a freak skateboarding accident. Carl had been with him when he died and apparently never got over it. Dave and Maggie kept Carl close after Eric died. Dave kept his promise and hired him into the firm when he passed the bar exam, all according to the original plan.

"Is that what you want?"

"Of course."

Silence.

I reached inside my shirt and pull the long gold chain that held Arthur's wedding ring over my head, unclasped the chain and slid the ring off. I had thought about this in the shower and knew it was the right thing to do. "Would you like to have this for Carl?"

Tricia's eyes bugged out. "No. No, Aunt Jen, it wouldn't be right."

"He would love to know that it had been passed on to you." I held it out to her, surprised that his ring was so easily given away.

"NO." She put her hand in the air, palm out. "No, thank you," she said more quietly.

"All right. If you change your mind, you know where it is." I slipped it onto my left thumb and found I kind of liked it there. I could always look at it instead of hiding it under my clothes.

"Tell me about your life. What are you leaving behind in Boston?"

Tricia stared at me. "Leaving behind?"

"Come on, you lived there for years. You have to be leaving quite a lot behind."

A shadow crossed her face. "No, I always planned to come home, so I never made any real connections."

That just didn't sound right. "I don't believe you. You're too friendly for that. I can't believe your entire life was school and studying. You'd go crazy." I leaned back against the couch, threw my arm over the back of it, and tucked my feet under me. "Talk."

She smiled. "Well, there's Lacey, of course, my best friend. Someday she'll come out here, I think, but for now she's staying put in Boston." She lowered her eyes and her voice. "There was a man, but he always knew I would be coming home and leaving him behind." Her eyes came up to meet mine. "He knew it, and he agreed to it." Her voice sounded too sure, too resolute.

"What's his name?"

"It doesn't matter." She waved one hand in the air and reached for her champagne.

"And it's over?"

She nodded, a bit too firmly, I thought. "I wouldn't have committed to Carl if I had any hesitation. This has been the plan for years."

"Plans can change."

"Not according to my mother." She smiled. "You know I love Carl, I always have, and I always will. Together we will run the firm and grow old. We understand each other, we get it, and we know what's important. I don't know of many marriages that are based on those principles."

Something in her voice bothered me, but I let it go. Until I could identify it, I wouldn't interfere.

"Mother has taken over the wedding, she's even talking about inviting the governor." Tricia rolled her eyes and frowned.

I can't say this was a major shock. Maggie ran Tricia's life, and Arthur and I had always wondered how Tricia turned out so well, and how in the world she would ever be able to make a decision on her own. She never rebelled, not once, always doing things exactly as expected. She even dressed like Maggie today, a wool skirt and tailored shirt, but she left the jewelry off and wore ballet slippers.

"I'm afraid you're in for it. She never had a wedding, so this is probably more her wedding than yours." I couldn't believe I said it, but there it was.

"I know. But honestly? I should have known she would barge ahead. I just wanted to get engaged, not plan the wedding so fast. It's all getting out of control. I want a small wedding, not the production she has planned, but I'm reconciled to it. The truth is, I don't really care about all the details. It's one day and at the end of the day no one's going to remember if the flowers were red or pink, or if the cake was three or four tiers, or if it was Bach or Beethoven playing. She can have all that."

"Very sensible."

"But I do want something specific, and she's going to have a shitfit about it." She mouthed the word silently.

"What's that?"

"Can I swear you to secrecy?"

"For the moment."

"Okay." She reached down into a large leather bag and looked up. "Really? This is just between us?"

"For the moment." Not knowing what was about to be revealed, I hedged. Coward.

Tricia pulled out a picture frame from her tote and handed it over to me. It was a pen and ink sketch of a long, lacy gown embraced a figure that looked like Tricia, but with dark spiked hair and darker eyes. Her gown crossed tightly across the bodice, stopped at the knees and draped back into a short train. The sleeves, pointed over the top of the hand, skimmed the arms. The neckline a low, V-shape that came down between and below her small breasts. The model wore boots. The sketch was signed Petchek. Not a name I knew.

"This is, um, unusual," was all I could think of to say. "I take it this is what you want for your dress. You're right. Your mother's going to have a fit. She would not allow it."

"Vera Wang," she said in an exaggerated nasal tone, "has already been contacted for one of her gowns. But I want this."

Choyou came in to deliver some finger sandwiches—and eavesdrop.

"So, will you make it?"

"Hunh?" I shook my head and blinked my eyes.

"Will you make my wedding dress? This one." She pointed to the sketch.

"Tricia, I'm not qualified to do this. I'm not a seamstress. Why don't you hire a dressmaker and then you can be sure your mother is out of the loop."

She shook her head. "No. I want you to make it."

"But honey, I'm not a tailor, this has to fit perfectly."

"You don't understand. I don't want it sewn. I want it hand-knit."

I must have been staring.

"You know, the sticks, the stitches, the rows?" She moved her hands as though she were knitting.

"Good God."

Trisha had never asked me for anything. I had made special dresses for her in the past for Easter, or her confirmation, but she was little then, with no curves. A hand-knit wedding dress?

"What's the rush? And why does this look familiar?" I said, holding up the sketch.

"Don't you see it? It's the Barbie dress Nana Buford made for you. You used to let me play Barbie wedding day, and it's a modified version of it."

"Very modified." My Barbie wedding dress must have been made with toothpicks, the stitches so small you needed a magnifying glass, and formed a lacy pattern that was most unique, but it had a straight hemline and a mandarin collar. Very conservative. "But, yes, I can see where you got the original design. Are you sure you don't want that design?"

"No. It's pretty, but it's not unusual enough. I want something unusual."

"Back to my first question. What's the rush?"

"If we start on it now . . . and I'll help," I taught Tricia how to knit years ago and she had become quite accomplished, "we can have it done before my mother starts the ball rolling on the wedding, and if I present it as a fait accompli, there won't be much to argue about. I'm trying to put the kibosh on all the planning. I have to study for the bar exam and Carl is nowhere near ready to get married. He gave me the ring to make a statement and save him from being harassed by my parents, a self-preservation tactic. I have to pull in the reins on my mother. It will be at least a year."

"Well, good luck with that," I muttered.

Tricia looked at me with her big doe eyes. "All I want is this one thing. She can have the rest. The ring isn't even my choice. Shouldn't I have this one thing?"

"Of course you should, but I may not be the right person to do this."

"You are and I won't have anyone else, certainly not Vera Wang." She exaggerated the name again and I couldn't help but laugh.

"If I do this, I can't keep it a secret. I won't be comfortable keeping something so big from your mother."

"I'll figure something out."

"I have something for you." I handed Tricia the envelope.

Her eyes watered when she saw Arthur's handwriting.

"I have no idea what it is, but he wanted you to have this either when you graduated or when you got married, whichever came first."

"Thank you," she whispered as she slid it into her bag. "Are you joining us for Christmas?"

"No, I don't think so. The thought of enjoying the holiday with all the good will toward man crap makes me nervous." Maggie always had an all-day affair, a catered lunch and a big Christmas goose brought in for a formal dinner. One was expected to be there all day.

No thank you.

She smiled and left a short time later, promising to keep in touch. I wandered back to the living room and my knitting, concerned for my future.

If Maggie thinks I'm interfering with her daughter's wedding, life will be incredibly uncomfortable for us all.

Chapter Nine

I MADE IT THROUGH CHRISTMAS BY WATCHING MOVIES ALL DAY AND eating popcorn. On December 28, I returned to my salon and had my hair colored. Esther swore it was the same color she had used for the past twenty years, but it looked too stark to me, too brassy, not natural, and I was not happy. I got into the shower and shampooed it again to see if I could tone it down a little.

This was supposed to make me feel more normal, more like myself. Instead, a stranger stared back at me in the mirror.

On an impulse, I opened the French doors to Arthur's closet. His clothes had all been packed up and donated, but the contents of his pockets from the last day he got dressed remained on top of his dresser. A few coins, his father's fountain pen, his keychain, a money clip, a small notebook, and his sunglasses in their case sat neatly, in a row, all lined up as though he would be getting dressed again in the morning. I hadn't let anyone move them.

My cell rang.

"Hi, Gigi. Free for lunch?"

"Sorry, no. Mother's called a command performance—Tricia's engaged, and we have to come up with a battle plan. Maggie, Trish and I are due there in," I looked at my watch, "Thirty-two minutes."

"Ouch." I could actually hear Renee wince. "Better you than me." She hung up.

Maggie is Mother's clone, at least in presentation, if not in personality. Tall, slim, and turned out with a long, highlighted bob, perfect makeup, acrylic nails and tons of expensive jewelry, Margaret Palmer Putnam was a caricature of the ladies who lunch. She never put a foot wrong and looked down her nose at those who did. Image was more important to her than reality. Renee called her "the plastic one."

But she was my sister.

We had ceremonial air kisses before selecting Sauvignon Blanc and canapés from a silver tray passed by a server in a black suit. I did not miss Mother's pupils pinpoint when she saw Arthur's ring on my thumb. (*"But my dear, she's wearing an ankle bracelet,"* she said once of a friend of hers who had not passed muster). The tiniest infraction of customary dress was cause for immediate dismissal. God help the person who appeared with a tattoo.

Mother's living room held small, upholstered chairs in moss green against dark wood, a cream-colored damask Victorian love seat and fresh orchids on antique tables. An oil portrait of my great-great grandfather hung over the fireplace. An evergreen wreath hung over the mirror and gold angel figurines were her modest decorations, along with atypical cylindrical candles for atmosphere.

Perfection.

Maggie started in before we had a chance for chitchat, as though she were reporting her homework. "I've contacted the Valencia for the reception, and, of course, the wedding will be at the Immaculata. They have both given me their availability dates for the summer." She ticked items off on her fingers. Her monogrammed leather notebook, well used, lay on her lap. "Warwick's will do the invitations, Adelaide's is on board to do the flowers in yellow and pink, and I am working on getting an appointment for one of Vera Wang's designers to meet with us next month in Boston. They normally ask for a year, but I think we can get it done by summer with a little grease." She rubbed her thumb against two fingers in the air. "Let's see, oh, the Jordan Almonds are ordered with your and Carl's initials. The cake can come from Hamilton's, one of those Wedgewood impressions you liked so much when we went to London, and I have the guest list at 200 at this point." She looked up at us, pride at a job well done evident in her smile. Expecting applause, no doubt.

Tricia eyed her mother, a brie-smeared cracker raised halfway to her mouth. "Mom, we haven't set a date yet. Don't you think it's a little early? I was thinking more like a year from now."

"Never too early, dear, especially if you want Vera Wang involved. We need to get her tied up quickly."

"But . . ."

"No buts, dear, it's pre-planning, and it never hurts to get our ducks in a row. I will not have the typical mother/daughter fuss over a wedding. We are going to do this in increments, and with systematic organization. Most everything has been covered." Maggie looked for approval at Mother, who nodded, then back at Tricia, who didn't.

"Of course, you have to approve of everything," she said, and looked at Tricia over her reading glasses.

"Really." Tricia folded her cocktail napkin. "I hate Jordan Almonds."

"Don't be difficult. I just started the ball rolling with things I knew you would enjoy. We do think alike, you know." She hesitated. "And Jordan Almonds are expected—they are a tradition at all formal weddings."

"Tricia, I have to agree. Your mother's arrangements are perfectly suitable." Mother continued, "I shall have a bridal shower here and you will register at Sterling's, of course."

Of course. It's where we all registered back in the day.

The discussion went so fast—ratatatatat—and they were so firm in their convictions a comment from me felt like trying to get into a clique at school, the nerd trying to get in with the cheerleaders. Tricia and I were the leftovers.

Poor Trish. She was outmaneuvered, and I didn't help much. But I gave it the gosh-darn-it-all-we-can-make-this-work treatment.

"Maggie, don't you think we should wait on this? It seems a bit rushed to me. Besides," I said, thinking fast and getting in the game, "a year will allow for any mishaps. Six months doesn't sound like enough time to pull off the wedding you're talking about." I wanted to ask Tricia what she wanted but thought this a better tactic.

Six months was not enough time to hand-knit a wedding dress, if I were to, in fact, agree to do so.

Mother's head moved from me to Maggie, like a tennis match in progress.

"Never too soon. But to be fair, a holiday wedding does sound lovely. Shall we agree on that?" Maggie's bright eyes looked from me to Mother to Tricia. "A holiday wedding next year?"

Tricia's wedding by consensus.

Tricia sighed. "Fine, Mother, but please don't go overboard. I have to study for the bar exam and can't really focus on anything else right now."

"As you wish," Maggie said, and closed her book with a slap.

"I will go see about lunch," said Mother, and Maggie excused herself to go to the loo. Tricia rolled her eyes at me and grinned. I lifted my eyebrows as a question, but she shook her head at me before Mother stepped back in.

"Luncheon is served." Mother pirouetted and led us into the dining room, where an oval table sat covered in a white lace tablecloth with four place settings showing off her priceless Victorian china plates. A bride's centerpiece of white roses, I'm guessing from Adelaide's, baby's breath and trailing ivy took center stage. The reflection played out against perfectly shined silverware, polished so many times it looked brand new.

So elegant. I would have been happy with a taco.

Maggie started in again: "About the music . . ." Trish shot a "help me" look across the table.

I had learned growing up with Mother and Maggie at the table that they were in sync. They tended to raise their forks at the same time, and if I wanted to introduce anything into the conversation, I would have to wait until the exact second they were both occupied.

Actually, Renee discovered that years ago and used to ask if their periods were synced, too.

"I have some news," I said in my most cheery voice.

"Oh, what's that, dear?" Mother sipped some water and looked at me.

"I'm thinking about taking a house at the art park."

"You're what?" Maggie's voice was a bit louder than usual.

"I'm thinking about taking a house." I tried to stare her down, but she won.

"Jen, you're not supposed to make any big decisions the first year. It's not good for you."

I shifted to the open-eyed, happy-to-take-in-information approach: "In what way would it not be good for me?"

"I like the idea," Mother said, shooting darts at Maggie. "Supporting an artist is not only helpful to the art park but it also gives you something to do without having to exert too much energy." She nodded approvingly. "And your name associated with the center will be a boon."

Maggie jumped in, "Possibly, but . . ."

This ought to be fun. Arthur's voice in my head again.

"I may not simply sponsor an artist; I may run it myself." I interrupted them, a first for me. I had to get it out, fast. I felt lightheaded being a bit of a devil. I took a bite of salad nonchalantly.

A silence descended over the elegant table. My mother and sister looked down at their plates. My niece looked at me directly, and we locked eyes. "A needlework shop?"

"How did you know?"

"Well, you're so good at it, and you're good with people. I think it's a great idea. I'll support it. It will be perfect for stress relief." Tricia's eyes showed approval, and her smile confirmed it.

Maggie dropped her fork on her plate, making a loud ping that clattered through the room. Mother shot a look at her, not so much at her reaction, but at the possibility of cracking her precious plate. "Well," Maggie said, "I never thought my sister would be a *shop girl.*" She took a gulp of wine. "Honestly, Jen, you must be mad." I was somewhat pleased to see a piece of something green stuck to her tooth.

Mother sat quietly and poked through her salad.

"Mimi, what do you think?" Tricia asked.

Damn. Almost home free.

Mother put her fork down with infinite patience. "I'm not entirely sure why you would want to, but I wish you luck, dear," Mother said. "If you want to sponsor a needlework shop rather than a real artist, I understand, and I approve."

Was she deliberately being obtuse?

I stared at my own salad, not sure what to say. "I don't know what else to do, honestly, and this opportunity came along . . ." I smiled as brightly as I could.

"What do you mean, you don't know what else to do? Do what I do, what Mother does, what you used to do. Get involved! You could get back into committee work again." Maggie's tone of voice made me nervous for some reason.

"I could, but . . ."

"But what, it's not good enough for you anymore? We do an awful lot of good, you know, supporting the infrastructure of the city, we don't just sit around eating bonbons." Maggie's voice rose a little but remained a monotone. She was furious, and I couldn't figure out why.

"I know that," I said, a bit complacently. "I'm just not sure that it's the place for me without Arthur. I supported him more than any cause."

"I'm sure you did, dear." Mother stepped in while Maggie pressed her lips together, folded her napkin and placed it neatly beside her spoon. "Coffee?" and rang the silver bell by her water goblet.

Chapter Ten

WHEN I AWOKE THE NEXT MORNING, I HAD A VISION SEARED INTO MY brain so clear it was as though a photograph of it had been taken. In fact, it had. On the cover of *Architectural Digest*, the October issue.

In my dream, my English manor drawing room had been recreated in the parlor of what I was now calling the widow's house. Bookcases lined every wall holding yarn and supplies. My furniture fit perfectly. The tapestry hung on the east wall. In my vision the fireplace blazed, lights were on, and rain was softly falling. I saw customers happily perusing inventory and relaxing in the parlor working on projects. Two King Charles dogs flanked the fireplace.

I laughed out loud at the picture-perfect scenario.

My dining room furniture featured needlepoint supplies. The serving board would house a silver coffee pot and cups and saucers, ready for customers. The kitchen would be the workplace for steamers and blockers and sewing machines, a production room to make something from items clients finished, too intimidated to sew or cut into it to make a finished product.

I saw it. I smelled it. Hell, I owned it.

My head started to tingle, and I grew restless with new visions, down to the house plants that would work, the lamps, all the lap blankets and afghans I had hidden in the closet upstairs waiting to be given away on display, draped across the couch, chairs, the bannister . . . .

If this wasn't a vision sent from above, I didn't know what was.

Do it. Do it. Do it. Arthur's voice in my ear cheered me on.

And Mother and Maggie's reaction yesterday just made me mad. Did they want to keep me in a box?

I dialed Renee on her cell. "Hi, Gigi. What's up?" She always took my call. I could hear papers rustling and her assistant talked to her in the background.

"I want that house."

"What house? Are you moving? Call a realtor." She pulled the phone away from her mouth "No, not this one," she said to someone over the mouthpiece, "the whoseamacallit . . . you know . . . thanks. Now, what's this?" She was back with me.

"The art park. I want the big, three story, burnt sienna house."

A hesitation. "You'll do it?"

"You think I can?"

"Hell, yeah."

"Then send over the realtor before I chicken out."

"Done." Click.

I hung up and felt my heart racing like I had just finished a 5K. I had, in fact, just finished a race of sorts.

God only knew what the repercussions would be.

Suzanne Finch, Realtor to the Stars, arrived in her bright red suit and her designer leather tote, raced up the drive, announced herself with screeching brakes, and charged into the house. This woman was a force of nature with a slight southern accent. I had been warned not to underestimate her. She was a Barbie doll, bleached blonde hair in a French twist, loads of makeup and a tiny waist. I took special note of her jingle bell bracelet and new year trumpet pin and fought the urge to vomit. I just wanted to skip the holidays, and someone being so cheery about it made me queasy. Like everything was normal, happy, dare I say jolly?

No.

"I am so happy you are taking one of the houses!" She chimed. "Do you know you are the first?" She enunciated her T's a tad longer so that they stood out and she spoke more slowly than she walked—or drove. Her eyes shone bright and clear, like a child entering a birthday party.

"I'm not sure I know what I'm doing, but I'll give it a shot," I said.

"What did you say?" she said into her tote as she leaned over it on the coffee table. "I didn't hear you."

One must speak up. Apparently I'm being a mouse.

"I said . . . Oh, never mind." She couldn't hear me over that damn bracelet anyway.

"Right, then. Here are the papers." She pulled out a file folder that had to be an inch thick. "Nothing out of the ordinary, I assure you." She leafed through them. "Oh, Renee says we don't have to bother with this . . . or with this . . . or this." She withdrew sections and left them on the table.

"What is the name of the business?" she asked with some officiousness, pen poised over the lease form, eyes glued with deep concentration, ready to do business.

"I . . ."

"Sorry. I guess I should ask what kind of business this will be." Her long eyelashes fluttered down, then up again, like curtains.

"A needlework shop?"

Her eyes bugged out. "Needlework shop? Really? We don't have a good one here. That's wonderful. A knitting shop?"

"More than that," I said as I made everything up on the fly. "Knitting, crocheting, needlepoint, crewel embroidery, some production, alterations, classes, groups, and custom orders." I spewed it all out in one sentence and had to take a breath.

Why hadn't I thought this through? I didn't even have a name yet.

"How wonderful! You will do well." She looked around the living room and took in the environment, "I assume you can finance this yourself?"

Shocked (*we don't talk about money, it's gauche*), I said, "Yes," and wondered if an inquisition might be part of the lease process.

"Just want to ensure you can pay the lease every month. You understand."

"Of course." But that put another thought into my head.

Jesus.

I have no idea how much money I have to spend on this venture.

I looked at the pile of papers on the coffee table. They were financial forms, apparently. Piles of them that had been deemed unnecessary.

Thank you, Renee. I would have no idea how to begin to fill those out.

"You are so lucky. That's my favorite house of the complex," she said, her eyes shining and her bleached teeth glinting.

Sure it was.

She looked around the house. "This is beautiful. If you ever want to sell, give me a call. I can get it sold for you in no time." She handed me her card and her jingle bracelet sung with a cheeriness I did not feel.

I didn't quite know what to say. It hadn't occurred to me to sell the house. It was my home.

It was Arthur.

Suzanne's car raced down the driveway and I heard her screech around the corner. I dropped down onto the couch and put my hand on my forehead.

What had I done? Instead of feeling I just accomplished something big, I felt trapped. Damn Renee. Mother and Maggie were right.

I don't know how to do this. What am I playing at?

I focused on the picture over the fireplace. My mind was a jumble of disjointed words that vibrated inside and didn't make any sense. My face burned and my heart started to pound in my chest. I couldn't breathe. Then a vice grip tightened around my ribs. I gasped and clutched my hand over my heart and leaned over, my head placed on my knees. I felt queasy and my stomach cramped badly. My eyes wouldn't focus; everything was blurry.

Didn't I have to have a business license? A DBA? A bank account? Didn't I have to have experience? Questions came at me visually, like inside a kaleidoscope, over and over until I was lightheaded and wanted to faint.

Was I having a heart attack? An elephant sat on my chest. I was alone in the house and my legs wouldn't hold me even if I wanted to get up. I sweat so much a drop fell off my nose and my silk shirt clung to me. My fingers tingled.

Somebody help me.

I stayed in that position, trying to breathe for a few minutes.

Calm down. Stay calm. Breathe. In. Out. In. Out. You're okay.

I sat up slowly, feeling my heart slow down and my brain begin to put itself back together again, the pieces sliding back in where they should be, like pieces of a jigsaw puzzle locking back into place. Enough so I could do something to help myself.

My cell was on the end table. I called Renee.

"Renee, I . . . can't . . . breathe."

She fired specific questions at me one after the other about my body and what I had been doing. When I could answer without having to take a breath, I decided I was going to live.

"What you just had, my friend, sounds like a panic attack, not a heart attack. I've had a few of those over the years. Remember when Eddie left me?" I remembered. She had been so devastated, so outraged, and so overwhelmed with her career and other pressures I forgot I had witnessed one.

It was just a panic attack.

She asked me a few questions about my chest, breathing, heart race, pulse, etc., and then pronounced me okay, but suggested I call my doc.

"God, Renee. They were going to find me here, on the couch, bent over. Widow dies of overblown confidence, loneliness, confusion and heartbreak."

Renee barked, "Jennifer Conrad, beloved member of this community, had just signed a lease to open the first shop at the new art park, a state-of-the-art needlework shop that friends and acquaintances said was bound to be a success, but, alas, will never be, due to this tragic case of overblown self-doubt resulting in death by sheer panic."

I held my breath.

"That was a joke. Now go on and live your life. Start making plans." A hesitation, then again she fired more questions at me, asking me to take my own pulse and check that I wasn't sweating any further and that my strength had come back. I swore to call her back in ten minutes.

I hung up and my eye went to the floor to a business card:

SUZANNE FINCH
REALTOR TO THE STARS
. . . AND YOU'RE THE STAR

With a tiny gold star dotting the I.

Good God.

After I felt better and Renee reassured me one more time that I was okay, I called my doc as promised.

I told them simply I wasn't feeling well and wanted a quick check. I knew telling them I had had chest pains would land me in the hospital immediately. She agreed to fit me in.

Pretty and competent Dr. Simpson reminded me I was way past my mammogram date. My chart sat on her lap and she examined my eyes, ears, and throat while chatting.

"I'm aware. My husband was very ill for two years and I let everything go. Besides, every year something shows up and it turns out to be nothing. I just didn't want to go through that again while he was so sick."

"I understand, but it's time for you to devote time to yourself," she said kindly, her hand on my wrist. "You'll need to make an appointment for a mammogram. And I see you're due for a colonoscopy."

I nodded.

"Now, tell me what frightened you so much you had to be seen today."

I explained the panic attack, and she agreed, but admonished me for not taking it more seriously at the time. "People your age needs to watch these things. It could have been very serious."

"I know." I almost wished it was. Almost. And . . . OUCH.

"Your blood pressure is very low. Are you feeling all right?"

"I've been very tired lately; grief does that to you."

She nodded.

"Let's do some stress tests to be sure your heart is working well. Are you exercising? Eating well?"

"Not really, I dropped everything when Arthur was so sick. I only went up and down stairs and sat a lot."

"Understandable . . ." We talked options and about how much I had enjoyed yoga and swimming. She did not mention the weight gain. Again: "At your age, it's time to pay attention to flutters and nerves. So, before I send you home, I'd like for you to take a stress test. Just spend some time on the treadmill, nothing really strenuous, to see where you are. You should be in good shape, even after the past two years of inactivity, but let's check it out anyway."

I had nothing better to do. So I ran in place for a few minutes, went home and had a drink.

Chapter Eleven

THE CONTRACTS HAD BEEN SIGNED FOR THE SHOP. ONCE THAT WAS DONE, I made the decision to gather my courage and get out again. I had made a few lunch plans in an effort to put something on those pristine white squares.

It was a start.

Unfortunately, my clothes no longer fit. Two years of sitting had taken its toll, and my uniform of sweats with elastic waistbands didn't warn me. My old habit of a daily walk, swim and yoga sessions at the club had fallen by the wayside on the day of Arthur's diagnosis.

I headed downtown to Lambert's and found a few things I liked, picked them up and placed them on the counter along with my credit card. "Would you like me to charge this to your Lambert Account?"

"No, thank you, this will do." I turned to look at something else to avoid more discussion about money, a knee-jerk reaction. ("One doesn't talk about money, it's a personal matter," said Mother when I asked if we were rich. I think I was ten.)

"Mrs. . . ." She looked at the name embossed on the card. "Conrad? If you open an account with us, you can save 15 percent today." I looked up to see a young, pretty, skinny girl with far too much makeup, and I realized this was her job and she probably got a bonus if she opened up new accounts. "Sure!" I said, forcing a cheerful response. I answered her questions as quickly as she asked them, and she entered the information into the system. Her friendly face turned to stone. "I'm so sorry, Mrs. Conrad, you've been declined."

"What?" Embarrassed, I continued, "Then just put it on the card. I don't have time for this." She looked at the card, typed the number in carefully, digit by digit, and waited to get an approval. "It's probably just a glitch," she said, pulling out the charge receipt successfully and presenting me with a pen. She handed the card back to me. "Happens all the time."

Yeah, sure it does. It's never happened to me.

I grabbed my purchase and wound my way back to the car. What's wrong with my credit?

And whom do I ask?

I headed for the bank to see our personal banker. He and Arthur had become friendly and in fact were Rotarians together. We had met socially a few times, and he made it clear he would help me in any way after Arthur became ill.

But I had never warmed to him. I once told Arthur he would be better suited to be an undertaker, that I found him too patronizing. Arthur found it hilarious and didn't disagree with me.

He rose from his desk, a soldier coming to attention, when he saw me, and he shook my hand. "I was so sorry to miss Arthur's funeral," he said, and placed his left hand over our right hands. "This must be very difficult for you." I wouldn't have been surprised if he had added "Little Lady."

"Yes. Thank you."

I stood at his desk.

"What can I do for you?"

"I was just declined for credit, and I wondered why. It's embarrassing."

"Oh? Let me look." He sat at his desk and started typing into his computer. He verified my social security number with me as though he wasn't quite sure I had it right. I could see his eyes traveling over the screen. "Ah. I see."

"Is there something wrong?"

"Not at all. You have no credit."

"What do you mean? We have the mortgage here, and the firm's financials are all here, I must have a dozen credit cards . . ."

"Yes, but that doesn't mean you have credit. It's all in Arthur's name."

I pulled out all my credit cards with my name on them. "Then these mean nothing?"

He took them and repeated as though I were a five-year-old. "All the credit is in Arthur's name. These are just secondary cards he allowed you to have."

"Allowed me?"

He had the grace to turn red. "Yes, the primary cardholder always allows others access to the account. These are not joint accounts. However, your checking account is, but that doesn't count much as far as credit." He handed them back to me.

"Then let's fix it. May I apply for a credit card?"

"Of course, but right now without any income it will have to be based on your assets, and they are in flux until Arthur's estate is settled. I'm afraid the rules are pretty strict. Why don't you keep using the cards you have? There's nothing wrong with them, and they are in your name. We can keep the accounts just as they are." His moist face, fatty jowls and slick hair gave me the willies.

"If you think that's the way to go."

The good girl again. I shook his hand, turned and walked past the desks of well-dressed bankers diligently tapping at their keyboards or talking with customers, earnest concern plastered on their faces. I exited the building, head down, wondering just exactly what had happened.

It didn't help to see the pile of mail on the table in the foyer addressed to "Mrs. Arthur Conrad," which is my title, not my name. What happened to Jennifer Conrad? Or even Jennifer Palmer?

I began to see what the feminists were talking about.

But this hiccup opened the doors of my brain to think about the practical matter of financing, something I had never had to think about. Arthur, or the firm, did it all.

My stomach rebelled when I realized I had no idea where I stood financially. I poured a drink and sat in front of the idiot box.

I'll think about it tomorrow.

Chapter Twelve

RAY CAME INTO THE INTERVIEW WITH HIS CURRICULA VITAE AND interviewed with Carl as he would any other candidate. He had filled out the application, his references were checked, and he knew the right words to say to apply for a CFO position.

Carl excused himself after about twenty minutes and went to Dave's office.

"I think I found him," Carl said.

"Found who?"

"Our new CFO. Come meet him and see what you think."

Dave threw his pen down on the brief he was reviewing. "Anything's better than the two you've already brought me." He scowled.

Carl followed him down the hallway, trying not to grin.

Ray stood when Dave came into the room and introduced himself.

Dave looked over his resume.

"Ah, so the entrepreneurial thing didn't work out, hunh?" He smiled. "A corporate job in a beautiful office with benefits is fairly appealing?" He looked over his reading glasses at Ray.

Ray smiled. "I need to get out of the house. I am becoming a recluse and losing my social skills. I was afraid I'd start to leave bottles of urine around like Howard Hughes."

Dave stared at him and roared. "I like him," he said. "Hire him." And left the room.

Carl and Ray looked at each other and grinned.

Carl took out his personal phone and texted:

> Phase two in place.

Chapter Thirteen

"**W**ILL YOU STOP COMPETING WITH YOUR SISTER?" DAVE TURNED AND looked at Maggie.

"What? I was just telling you how much attention she's gotten since Arthur died. She certainly is the focus of the entire community now that she's come out of hiding." Maggie took off her jewelry and plunked them into the velvet-lined china bowl. Earrings, rings, bracelets, it all went in the bowl. Plunk plunk plunk, for her maid to put away in the morning.

"It's because people like her. And that's all I've heard about for the past two hours. Jen, Jen, Jen. Can you give it a rest, please?"

"What's crawled up your ass?"

"Nothing." He threw his shoes in the closet and loosened his tie.

"Don't tell me *nothing*. What's wrong?"

"Maggie, don't start with me." He turned and looked at her. "I've given you everything. Everything, including your freedom, and you've abused it spending money left and right trying to one-up Jen Conrad."

"What are you *talking* about?"

"You. Everything you do is to compete with Jen. Well, you can't. You're not Jen and you never will be."

"So that's it. Now that she's free . . ."

"Get off it, Maggie. That's ancient history. Let it go. I have."

"Dave," Maggie sighed and sat on the edge of the bed. "I knew how you felt about Jen the day I married you. I know about the others. We made a deal, remember? I'm prepared to stand by it, but if you want to go after her, I'd prefer to not be here when you make a fool of yourself. Tell me now and I'll take my half and go away."

Dave stood, a statue of a middle-aged, slightly paunchy, silver-haired handsome, successful man. He ran his hands through his thick hair. "You might want to wait a bit; your half will not be a big as you might think."

Maggie slumped against the headrest and raised her feet on the bed, crossing them at the ankles. She crossed her arms as well and said, "Dave, I don't want a fight. What's this all about?"

"You really want to know? You're not going to like it."

"You're probably right, but go ahead."

Dave plopped on the edge of the bed, exhausted. "When we realized we were going big and would be a major force, Arthur and I arranged certain financial contingencies to cover you and Jen should something happen to us. You have to realize at the time the world was wide open, and the money just kept coming in."

"Yes?"

"We put a codicil into the new partnership agreement that said should one of us die, the surviving partner would buy the surviving spouse out. The good news is I believe the audit will provide a very high number—mid-eight figures."

"And that's a problem?"

"Half of it goes to Jen."

Maggie stared at him. "I knew she would get something, but Jen gets *half?* But she didn't do any of the work."

"See? That's what I'm talking about." Dave stood up and placed his hands on his hips. "If the situation were reversed, you'd be dancing in the streets, and whether or not you 'earned' it wouldn't cross your mind. But Jen gets what's coming to her, and you're pea green jealous." Dave glared at Maggie. She seemed not to notice.

"I take it this puts us in a squeeze."

"Yes, it does. Until the audit is done, we have to put our nose to the grindstone to build it back up."

"Oh, don't worry about that. Rich will do that quickly."

"Maggie, Rich is gone. He quit. No notice." Maggie stared. "Are you willing to hang in there with me?"

"Have I ever let you down?" Maggie hadn't moved, but her pupils constricted.

"Good. You can start by replacing the receptionist at the office. That will save some money right there." He turned away from her, a slight smile on his face.

"Ohhh, no. You're not putting *me* to work. How would it look? Why not get Tricia to do it?"

"Do you want to work with me on this or not?" He turned around; a scowl replaced the smile for Maggie's benefit.

"Arthur dies, Jen gets to sit on her laurels—again—and I have to go to work?"

"No, dear, you're volunteering. Isn't that your favorite thing to do?" He sneered.

"Listen. I can sell some jewelry. I can cut back here on the home front, but I am not going to be your receptionist, and that's final." Her fists clenched on the bedspread.

Dave laughed. "You're so easy to fuck with. Forget it. I wanted to make a point. We're fine, but we do need to build the firm up again. You can understand why." He looked at her with a look that implied she'd better understand.

"Of course. Arthur's death impacted the revenue of the firm. I get it. Now, how are your plans for Carl coming along?"

"How do you think Tricia got that ring on her finger? I intimated to him that if he didn't marry her soon, he'd be out of a job. He claims he got an offer to be a partner from another firm, but I knew that was just a negotiating tactic, so I countered and made him a junior partner. When he marries Tricia, he'll make Managing Partner. He's going to be great at this, and he will keep us in the style to which we have become accustomed." He shook his head a little. "It's too bad Tricia isn't equipped to be another Arthur. That would solve the problem, but, then again, the timing is off. I don't think we have the luxury of time to wait for her anyway, so Carl it is. There's no one else that can do as good a job."

"So, you're serious about running for D.A.?"

"Yes, I am. I've put out some feelers and am getting good feedback. The people who were going to back Arthur are prepared to back me. I think we have a good chance. Having the firm in the capable hands of my son-in-law is good press, and Carl and Tricia will be great on the political side."

Tricia pulled away from the doorway to her parents' bedroom. As their voices faded into the background, she descended the curved stairs. A frown formed as she slowly descended the plush, champagne-carpeted steps.

Chapter Fourteen

The test results were not all in, but Dr. Simpson told me it's probably nothing more than taking care of myself and maybe a few meds; my heart looked fine from what she saw, but she's consulting with a cardiac specialist and didn't want to give me final word until he had blessed it.

Nana Buford had heart disease, what if I inherited it? Worse yet, what if . . .

I realized again I was alone. All the people in my life I thought I could count on disappeared. All the social connections were just that—connections, not friendships. Maggie had no use for me, and Mother was, well, Mother. There would be no help there. Renee is my anchor and I know I can always count on her, but she's my friend, my pseudo-sister, and she has her own life.

My heart had suffered so much pain the past two years I hadn't even thought about the physical state of it. I had not been taking care of myself in my grief. My selfish, broad, over-arching grief.

I lost my best friend, my lover, my husband. He's gone.

You're on your own now, kid. Deal with it.

If I have a medical problem I have to handle it on my own. I cannot depend on anyone.

My life had been one of service; give things for raffle items, for philanthropy, for the community. What did I ever get back? It was for Arthur, to make him look good.

What about me? I was the hostess, the comforter, the yes-girl, the doer. A psychiatrist would say it's compensation for not doing things for my children, which is another story entirely.

No. I am alone. And I am going to have to make it work.

No more giving anything away—my time, my work, my love. Tricia's dress will be the last of my good deeds.

RIP, Gigi.

Mother and Maggie showed up early the morning of the fundraiser to make sure perfection reigned—it was their party, and the little widow might just forget to polish the silver.

It was a new year and I had decided to come out strong.

I had gone for a swim, building up my strength. My return to yoga would happen next week, but, taking it slow, I began. The doctor had ordered more movement, my heart would be fine.

My heart will never be the same.

I came into the house to find Mother had arranged for valets, a string quartet, flowers, plants, caterers, and admin-types running around with clipboards and headsets. She had Choyou so preoccupied and nervous I waved my hand at her and got my own coffee and rooted around for something to eat.

I was a little annoyed. They forgot whose house this was.

"No, that goes over there," Mother said to a man lumbering under a huge potted plant. "And you'll want to move the couch to the left." I snuck behind her with a plate and my coffee and tiptoed upstairs.

So much for coming out strong.

They want to do this? Fine. I'll just get back in bed and read. Take the day to myself. I put on Arthur's expensive noise-canceling headphones and opened the newest potboiler, given to me by someone at the reception after Arthur's funeral.

Now I knew how Tricia felt.

I dressed that night in a green evening gown and matching emerald jewelry—statement pieces I had worn once before, designed for the dress that had been made especially for a big event. Where I once stepped into the dress and Arthur easily zipped it up, Choyou had to yank and pull while I held my breath, no pre-dressing cocktail or chit chat, no easy banter, and I had gotten fat. I could barely breathe with the foundation garments attempting to even out the extra skin around my middle. When I shoved my feet into the matching shoes I found even they had muffin tops. My new sleek bobbed hair hung in my face and obstructed my vision. The extra emerald and diamond weight around my neck felt like a noose.

How in the world had this ever been comfortable?

"Ready for your big reveal?" Renee came into the bedroom with two glasses of vodka, thank God, and plopped onto the white velvet chaise. "You ok?"

"I suppose so. Mother and Maggie are doing everything." I threw my hands in the air. "I have no idea what's happening, and it's supposed to be my party. Plus, I don't think I can sit in this."

"All you have to do is show up, that's the point. They're using this to get you back into the fold so you won't slip away like Cinderella."

"Yeah, but Cinderella found her prince. I lost mine."

"That's not what I meant, and you know it. God, are you comfortable?" She said as she watched me hobble over to the mirror to get a final once-over.

I laughed. "No, but you look like you could curl up easily."

"Comfort is my watchword. I cannot afford to look uncomfortable or uptight. I have enough trouble." Renee stood up to model her feminine tuxedo, her hands in the air, bent at the wrist, palms up. Black pants with a satin stripe, a pristine white silk blouse with pinpoint pleats on the bodice and a black jacket with silk lapels looked perfect on her.

"To go," she said, snapped her fingers and pointed at the bedroom door that would lead us into the fray.

I limped out of the room behind her in shoes I hoped would keep me upright all night.

"Iris. How lovely to see you. I am happy to welcome you into our home."

Ouch. That should be *my* home.

"I am pleased to be here. Do you know Helen Sullivan?" I looked behind Iris and saw the woman who had tortured me at the kick-off meeting at the art park. The one with the hair growing out from her upper lip—she still had it. Apparently she was a friend of Iris's.

"Hullo," she said. "Met at the kick-off," and took a flute of champagne from a passing waiter and headed into the dining room.

Iris wore a floor-length coat of heavy pale blue silk over a matching dress. The color complemented her gray blue eyes and silver hair making her a knockout. When the attendant took her coat, I saw a painted stem and bloom of an iris graced her dress from the hem up to her left shoulder, using shades of green for the stem and blues and yellows for the bloom. It looked incredible against the color and grain of the silk.

"Iris, that is lovely," I said. "Who designed it? It doesn't look familiar."

She reared her head back to get a good look at me. "I did, of course, just this afternoon."

"You did?"

"Yes, this is an art event, after all, and I have been known to brandish a paintbrush from time to time," she said. "I have had this dinner suit hanging in my closet for years and decided to bring it out." She leaned in and quietly continued, "The last time I wore it was to the White House for Ronny's inauguration, that's how old it is." She straightened up. "I thought it looked a little too conservative for tonight. Besides, if it didn't turn out, I had plenty of other things to wear, and I cannot imagine I will wear any of them more than once again before I die."

"It is just lovely." At ninety something she still had the energy to take on a risky project.

I had trouble getting out of bed.

We glided into the living room, where we found Helen inspecting all the furniture and artwork.

"I assume all these are your work?" Iris asked, looking around at all the projects. Her eyes found the east wall and her voice changed. "What a lovely tapestry."

The large dark green tapestry over the bar showed nymphs playing, carefree and joyful. The irony did not escape me. Designed to be a rug, I couldn't see having stilettos piercing it after all my hard work, so Arthur hired someone to have it hung properly. I started that piece about ten years ago on a Mediterranean cruise with the Putnams, stitching my way through days and nights of sightseeing, good food, and tolerating my sister. Arthur pointed it out to anyone who would listen. "Jen's masterpiece—every stitch. Isn't it magnificent?"

"I did that. It took years, and I enjoyed the process. I developed a callous on my finger that still hasn't gone away."

Iris looked back at the tapestry. "My dear, it looks as though it belongs in a museum. Lovely. And the watercolor?" She pointed to a piece of a sailboat at sunset I had done after one class and sheer boredom. Clearly not very good, Arthur insisted on having it framed and displayed. I nodded. "Hmmm hmmmm."

"So, you're an artist. I'm impressed. Oh, here's our mayor."

Renee approached and bowed to Iris. She said, "Follow me, madam, and meet the chief of police." I laughed at their antics and nodded as Renee took her arm to lead her over into the dining room.

Maggie appeared next to me, a large double old-fashioned glass in her hand. "You? An artist? Remember the portrait you did of us all?" I remembered and winced. "You didn't show much talent then, and I'm afraid you're no Van Gogh," she said, as she nodded toward the watercolor.

I didn't correct her. Van Gogh's reputation as an oil painter far overrode that of a watercolorist. Besides, I was eight when I did the family portrait. I changed the subject. "You haven't seen the house since it's been redecorated. What do you think?"

Maggie sniffed. "It's nice, Jen."

Arthur didn't want any visitors when he was ill, so she hadn't been in the house to see the final result completed just before Arthur started the downhill slide.

Damn right it was nice. I paid a fortune for it. The fact it was on the cover of *Architectural Digest* must have bugged Maggie to no end. We had deliberately planned this for the many events demanded of a candidate vying for public office.

"Nice?"

"Yes, a little conservative, perhaps, but it will do. It certainly suits you."

I looked at my sister wrapped in a bright red, one-shouldered Grecian number, adorned with diamonds and rubies hanging from her neck and her earlobes. It wouldn't surprise me to discover her lipstick had been custom made to match the dress.

"Tricia, Mother, and Dave are all driving me crazy," She said, leaning over to whisper. I smelled the vodka along with a a hint of crab on her breath.

"How? Tricia seemed fine to me the other day."

"You've seen her?"

Oops.

"Of course. At Mother's? She looks great, Maggie. You should be proud. And Mother? What's wrong with her?" I nodded toward the great Patricia Palmer, who took court across the way in the dining room, a vision in a beaded top and a long black skirt.

"She's demanding as usual, but some of the threads are coming loose."

I let that one go.

"And what about Dave? Is he ok?"

"Sure, but for the first time in a long time he's worried about money."

My head started to tingle, and I remembered Dave's email about tightening belts. *It couldn't be that bad, could it?*

"What do you mean?"

"I mean he brought home a spreadsheet and reviewed how much I spend every month. Can you imagine?" She seemed irked and took a slug of her vodka. "Are you still working on your harebrained shop idea?"

"I think it will be interesting. Knitting, needlepoint, embroidery, the works. I'm even thinking about having a spinning room." My old flair for making conversation and instilling some enthusiasm where none existed came back with a bang.

"A spinning room? You?" she laughed, her mouth forming an unpleasant opening into which I wanted to slam my fist but refrained.

"What's wrong with that?" I took the bait and realized it too late.

"Jen, it's not what we *do*," she said as though she had to explain this to a five-year-old. "Hire somebody to run it, sponsor it, whatever, but don't lower yourself to working in retail. You can do all your little hobby knitting, or whatever it is you do, in private." Her left hand waved in the air as though to dismiss it. "Really, Jen."

No point in trying to discuss this. Our perspectives were too far off, and I found myself a little embarrassed at her reaction. Whether my embarrassment was for me or for her I couldn't tell.

"Well, Maggie, it's done. I signed the lease already."

"You what?" She turned to me, and I swear I saw fire in her eyes.

"I signed the lease. I'm going to open a shop."

"That. Is a huge mistake." She took a slug. "Big. Mistake. You'll regret it."

"Why?" Too late, I asked the question I shouldn't have. To my surprise, she changed the subject.

"Tricia is driving me to distraction."

"How?"

"She won't talk about the wedding, Carl is never around, I can't get an answer about anything. How am I supposed to get a wedding put together if neither the bride nor the groom will talk to me? Vera Wang needs a year to design and make a dress, and we haven't even talked about the visage yet." Maggie's favorite word: visage. "I'm worried they'll just run off and there won't be a wedding."

And you won't have the theater. Arthur always pointed out about Maggie's productions.

"I thought you all decided it was a holiday event. That gives you a year."

"Are you crazy? That long an engagement sends a message they are not ready. No. It has to be within the year. The Spring it is. At the latest." Tricia would have her hands full.

Poor Maggie. When she was younger she embraced being a professional victim. Fortunately, most of that went away, but from time to time it reared its ugly head. What I said to Tricia was right—this was not her wedding. It was all about Dave and Maggie and one-upping their friends with the wedding of the century. I had no doubt that if we were in New York, the fiasco would be at the Plaza.

I wanted to remind her that her daughter just graduated from one of the most stringent, most demanding law schools in the country, she's facing the bar exam, and Carl is trying to make partner. But I stayed in my role of good girl. "They're both busy. Give them time."

"Dave made Carl a partner."

"That's wonderful."

"Since Arthur's gone, Dave needed him to step up. He's done a good job, and Dave thinks he will be another Arthur."

"There never will be another Arthur," I said sharply, surprising even myself. Maggie's eyebrows, if it weren't for the latest Botox treatment, would have gone straight to her hairline. "I mean it, Maggie. Carl is who he is." My husband had just died two months before, and the thought of replacing him at the firm of Conrad and Putnam gave me a very sharp pain.

"Don't be so touchy. I just mean that he will have the contacts and the personality to bring in the business, while Dave tries the cases." She looked at me as though I were a simpleton and couldn't quite grasp the concept of another human being taking Arthur's place. She waved to someone and drifted off.

Don't be so touchy. Her tone of voice, rather than the actual words, rang in my head and made my eyelids twitch.

Breathe. She's just trying to get under your skin. Competing.

Iris and Helen came in, glowing with wine. They'd toured the living room and examined my handiwork again.

"You see? Wasn't I right?" Iris said to Helen.

"Yes." Helen looked at me and her voice dropped. "You're a goddamn fool if you don't open a shop." Renee had dropped that bomb earlier. Iris smiled at me.

I laughed. "Already done."

"Bully!" Helen said, and raised her arm, fist closed in celebration. "A real professional needlework shop!" Iris beamed at her side, both hands on top of her cane.

Tricia and Maggie appeared from the corner. Tricia threw her arms around me. "I'll be your first customer."

I leaned in toward her. "You already are."

"You'll do it?"

"Yes, but with some conditions."

"Do what?" Maggie's eyes blazed.

"Open the shop! Did you know, Mom?"

"Yes, darling, we talked about it at lunch, don't you remember? Shall we go find your father?" They turned and left us. Tricia turned around, winked and threw me a grin.

"The hell was that?" barked Helen.

"Just a little family drama," I said lightly. "Until the shop is ready to open, would you consider coming here on Tuesday mornings to knit? We can start a little group and when the shop opens we can move over there."

"Capital idea!" said Helen. Iris nodded.

We managed to obtain promises for $25,000 for the art park. Not bad, but a drop in the bucket for helping to refurbish the six Victorians at Heritage Park. If Arthur had been here, it would have been at least $100,000.

I hadn't done enough.

Chapter Fifteen

"HELLO, FATHER." MY VOICE CRACKED AS I STEPPED INTO THE DOVE gray dayroom of La Jolla Haven where my father sat in his wheelchair. He stared out the window at the orange and lemon trees in the orchard behind the memory care facility. Dressed in a starched white shirt and navy pants, his face was pasty, unresponsive. One slipper had fallen halfway off, and I resisted the urge to fix it. Someone had neglected to shave him this morning, but other than that, he looked well cared for.

It had been over two years since I last darkened this particular doorstep, but he never would have known that. I shook as I approached him. My stomach sunk down into the soles of my feet. Angry at my own reaction, I steeled myself as I always had since the summer of 1969. Deep breath, squared shoulders, high head.

He looked so old, so fragile. I cracked a little and almost felt sorry for him. I lowered and locked down the force field, like Sylvia Plath's bell jar.

I hated him with all my heart but could not stay away any longer. There was no excuse now, so I went. The good girl.

"How are you?" I asked as I rolled a gray upholstered chair close to his wheelchair.

I tried to engage and played the part of a good daughter. "Are you feeling all right? Are they treating you well?" I asked all the normal questions one would if the respondent had any faculties about them but received nothing in return. I did not touch him, kiss him, or relay any sort of affection to him the way most loving daughters would, my only self-imposed condition for making myself come visit the man who had destroyed my faith in mankind so many years ago. Treat him like a stranger; polite, and if I couldn't come up with respect, with civility.

I spent a total of fifteen minutes with him, a one-way conversation about Tricia and Carl and their plans. His eyes never left the window. God only knew what he thought. I gave up and stood to leave. I gathered my bag. "Goodbye, Father." He slowly turned his head to me, and his rheumy eyes met my face.

"Whore."

I drove home, my hands on the wooden steering wheel, knuckles white, hands bent so firmly against the wheel I thought perhaps they might be glued to the cool wood.

Could he have known what he said?

Of course he did. He looked right through you with the same look of utter disappointment he's displayed every day since you were fourteen.

He never gave me a chance, and I never took one. Correction—I took one, but I paid for it for years. In fact, in a way I'm still paying for it.

I slowly piloted the car into the garage, killed the engine and put my head on the steering wheel. After I took several deep breaths, I pushed the button to close the garage door and drifted into Arthur's office seeking comfort.

Frozen in place, I escaped into another world where Arthur still lived, happy and healthy, and I heard him tell me his favorite story, "Two guys walk into a bar . . ." for which he had a million endings. I felt my lips turn up and heard myself giggle, which brought me out of my trance.

I sat in my dead husband's office, with no husband, few friends, no job, and no value. Tears stung the back of my eyes and I shoved the chair out from under me and pounded my way upstairs to my pristine white bedroom.

Wait. I did have a purpose. The prospect of opening a shop I knew I was nowhere near ready, nor equipped, to deal with. The outcome of a promise made. The good girl. I had to make this work. It was all I had.

Choyou vacuumed downstairs. Life went on. Without me. But that would soon change.

I had no idea just how much.

Chapter Sixteen

IRIS HAD FOUND JADE SITTING, LOOKING LIKE A LOST PUPPY, ON A CURB outside a very high-end grocery story, and liked her on the spot. She took Jade home and hired her to be her companion; piercings, tattoos, green hair, attitude, and ripped clothes didn't make a bit of difference to her.

After she had gotten Jade settled in her room, she chuckled and called her friend Helen and gave her the news.

"You mean that horrible guhl I saw you with this morning?" Iris smiled; happy she had gotten the expected reaction.

"Yes, that one."

"Lock all silver. Hide jewels. Call insurance guy."

Helen's shorthand way of speaking was not unusual, and Iris smiled again.

"Oh, what do I care, Helen? It's just . . . stuff. Nothing means anything anymore."

Silence. Helen then said, "Right, but shouldn't get away with it. Makes them stronger."

"Them? You mean thieves?"

"Yesss. We have to stop them."

"Nonsense."

"What if she hurts you?"

Silence. "You know as well as I do I can take care of myself."

"Pfft . . ." Iris waited. "Youngsters can overtake you easily."

"Bet me. I still have some pretty good moves for an old lady."

"Yes. I know. You were taught well."

"That I was." They both reflected for a few seconds, remembering the old days.

"If all goes well, I'm going to bring her into the fold."

"That???"

"Yes, *that*. You and I are both without children, Helen, and we need someone to drive the ship and tell the story once we're gone, and we're behind on that project."

"But her?"

"Do you have a better idea? Have you brought anyone forward?"

"Well no, but . . ."

"Leave it to me," Iris said. "You know I'm a good judge of character, and this is a lost soul who can use some experienced granny-types."

"Pfft . . ." Helen hung up, and Iris placed the phone back quietly in its cradle, grinning like the Cheshire Cat.

Iris made another phone call, just to be sure her hunches were right. A few hours later, she found she still had her instincts. This girl was lost and needed to learn a few lessons. She and Helen were the perfect people to bring her around.

Iris now had a project, and that made her incredibly happy. She picked up her knitting and began to think.

Chapter Seventeen

"WELCOME!" I SAID AS I OPENED THE DOOR TO IRIS AND HELEN.

"I'd like to introduce you to my friend Jade," said Iris. "She is staying with me for a while and helping me from time to time." I saw Helen grimace as she walked by me, and I saw why.

Jade, maybe not quite twenty, short, with blunt cut dark green hair, heavy eyeliner, a piercing through her eyebrow, and black lipstick, stood holding Iris's elbow. She had a wrestler's build, thick but fit. She nodded to me and looked down at the floor. I had caught a glimpse of her at the art park, but this made me take a step back.

Not what I would have expected from Iris.

"Well, come in, come in," I said in my most cheery, uplifting, I-don't-judge-voice.

Iris chose a seat on the couch and patted the space beside her for Jade to sit. Her cane slipped from the couch onto the floor, and I again admired the silver fox at the top.

Iris had a bag from Lamb's Wool, a yarn shop on the coast, from which she pulled out knitting needles and a skein of black yarn. Jade looked at them as though they might bite her.

I smiled. A newbie. Iris took the needles from her and started to cast on. "I will get you started, dear, and show you the basic knit stitch. Once you have that, you can do anything."

Choyou came in with a tray of fresh coffee and her famous tarts. "Ladies, this is Choyou, who is an artist in her own right." I looked up at her. "Why don't you join us? Did you bring the shawl? It's so beautiful." Choyou's eyes widened, she nodded, and left the room. I saw Helen stiffen. I had broken a cardinal rule.

One doesn't ask the help to join you.

"Oh, I love to see new projects," said Iris as the handed over the needles to Jade and picked up her own needles. Helen started to work on a pair of argyle socks. I had the famous coat in a basket beside my chair.

Earlier that morning, I had unearthed a coat in progress with the ultimate purpose of bringing up the idea of a large project at the shop. I sat and pulled out the piece, still on long circular needles, removed the stitches from the needles and started to unravel. The project had been sitting for a bit and, in order to prevent a line showing where I had left off, I had to go back over and make sure the stitches stayed tight. A collective gasp went up when I started to unravel the huge piece. At the moment it looked like the back of a sweater—a large sweater. The coat would go all the way to the floor.

I looked around. "Is there a problem?"

"My dear, that looks like heaven. Your stitches are so even and tight." Iris zeroed in on my project, Jade's needles frozen in her hands as she eyed the pile of curly yarn accumulating on the floor.

Helen looked over at the piece in my lap and nodded. "Nice."

Whenever I pick up a project, I am reminded of the last time I worked on it: who I was with, what TV show I was watching, or music playing. My heart lurched a little as I drifted back into the memory of Arthur being so ill. Arthur and I chatted over my knitting for over a year, most of it good chatter. We laughed a lot and watched old movies, enjoyed each other while I worked the small stitches over and over. I put it away when Arthur noticeably declined, so the memories were mostly good ones connected with this project, but still.

"I started this a long time ago to match an evening gown. When Arthur became ill, I pulled it out to have something to do as we sat together. The two fronts have been done, the two sleeves are completed, and the back as you can see, is now about halfway done. It is sort of mindless." I laughed, "Arthur called it 'idiot's delight' because of the repetition and no color variation. I thought I could display it as a completed piece, sort of a 'nothing is impossible' display."

Choyou came into the living room carrying a silk pouch of Asian design. She pulled out an astonishing shawl of jade, coral, and silver metallic yarn depicting an Asian scene. She was almost finished with it and we all exclaimed over its magnificence. "I make these for ladies," she said. "This one for Mrs. Baldwin." She perched herself on the edge of a chair, both black ballet-slippered-feet firmly planted on the ground and started to knit. She didn't partake of any coffee or her own tarts. I hoped Helen would notice and appreciate that Choyou knew her place, so to speak.

Tricia's sports car screeched up the driveway and I heard the door slam; she entered the living room breathless but beautiful and fresh, with a huge smile. She wore a dove gray sweater and jeans and carried a bag from Alpaca Heaven of Boston. She introduced herself to everyone, hugged Choyou and pulled out a skein of soft gray mohair and started to cast on.

She saw me glance at her bag. "Sorry. The next purchase is from your shop, I promise."

I smiled and said. "Bags! Another thing to think about. And a logo!" The others smiled at my antics. I am not a scatterbrain, but sometimes I look like it.

"What was the impetus for such a large project, dear?" Iris asked, watching as I attempted to corral the stitches back onto the needles.

"I honestly don't know. I wanted something kind of mindless to do last year because I sat a lot." I worked, listening to Iris demonstrate and instruct Jade on her first knit stitches. I continued to place the stitches in the right order, facing the right way, all 347 of them. "I have an even bigger project in mind," I said.

"Bigger?" Jade looked astonished.

"A hand-knit dress. A gown." I bent down and pulled out the sketch Tricia had given me.

"Awesome." Jade's green eyes opened wide. It looked like something in her style: a bit off and edgy.

"I have no idea who Petchek is, but he's a good artist, and this just caught my eye. Look how he's put in the lace and painted just a blush color to show some life and give it dimension." I managed to deflect the real question. They moved forward, entranced.

"It could be a wedding dress," Tricia said as the picture passed by her.

I almost choked.

Iris examined the sketch. "The neckline needs to come up. It's almost down to the waist, and inappropriate for a bride. But otherwise it's very, what do they say, edgy."

"Hoochie Mamma," Helen sniffed into her argyle pattern of the socks she worked on with four tiny double pointed needles going every which way.

"I thought I might take it on. It's different enough to bring in the younger knitters. I could show it in the window." I hesitated, then jumped in. "I might even enter it into the *Elan Creative* contest. They specifically want projects that are unique." I opened a magazine from the coffee table and showed them the two-page bright red notice I had discovered and thought a nice way to cover up the real purpose for the dress. "For some reason I am entranced with the dress and I want to enter it in the contest just for fun." Tricia picked up the magazine and smiled.

"What a great idea! Black would make it punchy, dramatic," she said into the magazine.

"Black? Not a wedding dress." Helen's bushy eyebrows met, and that damn hair danced on her lip again.

"Actually, black is appropriate for a wedding dress, but the trend has been to have white or ivory for centuries," Iris evidently had a treasure trove of wedding trivia lodged in her brain. "To show purity and innocence of the fair maiden. If this is a wedding dress in black, the bride would look like the Wicked Witch of the West. Honestly," said Iris, pointing to the sketch on the table. "If this project is to be truly unique, I would suggest that soft gray" she pointed to the new skein of yarn in Tricia's hands, "and what a beautiful color for you! Why don't you be the model?"

Like shootin' fish in a barrel.

Tricia and I smiled at each other across the coffee table.

"Let's make this a group project for the shop. Our first one." Iris said, then nodded to me. "Jennifer, dear, you can take the lead and we'll help wherever we can."

Well, that was easy. Now if we can get this by Maggie we'll be home free.

Chapter Eighteen

"SO, HOW ARE YOU TODAY?" DR. SMALL LOOKED OVER HIS HALF-GLASSES at Maggie, crossed his legs, and reclined against the back of a claret red leather wingback chair while Maggie, slumped, pigeon-toed on the beige carpet. She hugged a plump pillow against her chest on the matching couch. A candle glowed on the coffee table inside a clay figurine of people in a circle holding hands. A carafe of water, a glass, and a box of tissues decorated the coffee table. A computer hummed on his mahogany desk, and a clock ticked on the full bookcase.

"I'm fine, but anxious. I have great news."

"Oh?"

"Yes, Tricia's engaged finally. I have a wedding to plan." She smiled brightly, then looked down at the pillow.

"Oh? And how do you feel about that?"

"Ecstatic, of course," she said to the pillow. "This is going to be the wedding of the century. I already have most everything planned out."

"Your usual efficient self, I see," he said. "When is the celebration?"

"No date has been set, but I'm thinking next spring."

"And how do the happy couple feel about that?"

Maggie looked up, her eyes wide. "I don't know. Tricia has to pass the bar exam first."

"Uh-huh." The silence became deafening. Maggie rocked a little on the edge of the couch, her eyes a little unfocused, dreamy.

"Oh, it's going to be wonderful. The ceremony will be at the Immaculata, and the reception is at the Valencia. I am pulling out all the stops. It will be the best, most exclusive, most beautiful wedding this city has ever seen."

"And why is that?"

Her eyes became dark and darted to the therapist. "Because Dave and I have worked hard all our lives, and now it's time to show the rest of the world just how successful we are."

"So this is not about your daughter, then."

Maggie looked at him, making her eyes bigger and brighter than usual. "Of course it is. This is for her. I've dreamed about this her entire life."

"But you just said . . ."

"I know what I just said," Maggie spouted. "This is to show off our daughter and give her the send-off she deserves."

Dr. Small sighed. "Maggie, I've never held anything back from you and I'm not going to start now. Whose dream is it?"

"What do you mean?"

"It sounds like this is your vision, not Tricia's."

"Tricia is going to be a huge force in this community once she takes over the firm. This will only help her. I've invited the governor." Maggie's nose raised high in the air.

Dr. Small leaned back in his chair, his index finger over his upper lip. "But you haven't set a date yet."

"I mean he's on the list. Don't be so nitpicky."

"Maggie, have you been taking your medication?"

"Yes, of course."

"Because you know how important it is." They locked eyes, and his voice softened. "How is the grief process coming?"

"Slowly. I miss him so much it hurts."

"Tell me about that."

"I loved him so much, and now he's gone," she shrugged.

"And he belonged to your sister."

"Yes."

"And how is she coping with it?"

"The Perfect One? Fine. She seems to be OK. She didn't love him as much as I did."

"How do you know that?"

"I just do."

Silence.

"Tell me about Tricia. How is she doing?"

"She's beginning to defy me."

"Defy you? How?"

"She spent the night at Carl's the other night."

"Is that such a sin?"

Maggie's head came up. "You know how I feel about that."

"Yes. Does she seem to be in love?"

"They've known each other so long I think they're just past that infatuation stage, and now they are making it official."

"So no, then."

"No. But infatuation doesn't guarantee happiness. I'm proof of that."

"Do you want to talk about your sister?"

"God, no." Maggie twisted a tissue between her hands. "She's started a little business," she whispered. "A needlework shop. Can you believe it?"

"Well, that's very constructive and healthy for her. It's often helpful to focus on something during the grieving process."

Maggie stared at him, her mouth open.

"What's the problem?"

"She doesn't know what she's doing. She's flying blind."

"And that's a problem because . . ."

"She's going to embarrass us all."

He sat back. "Well, we've come full circle, haven't we?" He received no response and listened to the ticking clock behind him. Finally he spoke. "What would happen if she were to succeed at this 'little business' of hers? How would you feel about that?"

"She would, once again, come out on top, of course. I would be left in the dust by her success. She'd get all the publicity—all the glory."

"So what's stopping you from doing something like that?"

Maggie lifted her head and lasered her brown eyes into his. "Be a shopgirl? Are you insane? I don't have to. I'd be laughed right out of town."

"So what are you going to do, Maggie? How are you going to handle these feelings of inferiority you've been fighting all your life?"

"I'm going to watch her like a hawk and make sure she does nothing that would embarrass me or Dave. He's going to run for District Attorney, and we can't afford to have anything get in our way, even my sister's attempts at making a name for herself."

Dr. Small stared at her as she continued to rail.

Chapter Nineteen

*F*INANCES. NOW THAT I'VE MADE THE COMMITMENT, HOW DO I PAY FOR it? I vowed to pull my head out of the sand.

The truth was I didn't have a clue how much money I had. I knew there would be money coming to me from the firm but didn't know how much and assumed that it would take a while to sort out. In the meantime, of course I had a rough idea—I'm not an idiot, but I had not kept up in the last year and I knew business had slowed down since Arthur left the firm. I was not aware of what had happened in the last eighteen months, so I don't know if I was up or down in my estimation.

I still received a monthly allowance from the firm that kept me comfortable. They continued to pay all our expenses, as happened when Arthur was alive. That would change when I received my lump sum, whatever and whenever that eventuality happened.

I went to the computer and brought up my emails, thinking I might connect with Dave and ask about my buyout, but there was an email from Renee that distracted me:

> Checking up on you. I'm coming over about nine o'clock with a pizza.

> Works for me

Renee always worked into the night, and the late hour suited me just fine.

I pulled up Dave's email address and, with my heart beating loudly in my ears, I had to ask my status.

Can you tell me what the status is of the audit and approximately how much to expect?

I hit send.

$$\times \quad \times \quad \times$$

We sat at the dining room table and scarfed down pizza and some good beer in the silence of the house. Renee had brought brochures and accounting information about the art park and they were strewn all over my parents' antique dining room table. A pizza box, cans of beer, wadded-up paper towels smeared with pizza sauce, brochures, files, and financial statements littered the table.

"I never thought I'd see pizza out of a box and canned beer at this table," she said. "Your mother would have a complete breakdown if she saw this." We were laughing when my sister popped in without knocking or ringing the bell. The look of horror on her face made me laugh even more, and Renee joined me. "What are you doing here, Maggie?" I asked as I stood and began to gather up trash and straighten piles. Renee, shaking her head, slid through the swinging door into the kitchen.

"I'm just checking up on you. I saw the light and wondered if you were all right." She stood in the doorway to the dining room in a perfectly tailored off-white suit trimmed in beige piping. Her feet were encased in beige pumps that matched a pocketbook with an embossed logo of a well-known designer.

"And why wouldn't I be? Maggie, it's after, what, ten o'clock?"

"Oh, you know . . ."

Renee came back through with a roll of paper towels. "Maggie, you don't live anywhere near here. What are you really doing here?"

"Nothing, I told you." She turned to look at me. "Just checking in on you and your, what should I call it, new venture?"

Renee plopped into her chair, picked up a slice of pizza from the box and crammed most of it into her mouth. I was sure it was deliberate as I saw Maggie wince.

Renee looked from me to Maggie and back again. With her mouth full, she said, "Should I leave? Is there something you two want to discuss?" A crumb of pizza crust flew out of her mouth and landed on the lemon-polished table. Maggie's eyes bugged out.

"No." I crossed my eyes at Renee and turned back to my sister. "Maggie, what exactly can I do for you?" I tried to look tough, but, damn it, I couldn't hold my eyes on hers. I caved.

"How are you going to pay for this?" She asked loudly.

"What, the pizza? Renee brought this."

"Your venture, the shop, your . . . folly." Her arms were crossed over her chest.

Renee sputtered a little and took a swig of her beer.

"Why do you want to know?" My ears tingled and I heard Arthur.

Careful. She's up to something.

"I wondered if you needed a loan." She smiled at me as though she were talking to her maid. I had seen that look before, the benevolent woman giving something to those beneath her. An offering to show she was human.

"A loan?" My ears started to burn even more. Didn't she tell me Dave is worried about money?

"She thinks you can't pay for this, and in her most respectful and humble way, she is offering to help," said Renee with no loss of sarcasm. She tossed back some more beer and belched, then smiled apologetically.

My electrical circuit went into overload, not because I was angry, but because Maggie hit my Achille's heel, and somehow she knew it.

"Why in the world would I need help?"

Her face turned to granite. "I'm just offering."

"Well, thank you for your offer, but I'll be fine, or I wouldn't be doing this." I wanted to choke at the lie. I had put myself into a corner by my impulse, but I was damn sure not going to let Maggie see that.

"Fine. I'll be off, then." She took a long look around the house and I heard the door close.

"How *are* you going to pay for this?" Renee looked at me while taking a more demure bite.

"I have absolutely no idea." We burst into laughter until we were both crying. A relief, a rinsing of sorts of all the troubles and fears I had harbored for a while now.

"Didn't Arthur leave you at least comfortable?"

"Yes and no. There was no life insurance. Every dime we had was reinvested into the firm, and they pay our personal bills. His 50 percent of the partnership should come to me shortly. In the meantime, I have to hang on with little cash and lots of optimism."

"Are you telling me," Renee said as she dropped her pizza back in the box, then wiped her hands, "That you haven't paid a bill in thirty years?"

I laughed. "It's not that bad, Renee. The firm gets all the bills, they pay them in lieu of a salary, and I get a small allowance for incidentals." I shrugged.

"Are you kidding me?" She slumped. "You are the most spoiled rich bitch there ever was."

I had just explained to her how my financial world worked, and she shook her head the entire time. I understood her reaction. Once I said it out loud, I agreed with her. I had taken no responsibility and displayed no interest.

"Did Arthur not explain anything to you?"

"Of course. He told me about our finances, but I didn't pay much attention. He reviewed our financials, explaining terms and what had been locked down and what was liquid, but I think my eyes glazed over."

She waited, eyes sharp and dark.

"Renee, I didn't think he would die. I always thought he would be here." As if that were a justification for being stupid. "But I'm not that imbecilic. I do know approximately how much I'm going to get once an audit is done, but for now I'm trapped in a holding pattern."

I felt like a child. A spoiled, uneducated, illiterate child who had been given every advantage and never once said thank you, as though it was my due.

"Okay, so what's your plan?" Renee's switch got flipped to "on" again, ready for action.

"I don't know. I know an audit has to be performed in order for the firm to buy me out, and I'm assuming that will take a while."

"Do you know how much to expect?"

"I told you, approximately." But she knew I had no clue.

She sighed. "At the moment I have $10,452.98 tucked away in a vacation plan and $533.44 in my checking account. I'm not telling you how much I have in investments or my 401(K), but you can be sure I know exactly how much—to the penny. That's my retirement, and I will live a good, healthy, comfortable life."

"Renee, I don't want your money."

"I'm not offering it, stupid. *I can't afford it.* I'm telling you to show you how the other half lives. Those of us who live by the paycheck don't rely on others to pay our expenses, we have to keep an eye on every penny. I suggest you change your outlook and start paying attention, and for God's sake, take control." She took a swig of her beer. "Welcome to the real world, Gigi."

I reminded myself that this was Renee. This was how she did things. If it had been anyone else, I would have been angry, depressed, embarrassed, and pissed off. But it was Renee. And she was right.

Jesus. I just assumed money would keep coming in the way it always had and that I could dip into something to get what I needed.

"Of course I will, but I have to get past this hurdle first. I need to figure out how I'm going to pay for the inventory. Everything was sunk into the firm and I have very little liquid."

"Get a list of all your expenses from Dave so you know what to expect, at least. I'm guessing your electric bill is just about my mortgage payment." She looked around the cavernous, empty house. "Which, by the way, will be mine in less than two years. Twenty more payments and it's mine."

Damn. I should have this information on the tip of my tongue. And be proud of it.

$\times$ $\times$ $\times$

The next day, I resolved to figure out where I was financially. I asked the Accounts Payable person at Conrad and Putnam to send over the last three months of bills paid on our behalf and received that information within ten minutes.

I guessed my take from the firm at high-six-figures, but it was only a guess. Arthur's social security, along with some investments, would see me through old age in comfort, if not in luxury. Whatever came to me from the firm would be icing on the cake. At least that's how I read it.

I pulled out a sheet of graph paper and made a spreadsheet of all the expenses. Most were known to me, but a second on the house was something I had not remembered, and the last entry made my heart stop and I lost focus.

Arthur had been paying the bills for Father to be at La Jolla Haven. Over $9,000 every month.

Holy shit. Why didn't he tell me? And . . . how could he?

$\times$ $\times$ $\times$

An hour later, I realized I would need to find some significant cash. It made sense to borrow against the house until the funds came through from the sale of the firm. I had a number on the spreadsheet of what we owed to the mortgage company.

I called the undertaker at the bank and explained the situation. He cautioned me against borrowing in case my "little business" didn't work. It was too risky.

Gee, thanks, Dad.

"The Small Business Administration might be interested," he said, and offered to send me the forms. They would approve the loan and he would finance it. It would be a good way to establish some credit in my own name.

I felt like I had been rejected by my fairy godfather.

I received the forms via email five minutes later—all thirty-six pages. They wanted pro formas, quotes, references, suppliers, tax numbers, and a guarantee, whatever that was. If I were not receiving any income, they wanted a co-signer.

All too overwhelming, and more than a little intimidating.

What the hell is a pro forma?

I lay on my bed wondering how I might do this. My eyes took in the pristine white bedroom that had once been a source of comfort, of pleasure, and of love. The pure whiteness now irritated me. The money I spent on this room alone would probably support the shop for some time.

You could sell the house and downsize.

That would take too long, and besides I'm not ready for such a big change. This is my home.

The smart thing to do would be to call my lawyer, but I resisted. Dave was Arthur's partner and my brother-in-law, and my assumed lawyer. I felt like I would be going to my father and asking for an advance on my allowance—a rather large allowance, granted, but the fact remained he would ask me "how much?" and I didn't have a comfortable answer. He would question me and I didn't have the answers. How stupid can one woman be?

Plus, he would tell Maggie and confirm her suspicions I was a ne'er do well.

In my mind, whatever came to me from the firm would be profiting from my husband's death. That felt "extremely distasteful," as Mother would say, and, frankly, I just didn't want to go there. It meant he was actually gone and some part of me still didn't want that door to close.

I spent two days in an attack of buyer's remorse and feeling stupid. How could I, a grown woman, college degree, smart by all accounts, commit to open a business without knowing how I'd pay for it? Money had never been a concern for me, and I didn't know what I was doing. I had no idea how much this might cost, where to get the money, or how to structure a business. I couldn't even get a goddamn credit card.

The temptation to go back to bed and pull the covers over my head became overwhelming. The shaking limbs, headache, heart pounding loudly in my ears, and crazed, unfocused thoughts prevented that from becoming a reality.

I'm acting like a ditz. Spoiled. I never had to work for anything—money was handed to me or my debts paid by someone else my entire life.

Just hang in there by your fingernails.

It would be easier if I still had acrylic ones.

Chapter Twenty

IT HAD BEEN A BRICK DAY; ONE I HAD BEEN TOLD TO EXPECT. THE HOSPICE counselor had told me some days I would come up against a brick wall and some days I'd be able to sail with the winds. This had definitely been a brick day. I teared up often, felt lonely and sorry for myself. I missed Arthur terribly and started blaming myself for not taking better care of him.

"Jennifer?"

"Mother?"

She never called me. I took a deep breath and tried to control my breathing and clear my nose. I put the phone away from my mouth and coughed to gain some time. "Sorry. Hello, Mother. How is your day?"

"Hello, dear."

Silence.

"Mother?"

"Yes." She coughed.

"Jennifer . . ." I could hear her voice cracking. "Could you come to me?"

This was unsettling. She never asked me to come over, never asked for anything.

"What's wrong." I made a bold statement, a first between my mother and me, and my voiced raised in alarm. I couldn't help it.

"Just come over, I'm not feeling well."

"Explain, please. Should I call 911?"

Her voice got stronger. The old Patricia Palmer came back. "Don't be ridiculous. I just want to talk to you."

"I'm on my way."

I broke all speed records getting to Mother's cottage in La Jolla, which really was a cottage, but because of its location in the heart of La Jolla it grew to be worth millions. She had bought the house for an investment years ago when she inherited some money, and when Father went to live in La Jolla Haven she evicted the renters and renovated it to suit her.

I came up the walk and found her door open.

"Hello, Mother." I looked her over and into her eyes checking for pain, for one side of her face to fall, for shortness of breath, for anything that would indicate I should have called 911 in the first place. Nothing.

"Sit down, dear. I have something to tell you about which you should be aware. I didn't want to do it over the telephone."

"Yes?"

"Would you like a drink?"

"Depends on what you are going to tell me." I meant it as a joke, something you don't do with Mother. She scowled and sat on Nana Buford's Queen Anne chair.

"Well, dear, the cancer is back, and I'm afraid this time I've run out of options."

Mother had had two lumpectomies since Arthur and I married, both self-contained malignancies caught in time.

"No lumpectomy this time?"

"No, they tell me it's metastasized."

"I'll have that drink now." I went to the bar and splashed vodka over ice in a double old-fashioned glass. "You?"

"No, thank you, dear."

"So," I said as I sat back down. "What's the treatment? Chemo? Radiation? Surgery?"

"Nothing. I'm eighty-six years old and I don't want to put myself, or you, or Margaret, or Tricia, through that. I'm going to let God take me when He thinks it's time."

Mother's unwavering faith in God had always been a thorn in my side. She came from an Irish Catholic family and had been raised to believe everything came from God's hands. She went to mass daily, a practice I had abandoned in junior high. God had let me down and I had never forgiven Him.

"Do you have that choice?"

"Of course I have that choice! Don't be a simpleton." Mother's brow drew in, her wrinkles became more pronounced and she, of course, smacked her lips together.

I was still three steps behind.

"What I mean is, don't the doctors have an obligation to treat you?"

"I hardly think they are going to make an issue of an eighty-six-year-old woman making a decision to not put herself through a grueling process to buy six more months of pain, much less a woman who has been active on the board."

She had a point there.

"So . . . what can I do?"

"You can tell your sister. I choose not to witness the histrionics."

To say I was knocked off my pins would be an understatement. Maggie had always been the good daughter, the one who followed in Mother's foot-steps, who catered to her. The fact that Mother had not shared this most important piece of information with her was a shock to me, to my world order. And her tone of voice talking about Maggie's histrionics a revelation.

And she trusted me.

"Oh, don't look so shocked. Maggie will not be able to handle it, and you are going to have to hold her hand through this. You're the strong one. You're going to have to prop her up." She nodded emphatically at me.

Me? Strong? You should have seen me an hour ago.

"What do you mean?"

Mother sighed and looked down at her clasped hands. "Dear, you know Margaret is delicate."

"Delicate?" *Like Attila the Hun delicate?*

Mother tamped her lips and looked extremely annoyed. "Jennifer. You must know that your sister has some emotional problems."

"Emotional problems?" I began to parrot my mother, and it annoyed both of us.

She looked straight at me. "Ever since you went to Nana Buford's that summer she's been, well . . . funny, and I don't understand it. It seems you both changed. That's when you became difficult and she became ill."

"Ill?" This was ridiculous. "Mother, we both know I didn't go to Nana's. Can't we at least be honest about that?" Nothing. "What happened to Maggie that summer?"

Mother stood up, walked to the bar, talking to me over her shoulder. "She was jealous that you got to go when we sent her to Europe with the Hamiltons to distract her and get out of town for a while. When she got back and you returned, she was never the same." She sat down and looked at me. "Neither were you." She smacked her lips. "So, Dear, tell me about the shop."

I shook my head at the abrupt change of subject and told her about the center, the shop, and the contest. I knew ahead of time that she had the same perspective of my being a *shop girl* that Maggie had displayed so clearly, but I suspect the fact that Iris Anderson was a supporter saved me from the same treatment. I did not offer any information about the financial situation.

She asked a few more semi-interested questions. I answered quietly, reassured that Mother facing the grim reaper would not change her basic personality.

I left shortly after, vowing to tell Maggie and prop her up with the news. How in the hell was I going to do that?

$$\times \quad \times \quad \times$$

Dave and Maggie invited me over for dinner, which they had never done before.

Maybe this was another "poor little widow" thing. Maybe they wanted something. The thought of spending an evening, just the three of us in their formal living room, being served by uniformed maids made my skin crawl.

This would be a good time to talk to Dave, and I knew I had to do it. I called Maggie back. "On second thought, why don't you come over here? I'm dying to cook again and I could use the company."

"But you don't have a dining room table," Maggie said, as though I had forgotten I had sent over my dining and living room furniture to the shop.

My house felt empty, but that just felt appropriate. I did not plan to do any entertaining in the near future. The shop was my first priority now.

"I have a perfectly serviceable table in the breakfast room—there are only three of us. Very casual. I'll plan to see you at seven." I hung up, a first for me.

Let her try to force that.

I set to work making a simple dinner of meatloaf and mashed potatoes. I wanted comfort food. Maggie'll have a heart attack expecting *foie gras* and Beef Wellington.

The Putnams showed up at seven, Dave in a suit and Maggie wearing a pantsuit and the requisite jewelry. I stayed in a track suit. Her expression was priceless. At least my hair was done.

We sat in the family room with drinks.

"Dave, I need to know more about the buyout. When will it be done, and approximately what should I expect?"

His eyes shifted to the carpet. "I don't know. There's an audit to be done and it hasn't even started yet."

"But . . . can you tell me anything? Like the amount?"

"No, I'm sorry, Jen, I just don't know. Our CFO quit and we are breaking in a new one; the books have to be reviewed and approved before he can take over, so it's been extended for a bit."

Whoa, buddy. You're the one who had his finger on the General Ledger.

My ears tingled again. "Dave . . ."

Maggie interrupted. "Jen, have you seen Mother?"

"I'm glad you're here. I have to tell you something, and I've been putting it off for a while now."

Maggie's eyes grew wide.

"Mother has confided in me that," (*was I sure I had to do this?*) "unfortunately, the cancer has returned, it's metastasized."

Stone cold silence. Dave put his arm around Maggie. She sat, a cold slab of marble. "No."

"Yes, Maggie, I'm afraid so."

"NO. NO." She put her head in her hands and aggressively shoved Dave's arm away from her.

I waited. Dave looked at me with real concern in his eyes. "What does she want to do?"

Maggie's pale face popped up, waiting.

"She wants to let it go. No more treatments. She's eighty-six and doesn't want the drama of it. She'll take pain medication and take care of herself, but she's reconciled to it and wants to go out gracefully."

Maggie stood up. "That sounds like her." She took a deep breath and walked over to the bar to pour herself more vodka.

"Are you okay, honey?" Dave asked.

"Yes, I am." She turned to me. "Why did she tell you and not me?"

"I don't know, Maggie. I was just there, I guess."

"She doesn't trust me to handle it."

We remained quiet.

"I'm sorry, Maggie. I probably should have waited until after dinner, but it just seemed like a good time."

She sniffed and her head came up, almost in defiance. "I'm all right, and I'm glad you told me. What do I need to do?"

"I honestly don't know. Let's let her drive the bus on this one, okay? Let's eat."

We carried our drinks into the kitchen and around the corner to the breakfast room. If I hadn't affected Maggie with Mother's news, this most certainly would give her another jolt. I had our informal dinnerware set up with—gasp—stainless steel utensils instead of sterling silver. No stemmed goblets, just Mexican tube glasses and bright colored napkins. I had thought of using paper napkins but thought it a bit much. It might send Maggie right over the edge.

We gathered around our simple dinner. Dave and I ate most of our meal while Maggie picked at hers, shoving bits around her plate.

"How is the firm doing, Dave?"

"We're plugging along, but our new CFO is making some changes, probably good ones. We're turning in the leased vehicles." His face turned red. "I'm so sorry, Jen, I didn't think. You should have been notified."

"What are you talking about?"

"The Lexus. It belongs to the firm, it's one of the leased vehicles."

"Of course it is," I said, trying to be relaxed. I had forgotten all about it. Arthur was supposed to drive it, but he preferred his father's 1974 Cadillac, Big Bessie. I had driven the Lexus so long I forgot it wasn't mine. "When would you like to pick it up?"

Good God. I have to buy a new car.

"I'm sure you'll be hearing from Ray, and I'll make sure it's convenient for you." He thought a minute. "Unless you'd like to buy it, I'm sure I can arrange for that."

"No, Dave. I'll make my own arrangements."

I thought Maggie's eyes just might just pop out. "Me, too?" she said. Dave nodded, his head down. "Great. Just great." She stood, threw her napkin on her plate and went into the powder room.

"There it is," said Dave. He grinned at me between his bared teeth. "Delayed reaction." He continued to eat, head down.

Sobs came from the closed room, pounding fists against the counter. Eventually the door opened. "Ignore her," Dave said quietly. She emerged in normal form: lipstick, mascara, buffed and powdered skin to perfection.

Perfection is important.

Chapter Twenty-One

I SAT IN STARBUCKS WITH A LEGAL PAD AND MY FAVORITE PEN, A BRIGHT red fine point Mont Blanc with my monogram that Arthur had given me one Valentine's Day. Ironically, he told me to sign checks and credit card chits with it because the firm performed so well.

Ha. Ha.

I made a list of things on my mind and wondered how one goes about getting a retail store off the ground.

What had I gotten myself into? And what was the alternative?

From behind me, I heard a familiar voice. "Here's my application. Can I give you references now?"

"No, wait until you get a call."

Poor thing. Imagine working at a coffee shop. How low can you go?

Now I sound like my sister.

As the job applicant passed me, I said, "Lupe?"

"Mrs. Conrad, hello." Her face showed some strain at the edges, her skin somewhat paler than I remember. Lupe had worked as Arthur's assistant for many years, always dressed in professional pantsuits, her dark hair gathered professionally, her voice quiet and respectful. Now she looked ripe, her long curly hair bouncing at her shoulders, a poet's blouse over a long flowy skirt. She looked adorable, if stressed. I noted her olive skin glowed with perspiration and her makeup had become a little smudged around her worried eyes.

"Are you applying for a job here?" Lupe pulled out a chair and plopped down. "I know they were laying people off, but I hope you got a good severance." Did Dave live up to my request?

"Yes, but it doesn't hurt to get a job right away. I'm banking the severance for an emergency." She looked down at her hands, her bitten nails showing some bloody blisters from hangnails and picking at her cuticles.

115

I sat back and appraised this woman who had become so close to Arthur, who he trusted with everything he had, including all our personal and professional history. He gave her away at her small wedding; her family was gone, she said. He hired a limo to take them away to the Hotel Del for their weekend honeymoon.

"What kind of job are you looking for?"

"Something where I work with people. Something creative. I can make websites, I can balance books, I can roll up my sleeves and create something from nothing." She laughed. "How do you define a perfect job from those experiences?"

"I don't know, but I'm sure something will come up." My head started to tingle again.

I phrased the next question very carefully, not wanting to lead her on to where I really, really wanted her to go. "Lupe, what are your hobbies?"

She looked around at the shelves holding various coffees, cups, and brewers, at the ceiling where the speakers broke out some Nina Simone and seemed to just as carefully to frame her answer. "I like quiet things, like reading, writing, researching . . ."

"Yes?" My ears rose in alert. *Say it.*

"I really like to be creative. I've dabbled in watercolors, and I can design a dress for someone in no time flat. I've even made wedding dresses, but that's not something I'd like to do as a profession. Brides are too nervous and uncertain. They keep changing their minds, and it's just not worth it!" She giggled. "I'm not very athletic or outdoorsy. I sew, knit, I do some needlepoint." She laughed. "But that's not going to get me a job."

"Lupe," I took a gulp of my coffee. "Have I got a deal for you. What are you doing the rest of the day?"

Chapter Twenty-Two

*W*E NAMED THE SHOP STITCHES.

Lupe and I had met several times more and I learned more about her. I put my faith in her to run the shop. It turned out she had some experience in retail and dabbled in needlework, so it seemed a safe bet. It was one more connection to Arthur, one that I appreciated and gloried in.

Over the course of the next month, we spent a lot of time on the phone and online researching vendors and suppliers. Help came out of the woodwork. I accepted offers of samples, feeling greedy. One vendor hooked me up with other vendors, and before long an entire team of cooperative salespeople more than willing to help this newbie get started.

All this through Google. Google is my friend.

A little at a time, I started to place orders. One night, tired of indecision and wishy-washy thinking, my laptop placed against my legs in my igloo bedroom, I went full boar. I gulped and ordered everything. Every kind of yarn: wool, cotton, silk, cashmere, sock, worsted, whatever they offered, I ordered. Every single notion, no matter how silly or unnecessary, and every pattern book in the catalogs would be in my shop.

My obsessive/compulsive nature took over. I ignored the rest of my world, letting go of what no longer beckoned to me. A few old friends and acquaintances kept in touch, but only to check in. I found it interesting no one asked *what* I was doing, but *how* I was doing, as though I had to recover from a serious illness. Renee was the only one interested in the process, not because this was her project, but because, as always, she showed herself as my true friend. I had been abandoned by people I had known for years, but I honestly didn't mind. I had to laugh when I thought of some of them actually physically working, like my sister. Inconceivable.

I loved it. It felt good to move, to create, and to think of a future entirely different from one I had ever experienced.

I just didn't know how I was going to pay for it, and I felt guilty anticipating a life without Arthur.

The opening would be in a month. Bruce Miller, the superintendent on the construction and renovation of Historic Park into the Historic art park, had been retained to customize each shop. He built bookcases for me to house inventory, hide wires, and display items using spotlights. Big and awkward, with light red hair turning silver, affable and a little goofy, he was creative and found ingenious ways to hide wires and display items. We didn't talk much, but I was always aware of him when he entered the shop.

Lupe proved to be a godsend. We made a good team, and I found her well versed in textiles. She developed our website and set up an online shop. The three of us worked hard to set up the shop and get ready for the grand opening.

Boxes started to appear in the porch area, the dribs and drabs I had ordered while being careful, before I went crazy and ordered what felt like several warehouses. I was too careful.

It turned out to be only a small part of what the shop could contain, a sad display on the boxes and partitions set up all over the parlor and dining rooms.

I went to the computer and placed orders for more yarn, just to be sure every cubby was full and interesting.

Please please please.

"I've never worked up such a sweat in my life," I said as I moved muscles I never knew I had. Bending, scooping, lifting, and stretching made me ache at the end of the day, but I was pleased. Lupe just laughed.

Stitches was coming together, and it was good.

I caught myself having a good time, enjoying the process, and immediately shut down. I'm supposed to be in mourning.

I spent a lot of time by myself, sliding into my new space and making it exactly what I would want as a customer. Every muscle screamed, then sang as I eased into my new life of movement.

I felt guilty creating a life without Arthur. I had days where my grief grabbed my heart and wrung it out, but I worked through it, crying while I unpacked and loaded the shelves through blurred vision. Bruce and Lupe either didn't notice or chose to give me my space.

But I did it. That's not to say I wasn't scared shitless. I had no idea what I was doing. But I had ninety days before they would come calling for payment.

This shop had to succeed. If it failed, that meant I failed. Nothing to show for this woman's efforts. Then I knew I would be afraid to try anything else. My mother, my sister and the rest of my friends would shake their heads and say, "Poor Jen, she just couldn't cut it." What little faith my father had placed in my abilities would be validated.

I had no choice but to succeed. Then I could sell the shop and do whatever I wanted.

In the meantime, I just had to keep my head above water.

I sent another email to Dave and asked when the buyout would take place. "Soon" was the answer.

"The shop opens in a month and we still don't have much inventory," I said to Lupe. "What if it's late? What happens if I don't have anything to sell on opening day?" The cupboards were only about half full and began to look pathetic.

Lupe looked at me and smiled. "Why don't I call the reps for what hasn't come in and confirm delivery dates, just to be sure?" I fell into a chair and started to laugh. "I know what the delivery dates are, I'm just anxious that something's going to go haywire. It would be embarrassing to open up and have nothing to show."

"Just to be sure, I'll confirm." She disappeared into the office and came back a few minutes later, her face pale. "One of the orders never got placed."

"What do you mean, never got placed? I called them in myself."

"No. I mean the rep didn't place the order with the warehouse. It will be another six weeks."

My stomach fell into my sneakers. "Which vendor?"

I saw her swallow hard. "Creative Concepts."

"That's the big order. We can't open without that yarn." I rocketed myself out of the chair and into the office.

This had to work. I had to make this work, and no one was going to get in the way. I picked up the phone and made myself clear to the rep that that big order had to come at the very latest, by the day before opening day. She made no promises. I asked to speak to her supervisor. She didn't have one, she was an independent contractor.

Damn. I had no clout, no track record, and I was no threat.

The notions arrived the next day and I felt better as I looked over all the new tools and needles, all bundled up in their sealed packages, just ready to be part of a new creation. But I still didn't have much yarn to display, all I had had come from minor vendors. I called the rep for Creative Concepts again, just to bug her. I planned on calling every day until I got my inventory.

This was unacceptable.

Bruce came in the shop as Lupe and I started to categorize the notions, a scowl on his face. "Come here," he said. His steps sounded hard and purposeful as he headed into the living room, one hand across his stomach. He leaned over the couch, put a hand into his shirt and pulled out a tiny black puppy, whimpering and weak, then another one.

"Goddamn bastard just threw these guys in the trash bin." His voice croaked. "Their eyes aren't even open."

Lupe put her hand on one and said, "Oh, God. He's shaking. They must be starving. I'm going to run to the vet and see if I can get some formula. Okay if I take your car?" I nodded. She took off, grabbing my keys on the way out.

Bruce and I sat on the couch in the living room and placed the puppies between us. I wrapped them up in a hand-knitted blanket, and they snuffled and dozed. "How could someone do this?" he asked, his glassy blue eyes looking down at them. "He just tossed them in there like trash."

"You saw it?"

"Yeah, and I would have gone after the bastard, but I was too concerned about the little guys," he said. He rubbed his big finger down the nose of one of them. The puppy's face all but disappeared under his thumb. "I had to climb into the dumpster to get them. There was another one." He frowned. I didn't ask.

His gentleness and sensitivity touched me. I saw him as a dad, taking each disappointment to heart.

"Do you have any kids?" I whispered.

"Yes, a son. You?"

"One. I gave it up for adoption at birth."

Whoa.

My cell rang. Lupe must have flown down the street. "The vet says to bring them in right away. She wants to look at them before she gives us formula."

The vet's office was just down the street, but Bruce drove around back to the dumpster and climbed in without saying a word. He came back with a third puppy, not moving.

"We're taking him, too." He handed the little guy to me. He was cold, but I bundled him up with his siblings.

I felt the little guys moving next to my chest and some small puppy grunts came from under the blanket. We rushed them into the examination room and placed all three of them on the cold steel table. I lifted them and placed the blanket under them.

The babies were looked over and determined to be less than two weeks old, two boys and one girl. The tech listened to their hearts and played with the two that were so clearly alive, then went to the third.

"There's a faint heartbeat."

"No. He was dead."

"Well, he's hanging in there now." She picked him up and shook him gently, swiped out his mouth and blew into his nose. She lay him back down and pushed gently on his chest.

A tiny little sneeze, the happiest little sound ever, came out from him and I wanted to jump up and down. His brother and sister made even more noise.

"If they make it through the night, they have a better chance," the vet said after she examined them. "Let me keep them overnight. I will have a better idea then what their real prognosis is." She looked at us. "But don't expect miracles. We don't know what the real story is here. They may not have gotten enough nourishment from their mother, so there may be some real problems ahead, even if they survive."

I went home obsessed, worried, and concerned about the three little guys we had left behind. I couldn't focus.

"Missy C?" Choyou stood in the doorway to the family room. "We talk?"

"Of course."

She wrung her hands. "I think I retire. Mr. Arthur gone, you gone all day. Not much to do."

This had come out of the blue and it took me a minute to wrap my brain around it. Of course she wasn't going to stay with me my entire life.

"I see. Yes, I can understand how you feel. You've been invaluable for the past thirty years, Choyou, and I completely understand you wanting to not work so hard. How long would you like to stay?"

"Oh, I still work hard, Missy C. I start Asian tea shop at art park. Missy Murphy get me into shop next to you." She smiled.

"What? A tea shop? At the art park? That's wonderful. When do you open?"

"Soon. Coming soon." She nodded and clapped her hands together silently. "My sister join me. Beautiful. Chinese herbal remedies, ancient medicine. I bring Auntie in to advise."

"I think that's a wonderful idea. Oh, but I'll miss you." I stood up to give her a hug. "How things have changed, no?" I said. Choyou broke away and put her hands over her face, sobbing.

$$\times \quad \times \quad \times$$

I took Lupe with me to the vet the next day. We were sad to learn that the third guy didn't make it. He died during the night.

"I'll foster them until they're over the hump, then we give them to a good home," I said as I handed over my credit card. We took away several bags of medicine, formula, licensing fees, an agreement to spay/neuter, and the microchipping paperwork.

We went back to the shop where I found a box and put them on the blanket in the box. I found a portable heater and pointed it at the box. Bruce came in and we all studied the orders and medicines. I went back to work stocking and inventorying until I heard them whimpering. I fed them and nuzzled their little puppy necks and breathed in their little puppy breath. I knew it would break my heart if they didn't make it. Lupe and I cared for them all afternoon, even whispering so as not to wake them up.

I took them home and placed them on Arthur's pillow. They were so weak they couldn't possibly fall off the bed, but I surrounded them with pillows just in case. I loved having those warm little bodies so dependent on me. I followed the directions to the letter. I fed them every two hours, kept them close and warm, and at dawn I was awakened by a tiny little mouth trying to suck on my nose.

They were survivors, these little guys.

Just for kicks, I named them Sticks and Stitches. I kept them close to ensure they were fed and got their meds on time. I became an obsessive mommy.

Within forty-eight hours I knew I would never give them up. Their eyes opened and their little legs got stronger. The day Stitches took her first wobbly steps I felt like I had just given birth.

A female. A strong one.

Chapter Twenty-Three

THE MORNING OF THE OPENING, WE RECEIVED THIRTY-FIVE BOXES FROM Creative Concepts about ten o'clock—all thirty-five of them—we built up a sweat opening, tagging and filling up the empty spots in the bookcases. We hid the boxes behind the house, we didn't have the time to break them down.

Before I knew it, I heard the high school band strike up as they led observers on the walkway to the big coral tree, the signal that we had run out of time. I looked at my watch. Two o'clock. Lupe kept arranging the inventory while I took a final run-through, plumped up pillows, fluffed afghans and arranged sweaters and scarves for the umpteenth time.

This had to work. Please God, this had to work.

Bookshelves showed either pattern books or skeins of beautiful yarn. Needles, row counters, stitch holders and charms scattered about on the tables. Every item had been labeled, priced, and ready to go. I didn't know what would sell, so I ordered every size, every color, and every variety of every tool I could find from inexpensive plastic to expensive ivory needles. I switched on the lights on the end tables and lit the fire. I rearranged pillows again.

The dining room held various needlepoint samples and yarns in bowls and on plates, some spilling out of goblets, as a table is set for dinner. The walls held more kits, tapestry yarns, embroidery scissors, magnifiers, needles, thimbles, and books of patterns and inspiration.

Goose bumps erupted on my arms as I looked at the beautiful display. It should have been on the cover of a magazine. I adjusted a few things that didn't need adjustment. My stomach felt like a flock of seagulls had settled in there and wanted out.

One last look at the large kitchen showed materials for crewel embroidery: wool from Wales, Belgian linen, sharps, embroidery hoops, and traceable designs all spilled out of the open cupboards. Bright copper pots and pans and kitchen drawers held luscious, colorful embroidery yarns and supplies. Pillows in the breakfast nook showed examples of crewel work, and even some blackwork.

The old historic house would become a haven for anyone holding a needle of any kind or anyone with a shred of imagination. It opened on its first day of business on February 11. Even though only one shop opened that day, the grand opening was held to allow people to come see the houses, the community and the park.

I owed a bloody fortune. I had a running tab in my office, not on the computer but in a ledger, that totaled up to the price of a small house on the beach. I broke out in a sweat every time I looked at it.

Renee cut the bright red ribbon at precisely three o'clock. She thanked the entire committee and gave me kudos for working so hard to be their first tenant. She announced the other tenants under review and predicted that in one year the art park would be productive, energetic, and make money for the community.

Suzanne had loaned out the houses for the afternoon to various artists to show off their wares.

Choyou's tea house was behind the coral tree, and she served various teas and her famous tarts, and writing each participant's name on rice paper in Japanese calligraphy, promising more when the shop opened for business in two months. An oil painter did quick portraits on small canvases and a watercolorist stood outside painting the scenery, including the large gazebo on the middle of the lawn that had been brought in for the day. A thrower had his potter's wheel set up on the grass and proceeded to make clay bowls, cups and plates to be fired and painted later, and a glass blower demonstrated how a vase was formed on the lawn.

Inside Stitches, flowers graced the center of the dining room table, several potted plants and bouquets that had arrived from friends and vendors decorated an already perfect house.

I took a moment to appreciate all the hard work. And pray.

Soft piano music played through speakers Bruce had ingeniously hidden throughout the house. I was amazed when Lupe set up her phone to the system and played the music from it. I had no idea you could do that. The smell of freshly brewed coffee permeated every room, and flowers kept coming.

The shop exceeded everything I had imagined in that dream such a short time ago, and then some. But was it a dream that can stay true?

Iris and Helen were the first customers in the door. They plopped themselves in their customary chairs. (the ones I had brought in from my house; it just felt natural to move what I already had and use them. No sense in a formal living room for a shopkeeper widow.) They brought their projects and sat knitting in the parlor as people walked through, a glass of wine by Iris and a cup of tea by Helen. They chatted people up and invited them to sit—*Oh, just for a minute—would you like a glass of wine? A cup of tea, perhaps a cookie? You must see the needlepoint displayed in the dining room. Have you ever seen such a beautiful shop? The owner knows what she's doing. She made everything in this room, can you believe it? Even the tapestry! Look at that masterpiece!*

I heard it all and it made me smile.

I took a moment and took the temperature. Would Arthur love this? Yes, of course he would. He'd be at the door charming everyone with witty banter and bragging about me. I wiped away a tear and put one foot in front of the other, knowing I was stepping in the right direction.

Robert Graham, the current social editor for the *San Diego Union*, followed Iris and Helen with his two photographers. Robert had a byline in every major newspaper. I had met him several times in my previous life and he knew me, and Iris, very well. He requested a quick interview, and we wove our way through the crowd to the office.

He was about thirty, thirty-five, tall and slim, with blonde hair that swept over his forehead and light blue eyes. He wore casual pants, boat shoes, and a light blue velvet jacket, certainly not a conservative man. He was warm and friendly, if a bit quirky.

"So, how does it feel?" he asked as we sat the small round table in the corner of the office.

How does it feel? I was prepared to answer direct questions, what made me do this, how much time had I put into this, what my hopes were, have I always wanted to do this, etc., for which I was prepared.

I was not ready to answer a question about how I felt.

He leaned over and put his hand over mine in my lap. "I'm sorry. Did I jump in too fast? I know your husband just died and I was trying to avoid boring questions."

I wiped a tear away, an escapee. "No," I said. "I just wasn't expecting that question. How do I feel? Scared shitless." My filters were deserting me.

"Well, I can't say that in the article." We laughed. "How about if I just put something together, run it by you, and then you can approve it before it runs? You're busy with the opening and I know this is not a good time." He smiled so nicely I almost forgave him.

"Maybe you can interview Lupe, the shop manager, talk to Iris and Helen, and get a feel for them about what they have experienced with me and with the shop. They have been a great help to me in formulating ideas and themes." I tried to be helpful, the good girl.

"Good. I will. And I know your background, so I'll just put a bit of history in there. Anybody else I should talk to?"

"Don't talk to my mother or my sister. Or at least don't use their quotes. I'm not sure I have their support." Now my filters had clearly gone AWOL.

"Who is your mother, and who is your sister?" Pencil poised over pad.

"Patricia Palmer and Maggie Putnam." His pencil stayed immobile; his face turned up to mine.

"Patricia Palmer is your mother? and Maggie Putnam is your sister?" He shook his head and snapped his book closed. "Understood."

When I followed him out of the office, Renee sailed through the front door with a huge basket of flowers. She dropped them down on the hallway table and gave me a hug. "You did it, Gigi, and it's fabulous." She looked around at my recreated living room. "It's *de ja vu* all over again," she said.

I laughed. "It works."

"It certainly does." She reached under the plastic of the basket and pulled out a bottle of champagne and two plastic glasses. We went into the kitchen where she popped open the bottle quietly, poured, and said, "To you, and to forward movement."

Tears ran down my face. "Damn you," I said as I put my drink down and grabbed a towel. "I was doing just fine until *you* showed up." She laughed and hugged me again, then went into the living room to see what all the noise was about.

Iris, Helen and Robert entertained the growing crowd. The trio did not move, preferring to draw people in to sit and have tea or coffee and chat, talk about various projects and bond over knitting and the creative process. I appreciated their natural instinct to make the room cozy and inviting.

At one point I looked up to see Robert buying some dark green yarn and two sets of knitting needles from Lupe, who manned the door, greeted customers. She held her electronic tablet to add up purchases and charge their credit card electronically.

We had the computer set up to do the same thing, but this allowed her to go anywhere in the shop. Ingenious. She asked for email addresses to send receipts to customers.

"You can do that?" I asked. She laughed. "Yes, that way we capture their email addresses so we can keep in touch for sales and events, and we are seen as environmentally responsible."

Thank you, Arthur. She's perfect.

The astounding dollar amount I owed to the vendors kept popping into my head like a bad dream. I went out the front door to catch a breath of fresh air.

I turned to go back into the house when I noticed a blue butterfly with gold pattern sitting on the rail. "Hello. Do we know each other?" I whispered to him. He fluttered his wings and flew away.

Maggie and Tricia appeared from nowhere, and I saw Tricia wink at me as Maggie almost watched the clock waiting to make her exit at just the right time, not too soon, but no longer than absolutely necessary. She took a cursory glance at the bookcases and wandered into the needlepoint room, nodding at people as though she were the duchess making inspection. She never spoke to me or acknowledged me in any way.

Mother dropped in but was distracted by admirers demanding her attention. As far as I knew no one knew of her returned cancer, and she looked well to me. Suzanne kept popping in and checking on the group in between showing people the houses and talking up the possibilities.

The babies proved a hit and charmed people who would ordinarily never step foot in a yarn shop. They never barked or growled and greeted everyone with unbounded enthusiasm.

My first marketing ploy—use adorable puppies to get attention. Check.

If only Arthur could see this. He'd absolutely love it, and he'd find a way to pay for it.

$$\times \quad \times \quad \times$$

"The contest rules state we should submit a sketch of the project with the application, then send a picture of the completed project on a live model as soon as possible. They want the finished product in their offices by year-end. Tricia, if you're willing to be our model, we can start making choices," I said. Tricia nodded as she pointed her nose at her stitches.

"I've gathered some yarn I thought might work and made some samples since we last talked about it." I opened a wicker basket I had on the coffee table and spread out ten squares of lace I had worked up. I had selected colors of silver, gray, candlelight, and even some eggshell with a glimmer of silver running through it, hoping Tricia would change her mind about the black.

Iris thought the colors all wrong, Helen dug in her heels set on white, Jade abstained. The neckline definitely needed to come up, the sleeves discussed ad nauseum. I stayed out of the conversation, allowing Tricia to make her voice heard.

"It would be so dramatic in black."

"It would be too hard, edgy."

"But that's the point, I thought." Tricia wasn't giving up.

"It would lose its softness, the lacy froth of it would be lost."

"Look at the sketch again."

On and on it went. Everyone, it seemed, had an opinion.

Back to the drawing board. Tricia looked dejected when she left. "Don't worry. Let's keep looking at options. We will find something that works that you like. There's plenty of time." Although we had already lost quite a bit of time getting the shop up and running, we did have time. I hoped. Maggie was still thinking Spring.

Evelyn, a yarn rep with whom I seemed to connect, seemed to understand the concept. We had formed a friendship over the phone when I first started my vendor research, and when I explained the project to her, the voice coming over the phone was animated. "Of course you'll have to line it with fabric, and I suspect that will make a huge difference in how it looks. My roommate is a sales rep for Phoenix Fabrics. Let me talk to her, she's incredibly creative and together we'll come up with a combination that will knock their socks off."

"Great! Would you like me to email you a scan of the design?"

A silence thundered over the phone. "No. Absolutely not. I don't want that kind of responsibility."

"It's only a scan," I laughed. "You can't steal it."

Her voice came over loud and clear. "This contest is worth a huge amount of money, and I'm right in the thick of it. Please promise me you won't show the design to anyone. They may copy your idea and submit it. No, keep it to yourself. Honestly. I've seen this before, and I don't want it coming back to me if by some weird coincidence someone else comes up with the same design. You may think I tipped them off. No, please don't."

I had found several other yarn reps to bring in samples of everything from silk to wool to make the dress. Off white, eggshell, bright white, candlelight, and some even with small amounts of glittery strands came in, along with some grays and pure silvers. I made careful samples of each copying the lace in Barbie's dress.

Then I went to fabric reps to bring in samples to match with the yarns. The group examined colors, weights, widths, and feel of each piece and compared them against the yarn samples. None of them made an impact.

"We've seen so many of them," I said. "Let's sleep on it and look again."

"None of this fits the picture." Tricia said with a scowl.

I called the fabric reps and told them to come pick up their samples.

The next morning, I received two packages via UPS. The package from Evelyn had six different skeins of yarn in shades of gray and some silver tones. The other package from Phoenix contained four samples of light silk: a blush color, white, a light mauve, an ice blue and a pale, pale green. I went home and whipped up several four-inch squares of the new yarns.

The next day, I unwrapped each sample and laid out the new and the old samples on the different colors, switched them back and forth to see which yarn fit with which fabric.

I stepped back, stunned. These showed beautifully, and I had seen nothing like them before. One combination popped out, but not to influence Tricia's choice, I piled them all aside until next Tuesday. I noticed Lupe kept going back and looking at them as well, but we never talked about it, afraid to jinx it.

$$\times \quad \times \quad \times$$

Suzanne the obnoxious realtor surprised me by joining us the following week. I had no idea this flashy and chatty broad could sit still long enough to knit. Tricia, Iris, Helen, Lupe, Jade and Suzanne sat around the coffee table and worked on their own projects. The babies snoozed under the coffee table. All was quiet, each in our own thoughts.

"Oh, lovely," said Iris, as she fondled the various skeins of yarn.

"Come see them worked up against some new fabrics," I said, hoping to not sound too eager. The group enjoyed playing with the squares and the fabrics on the big table. The contest forced us to make it the most unique and impressive design possible, no emotions involved.

The slight blush fabric played exceptionally well with a dove gray, which created an art deco, antique look. "I think this combination is what you're thinking of," said Iris. "Sort of jazz-age-looking, something Zelda would wear." My head tingled. Iris had picked the combination that had wowed me from the beginning.

Tricia stared at Iris. "That's exactly what I thought when Carl gave me the ring. Fitzgerald is my favorite writer, and when I discovered Zelda, I fell in love with her. At one point I thought I may be her reincarnation!" She looked at the combination again and I knew we were close.

"Then, perhaps some research into Zelda's dresses would prove to be effective in the final design?" Iris looked at me. "The dress will have a theme, something I believe no one else will have: Zelda's wedding dress, and it would have been perfectly appropriate for the time, but that neckline won't work. It's not what she would have worn."

"And I think a lighter gray would work better," said Suzanne as she picked up a skein of yarn we had discarded and placed it next to the fabric. "See? Or even better . . . she put it on the mauve silk.

"Awesome!" said Tricia, her hand at her chest. "That's it!" then she remembered the subterfuge. "That's the winner!"

Chapter Twenty-Four

TRICIA'S FINGERS HAD BEEN FLYING, THE STITCHES TRANSFERRED FROM one needle to the next with alarming speed on the hat she started last week. "I have a confession," she said, still working furiously.

Robert sat with us this morning, and Iris and Helen were in their preferred spots and looked up at her expectantly. I was wondering the same thing—*what confession?*

"This dress." She looked up at the group. "It's supposed to be a secret, but I see no reason to keep it that way. I might as well be honest about it."

"But, my dear, what's the secrecy about?" Iris's blue eyes opened wide.

"Well, it's complicated . . . ."

I was dumbfounded to see Maggie breeze in, head high, her bright red lipstick a thin line across her face. "Good morning. I'm Jen's sister Maggie Putnam, and Tricia's mother." No hesitation, no question but that she would be a part of the group. She did not greet me, just sat next to Tricia and plopped her Louis Vuitton tote at her feet and brought out a needlework canvas.

"It's the only way I get to see you," Maggie said as she received kisses on the cheek from her daughter. "You certainly don't need that here, darling," Maggie said, as she looked at the wool cap Tricia worked on. "You forget San Diego doesn't get that cold."

"Oh, it's for Lacey," said Tricia. "Her birthday is next month, and I want to get it off to her before I get bogged down in the bar exam process."

"Lacey? Are you still friends with that . . . girl?"

"Yes, Mother, and she's my maid of honor."

"Well, we'll talk about that later. I thought perhaps Carl's sister would be your maid of honor. You need to keep it in the family, and she will be upset if she's not asked." Maggie started working on her needlepoint canvas of a bowl of roses quietly, as she contributed to the conversation about projects and books. She remained pleasant and used her party manners: amusing, but not too much so.

I watched Tricia as her mother began to work her way into the group. Her face, set in stone, didn't betray any surprise at her mother's machinations.

Careful. Arthur's voice batted around in my head.

"Those are lovely," said Maggie, pointing to the bowl of various grays, creams, and charcoals.

The group worked studiously on their projects. Tricia looked up at her mother. "Aren't they?"

"What are you going to do with them?" Maggie looked at me.

"*Elan Creative* is having a contest; I am considering entering a project. The prize is huge." I didn't look at Maggie. I kept working on the coat furiously so that I didn't have to confront her. The project sat in plain sight on the table, but Maggie hadn't seen it yet.

"I see your Barbie wedding dress there. I haven't seen that in fifty years."

"Yes," I said as I leaned forward to pull out the tiny dress from the basket of yarn. "Isn't it beautiful?"

The Barbie wedding dress had been saved from my childhood: white, fitted, long, with a mandarin collar and pointed sleeves. Nana Buford had made it for me, along with some hand-sewn suits, pillbox hats, and tiny purses.

"We had a crazy grandmother," Maggie said as she looked at each woman. "Crazy as a loon, but she knew how to work needles. That's where Jen gets it."

I worked even more furiously; my blood pressure hit the big red bulb at the top of the scale. Nana wasn't crazy, just honest and real, something that didn't set well with the rest of the family.

Plus, she didn't go to charm school.

"When do you plan to design the dress? Are you using that," and she pointed to the Barbie dress as though it were a rattlesnake, "for the model?"

"No. There's a sketch that everyone liked," Tricia said, I think between her teeth, and she leaned forward to get the sketch off the table. She presented it to Maggie, who put her right hand to her mouth as she held the framed sketch in her left.

"This? You must be joking."

Maggie handed the frame to Tricia and picked up her needlepoint. I heard the ticking of the grandfather clock in the hallway and racked my brain for something to say to change the subject.

"Why not that?" asked Helen in a loud voice and pointed to the sketch still in Tricia's hand. "Too *avant-garde*?" Helen's eyes pinpointed directly to Maggie's face. "Too fancy? Too unconventional? We all liked it."

"Not at all," Maggie said smoothly. "I just expected a more sophisticated design from women who might have higher standards." She looked at me.

"Higher standards indeed," said Iris with a wink at Helen.

We worked for a while on our projects and made safe small talk, again, about books and movies.

Maggie looked at her watch. "I have to get to the hospital board meeting." She rolled up her canvas and put it in her bag. "Tricia, will you walk me to my car?"

Tricia put down her knitting and followed her mother out the door. No good-byes, no niceties. Not like Maggie, so I knew she had become furious about something.

I watched out the picture window while others chattered and worked away. I saw Maggie's arms flailing at Tricia, while Tricia stood, feet planted, arms crossed against her cranberry sweater, failing to react. Maggie's arms came down to her sides, the shoulder strap of her bag slipped off and onto her elbow. Tricia uncrossed her arms, took the strap and put it gently back onto Maggie's shoulder, leaned forward and gave her a kiss on the cheek. Tricia turned and started up the walk while Maggie stared at her daughter's back.

When I turned back to my knitting, I saw the others conspicuously turning back to theirs.

Tricia plopped back onto her seat and said, "I apologize for Mother's bad behavior."

"What was she upset about?" Helen asked into her knitting.

"She thinks I should be spending more time at the law library, not frittering my time away at . . . knitting." Tricia's face flushed.

"Bull Hockey," said Helen. "Down time. You've earned it."

"Never apologize for another person," Iris said, waving her knitting at Tricia. "You are not responsible for anyone other than yourself."

"Thank you for that." Tricia smiled. "But as I was saying before Mother came in . . ."

"What, dear?"

"The dress? It's for me. For my wedding."

"Huzzah!" Helen clapped her hands silently. "I knew there was something special. Didn't I?" She looked to Iris, who patted her arm, and said, "Yes, you did."

Helen remembered her distaste for the project. "But I still say it's inappropriate for a wedding dress," and sniffed loudly.

Chapter Twenty-Five

"IT'S HERE." LUPE CALLED ME ONE MORNING ON MY WAY IN. "UPS JUST delivered the yarn for the dress."

"That was fast. I expected to wait another two weeks. The earlier we start on it, the better." The knitting group was due in for our Tuesday session in half an hour, so it the timing was excellent.

Five minutes later I walked in with the babies, or rather, they led me in, so excited to see Lupe, who always had a treat for them in her pocket.

I still didn't know Lupe well; we had been busy with the set up and with all the details we had not chatted too much about our lives. Arthur knew her and I had heard a few snippets from him, but she kept herself at a distance. I had a great deal of faith in her ability to think on her feet and solve any problem without wringing her hands and screaming.

She stayed solid, sure, dependable, and very, very private. Lupe seldom spoke or laughed, she just worked. And she was precise. She arrived at exactly 9:00 to open the shop if she were to open that day, and precisely at 6:00 if she were to close. Absolutely no deviation to her schedule. She wore the same clothes, nothing stylish, and nothing new. I often thought she looked like a sad little spinster.

The only complaint I had about Lupe is that she constantly answered her phone or texted something as though her life depended on it. But that was a small price to pay for such great help.

That morning the puppies scampered in and went directly to Lupe, expecting a treat. They jumped up onto her legs, and I was surprised to see Lupe back away, as if in pain.

"Uh-oh," I said, "They're being too feisty this morning. Come!" Lupe turned away and bent, I assumed, to get something off the floor.

I corralled the dogs and got them in their little beds in the workroom before they could do any more damage and hooked them up to their harnesses. I went into the kitchen and put the kettle on to make coffee in the French Press, then turned the corner to see Lupe still bent over as if in pain.

"I'm all right," said Lupe. "Just a hitch in my gitalong."

Lupe, usually correct, cordial, and deferential, didn't complain. She wore dark glasses this morning, and they slipped off in her effort to upright herself.

The blue-black-purple-green surrounding her left eye hit me like a brick. The constant phone calls, texting, the down-to-the-minute schedule, and the fact that Lupe didn't drive herself to work suddenly made sense.

Ding ding dingdingdingding.

I helped her into the kitchen. I knew better than to start asking questions. I handed Lupe her coffee and she slowly slid it onto the table, leaning carefully and grimacing. I looked more closely and could see that she would not be able to drink the coffee through the large, bruised, swollen lower lip. I went to the freezer and put some ice in a dishcloth and handed it to her. One tear streamed down Lupe's face. "I'm so embarrassed," she said quietly.

Lupe shifted in her chair, and her long skirt shifted with her. I saw the bruises on her legs, some old, some newer, varying in color from purple to yellow. Now I understood why she always wore pants or long skirts.

My gasp came out in two pieces like a hiccup, shocking even myself. Lupe stared up at me with some degree of defiance. "I'm not going to pretend I fell down the stairs. I'm pregnant," she said, "and he didn't like the idea—said it was my fault. He doesn't want the baby and I when I told him I wouldn't get an abortion, he decided he had to teach me a lesson." She winced and touched her lip with the tip of her fingers.

Tears poured down her face, but she spoke strongly and firmly. She was sure of herself, which I saw as a good sign. She had some moxy left in her, and that meant there was something to build on.

I found a straw in a kitchen drawer and poured a glass of water. I also shook out two Advil and handed them to Lupe. She carefully placed the pills on her tongue and gulped the water through the straw.

"When did you last eat?"

"I'm not hungry," she whispered.

"Nerves or morning sickness?" It was a serious question, but Lupe looked at me and started to laugh, placing her hand over her mouth to protect her swollen lip. We harrumphed together at the absurdity of it. Lupe stopped and said, "Not sure. I'm supposed to be on a diet—Harold says I'm too fat."

"Bullshit," I said. "You have a baby to nourish and you have to get healthy. And you are not fat." My blood pressure went into warp speed

Lupe's phone trilled. She went to answer it. Instinctively I put her hand on her arm, stopping her. "Let it ring," I said. "You can call him back in a minute."

Lupe looked horrified "Do you know what will happen to me if I don't answer?"

"I'm fine, I'm ok," she said into the phone. "I know, I know."

"Yes, that would be great. Thank you," and then she said, "I love you too," and hung up.

"Don't tell me, he's sorry, he'll never do it again, you just made him so mad, he wants to make it up to you, and he loves you, or words to that effect."

Lupe's eyes opened wide, and she said, "You sound like you've been through this yourself."

"No, I haven't. My husband never laid a hand on me in anything other than a loving manner. Have you reported any of this to the police?"

"I did once. The cops came and didn't do anything. They called it a domestic disturbance and made me feel like I started it, which Harold did nothing to change, of course. After they left, I couldn't go to work for a week, and Harold blamed me for not making any money that week."

"Do you want to talk about it some more?"

"No, I think I'd just like to pull myself together and get back to work. I do still have a job, right?"

"Why wouldn't you?"

"Because this is such drama, and I thought maybe you wouldn't want to deal with it. I wouldn't blame you."

"Lupe, you have a job here no matter what. I couldn't run this place without you. We'll deal with this together, if you want."

Lupe slumped. "Thank you. I will be all right. I always am."

That last sentence broke my heart. I pat her on the shoulder and left the kitchen just as new customers came into the shop. Sticks and Stitches greeted them in their usual enthusiastic fashion, and the shop shortly resumed its normal casual, carefree atmosphere.

The knitting group came in shortly, and we got to work with our individual projects; I handed each a skein of the dress yarn with which to make sample pieces.

When Harold came to pick up Lupe after her at the end of the day, I made sure to note the car and the license plate number. I saw that he didn't even get out of the car to help Lupe in, he just honked and waited for her to slowly make her way down the walk to the waiting, idling car. He waived to her impatiently, as though she needed to move faster.

Chapter Twenty-Six

A WEEK LATER, WE GATHERED AGAIN.

Tricia held a skein of the light gray yarn like a brand new kitten. "This is really going to happen," she whispered.

"Yes ma'am. We can start today."

Bruce stood on a ladder in the dining room installing shelves. He was good at doing quiet work when the shop had customers and bringing out the noise makers when we were empty.

Helen and Iris came in together and sat in their usual spots. Unbelievably, Helen began to grow on me. Direct and to the point, I found her brashness somewhat refreshing, although the hair on her upper lip still wanted to reach out and wind itself around me.

I felt guilty that her response to my sister's attempt at one-upsmanship was so strong—and that I felt giddy about it.

"Oh, marvelous," said Iris, as she held up a skein of yarn. She sat upright on the couch, as though she expected to be handed an award of some kind. "This is exciting. How are we going to divvy up the project?"

"First, let's look at the samples," I said. "Then we can work out the gauge and pattern so it's all consistent."

We all put our samples on the table. "Houston? We have a problem," I said. Six completely different sized squares lay on the table like beached whales.

"We have some arithmetic to do," said Iris, and leaned back in her chair. "We are all so different."

"Ain't that the truth." Suzanne looked around, amused. Her bracelet sang as she adjusted her knitting.

I pulled out a pad of paper and pencil and began measuring and counting stitches. I had lots of help. "No, you want to divide the number of stitches by the number of inches and then multiply the total by the number of inches wanted."

"I think you might be in error, Helen, dear . . ."

"But what about . . ."

"Now, we have to consider . . ."

"What's going on here?" Maggie stood at the doorway to the living room surveying the room full of confused women. "Is this a convention I'm not aware of?" I knew that smarmy smile and the mood it implied, the others didn't have my unfortunate history and took her at face value.

"We're trying to establish the correct gauge for the dress so we all knit the same way," said Tricia. "It's important to get it right so it fits properly."

Maggie sat down and began to pull out her needlepoint. "But it's just for a contest, correct?" Maggie's eyelids closed into slits. "What is the problem?"

"I am the model for it. It has to fit me perfectly so when we take the picture and submit it, they can tell it was custom made for me."

"Well, I don't see why that matters so much. You can always pin it in place and fool the camera," she said, waving her hand in the air.

"It matters, Margaret, because it has to be perfect. Can't fake perfection," said Helen.

My throat closed and my eyes watered in my attempt to avoid laughing out loud. Honestly, Helen was so obvious it was almost painful.

"Of course you can. It's done all the time." Maggie spoke with the voice of authority.

"Really?" Iris looked around the room. "I was not aware of that. I know there are impostors, but I don't know of any fake perfectionists."

The whole thing was accomplished so perfectly you had to admire the skill with which Iris and Helen teamed up to put Maggie down without her even knowing it.

"What are those?" Maggie asked, pointing to the squares.

"Those are the samples we all made to make sure our gauges work together, and they don't." I said. "We are having trouble figuring out how to make it work for everyone so we can all contribute to the project."

Bruce stuck his head in. He had Sticks under one arm and Stitches under the other like two footballs. He couldn't resist holding them, I knew. It wouldn't be long before they grew too big to carry.

"I think, if you don't mind my butting in, I may have a way to solve your problem. I have an algorithm on my computer that will work this out. It's an architectural software that has all kinds of functions, and I think maybe it might be able to handle this. I'd be happy to give it a shot if you'd like."

Maggie gave a huge eye roll.

We labeled them and gave Bruce a quick lesson on needle sizes and a chart showing the metrics of the needles. He took the samples to the dining room table, went to his truck and brought back a laptop.

"What, a construction guy is going to figure this out?" sneered Maggie. I knew Bruce heard her—he had to.

"Yes," I bristled at Maggie's implication that Bruce was less than intelligent. "and I have every faith in him."

Tricia had been quiet the entire time the discussion about math and gauges and sizing had taken place. She knitted away at yet another hat, this one black, and didn't look up.

Maggie left shortly thereafter, claiming another hospital meeting, and Bruce came back in with notations on the labels. "If the calculations are correct, this is the size needle each of you should use to get the same results. I would suggest making another sample to make sure, but I believe this is going to get you close to, um, perfection."

Helen guffawed. "I like him," she said.

"My dear, he's a goddamn jewel," said Iris, staring at the big gentle bear.

I could do nothing but stare in awe, my head spun a little at the discovery of a man taking an interest so genuinely and helpfully in a project he had nothing to do with.

Something Arthur would have done.

X X X

The next week the group brought in their samples, and they measured perfectly. The squares were exact and, if you looked closely, you could see a little difference in tension, but the measurements worked. Tricia allowed as how she could tell each person's contribution and it just added to the charm of the dress.

Now we had to get it to fit Tricia's body.

Bruce performed his magic on that, too, using measurements I had researched through old patterns and using the current gauge.

I took a deep breath and doled out yarn to Iris, who said she wanted to do the sleeves. Helen allowed as how she might take over for Iris at some point. ("It's too much!") Suzanne abstained, for the moment. She worked on her Fisherman's sweater.

I began on the back, from the bottom up, starting with the train.

Iris and I cast on that Tuesday morning, and began our Zelda Adventure, creating something from experience, expertise, and excitement.

Something like me. And the shop.

Chapter Twenty-Seven

*L*UPE HAD OPENED THIS MORNING, SO I HAD A LEISURELY MORNING AND I used it wisely by panicking.

The bills for the shop started to come in and piled one on top of the other on top of the other. It was overwhelming and becoming a reality. I needed money fast. My spreadsheet missed some key figures, and I had not included the cost of freight and taxes.

One learns by living, Eleanor Roosevelt once said.

I knew I was going to have to call Dave and beg for a sizable advance on whatever was coming to me. I sent him an email asking for a time to meet.

Then I paced back and forth in my office. I reached for the phone several times, but for some reason pulled back. The few personal investments, if I were to cash them out, would not be enough and I would pay a chunk of taxes off the top. I had learned that lovely little piece of information when some flunky, after four phone calls, deigned to talk to me about investments I knew nothing about. Arthur had said time and again the firm was our future.

Damn it, Arthur, how could you leave me in this position?

Think. Think.

I went to lie down, hoping I could relax enough to think straight. I had to do something today. My procrastination had only added to the pressure. I rolled over and crossed my hands under my cheek to support me. My tennis bracelet bit into the soft flesh of my cheek and I removed it as well as my watch and placed them on the nightstand. My head tingled.

I got up and went to the wall safe behind the artwork hanging on the south side of our bedroom. I opened it and pulled out my three jewelry boxes. One of them held family pieces I would never part with, smaller more diminutive pieces I never wore, but were good pieces.

The second one held earlier pieces Arthur had bought for me in the early years I could wear for daily events and often did.

The third box held show jewelry for very special events, large gemstones surrounded by diamonds that matched gowns worn only once.

What an embarrassing waste.

I knew I would never wear those huge pieces anymore. Other than the fact that Arthur gave them to me as gifts to honor certain dates, they held no sentimental value, and I would not miss them. I counted twelve complete sets.

I looked at the ceiling. "Thank you, Arthur." I dressed and put the box into a large tote. I went to see Mark Hepburn, the jeweler who had made most of these.

He looked over the pieces with a loupe and smiled. "Good work, if I do say so myself." He lowered the eyepiece and said, "I'm sorry, though, I cannot buy them back. I'm in the business of selling, not buying."

"Do you have a suggestion?"

"You can sell them at an estate sale, I suppose, or put them up at the annual jewelry auction. I'd be happy to represent you, but I'd take a fifty percent commission, and I'm sure you don't want that." He smiled at me as though out of pity. He probably saw widows all the time, or divorcees, attempting to wring some money off items they once treasured, now categorized as assets to be liquidated.

Arthur was gone, I was clearly not going to be a valuable customer, so I was of no use to the man who had designed some excellent expensive pieces of jewelry—for Arthur.

I pulled my cell out and dialed Dave at the firm.

"Dave Putnam, please."

"May I ask who's calling?"

"Jen Conrad."

"I'm sorry, Mrs. Conrad, Mr. Putnam is not available."

She didn't even check.

"Thank you."

I have no backup, and no information. I have to get this done. Today. I dialed another number.

"Lupe, are you all right to cover the entire day? I have to make a trip to Los Angeles."

"Of course. I'll call you if I have any questions."

While I still had the Lexus and the firm's gas card, I drove up to L.A. to a pawn shop that had advertised heavily that they would buy jewelry. I didn't want to do it in town lest my pieces show up at a party. I would be mortified.

I didn't know what else to do, and I was desperate. The vendors' bills were over sixty days late.

Six hours later I had hard cash in my purse. By my calculations, it was less than one fourth of the value Mark had ballparked the entire collection, but it was enough to start with.

I headed south to San Diego and directly to the bank. As I pulled the envelope out of my purse, I thought about my last experience here, and of the instinctive distaste I had for the undertaker. I looked at the bank facade and turned around to see First Fidelity Bank across the street.

This bank building turned out to be large, open, friendly, and was managed by a woman. I went directly to her and explained the situation. She listened attentively, gave me a packet of guidelines for small businesses, took my cash and opened a business and a savings account in my name d/b/a Stitches.

A credit line of $10,000 and a revolving credit card came with the small business package. No proformas, no explaining myself, no groveling.

We shook hands and I walked back to my car, astounded. A Woman Who Mattered.

I felt lighter, as though a heavy weight had been lifted, and it wasn't about the money. Jennifer Palmer Conrad existed. As a businesswoman in her own right.

My soul had taken a beating as well as my memories and my pride, but I was still standing.

Chapter Twenty-Eight

LUPE, IT APPEARED, HAD MORE SKILLS THAN I KNEW. SHE BUILT A website for us, she started an on-line community of needle workers, and an e-shop. She started a Twitter war to come up with a tag line for the shop. She featured the babies on every page and put cartoon bubbles over their heads to direct people to new items and ideas.

She contacted Robert about the dress contest, and he jumped on it. Iris and Helen's names didn't hurt the publicity, and Robert gave us a half-page article just on the shop and the dress to be submitted to win the unheard-of prize. He obtained a quote from *Elan Creative*, who did not endorse us one way or the other but did say "Shops like Stitches all over the country are the backbone of experienced needle workers, and they wished all entrants the best of luck."

The article picked up interest from several journalists who came to the shop to take pictures of the yarn, the *Elan* contest package, and the women working on it. We agreed to not disclose the actual design, but to allow pictures of the shop, of the group, and our inventory. Sticks and Stitches were a hit, and the puppies were included in articles about the shop in several papers and magazines. Smaller local papers picked up on the community project and ran the article. They all wanted to come back when the dress was finished to take pictures and get our story.

Free publicity is the best publicity.

This dress has to be perfect, on time, and we have to win the contest, not to mention keep the design under wraps. And I had to keep the shop open long enough to make that happen.

No pressure there.

Chapter Twenty-Nine

BIG BESSIE, THE CADILLAC THAT HAD BELONGED TO ARTHUR'S FATHER, sat in the garage, lonely and neglected. Once the Lexus was taken away, I thought I would drive it myself until I figured out what I wanted and how I would pay for it. Arthur had constant problems with Big Bessie, which provided great amusement for him. He loved that car and kept trying to outsmart it.

I could never stand to sit in it because it felt so big, the leather ripped, it smelled like cigarettes, and nothing worked. I hadn't been in it in twenty years.

Like an idiot, I tried to start it after it sat dormant for two years. I called Triple A.

The young man with an embroidered name patch that read "Matt" had no luck and hauled her up on the truck bed while I went inside to find exactly which repair shop to entrust with her.

Arthur's pride and joy was going away, and it broke my heart. One more thing to lose. I paced around the island in the kitchen. I tried to force my head to work, but the fog wouldn't go away. I had had no time to prepare for this. Matt appeared in the doorway, concern showing on his face as he took in the deranged woman before him. The look on his face went from scared kid to resolute adult. His shoulders went back, his chest came out. "Ma'am," he said, "This is a classic car, made before I was born."

Ouch.

"Can I buy it from you? I can give you $500 for it." He looked so hopeful. I couldn't help myself.

I found my voice. "Take it. It's yours."

"Awesome!"

He walked around the car and shook my hand. "Thanks."

I watched Big Bessie go down the road. The front end faced out like the face of a small child turned around in the back seat going away to summer camp, waving, a look of total confusion on her face. My heart cracked a little more.

Choyou tried to comfort me. "Missy C . . ." But I cut her off. I put a hand up, palm out. "Let's get some lunch ready, shall we?" I mushed on. Choyou had something on her mind, but I didn't care.

It's only a car. It's only a car. It's only a car.

I wanted Matt to have it, a gift, probably not even worth the $500 in parts, but it was priceless, no way could I put a number on it.

A few hours later, the doorbell rang, and I found Matt on the doorstep with $500 cash in his hands.

My eyes filled not only because this young person valued Arthur's treasure, but because I was so astounded someone of his generation would fulfill a responsibility to who he must see as an old widow who would not have cared whether he paid up or not. I guess I sort of assumed he wouldn't.

"Tell me about the history of the car," he said after I took his wad of cash. We sat on the couch and he heard the story of the car, and a lot about Arthur, my voice ebbing and flowing and cracking with emotion. He listened. I felt like an idiot when I finally wound down. He sheepishly asked for the pink slip.

I hadn't thought of that.

While I went upstairs to retrieve the registration, I heard a door slam in the driveway and looked out to see Choyou and Matt walking back up to the house. By the time I got back downstairs, Choyou was drying bar glasses.

Now I had no husband, no living or dining room, no credit, and now no car. I slumped on the couch in the family room and sobbed.

Come on, dipshit. You can do this.

My back went up, I swiped my face and sat up to think. For the first time in my life I had a decision to make, and mine only. No one else to share the responsibility, but no one else to tell me what I wanted.

Chapter Thirty

THE LYFT DRIVER DROPPED ME OFF AT THE MILE OF CARS, AND AN HOUR later I drove out in a bright red convertible bug, a car I had always pined after for the carefree, easy life it implied, a far cry from the Lexus. Getting financing hadn't proved to be too difficult. They charged me a huge interest rate, but approved me with only a small down payment, augmented by Matt's $500.

Top down, radio blasting not classical music as in the Lexus, but a classic rock station. I laughed as I puttered down the freeway to Stitches. As I parked behind the shop, I looked in the back seat. Perfect for two little dogs to go anywhere I went.

What a difference a few hours make. But now I had an additional monthly expense. I made a mental note to add it to the spreadsheet.

A few weeks later, the blue coat was coming along slowly, and I worked on it on a chilly Tuesday while Lupe worked on the back of Zelda and the rest of the group settled in for the afternoon.

"I thought I would see her at the party, but she didn't show." Tricia was talking about Claire Johnson, who had been a member of my former social group, a workhorse who performed on every committee and the person to whom one appealed to get the dirty work done. She was not a grand-stander, and therefore fell in Maggie's favor. It became a well-known secret that Claire, a proper, quiet woman, married a man who controlled her every move. It was not a well-known fact that she was routinely abused.

Helen and Iris looked at each other and I cleared my throat. "Perhaps she's been busy," I said.

"Perhaps she's been unable," said Iris.

"Perhaps she's been beaten to a bloody pulp," Helen contributed. "Man ought to be shot."

Lupe leaned over. "How do you know this?" she whispered.

Helen sat up and adjusted her glasses. "Came into the emergency room on my volunteer day. Did the intake. Don't get involved. None of my business. Bastard said she suffered from a 'woman's thing' and left. Looked at her chart." The vast lawn on the other side of the window seemed to hold her attention as she mused quietly.

"And?" Iris's eyes grew as big as an owl's.

"And it said internal damage due to several blows to the abdomen." Helen focused on her knitting.

"Excuse me," said Lupe as she placed the Zelda's train on the table and left the room. I felt badly for her. This had to be excruciating to hear about another woman suffering, one that had been married for over fifty years.

Iris and Helen stared after her, and then turned their heads to me in tandem. I shrugged.

"I don't know how women put up with that nonsense. I'd leave in a heartbeat." Maggie said into her canvas.

"With his jewels in my pocket," said Iris.

Suzanne spoke up quietly. "Sometimes it's just not possible."

"Of course it's possible. You just go." Maggie sat up on her high horse. She just couldn't imagine anyone living any other way.

Iris leaned in toward Suzanne. "What do you mean, dear? Do you have some experience with this?" I heard a Bach sonata in the background as we waited for Suzanne to speak. She had become someone else; quiet, introspective, focused.

"I do." She put her knitting down. "If it stays here in this room I will tell you the truth."

"The truth, dear?" At that moment Iris reminded me of Miss Marple.

"Yes." She looked around. "This is not to leave this room. I've been able to live here quite nicely, thank you, and I've paid the price, but I don't want this to be public knowledge."

We all nodded.

"Suzanne Finch is not my real name; I've recreated myself." She took a long deep breath and continued. "I spent six years in prison for killing my brother-in-law and I'd do it again. He put my sister in the hospital on life support. The cops wouldn't do anything. She called asking for help, and I warned them something was going to happen. They did nothing, calling it a domestic dispute. She couldn't go anywhere; she had no money, no freedom. She was a prisoner. I finally had enough and tried to get her out of that house. He came at me with a knife and I grabbed the fireplace poker. It did not end well." She looked around at the astounded faces and added, "She ended up in bad shape, but recovered. And I'm still on probation. Every move I make has to be reported in."

Lupe came back into the room and heard the last part.

"No joke," said Iris. "This woman is a true hero. She killed the man who put her sister in the hospital. I applaud you, Suzanne."

Lupe sunk down into her chair. "Really. Too bad I don't have a sister. I could use one right about now.""

Like a magnet, we turned our heads in unison to Lupe. Her eyes were brimming as she lifted her skirt to show the many bruises on her legs.

"Oh, Lupe," said Suzanne in such a quiet, sad voice I felt badly for her. She must have been reliving strong emotions.

"Well." Helen sputtered. "Want my Swiss Army Knife? Untraceable."

"I am pregnant."

"A baby!" said Iris. "Marvelous!" The energy in the room changed immediately.

Suzanne looked at Lupe. "You don't have to put up with this, you know."

"I'm beginning to realize that. You all are so strong. I'm learning a lot from you."

"When you are ready, dear, there is a room waiting at Chez Anderson for you and the child. Open invitation."

She nodded with a small smile on her lips. "Thank you, Iris, but I have to do this my own way."

"Understood. But know that any one of us, or all of us," she said, looking around the group, "will be here when you need us."

"Bet your bippie," said Helen with real conviction.

Maggie hadn't said a word. Bitch.

Later that afternoon, Jade shot into the shop.

"Iris left her cane. There it is." She hopped over to Iris's chair and grabbed the silver-topped cane.

A horn blasted behind the shop from the delivery area—three long, rude blasts. It could only be Harold. Lupe was in the bathroom. "That him?" Jade asked.

I nodded, recognizing the truck.

Lupe's husband Harold was a huge guy, from what I could see through the windshield, with long bushy hair that didn't look washed.

Three more blasts, this time more insistent. "Let him wait," Jade said.

Lupe came running down the hallway, grabbing her bags on the run. Her bulging tummy slowed her down and she looked a bit comical trying to move fast.

"God no," she said. "He's already mad. Don't make him madder." She opened the back door.

Harold's head appeared over the roof of his truck. "Come on, butterball. You waitin' for an engraved invitation?"

Jade pushed past her. "I got this."

"No!" Lupe's voice creaked out. I could smell the fear.

I didn't like the tone of Jade's voice: menacing and mean. She stomped down the three steps toward his car, her short jean jacket blowing back in the wind.

Harold hopped out of the truck and marched toward Jade, matching her footsteps. His cotton shirt was too small for him and I saw a hairy stomach through the bursting button front. Drips of something red ran down the

KATHY WEYER

front of his shirt, like he had spilled ketchup and didn't bother to wipe it off. This guy was huge, and Jade was tiny. She was going to get her clock cleaned.

His fists were bunched at his side, his steps loud on the concrete walkway. She got in his face. "What's with the honking? She not moving fast enough for ya? She can't take a minute to go to the bathroom?" She growled.

"Who the fuck are you?" He actually sneered.

She stood her ground. "Someone you really, really don't want to mess with."

"Oh yeah?" he laughed, a deep, grim sound.

"Yeah. Try me, big boy." Her feet, planted shoulder width apart, anchored her to the ground. She started to shift her weight back and forth from left to right foot.

He swung. She ducked and hit him hard in the gut with her right elbow. He dropped to his knees on the concrete and gasped for air.

"Jade?" Lupe flew out the door.

"I got this," Jade said as she waved all ten fingers at him, knees bent, begging him for more. "Come on. You think you're so tough? Try it again." She rocked from side to side again and worked up a perfect balance and a good head of steam as he appeared to get a grip and stood up.

He charged and gave a great growl, both arms open like he was going to get her in a bear hug—she ducked again, placed her head to the left of his chest, bent down, jerked upright, and threw him over her back onto the grass. He landed with a loud thump, which took the wind out of him. He moaned, arms splayed, gasping.

Very satisfying. I wanted to applaud but refrained.

"Anything else?" she said as she leaned over him with her hands on her hips and her foot on his chest. The exertion had been minor, her breathing normal.

"Bitch."

"Ouchie," she said, looking over at Lupe. She backed away, releasing him.

Harold hauled himself up, hands clenched, breathing hard and focusing on Lupe. "Come with me. Now."

Lupe had her head in her hands. "No. You're too upset." I put my arm around her. "She's not going with you. She's staying with me."

"And you? You're to blame for this," he said pointing at me. "She should be still at the law firm, making much more than she is here." He turned back to his wife. "You're coming with me. Get. In. The car. Now." He pointed his thumb to his chest. "You're mine, and I'm not leaving here without you."

Jade laughed. "Like property, huh? You have a lot to learn, buddy boy."

He took two steps toward Jade, his index finger pointed right at her core. "You. Stay out of this."

"I'm tho thcared," She said to Lupe on my left, who stared back in horror.

Jade took a deep breath and slowly turned her face to his. "You wanna do this again?"

Lupe gasped beside me.

They locked eyes like in some kind of chicken game.

In less than one second Jade's index and third fingers clamped around his index finger and bent it back. She twisted and pushed, and he fell onto his knee. She kept the pressure on and counted slowly and calmly. Her hand was the only part of her that moved the rest was cold, immovable stone.

"One. Two. Three. Four. Five."

With a grin, she slowly released him from the vice grip. She dragged her hand on her thigh, as though it had been contaminated. He took a moment to stand, spat on the ground and stalked to his car holding his hand. I heard his car door slam like a tin cup on a metal table.

"Lupe! Get your ass in the car." He yelled so loudly I was embarrassed for him. Thank God no other shops were open.

I turned to Lupe, who shook like a vibrator on extra high and I pulled her back into the shop. Harold's car sped off with tires screeching.

Jade followed us and picked up the cane she had come for earlier.

"Where did you learn that?" I whispered to her.

"Around," she mumbled.

I knew there was more to the story but didn't ask.

Chapter Thirty-One

OFFERED TO TAKE HER HOME WITH ME, BUT SHE DECLINED. SHE WANTED to be alone.

One of the bedrooms upstairs held a guest suite from my house, brought over with the living and dining room furniture just in case I needed to stay the night. It would be perfect for Lupe until she got sorted out.

I picked up my cell, my arm still around Lupe's shaking body.

"Can you do a favor for me?"

"Anything." Bruce's voice on the other end of my cell sounded warm and receptive, which caught me off guard for a moment.

"Jen?"

"I'm here. Yes. Lupe has run into some trouble and we need to go to her house and get some things for her. She's staying here for a bit."

Bruce hesitated a second, and his voice lowered. "That son of a bitch." He went from warm to cold with one sentence.

I said nothing.

A sharp intake of breath. "Is she okay?"

"Yes, just scared."

"Want me to call Guido?" Back to warm.

"What? No. We need to go get some provisions from her house and I don't know what to expect."

"Look, I'm happy to help, and I'll do anything you want, but wouldn't it be better to call your friend Ron Walker and have him escort her?"

"Of course. Why didn't I think of that?"

"Because you're too caring."

Brother, you just said a mouthful.

A nice young recruit showed up and a restraining order was issued.

✕ ✕ ✕

Carl was helping Tricia prep for the bar exam. She had moved into an empty office to be able to study and get to law books easily. It also gave them a chance to chat easily after everyone had gone.

"How is Ray coming along?" Tricia asked Carl one day.

"He tells me he thinks we were right, but it could just be accounting issues. He wants to make sure everything is in place before we go forward."

"It's been months . . ."

"I know, but these things take time. He also has to do an audit for the past five years, and keep up with the daily work, so he's a little busy." Carl sipped his water and looked around for anyone who might overhear.

"Also, your mother has been in touch with him, making him feel like part of the family." He used air quotes. "You know what that means."

"God, this is torture," Tricia said.

"The waiting? That's not like you. You are the most patient person I know."

"The waiting, the wedding, the bar exam, Mom . . . God." She drew her hands through her short pixie cut and cursed.

"Maybe you need to get out a bit—take a break."

"I can't. If I couldn't study or stay afloat, I'd lose it all. I have to keep the momentum going."

"Have you talked to Lacey?"

"Yeah, we talk almost every week. She's studying too, so there's that . . ."

"Is she going to specialize?"

"She's big into feminist studies, so I suspect she's going to develop her caseload on women's rights; it's her passion."

"Ah. Hmm . . . maybe we can move the firm in that direction." Carl mumbled.

"No—she loves New England. She'll never leave. So . . . back to Ray—does he have an inkling yet?"

"Just an inkling. He's following it, but swears he has to keep up with everything else he's doing; he's asked for an assistant, but Dave denied him. After laying off five people, we can't justify hiring someone now."

"And none of them were in finance?"

"Nope. And Dave seems to be putting pressure on him—where is this, where is that? I think Ray's starting to feel Dave's manipulating his work."

"Uh oh."

Carl smiled. "He's smart. He knows the whole story, so he sees road-blocks when they are put in front of him. He'll work it out. It will just take time and we cannot say anything." He looked over at her. *"Anything."*

"I know that," she snapped. "Who came up with this idea in the first place?"

"Let's not get into that again. We've started, let's finish it. It will all come out one way or the other and it will be over."

"I know," she said, with tears in her eyes. "But it's Dad."

"For Eric, remember?" Now his eyes were overflowing.

She nodded. "For Eric."

$$\times \quad \times \quad \times$$

"Lamb's Wool is going to hell in a handbasket," said Iris. She reached into her large carpet bag and pulled out large circular needles with the two sleeves started. She had executed the points well, with crisp and perfectly clean edges.

"What do you mean? Have you been there?" I confess for a fleeting second I felt a little betrayed. These women belonged in my posse. I adjusted the back of the dress on my lap, which was getting cumbersome and heavy. Between us, Lupe and I had almost completed it.

"Oh, yes, dear, we are scoping out all your competition." Iris nodded to Helen. "We are doing some comparison shopping."

"Right." Helen said as she lowered herself with a grunt into the over-stuffed, cushy chair. "First stop. Hit them all to suss out what they are doing."

Iris smiled at me. "Lamb's Wool brands are inferior, they charge $12 to sit at a large wooden table with hardback chairs in a group, which I find to be a large pile of, um . . ."

"Bullshit," Helen interjected.

" . . . nonsense," Iris said, looking over at Helen. "They don't even offer any help." She sniffed. "I found them to be lacking, distasteful."

Stitches

"No good." Helen proclaimed.

"What's distasteful?" Maggie breezed in, her perfect hair shiny and swinging as in a television commercial. It irked me. Tricia came in three paces behind her.

"Lamb's Wool yarns. Have you been there?"

"I try not to frequent those places. I get my canvas and tapestry yarn from the United Kingdom." Maggie sniffed.

"Perfectly acceptable places here in this country." Helen looked over her glasses. "You don't have to import quality, you know. You can find it right here."

"There's nothing quite like the very best, is there?" Maggie shot back. "I find that if I am going to put my time and expertise into something, I don't want to waste it on an inferior product."

"Quite right, Margaret," said Iris. "That's the discussion of the day, and, I believe, the reason Jennifer started this marvelous shop. Quality for the discriminating needle worker."

Lupe walked in. "You may have just won the contest for the tag line," she said.

"A contest?" Maggie looked around the room. "Surely you haven't stooped that low?"

She looked directly at me.

I never knew how to answer Maggie's barbs, and while I formulated a comeback, the most perfect of which I knew wouldn't occur to me until two o'clock the next morning, Lupe jumped in.

"It was my idea to draw people to the website. I know it's silly, but some people love to take part in these things, and it makes them feel as though they are part of history when the tag line is announced."

"I don't approve of drawing attention to yourself," said Maggie.

This from the woman who appears almost every week in the society columns and would run naked through the streets if it meant she could be featured in the New York Times.

"Agree if we spoke of personal attention, but this is business, and any publicity is good publicity. Any way you can get the word out increases your

160

market exposure." Helen the schoolmarm put the issue to rest. Sticks and Stitches sat together on the floor, their heads following the conversation.

I saw Maggie's eyes focus in on Iris's needles. "What is that?" she pointed at the two peaks dropping down from Iris's capable hands.

Iris pulled the needles up to eye level. "These are the beginning of the sleeves," she explained patiently. "I started at the wrist and will go all the way to the shoulder."

"It looks like the beginning of the Evil Witch's costume. Good thing it's not in black."

Helen snorted and Tricia worked even more furiously on her cap.

Iris said, looking intensely at her work, "I suppose you could look at it that way, but you will see."

"If you say so."

Tricia's face went pale. I tried to give her a supportive smile, but she wouldn't look up.

Sticks and Stitches were beginning to learn their way around. They went to Iris, who lovingly and sweetly pat each of them on their heads, bypassed Helen, jumped up onto Lupe's knees, up on my lap on the couch, at which point Maggie frowned, and then they jumped down. I noticed they gave Maggie a wide berth.

Then Robert came in and they went apeshit.

"Hoo, who da best widdle babies?" he got down on all fours and they played with his long hair and barked at his antics.

Maggie's frown grew deeper. Her latest Botox treatment prevented her from showing a furrowed brow. Only her mouth could show her feelings, and often that was a frown.

Robert laughed, straightened up and plopped in the smaller upholstered chair. His Stitches bag fell to the floor, and we saw dark green yarn had been worked on small needles into a wide ribbing.

"Lovely," said Iris when he brought his project up to his lap. He shrugged.

"What are we talking about?" He knew about everything: fashion, parties, buildings, books, but most especially—gossip, and he doled it out liberally.

"Quality, dear, we are talking about the cream of the crop, the best of the best, the top-drawer." Iris answered, drawing out the last two words.

"What, people?" Robert asked.

Iris giggled, "No, I'm afraid there aren't many of those anymore. In my day, people competed for that station." She put her knitting in her lap. "Oh, I remember Truman's Black and White Ball honoring Katie Graham. Now there was a grouping of the cream of the crop."

"You were there?" Maggie's fascination with that part of the world showed through her practiced nonchalance. Beautiful people were to be watched and admired.

"Why, yes, of course I attended. Frank Sinatra, his new bride, that tiny little girl, oh, what's her name? With the short hair. Mia Farrow, that's her, and Katie Graham . . . it was so very glamorous. In those days people dressed elegantly, spoke properly, and knew how to use the right silverware." Her chin came up and she focused on Maggie. "But you see, my dear, it wasn't real."

"I would have loved to be a part of that," sighed Robert. "I've read all about it and have seen the pictures. Truman must have been a fascinating person."

"He was an asshole, but he *was* amusing."

I choked on my coffee. "Iris!"

"Well, he was. No sense in sugarcoating it. He had a reputation of being difficult, I believe is the way it you say it now, which people excused because he entertained the guests." She stopped for a moment. "I never understood it. He only wrote one book of any consequence, you know, but he used his entertainment value as his currency. He managed to allow others to think it a privilege to pay for his parties, his clothes, his drinks, and sometimes his trips. He was an uneducated, crass, crude harpie, but people loved him. Harper Lee, frankly, was better educated and more down to earth and a nice complement for him at parties. I adored her. How she never had more success is beyond me."

"Wow. You were there." Robert shook his head.

I wondered if this was another one of Iris's tall stories. I had heard for many years she told stories people didn't believe, but this took the cake. I counted back and figured out mathematically it could have been possible for her to have been there. She would have been in her fifties.

"Quality and good manners have gone by the wayside," said Helen.

"I agree," said Maggie. "People are just so common these days."

Ouch?

Chapter Thirty-Two

"NO! STICKS, GIVE THAT BACK."

I ran behind him as two-month-old Sticks ran away with a skein of yarn that had fallen to the floor. He took his prize and sat under the table in the dining room, the yarn twice as big as he, and plopped his little butt down on the floor. I had no choice but to get down on my hands and knees and retrieve it. I reached out with my right hand, and he ran. I lost my balance and ended up face down under the table, laughing.

A male voice: "Wish I had my camera. Oh wait, I do." Click. "I'll email it to you. You can put it on the website." Bruce's eyes shone full of laughter as he pocketed his phone.

He looked at Sticks, who was now joined by his sister.

"Sit." Like a solider, Sticks sat. "Drop it." His mouth opened and the yarn dropped to the floor. "Good boy." Bruce produced a treat from his pocket and gave it to him.

"Too bad you can't train children like that," said Maggie and headed into the living room. Bruce looked at me, eyebrows raised. "Who's the bitch?" he whispered.

"That bitch is my sister."

"Oops."

I giggled. "Never mind. She seems to be worse these days, but she's really not that bad."

"You came from the same family?" Bruce's eyes were sparkly.

" . . . and what a family it is."

Tricia burst through the door, her face flushed and happy. I hadn't seen that look in a long time, and I soon found out why. A young woman stood beside her whom Tricia introduced as Lacey, her friend from Boston. Tall, thin, with flowing blonde locks and a grunge look, she, too, smiled and laughed her way into the store.

Built like Tricia, short and slim, she showed the yin to Tricia's yan; while Tricia was pale and dark headed, Lacey was light blonde and intense. Her eyes penetrated mine as though she tried to see my mechanics. I watched as she took in the shop and analyzed everything like a computer, the zeros and ones of binary coding in her head. While Tricia wore her typical cashmere sweater over jeans, Lacey wore a t-shirt over ripped, ragged jeans and combat boots.

The rest of the group had already been seated in the living room except for Lupe, who helped a customer as we settled in. Helen, by her furrowed brow, told me she remained unamused by the looks of this interloper. Suzanne, who had dropped in for a moment, remained static, Robert greeted her enthusiastically, and Sticks and Stitches jumped all over her.

The train for the dress had been completed and added to the back with careful weaving and decorative pearls. It was heavier than I anticipated, and when I held it up by the shoulders, it stretched, and my heart stopped. "Tricia? Would you come here?"

Tricia stepped over and turned her back to me. I placed the shoulders of the dress over her shoulders and stopped breathing.

It had stretched way too much. The decreases for her waist dropped down to her hips, and, while you could get away with the train stretched out, where the sides were supposed to skim the floor, they draped like balloon curtains.

"Can you block it back into shape?" whispered Suzanne.

"No, dear, blocking only works to get pieces to stretch, not to shrink." Iris said quietly. She put her fingers over her upper lip and pondered with her head to one side. She picked up her needles with the sleeves and looked at them. "I suspect these are light enough not to have been affected." She retrieved a tape measure and went to work measuring. "Everything is fine here so far," she said.

Thank God.

Lupe and I looked at each other, so disappointed. All that work. There was no way to salvage the back. The train could be used and reattached once we had a new back. Tricia hadn't picked up on the seriousness of the situation yet.

Damn. I should have considered the weight factor.

"And I see you are working sleeves that match. What is it going to be?" asked Lacey.

I saw Tricia freeze. Her face went white. I tried to get her attention, but I could tell she couldn't see anything clearly. I saw clear, unadulterated fear in her eyes as she finally turned her face to me. She looked like a cornered rabbit.

I jumped in as quickly as I could.

"We are entering a dress in a contest, and Tricia is our model. We are all working on pieces of it at some point. First prize is a hefty sum." I put on my cheerleader voice. "Here's the picture we used as inspiration," and handed the framed sketch over to Lacey.

"Oh!" She said. "This . . ." She looked at Tricia, who met her eyes straight on. I knew right away Lacey had seen that sketch before. I sensed Tricia's reaction: she was caught in something. Lacey's head cocked to one side as she silently questioned her friend.

". . . is perfect for you. It's almost as though it was designed for you."

"What? That's nothing like Tricia. She's has much better taste than that." Maggie's eyes became hard, and she started to lecture. "Tricia has always worn good, classic, well-made clothes."

Lacey stared at Tricia, who started to work on her project again.

"How long have you two known each other?" asked Iris.

"Eight years. We met in our freshman year in our first class." Lacey answered, still looking at Tricia, eyebrows raised.

"Where are you from, dear?"

Lacey turned to Iris. "Originally Chicago, but I moved around a lot."

"What does your father do?" Maggie asked, trying to suss out Lacey's pedigree, I felt sure. The fact that Maggie didn't know this information spoke volumes. I knew Lacey had come to spend Christmas their freshman year and Maggie clearly hadn't been interested enough to find out.

"He was a garbage man," Lacey said with her chin up, looking down at Maggie. "He died when I was ten."

"Oh dear." Maggie, I was sure, referred to the occupation rather than the death. She lowered her head to the canvas in her lap.

"And your mother?" Iris asked quietly.

"A drug addict who abandoned us as babies. I have a twin."

Maggie stopped stitching. I saw her face flush and instantly felt sorry for every evil thought I had about her. Losing Eric had to be the single worst thing that had ever happened to her.

Iris dropped her knitting into her lap. "How did you get into Harvard? Surely it couldn't have been easy with that background."

Lacey smiled. "I had a guidance counselor who encouraged me to apply for scholarships and grants. Without her, I would probably be on the streets. There could be no future for me without an education. Then I met Tricia here and hitched my wagon to her."

"I applaud your determination and your success," Helen said.

Suzanne said, "Yes" quietly.

"And your own judgment," I said with a smile.

"What kind of law are you going to practice?"

"Family law, focusing on women and children who have been abandoned or abused. I feel very strongly that we don't do enough to protect women in our misogynistic society."

Maggie snorted, something she never did, her reaction to a statement that may have been rehearsed or worn out over years of repetition it, but there was no mistaking the passion.

"What . . . you have a problem with it?" Lacey looked at Maggie. *So much for respecting your elders.*

"Misogynistic society?" Maggie gave Lacey a condescending smile, as though she were demanding a retraction from a five-year-old, but in a nice way.

"Yes, men rule the world, but we have come so far," said Iris. "In my day, if a woman worked it meant her husband couldn't afford to keep her, it was known as shameful." She knit a few more stitches. "Too bad, I would have made a great tycoon."

By now my arms were tired and the pile of yarn was growing on the floor. We wouldn't be able to use it. It had to be perfect with new yarn. I made a mental note to order more.

Lacey continued, looking at each of us around the room. "We haven't come far enough. Women are beaten down in the workplace and, worse, figuratively and literally at home. I did an internship where I saw some real injustices done to women who can't get away. They're trapped doing whatever their mates tell them to do and they get beat if they don't." Lacey was on a roll, and angry, I saw from her flushed face and brimming eyes. "One woman I knew had been beaten into a pulp and left for dead when we saw her. She later died on the way to the hospital. Her children were left with an abusive father. There was nothing I could do." She looked around the room. "That's why I'm going into this part of the law. I may not make any money, but I will change the world, one woman at a time."

"Commendable," said Helen.

Iris stared at Lacey. "To be so young and so sure of what you will do with your entire life. I'm extraordinarily impressed."

I thought about Lupe, who, I am sure, heard the discussion. I thanked God I had been married to a man who respected and treated me as though I were a queen.

But he took care of me, he made all the decisions about our life, and I was just now learning how much. There was so much I was not comfortable with, and these girls knew exactly how to run their own lives, if they didn't know, they would figure it out quickly.

They will make their mistakes and unravel what they needed to and start over. Just like this dress.

After the session, Tricia and Lacey ran out of the shop and jumped in Tricia's car. "Don't say a word," Tricia muttered under her breath. She cranked up the stereo, shoved the car in gear and ran up the freeway to a small rural town, turned right and followed that long road up into the mountain. She slammed on the brakes in the middle of nowhere, got out, and retrieved a backpack from the trunk.

Tricia started to march into a small forest. Lacey followed behind, her hands in her back pockets.

Tricia threw her pack down and plopped on a bed of dry leaves. Lacey stood over her.

"What the fuck, Tricia?"

Tricia sighed and opened her backpack. She lit up a joint and handed it to Lacey, squinting up through the smoke.

Lacey hesitated about ten seconds, then sighed and circled herself down, her legs crossing and took the joint. "I saw Adam the other day. He took me to the airport."

"Oh?"

Lacey nodded. "He asked about you."

"Did you promise to give him a note after study hall?"

"Come on, Trish. What's going on? Really."

So Tricia told her. It took about twenty minutes to get it all out.

"Holy shit."

"Yeah."

"And that's your plan?"

"Can you think of another one?"

Lacey thought for a bit and said again, "Holy shit. This is big. This is disbarring material."

"Don't you think I know that?"

"And Carl's on board?"

"Yes, and now you know why. We are going to make this work. It's the only way."

"You're going to need some help, then."

For the first time that morning, Tricia smiled. "I had hoped you'd say that."

Chapter Thirty-Three

"HAVE YOU HEARD THE LATEST?" ROBERT GLOWED IN ANTICIPATION TO his newest gossip.

"No, dear, but I'm sure you'll tell us," Iris said, smiling. Helen smirked.

"Somebody just put his hat in the ring to take Mayor Murphy's place," he sing-songed. "and you'll never believe who it is." Robert looked around at all of us, gathered together on a Tuesday morning. "Or maybe you will. He's got cajones the size of grapefruits."

"If it's who I think it is, those grapefruits are really overinflated raisins," Iris said, gazing over her glasses. "Ed Knowles?"

"Yes, and you win $2,000 for playing our game today," said Robert, as he cocked his finger toward Iris.

"Nonsense. I'll give him $2,000 to not run. Imbecile."

"Now, Iris, don't get your heart rate up again."

"I can't help it. That man doesn't know his willy from a water fountain."

Tricia used her growly laugh. "Iris, you're on today."

"We need to form a coalition. Who can we place to run against him? It would have to be someone who could knock him out of the water immediately. Someone strong, someone people know with a solid foundation."

"Mickey Mouse could run and take it away from him. Wouldn't worry," Helen piped up.

"I am worried. Who is he? He shows up at all the important events and manages to get his face into every camera lens. Without an education, they would vote for him because he gives the illusion he knows what he's doing. If you pay attention, he's captured in photographs cozying up to rivals, seeming to endorse them both."

"What are his qualifications?" Suzanne looked around the group, eyebrows raised. "It seems to me there would be qualifications to fulfill, a vetting process?"

"And motivation to figure out," Tricia said. "What would possess someone to take on that job?"

"For him, it's self-importance. Our current mayor has proven to have the right perspective. She stands up when she needs to, and fades into the background and works away at all the important projects behind the scenes. She's perfect, but we do have term limits. Knowles would be shining the light on himself every day, calling press conferences and announcing decisions. Pfft." Iris's voice was beginning to quiver.

"What motivates anyone to do anything?" Tricia asked the group. "Why is my father running for D.A.?"

"Tricia!" Maggie spoke sharply and glared at her daughter.

"Oh, I'm sorry, is that a secret? No one told me. I just assumed it was common knowledge." Her eyes proclaimed innocence, but I knew better.

My heart pounded so loudly I thought the others might hear it.

So, Dave's taking Arthur's place running for D.A. I'm not sure if I feel betrayed or not. Somebody has to run and if it's not Arthur, it might as well be Dave.

"What about Ron Walker, the police chief? I hear he's retiring soon," Robert said.

"How do you know that?" Renee had told me in strict confidence, and I was shocked to hear it coming from the outside. "Has he announced it?"

"No, but I hear rumblings, and it's a natural assumption. He's frustrated with the young recruits, and I hear he wants to go fishing and have a life."

"Well, if he's made up his mind to retire, he's not the right man to approach," I said, with the mild hope that I could end the conversation.

"Oh, but he's perfect. Morals, integrity, experience, a proven leader . . . and so, so handsome. He'd win in a landslide. How can we convince him?" Iris had put down her knitting and devoted her complete attention to the subject.

"Just like that?" I asked. "Doesn't there have to be a vetting process?"

"What do you think we're going to do? We'll vet the man, get a committee to get the word out, test the waters, and get his campaign funded. Anybody can throw his hat into the ring, Mr. Assface has proven that, but it takes a group like us, plus some experienced politicos behind him to make it happen. How about our current mayor? Do you think she'd be interested in helping him get set up?" Iris looked at me.

"I have no idea, but I'll run it past her."

The group went back to knitting.

Iris asked quietly, "What motivated you to open the shop, Jennifer? It's a far cry from your old life."

"Yes, I'd like to know the answer to that myself." Maggie smiled at me in such a way that I knew she was out for blood. She would use my words against me later on.

"You know what? I don't know." I laughed. "Fate got in the way, Renee has a way of talking you into things, I needed something to do, and I found myself declaring my allegiance to the art park."

"With no qualifications," Maggie pointed out.

"With no qualifications, no training, no experience, and no money." Agreeing with Maggie was foreign to me, but it stopped her from another attack at my expense.

"Admire your grit. Wouldn't have the courage to take it on," said Helen, shaking her head.

"Grit, nothing. I had to. I just had to." I found myself close to tears. "I had to." The tears escaped as I repeated myself out of sheer terror. "I had no choice. I spent my time wallowing in self-pity in that great big house and felt worthless."

Maggie's expression and frozen fingers over her canvas betrayed her shock. I understood that she was shocked not by the words or the sentiment, but by the fact that I uttered them in front of virtual strangers.

We don't discuss our feelings.

"I understand completely, my dear. When you devote your entire life to someone else, it can be a form of self-deflection. You have to slowly untie the knots and lovingly let them go." Iris mimicked the process of untying a scarf around her neck as though a silk scarf would be carried away in the wind behind her.

"Are you scared?" Tricia asked quietly.

I hiccupped and laughed. "Scared shitless, as they say. Until Arthur's estate is settled, I have nothing liquid. I'm in it to win it."

"I am sure it will all work out, dear, but I do admire your perseverance," Iris declared.

Maggie didn't say a word. She looked at her watch, packed up her needlepoint, said her good-byes, and left.

"So, who should approach Mr. Walker?" Iris asked as we got back to our work.

"I know him fairly well," I said, lying through my teeth. "Why don't I test the waters?"

"Good." Iris nodded her head. "Then I will have him to lunch and land the final punch. He'll listen to me."

"Bold statement." Helen looked at Iris, who just smiled like the Cheshire Cat.

New beginnings. Just when Ron thought he would retire and fish, he's called to action. Just when I thought the dress was going well, it had to be redone. Just when I thought my life was on target, it got ripped out from under me.

Yes, there is nothing quite so sure as change.

"What are you saying?"

Helen had stopped at the shop one afternoon with some news I just couldn't believe. I worked at my favorite chair on the calculations for the new Zelda back, recalculated to offset the drag of actually wearing it. Lupe and I would have to work double time to make up for lost time.

"Lamb's Wool stole the design."

"What? How could they get it?"

"Don't know." Helen shifted her purse from one arm to the other. "But I have my suspicions."

"How do you know this?"

"We went to Lamb's Wool this afternoon to check out the competition. We actually paid the $12 fee to sit at that damn table." She looked up at the ceiling. "It's exactly the same, down to all the changes we made."

"Well, well, well." I felt sure that Helen suspected Maggie. Someone in the group could have dropped it on the ground, or, well, I couldn't think of another option, but there had to be one. Maggie wouldn't do that.

"One more thing came out."

"Yes?"

"They received the $1,000 entry fee from an anonymous donor."

"Anything else?" My nerves began to vibrate. I didn't want to hear anything else.

"They are badmouthing Stitches. Says you are overpriced, highway robbery, and hoity-toity."

"What?"

"And the owner said she sent someone over to buy some wool, and it had moths in it."

"Who's the owner?"

"That slimeball who always manages to get himself on TV? The 'political expert' who follows around the most promising candidate and then professes that he's the man behind the curtain? Ed Knowles? His wife owns it. She's not much better, I must say."

"So, they're sabotaging us."

"Looks that way. What are you going to do?"

"I have no idea."

I called the rep who had sold me the original yarn and explained the problem. She said she had the same yarn but in a much lighter weight, but we'd have to recalculate and redesign the dress.

We still had eight months, but what a goddamn waste.

A sample skein of yarn was delivered the following day and I went to work, again, knitting up a square. By the end of the day the square was finished, and Bruce went to work doing his magic for stitch numbers and inches.

All this for a dress I wasn't sure was appropriate and that I had to keep from Maggie.

Chapter Thirty-Four

$\mathcal{T}$HE FOLLOWING TUESDAY I APPROACHED THE SHOP WITH WHAT IRIS would have called "a great deal of trepidation." Since we close the shop on Mondays, I spent the day with Tricia and Lacey. We opened the wine after lunch and somehow I got talked into cutting my hair. Lacey had worked her way through college as a hair designer, and they convinced me to take a chance. All my hair had been cut off.

I had sprouted about two inches around my head since my last visit to the salon, all gray which they placed in soft spikes. They took away my pearl studs and added more bold makeup and drop earrings. My hair, now all gray with a hint of my natural auburn, stood straight up and framed my now-round face. I also sported more brave makeup than I had in the past. Gone was the pink lipstick, in came a bright peach bordering in orange and heavier mascara.

I loved it.

Wait'll your sister and your mother get a load of this.

Lupe greeted me with an open mouth, which turned into a smile. "This is awesome. How did you get the nerve?"

"Two young law students and three bottles of wine."

"That'll do it every time."

Maggie came in and stopped short. "My God, what have you done?"

"Do you like it?"

I should have known better.

"Oh, Jen, what are you going to do?"

"Do? About what?"

"Your hair. You look like a dyke."

"I BEG YOUR PARDON." Helen stood behind Maggie, her eyes on fire. "That is not a word I appreciate. Who do you think you are?"

"Helen, really, it's ok." I said and smiled. It really was. If Maggie wanted to make an ass out of herself, let her.

"No, it's not. I take offense at that remark. No. I *resent* it." Helen turned to me. "Jennifer, I applaud you and your new haircut. I think it's beautiful."

"You would." Maggie muttered, turned, and entered the living room.

Iris saved the day by swooping between them and putting her hand on Helen's arm. "Now, Helen, don't let her ruffle you. You've endured worse," she said softly. She turned to me and whispered. "I know she's your sister, Jennifer, dear, but honestly, if I didn't know that I would never have guessed."

Iris said loudly as she entered the knitting area, Helen behind her. "The subject today is change, I gather. When your friend was here," she nodded at Tricia, already seated at the couch, "we talked about men and our place in society. It seems appropriate we talk about change."

Robert popped in. We hadn't seen him in a few weeks. "Change?" He looked over at me. "Oh, I see," and he smiled. "Change, indeed. Very chic."

Maggie snorted.

"Thank you. I like it," I said pointedly to the group.

"I've got some good gossip for you," he said. "You will all be interested since it centers on the law and judicial matters." He looked around the room at six pair of eyes focused on him, waiting. He sat the edge of the couch, raised one knee and grasped it in his clasped hands. "There are whispers about judicial bribery and witness tampering."

"Who?" Maggie's reaction, so swift, so high-pitched, should have told me something.

"No names have come out yet, but I assure you it emanates from the most knowledgeable sources. The ball is about to drop, there's an undercover investigation going on. All very hush-hush and clandestine."

Tricia stared at Robert, Maggie got busy with her needlepoint, and I bent my head down to focus on my knitting.

"Rumor, pure rumor. I do not pay any attention to rumors," sniffed Helen.

"Nonsense—give me the scoop, young man. This is positively delicious!" Iris's eyes danced, and she actually cackled.

"That's all the news that's fit to print," grinned Robert. "I'll fill you in when I know more."

"Change," Tricia said. "I'm going through a huge change, and about to go through more. I feel like my real life is about to start."

"As it is, dear, as it is. Jennifer, how are you, really? You've opened the shop and cut your hair. Are you different? Or are you still the same person?" Iris asked.

Maggie piped up. "That's rather abrupt, don't you think? Of course she's the same person. Why wouldn't she be?"

"I don't honestly know how to answer that. I feel as though my old life is peeling away, with a new one underneath. I can't seem to jive it out yet. I'm not going to social events the way I used to, and I'm not getting many invitations to go to parties. I'm the proverbial fifth wheel. And you know what? I'm okay with it."

"Ah, yes," said Iris. "I understand completely. But I don't mind saying that's when I found my own source of strength and developed some degree of power, much less character of my own. Oh, don't look at me like that, Margaret, it's true. Once you don't have to satisfy someone else's idea of the way you should live, you are free to live your own life."

Maggie guffawed.

"Don't sell it short, Margaret. I loved my time with William, all forty-seven years, but when he died, I discovered things I enjoyed, and I found I liked myself without censoring or thinking of how my language or actions would reflect on him."

The Fed Ex delivery man entered with a large box. It had to be the yarn for starting the second Zelda dress. I listened to the conversation as I took a box cutter to it.

"I don't know how you women do it, trying to please your men. Is that a rule?" Robert piped up.

"Don't you try to please whoever you're with?" asked Iris. "It's the same thing."

"Sure, but I wouldn't change who I am just to please someone."

"Robert, you are in an enviable position. You don't have those old tapes playing about being a domestic goddess and you can be yourself. What a novel idea." Iris said.

I listened to this exchange and thought about Maggie, who had built her life around Dave and the practice. The twins were an added bonus, a side dish. Her time had been spent focused on her husband more than her children.

Somewhat how I had lived. If I had had children, would I be the same?

Mother had done the same thing. She had turned an Arkansas hillbilly into a perfectly respectable Superior Court Judge. She had come from, not exactly privilege, but a nice, comfortable Catholic life, married my father, taught him everything she knew about society, and groomed them both to enter the world a notch above.

What would any of us be if we had devoted our efforts to our own success?

$$\times \quad \times \quad \times$$

Sticks and Stitches were getting to know the members of what we now called the Sticks Gang. As always, they adored everyone but Maggie, who looked at them as though they belonged to a primal tribe. Sticks had an accident on the Persian rug one Tuesday and I thought Maggie would have a stroke. The others tut-tutted and I blamed myself. I neglected to take them out before the session started. Maggie had a fit, this just didn't work in her pristine world.

"How are the wedding plans coming?" Iris asked Tricia.

"More importantly, how is the studying coming?" intercepted Helen. "That must be grueling."

Tricia sighed. "It is. I'm up to here with torts. I just can't believe the kinds of cases that come up in court, much less the lawyers who take them."

"May I ask, dear, are you planning on working at your father's firm?" Iris looked at Tricia. "Or are you going to work for someone else? Maybe start your own firm?"

"I'm not sure yet. I'm not interested in criminal law, to be honest. Like Lacey, I think Family Law may be my forte, but I'm just not sure yet. Maybe Criminal."

"Change," said Robert. "There is nothing quite so sure as change."

And this dress. It will get finished and it will fit properly.

Chapter Thirty-Five

I HADN'T SEEN RENEE IN A WHILE. I INVITED HER OVER SO WE COULD catch up. She plopped down in the family room with her scotch.

"So, how are you, really? You look and sound OK, but inside. . . ?" Renee asked.

"Inside, I'm . . . OK. Life will never be the same. I feel a little guilty that I'm enjoying things. Arthur was such a big part of my life I'm surprised I'm able to make a decision on my own." Shocked, I sat back and shut up. I sounded so disloyal and didn't know how to fix it.

"You made plenty of decisions on your own, don't sell yourself short."

"What to serve, who to ask, and which gown to wear, I suppose, but not much more than that."

"That's all your life required of you. Sounds like a slice of heaven to me."

I supposed it would. She's responsible for an entire city's budget, finances, and about 5,000 jobs directly under her. No way could I sign up for that.

"If only we could find something in the middle," I said, laughing. "Not too much stress, but not a life of leisure, either." Renee looked over and pointed at me.

"I think you've found it. Isn't the shop just exactly right?"

"It would be, if it weren't for the financial end."

"The audit should have started by now, and you seem to be running into brick walls. Do you think Maggie's behind it?"

"What? No."

"OK, I'll drop it, but I wouldn't put it past her. Listen, I need to give you a heads up. I've gotten some calls about Stitches. Nothing serious, very minor stuff, but I suspect someone's trying to make trouble for you."

"Like what?"

"Like questioning if someone was living there, if you have all your licenses and permits, little things that tell me someone's poking around trying to find something to make an issue of."

We sat in silence for a bit, listening to Choyou bustling in the kitchen.

My turn. "I need to give you a heads up. I'm sure you've heard Ed Knowles has thrown his hat in the ring for Mayor. I've warned Ron that Iris Anderson is set on Ron running against him. She's going to approach him shortly." I took slug and wound up. "We cannot let Ed Knowles become mayor of this town. He's smarmy, self-aggrandizing, and uneducated in the art of politics. I cannot imagine someone so awful taking your place."

Renee stared at me in disbelief. "I can't believe I just heard the great Jennifer Conrad, the good girl, the nice socialite, the polite Pollyanna, say a negative word about someone. Who are you and what have you done with my friend?" She smiled.

"It's true. He's the worst candidate ever, but nobody knows it; the general public thinks he's a perfect candidate just because he's in the papers all the time and shaking hands with the hoity-toity."

"The hoity-toity?" Renee grinned.

I waved my glass at her. "The hoity-toity. We have to get a candidate to run against him and crush him like a bug."

"My God, Jen." She put her glass on the table. "What are you saying?"

"I'm saying I'll do anything to override and crush that horrible man." And I meant it.

"Why don't you run?"

"What? No. This time you're not talking me into something so huge. No. I'll help any way I can, but it won't be me. I'm definitely not qualified, and no one would vote for me just because I'm Arthur's wife, uh, widow."

"I didn't mean now, but you should start working the circuit and run in four years. You can start positioning yourself now. I think you'd be spectacular."

"Let's get back to Ron. What's going on with you two?"

"Not much yet. We've had a few quiet moments; a connection has been made." Her face turned red.

"You mean a spark." I wanted to laugh. We were back in Junior High, confessing to kissing someone.

"You could say that, but nothing's happened yet. He still reports to me."

"If he were to become mayor, would that screw it up?"

"Maybe. I will retire then, maybe do something fun. I've always wanted to paint and travel. As long as one of us doesn't report to the other, we're fine, but the truth is I don't know how to act. I haven't been on a date in forever. I'm so insecure I don't quite know what to do." She laughed.

"Tell you what. Come to the shop one Tuesday morning. I guarantee those ladies will give you enough security and laughs to prop you up for weeks, and we are very discreet, believe me. They have an interest in Ron running, and would love to see you. Iris is part of the group."

"Iris is there? Then I'll definitely come check on the park and drop in on a Tuesday morning."

"Do you think Ron would run?"

"If Iris Anderson asks, he will obey. He adores her." She smiled. "The truth is, I can't see him relaxing. He's too young and has too much to offer. He'd be a wonderful mayor. I'll prod him a little. When he heard about Ed Knowles, he actually growled. I don't think it will take much."

Chapter Thirty-Six

"HOW ARE YOU TODAY?" ASKED DR. SMALL.

"How many times do you start a conversation like that?" Maggie asked.

He laughed. "It seems to open things up. How is the wedding coming along?"

"It's not. I suspect there are powers at work defeating my every move."

"What do you mean?"

"I mean every time I try to do something or maneuver things, I come up against a brick wall. It's like there's something that's in my way all the time. I can't believe it. I used to snap my fingers and make things happen, now not so much."

"Like what?"

"Oh, little things I'm not willing to share, just trying to get this wedding done. My sister's shop is failing, and I can't do a thing to help, although I've tried."

"Why do you care about your sister's shop?"

"Of course I care!" She shot him a look of complete shock.

He thought for a moment. "I don't believe you." He said quietly.

She pulled over her favorite pillow and hugged it to her chest and bent her head so that her lips picked at the piping of the pillow.

"Maggie?"

"All right! I want her to fail! I want her to come to her senses and come back to her old life and have things the way they were." She looked up at the therapist. "You happy now?"

"Why? Why would that be good for you?"

"Because she can be second banana to me."

"And if her shop is a success, can't you enjoy the other part all by yourself?"

"Yes, but she'll never know then. She doesn't seem to care about that life anymore, just the stupid shop and these so-called 'friends' she's made in the little old lady knitting group she's formed."

"So she's moved on. That sounds healthy to me."

"Oh, no. It's crass."

"Crass? You mean actually working for a living?" She hadn't seen him sneer before, and it unnerved her. "How many hours does Dave put in?"

"Why? What difference does that make?"

"Humor me."

"Probably sixty hours a week."

"And what are you doing those sixty hours?"

"Look. I provide an exclusive home, good meals, good companionship, and an excellent front for the community. I give parties, give money, and give my time to good causes. I earn my keep."

"Yes, I know that, but what do you *do*?"

"I just told you."

"Let me try this another way. If you were to die tomorrow, what would you tell Peter at the Pearly Gates to gain admission?"

"I lived a good life and went after what I wanted."

"Aha! And what is that?"

"Respect."

"Think about that, Maggie. Do you have that? Really?"

 Maggie hugged the pillow closer.

"I didn't hear you mention your children."

"Child."

"Children. You bore two. Eric was your son."

"Eric was my disappointment."

Peter leaned back in his chair. "I don't believe you—again. I think you said that so it won't hurt as much. Losing a child hurts, Maggie. Have you ever grieved or thought about him?"

"No. He's gone. Tricia is my world now."

"And you're controlling her life."

"No, just guiding her in the right direction."

He sighed and looked out the window. "Maggie, I want to help you. Really. But it's been almost two years now, and we don't seem to be making any progress." He sat back, and receiving no response from Maggie, he asked, "Are you happy? I mean really happy with your choices?"

"Yes, of course," she sniffed, straightened up and laid the pillow back where it belonged. "I have everything I want."

"OK, then. Maybe we should stop our sessions. I hate to keep taking your money if you don't need me."

Maggie stood up. "Perhaps you're right."

"Well, since I'm joining you, wouldn't it be easier if I moved now and applied for the California bar rather than the Massachusetts bar?" Lacey said over the phone.

Tricia was astonished. "You'd move that fast?"

"Why not? I have nothing holding me here."

Trish thought for a moment, a pang got her in the gut. "I suppose not. You can live with us."

"Hold on, Cowgirl. I love ya, but I'm not sharing a house with your mother. Sorry. That's a deal breaker."

Trish laughed. "Can't say as I blame you there. I'll figure something out."

Lacey sighed. "I'll need to get a job, too. Hopefully better than shampooing old ladies and delivering pizzas."

Trish thought back to the overheard conversation and laughed. "I have just the thing. My dad's looking for a receptionist."

Lacey got very quiet. "Are you sure?"

"Why not? He needs the help and it's another pair of eyes in the office. You can study there and have access to all the law books and maybe even do some filings. It's perfect. You can borrow some of my clothes—we are the same size, and I have plenty of clothes that are more than law office appropriate." Lacey said the last two words with a slight twang of sarcasm.

"Oh, joy."

Chapter Thirty-Seven

URING SPRING BREAK OF 1969, THE WHITE WALL PHONE WITH THE rotary dial rang loudly and I ran to get it. "Is Jen there?"

"This is she."

"This is Adrian." My heart beat so loudly in my ears I wasn't sure I had heard correctly. I pointed to the phone and mouthed to Renee, "Adrian Shoemaker!" and jumped a little on my toes. Her jaw dropped and she clasped her hands between her knees and bent over.

"Oh, hi," I tried to sound calm and nonchalant.

"Hey, um, my parents are out of town and we're having a party. Wanna come over?"

"Sure!" What was I going to say, *no, my parents wouldn't let me*? I stared at Renee and pointed again to the mouthpiece. "Party." She shook her hands in the air like she was having a hissy fit and danced around in a circle.

"Okay, then, um, I guess I'll see you here."

"What time?"

"My brother says his friends are coming at nine, so come later. You can sneak in and they won't notice."

"Okay. Can Renee come?"

"Sure—see you later."

I hung up and we both screamed like banshees.

That was the last time I felt carefree.

Chapter Thirty-Eight

*A*DRIAN SHOEMAKER WAS A HUNK. THERE WAS JUST NO OTHER WAY TO put it. Girls swarmed around him, the most timid of whom (like me) held back and stared in adoration, clutching their blue-fabric covered three-ring notebooks to their chests. He played football and was a world-class wrestler. He wore chords and short sleeved oxford shirts, neatly pressed. His blond hair was a little long and curled on his collar and hung in his eyes in waves. He was a good student and was on the ASB. When he ran for president his picture was everywhere, and girls touched the posters as they passed by. His father was a congressman and his mother picked him up from school in a large Pontiac LeMans.

There wasn't much more to know.

He was Mr. Big, and he had asked me to come to his party. Renee could come, too, which was a switch.

We snuck out the window that night, all dolled up in our sundresses with spaghetti straps. We ran fast to get to his house in the next neighborhood, laughing and snickering, hoping it would be worth it if we got caught.

We found several other people we knew around the pool, each with a bottle of beer and some smoking cigarettes or passing around a joint. I tried to look nonchalant while Renee instinctively went to people she knew and joined in. I followed and listened to her chatter with guys, natural as could be.

I was terrified and wanted to be back home in my pink pajamas listening to music and writing in my diary. This was not for me.

Renee grimaced as she took a slug of beer offered to her from some guy, and they laughed at her. She handed it back and I leaned over to her and whispered, "I want to go home." She turned to me. "Look," she nodded to someone over my shoulder. I turned and saw Adrian coming toward me. "Still want to go?" she whispered in my ear. I felt her leave and Adrian stood over me.

"How ya doin'?" he asked. I smelled the beer on his breath and watched him sway.

"I'm good."

"Wanna take a walk?"

"Sure." He held his hand out and I took it. I was holding hands with Adrian Shoemaker and I wanted to shout. I looked around to see if anyone had noticed. Nobody looked our way. We walked toward the woods in the back of their house and eventually he led us to a log in a clearing. We were all alone.

"Are you scared?" Adrian asked me. My knees knocked and I took a long time to make sure my voice didn't shake.

"No, should I be?"

He leaned in closer. "You are so cute." His tongue entered my mouth and the unfamiliar sensation made shivers go up and down the back of my neck. He stayed there for a while and I responded, my tongue playing with his. He started to grunt a little and moan. His hand moved to my left breast and I let it stay there.

He took my hand and put it over his crotch. I stopped playing. This was no game. "No," I said.

"Please? Just a little." His breath was hot on my neck and I got cold and started to shiver. I didn't want to be there anymore.

"No."

"Yes." He had me in a strong hold and rolled me over onto the forest floor and straddled me.

"NO." I struggled against him, kicking and screaming. "Stop. Please stop."

He raised his head to meet my eyes. "No. You want this, trust me."

"No!" I screamed. "Help!"

"No one can hear you, Jenny." His breath covered my face, I was swathed in the smell of alcohol and cigarettes.

I wanted to go home. The idea of my own room, my parents watching TV, and my sister doing God knows that sounded good.

I wanted to go home.

Tears overflowed from my eyes and down into my ears. I heard myself snuffling and crying while at the same time I heard the sound of a zipper. He grabbed my hand and tried to put it around him, but I resisted. He pulled my skirt up and ripped off my panties and I screamed again.

"Shh, it's okay," he moaned. "It's alright." He pulled himself up and into me so fast I never knew what was happening until it was happening. The sharp pain took my breath away and I stopped kicking and screaming. He jerked a few times, groaned, and fell off me. "Whew!"

He lay on his back and zipped up his pants, grinning. "That was great, babe."

I curled up into a fetal position, sniffling and crying. He looked over at me. "What's wrong?"

"I didn't want that. I thought you liked me."

"I do, babe. Didn't I just prove it?" He grinned at me. "You'll be okay. I didn't realize you were a virgin, though. Hope you're not regretting it."

I sat up and pulled my panties on, ran back to the house, found Renee, and ran home. She was drunk and made too much noise getting back into the house I thought we might get caught, but no one woke up.

Renee spent the night worshiping the porcelain god and I cried myself to sleep.

The next day Renee was sick as a dog and I spent it tending to her and trying to forget what happened to me.

I hadn't had my first period yet.

"He's on the bench this morning, ruling on what appears to be a complicated embezzlement case." A nurse in pink scrubs led me to the solarium where my father sat with three others. His arms waved around as his voice boomed in agitation. "Objection overruled! Mr. Peterson, you are out of line. Continue, counselor."

"Hello, Father." A silence descended as they all turned to inspect me.

He stared out the picture window as the others wheeled themselves out of the day room.

"How are you today?" I saw his chin waver a little, and his eyes glowed like glass garage doors: when the door came down you could still see inside but couldn't get to it.

"He's been rockin' today, a real hoot," said a voice coming from a retreating wheelchair.

When I showed up he shut down. Every time.

Why did I come back? I had never been forgiven for my sin, and yet I continued to crave his forgiveness.

A virtual egg broke on the top of my head and dropped down my scalp, tingling new parts of my brain and opening up curtains to let some light in, throwing open new doors in my psyche.

It occurred to me I had some power here, too. My feelings counted, and he had disappointed me and let me down far more than a parent should.

And, with a shudder, I realized Mother sat back and allowed it to happen.

I may have made the mistake, but they did the damage.

We sat in silence as this new revelation hit me, and I inspected his face. The folds, the wrinkles, the disappointment in his eyes.

All this time I waited for approval, for forgiveness. My adolescence had been ruined not by my own mistake, but by how my own parents handled it. The situation had been so badly handled that I fell into what I now know could be diagnosed as a deep clinical depression. I skated by in school, never ditched like the others, just barely achieved C's so I wouldn't call attention to myself by failing. I kept my head down, both literally and figuratively. I had no friends except Renee and I did not participate in school activities. I never went to a prom, a football game, or even graduation.

I became an outcast because I was told I was a sinner, a bad girl.

And I believed them.

I escaped to Boston University, where I majored in liberal arts and met new people. I started over. That was my salvation. I learned all about art, literature, music, and French. And that's where I met Arthur. Thank God. I met him at a party at Harvard where he was a law student. I was immediately enthralled with his charm, his intellect, and his ethics.

He brought out the best in me, my savior. He believed in the good girl I had become by practicing, trying to please my parents. I glommed on and didn't let go. I never told him of my sin, scared he would no longer find me attractive, virginal, or valuable. Used. Thrown away.

A sinner.

I sat with my father, doing my duty and sitting with him, reeling from this epiphany.

Neither one of us said a word.

Chapter Thirty-Nine

MOTHER HAD GIVEN ME A BOOK IN THE SPRING CALLED *YOU'RE A Young Lady Now* and said to ask her any questions I had. Her eyes bored through me and I didn't quite know what to think. I put the book in my drawer and forgot about it.

My friends were getting their periods, but I hadn't gotten mine yet. Renee complained of cramps all the time and I just thought she was a big baby. We had a big dark blue box of Modess in our bathroom, never opened.

I had a few weeks of unexplained nausea. Mother explained it away as food allergies or test anxiety and had me taking things away from my diet and then putting them back in to test the effects.

One day I was in the shower and Mother came in with fresh towels. She took one look at me and dropped the towels, her face paled and I thought she might faint. She ran out; I had never seen her run before.

The party had ended my burgeoning party-girl image. I had no desire to become popular or hang out with Adrian and his friends. I stayed home while Renee did her own social thing. I read, watched movies, and tried to evade my sister. I knew my tummy had gotten big, but I had started to stay home and got lazy and put it down to eating too much.

When Father came home, he and Mother had a meeting in their bedroom, which was highly unusual. Renee looked at me with raised eyebrows and I shrugged. All of a sudden, our bedroom door slammed open.

"You're pregnant? You're PREGNANT?" Spittle flew out of his mouth. "You little whore. How could you embarrass us like that? You have RUINED this family." The waddle under his neck vibrated as he shook his hand at me. "Do you know what you've done? You have sinned. Now you are damaged. No man will ever love you."

I was still trying to wrap my brain around being pregnant. I had all the sex ed classes, so I knew it was possible, but I hadn't even had my first period yet. How could this be?

I'm having a baby?

"You are a disappointment to me. You are a sinner, a fornicator, a slut. You cannot be a proud girl anymore." He stopped, breathing hard, and lowered his voice. "We will take care of this, but it's the last time we solve your problems." He turned and slammed the door closed.

I slumped on my bed, still trying to understand what had just happened.

Renee stared at me, eyes huge.

That summer, it was announced to everyone that Maggie and I were going to Europe with the Hamiltons, old friends of my parents and, in fact, our Godparents.

On the morning of our fabulous trip, Maggie and I got in the car with our luggage and headed off to the Hamiltons' mansion in La Jolla. We were giddy with excitement. I started to follow Maggie out of the car when Father said quietly and firmly, "You. Stay here."

Maggie looked back at me with a questioning look and followed Mother and Father up the walk. After a few minutes of discussion with the Hamiltons, I saw Mr. and Mrs. Hamilton nod at my parents, who gave Maggie kisses goodbye and walked back to the car. Maggie waved to me from their doorway.

I was terrified.

Mother and Father got into the car.

"What's going on?" I asked.

Father pressed his lips together and said, "You don't deserve a trip to Europe. You're a sinner. You're going off to a place for unwed mothers in New Hampshire. By the time school starts you will be back here, and no one will know the difference. Your humiliation will be kept within the family and you will not expose the rest of us to your shame."

Mother stared out the window. She never did address "the problem" with me.

"What about Renee?"

"What about her?"

"Is she going to live alone with you?"

"She'll be taken care of." I wasn't sure what Father meant by that, but it occurred to me that my best friend might just be gone when I got back.

"Please don't. I'll be good." I started to sob. "I don't want to go. I want to stay with you."

"You should have thought of that before you spread your legs."

Father met me at the airport when I came home from New Hampshire. No hugs, no greeting, just a trip down to baggage handling to retrieve my suitcase. He actually shoved me out the door and into the parking lot to the car. I got in the back seat like a child.

"Let us be clear," he said into the rearview mirror when we were belted into our seats. "There will be no privileges extended to you. You have proven you are not worthy of any freedom, so you will not attend any events, any parties, or any activities other than school events. You will not go to prom, you will not come out, and you will not have any friends over unless we are present. Understood?"

"Yes sir." I felt myself shrink down in the vinyl seat. I wanted so badly to ask about Renee but didn't. It was so hard to just sit there knowing I was not worthy any more of his love.

Mother met me at the door and gave me a dry kiss on the cheek. "Dinner is at seven."

I dragged my bag up to my room and opened the door.

Nothing had changed. My bed was made perfectly. Renee's bed was made perfectly. There was not a speck in the mausoleum of a room previously shared by two best friends. I threw my bag on my bed and fell backwards onto Renee's.

"About time you got home." The door creaked and closed, and lo and behold, there was Renee. I wanted to shout but dared not disturb the quiet in the house.

She lay down next to me and spooned me. "It must have been hell," was all she said. I cried, for the first time.

We went downstairs at precisely seven o'clock for dinner. Maggie smiled and talked all through dinner about Europe, and my parents doted on her, leaving me and Renee in the dust.

Fine by me.

School was to start the following week. My suitcase was full of clothes I wore before my life changed forever, and they no longer fit. I expected to go shopping as usual for school clothes and supplies and was looking forward to life getting back to normal.

That never happened. Renee and I learned to sew, and I remade some old clothes and bought fabric and patterns with my babysitting money.

That's when I learned to be creative. I've never stopped.

Chapter Forty

TRICIA HAD COME IN EARLY FOR OUR GROUP SESSION. "MOM'S ACTING weird." She opened her mouth to say more, but then Maggie entered the shop, swinging her tote as though she owned the world. She stood at the counter with me and Tricia and said, "How is Lacey's dress coming?"

"Lacey's dress?" I asked

"Yes, the one you're modeling and entering for the," she used air quotes, "contest."

"What?" What in the hell was she up to?

Tricia stared at her. "Mother, the dress has nothing to do with Lacey. Why would you think that?" She studied her mother carefully.

"No reason. It just looks like something she would wear. Is she a lesbian?"

"What? Mother, where is this coming from?"

"Never mind, dear. I was just wondering. I came in to get more needles. I have to get to the hospital board meeting, so I can't make it to the meeting." She looked into her bag. "Oh, look at that, I have enough needles. Silly me."

Maggie has left the building.

The rest of the group had not heard this exchange and wondered aloud why Maggie left in such a hurry.

"So, get this," Tricia said, leaning in toward the middle of the group. "Mom thinks the dress is for a lesbian wedding, and that Lacey's the bride!" The others sat back, slumped in confusion. "How in the world did she come up with that one?"

"Wild imagination," said Helen. "Oh, give me that," she said to Iris, who was wagging her wrists in the air like puppies begging for treats. "Your arthritis is acting up, and these need to be finished some time this century."

I laughed, stopped working and thought for a minute. Nope, my conscience is clear, no references to lesbians or Lacey being the bride. I had no responsibility in that line of thinking at all. I adjusted the knitting in my lap. The back was coming along well, if a bit slower, and appeared to be the right size, thank God.

Lupe put her head in her hands. I thought she might be sobbing. "Lupe?"

"Oh, my dear, whatever's the matter?" asked Iris. Suzanne just stared at her.

Lupe pulled her hands away. Relieved to find her laughing, my blood pressure went down. "Lupe, what do you know about this?"

She couldn't get her breath. "I . . . I . . . I . . ." More spastic laughing. "It's all on me. Trish, if you want me to confess to your mother I certainly will, but really, I just wanted to scare Lamb's Wool and throw them off the track."

"What do you mean?" I realized too late that Tricia didn't know about the duplicity and turned to her to explain. "Someone gave a copy of the sketch and the new design pattern to Lamb's Wool, along with the $1,000 entry fee."

"But why?"

"Good question. I think it's to compete with us and put a roadblock in our way."

Helen sat up straight. "Hate to say it but suspect it's your mother. No one else would wish ill on this project or this shop." Iris put a hand on Helen's arm, attempting to quiet her, as usual.

Lupe went on. "I went to Lamb's Wool and used the business card of an attorney who is no longer at Conrad and Putnam, I know I shouldn't have, but I asked them to 'cease and desist', and I said the dress was for my fiancée. I meant to say friend but got flustered. I didn't mean it to come out like that, but once it did, I couldn't take it back and sound like a real attorney, so I left it lying there." Her laughter slowed and she had better control.

Iris whooped and Helen shook her head.

"But how could Mother find out about it?" Tricia asked. "And by the way, what you did was illegal."

Lupe looked solemn as she delivered the bad news. "Apparently I, as a pregnant, engaged lesbian, am incredibly scary. I told her to call her benefactor and tell her they decided not to enter the dress."

Silence engulfed the room.

". . . and, yes, I know it's illegal, but I was willing to risk it."

"So you think the shop owner called Mom."

Helen nodded. "Proves it's her. Where else would she get the lesbian bit?"

Tricia sat still. I felt bad for her. "Can I ask you all to just not mention this again—to anyone?" Tricia said.

We all agreed and finished our session in quiet solidarity.

Several weeks later, Maggie, Tricia and I sat in the parlor and finished up for the day. The others had left, and the room was quiet. Sticks and Stitches were curled up on the fireplace mantle in their little beds—not quite the King Charles Spaniels I had envisioned, but they were adorable. And they were mine.

Tricia's voice came out of the blue. "Mother, I have to tell you something."

"What, dear?" Maggie started to roll up her needlepoint canvas. The newest *Modern Bride* magazine peeked out from the top of her tote.

"You're not going to like it."

Maggie looked at her daughter and waited.

"The dress we're working on in the knitting group. It's my wedding dress."

"Your what?"

"I asked Aunt Jen to make my dress, and it turned into a group project." She nodded to me.

"A handmade wedding dress? Tricia, you can't be serious. This can't be made by 'loving hands at home'. Your Aunt Jen is good, but she's no Vera Wang."

Gee, thanks.

Tricia's chin went up. "I don't want Vera Wang. I want my own design made by someone who loves me."

"Out of the question."

Tricia took a deep breath. "Mother, I am not going to fight you on this or on anything else. You can have the Jordan Almonds and can pick out my crystal and sterling patterns, and even the place and the time. But this is the one thing I'm going to insist on."

"Absolutely not. This is going to be the wedding of the century for this town and I will not have you looking like a ragamuffin in a cheap, handmade dress."

"Whoa," I said.

"It may be handmade, but it won't be cheap." Tricia picked up her backpack and stood over her mother. "It's getting made. I just wanted you to know so it isn't kept a secret, which was my first choice, but that puts Aunt Jen in an awkward position. I knew how you would feel, but I think you'll change your mind when you see it."

She was halfway through the doorway into the foyer when her mother's growly voice hit her. "Patricia Elizabeth Putnam get back here. We're not finished."

She turned around. "Yes, Mother, we are. I'm sorry to go against you, but I'm only asking for this one thing, and I wish you would honor it."

Maggie's mouth opened, then shut.

Tricia had gone.

Maggie's red face turned to me.

"What the hell is going on?"

"Maggie, calm down."

"Don't you tell me to calm down. How dare you insert yourself into *my* daughter's wedding." I heard Maggie breathe heavily, and it brought back several memories of difficult times. My stomach plummeted and I became a little dizzy.

"If you will hang on a bit, I can explain how all this came about."

"Talk."

"Okay. *Elan Creative Magazine* is having a contest . . ."

"That's nice, and I already knew that, but what does it have to do with *my daughter?*"

I let the inference that I maybe thought Tricia was my daughter slide.

"Maggie," I sighed. "It doesn't really, except Tricia had a sketch that she presented to the knitting group and someone said it might even make a beautiful wedding dress." I didn't lie, I just left out a few things.

"Ohhh, no. I will not have Tricia showing up in a piecemeal lace project from a bunch of old biddies who have nothing better to do." Maggie's breathing became tighter, "And that. Is that." She took a deep breath. "I'm going to put a stop to this nonsense. How you got her involved in this is beyond me, but Tricia is wearing an original Vera Wang to her wedding. I'll see to that."

I stared at my sister and wondered how in the hell we came from the same gene pool.

Well, you managed to skirt a real argument with Maggie—again. When are you going to stand up for yourself?

$$\times \quad \times \quad \times$$

Tricia was the last to enter the following Tuesday. "Mom's so upset she's not coming anymore," she said to the group. "I'm sorry to put you all in that position."

"Nonsense, dear. You should have what you want, but I will say it's more comfortable now knowing that she's aware of it." Iris the diplomat.

"Not to me. Happier if she's left out of it." Helen looked at Tricia. "Sorry. I know she's your mother, but I fear something's underfoot here, and I have to speak my mind. You are so gentle and true, how could you possibly come from that woman?"

"Helen . . ." My knee-jerk reaction was to defend my sister.

"Sorry. Sorry, she's up to something, I can feel it. Your sister has a reputation of getting her own way, she doesn't care what methods she uses."

Helen's turkey neck wobbled in indignation, and that damned hair on her lip quivered.

Suzanne spoke up, "I don't think that's nice," she said quietly. "We shouldn't be speaking ill of one person's sister and another's mother."

"Hang on." Tricia dropped her needles. "This dress is so special. A friend designed it for me. I don't want anyone else making it."

"What do you suggest?"

"Let me think about this for a bit." Tricia bit her lower lip.

Chapter Forty-One

"WHAT'S THIS ABOUT AN ART PARTY?" SAID MAGGIE AS WE SAT HAVING lunch. She had invited me, something that hadn't happened since the old days. Her eyes were wide, as though she were asking for a state secret. "I hear rumors there's a big shindig at the art park, and I haven't received my invitation yet."

We sat at Maggie's table at Harry's, a venerable old bar downtown where the powerful and elite met to discuss deals, celebrate victories, or drown their sorrows. The wives of those powerful and elite professionals invaded the bar for lunch just to be seen.

The starched white arms that discreetly lay our goblets at their places and our lunches on the gold-plated charger plate were stiff and quiet. I looked up and smiled. No smile back.

So stiff. So formal. Was this ever a part of my world?

"You weren't invited because you're not an artist," I said as I took a gulp of wine.

"And you are?"

I took a deep breath. "We're trying to get artists interested in the park and get them to lease space. We thought having them all together with something in common would create a community of sorts that would generate enthusiasm."

She took a tiny bite of tuna off the tip of her fork. "But why not have some social heavy hitters in the pack?"

"Because we don't want the artists to feel intimidated. We want them relaxed and free to browse and talk."

"But Iris is coming, and Helen."

You don't have to explain anything. Let her twist in the wind a little.

"So, how is the wedding coming along?"

"Don't change the subject. I want to know exactly what's going on out there."

"Maggie, I don't owe you an explanation. This is what we are doing, and it's closed to the public. We need to get the center filled up; my business is suffering because there's no draw."

"Your business." She sniffed.

"Yes, Maggie, my business. You don't seem to understand that this is my life now, one I chose. I'm sorry if you don't like it, but it's my decision and my life and I'm doing the best I can. I have no interest in living the old life anymore. I want my life to be real and based on something other than ethereal proof of success." I have no idea where that came from, but it came out in a rush. My bad.

Maybe I went too far.

Maggie sat back against her chair, her mouth open. "Are you serious? Do you really think you can succeed in this little business of yours?"

Shut her down, babe.

"So, how's the wedding coming along?" I asked again.

Maggie's eyes bored into mine. She didn't answer.

"If you don't want to talk about it, I understand, but I'm changing the subject because I'm getting angry," I said, staring her in the eyes.

One does not address one's feelings, much less admit to them.

She looked down at her plate. "I don't want to talk about it." Maggie said with a pout.

"Fine, then. Your choice."

"You're making a big mistake, Jen."

"It's my mistake to make, isn't it? Can you get the check? I'm late to relieve Lupe." I stood and left.

As I paced in my heels back to my car in the underground garage, I realized I was angry. Really angry.

For the first time I saw how my sister had manipulated me. But today I pushed up against her and she reacted the way I had seen her react to others to intimidate them to get her way.

Why was this so threatening to her? Was it the thought of me being a "shopgirl" was embarrassing for her? Or was it that succeeding in building a business by myself might make her feel less of a person?

I just didn't understand it, but I was beginning to recognize the incongruity.

Bruce stopped in one afternoon to make some minor adjustments. Sticks and Stitches jumped all over him, their favorite person of all time, their hero. I was always astounded to watch this great big bear of a man be so gentle and loving to those two. He had started to train them to fetch. I loved watching him get them to obey. I certainly couldn't do it.

I had found over the first few months that he was an interesting man: well-read, funny, and honest. He had some hard edges to him. His grammar could use some improvement, his manners weren't quite up to Mother's standards, and he tended to use foul language. But he certainly was a sweetheart and always looked for ways to help. He and Lupe laughed a lot and seemed to enjoy a particular camaraderie.

Bruce finished up and put away all his tools and paraphernalia and lumbered out to his truck. I locked up and followed.

"What are your plans for the rest of the evening?" I asked, somewhat awkwardly, I admit, as I unlocked my car.

"Dunno. Maybe go get a pizza or something."

"When was the last time you had a home-cooked meal?"

He cocked his head at me. "It's been a while."

I laughed. "Some day I'll have everyone over for a good meal, and we can relax for a change."

"My house is just right down the street, why not now?" His grin was enticing.

I thought about it for half a second. "Can the babies come, too?"

He looked at me as though I had lost all sense.

I laughed. "Silly question."

His house was two miles from the park. Of Spanish design, with well-tended potted plants, real adobe tile, arched doorways, and hardwood floors that gleamed, it was a slice of no-frills elegance. A large plank of thick knotted wood served as his dining table surrounded by large ladder-back chairs. His kitchen sparkled in pristine white tile with colored name-brand dutch ovens in various sizes on the countertop, modern appliances and colorful Fiesta dinnerware on display.

Not what I expected.

Bruce poured two glasses of Spanish burgundy, told me to help myself, and excused himself to freshen up. I found the refrigerator fully stocked and set to work making a paella with some frozen shrimp, chicken, andouille sausage, and lots of other interesting things I found. I hadn't done this in years, and it felt good.

"Hope you don't mind; I raided your supplies." I said when he appeared, fresh and clean with wet hair.

"I didn't mean for you to cook," he said, sniffing the air and admiring my work. "But I'm not complaining." Again with the grin.

We took the babies for a walk while the paella was in the oven, and I found the neighborhood charming. Older houses, quite a few large ones that would have been termed mansions in earlier days, still stood proudly, next to Craftsman houses from the 40s and 50s with well-manicured lawns, brick pathways, and large Birds of Paradise plants in full bloom. I saw bicycles thrown on their sides in haste to come in for dinner, I imagined, skateboards abandoned, music blaring out of windows, and the unmistakable sounds of families going about their nighttime routine.

This was not my neighborhood. It occurred to me I never saw a bike, or even a front yard in Rancho Santa Fe. Houses were hidden behind electronic gates by security for the celebrities that lived around us or just paranoid people who didn't want to be disturbed. It seemed so mundane, so boring in comparison.

I liked seeing bikes and skateboards. It showed life. It was messy. It was nice.

We stopped in front of a one-story brown single house with small palms, neat shrubs and white trim. The tops of large palm trees peered over the roof from the back.

"My office," he said, as he waved up the stone walkway to the glass-paned front door.

"Your office?"

"When I had an architectural firm, this is what we used."

"An architectural firm?" I tried to make sense of this surprising evening.

He nodded. "It's going up for sale. I don't need it anymore, but I like to visit it from time to time." His eyes narrowed and his jaw clamped.

We ambled on and back to the house, where the puppies snoozed on the warm brick on the patio.

We had dinner out on his back yard in a beautiful setting with a white stucco wall that surrounded glorious blossoms in every color. Lanterns burned from the limbs of Ficus trees. We could hear the dove birds cooing in the palm trees. Jasmine wafted in the dusk.

He told me about his marriage and its breakup, his son, and his parents. I told him about Arthur. It's all I had to offer.

He was good with that.

Chapter Forty-Two

*E*ARLIER THAT MORNING, I HAD STOPPED BY THE DRY CLEANERS, A FEW days late, to pick up the finished pieces I had dropped off earlier with very specific blocking instructions. I waited for ten minutes as my temperature rose and my ears began to tingle, when the owner emerged, head down.

"Madam, I am afraid we can't find them at the moment. I know they were done, I saw to it myself, but someone has put them somewhere, and I just don't see them."

"The let me suggest you go back and look again."

"We've looked everywhere, and they are just not here."

I had an internal meltdown and firmly suggested they look again. He went back, I heard a lot of yelling, but he came out empty and held his hands up as though he were offering up a sacrificial lamb to the gods.

Nothing helped, not even an explanation as to what the dress was or what it meant. I couldn't get them to care. When I mentioned the *San Diego Union* had done a feature article and they were expecting to photograph the finished product, that didn't seem to make much difference. I told him I would come back tomorrow, and the day after, and the day after that until they found those pieces.

I decided to try to forget about it, not mention it to anyone, and try to enjoy the evening. Tricia had called me and asked to come by to talk. I hate that my family, or everyone, actually, feels they have to make an appointment. Why can't they just drop by? It's like I may be too busy, too depressed, or too uninterested to see them, which is nowhere near the case.

"You're going to hate me," she said as she came in.

I gave her a hug. "Never."

"I've been thinking about the dress."

"Yes?"

"You were right. It's too much for me. My father's running for D.A., I'm about to take over one of the largest law firms in the county, and I'm an attorney, for God's sake. I don't know what I was thinking."

"You were thinking of shocking your mother."

She stared.

I laughed. "Honey, if I had the guts I would have done the same thing. She could use a shock now and then. What do you want to do?"

"It's not totally wasted. We can still enter it in the contest."

"Of course we can. We're not going to drop it, but are you going the Vera Wang route?"

"God, no." She lowered her head. "You're really not going to be happy."

"What?" then I knew, and it warmed me to know I knew Tricia so well. She had come back to basics. "You want the Barbie dress."

"Yes."

"Okay, then. Zelda's in the final stages. We can do this, but I'm afraid to ask everyone to take part again. It will have to be you and me, I'm afraid."

"And Lacey's coming in a few weeks, she can help."

"We'll tell the others on Tuesday and you can choose the fabric to go under it and the same yarn in a white or candlelight. It shouldn't be too difficult. We already know how the yarn performs and your measurements, but we have to move fast."

We announced the design change at the next Tuesday meeting.

"Huzzah!" said Helen when Trish told the group of the new project. "Now you're coming to your senses. The other one was just crap."

"We are almost finished with the Zelda dress," I said. "Tricia and I will concentrate on the bride's dress."

"Nonsense, dear. No bride should have to make her own dress. I'll help, but I don't know how fast I can go, my hands seem to be seizing up on me." Iris held her hands up, fingers at almost right angles, and displayed the claw-like appendages at the end of her wrist.

Starting over. What a concept.

Chapter Forty-Three

"READY, GIGI?" WE BUCKLED OUR SEAT BELTS FOR THE FIVE-HOUR flight into Chicago.

"Ready as I'm ever going to be," I mumbled. Renee laughed. "This is going to be fun."

"Fun for who? And how the hell did you talk me into this?"

She fumbled around in her tote, pulled out a book, and shoved the tote back under the seat in front of her. "You're going to be surprised when you see these guys. They're so *old.*"

Renee had gone to every high school reunion there was, and I had abstained all these years. I hated it when I was there, why would I want to recreate it? But she was adamant, and I finally gave in. Lupe encouraged me, too, and I think she was just as happy to have the place to herself.

Now I was feeling as though I had abandoned the shop, the babies, and my own conviction that I would never, ever go to one of these reunions.

Renee read the newest potboiler and I knit the entire way, brought back into the world of my own making. I had few memories, but a sort of gray blanket hung over me when I thought about those years. Forgetting the Incident, I was not part of the crowd, I kept to myself and did what I needed to do to get through it. Renee, on the other hand, was incredibly popular, the one who knew everyone and all the gossip. She did not drink or smoke pot, but those who did liked her anyway and always invited her to parties, knowing she would not go. Not a raving beauty, she was never considered for homecoming queen or cheerleading squad, but she was more of the girl everyone knew about who was smart without being cocky and friendly without being effusive.

I should have known she'd be a politician.

"Maybe we'll see Adrian Shoemaker," she said with a grin, and placed her finger in her book. "What's wrong?"

"Nothing." I shook my head and knit a few more stitches.

"You had such a crush on him. I haven't seen him in all these years, but since this is the fortieth, maybe he'll show up."

"Maybe," I said, and fervently wished not.

We entered the Grand Ballroom at the Hyatt, picked up our name tags showing our old selves and headed to the bar.

"God, Renee, why am I here?" I muttered.

"You're here because you said you wanted to branch out. So branch."

Drinks in hand, Renee pointed across the room to a platinum blonde wearing a caftan that covered her enormous frame. "Sally Hart, head cheerleader and homecoming queen."

My jaw dropped. I had been so jealous of her perfection, her cute frame, and the fact that she dated Adrien Shoemaker, the quarterback and captain of the football team. They held hands down the hallways every chance they got, and we thought that was really cool. She drove a yellow Opal and her green and white cheerleader outfit showed off her perfect legs. I had a girl crush.

"Head cheerleader, homecoming queen and dated the captain of the football team, much less the quarterback. How corny can you get? Quick, somebody make a movie," Renee sneered. She was not one to get a girl crush.

"Renee Murphy, I can't believe it." An overzealous middle-aged woman grabbed Renee into a bear hug. "Never married, I see?"

I made my escape and stood on the outskirts; eyes glued to Sally.

What a shock. What the hell happened to her? Only one way to find out.

"Sally?" I stood in front of her. "Jen Palmer. Do you remember me?"

She took a good long look at the name badge with my seventeen-year-old self pictured on my chest.

"Yes, yes I think so. Were you in Mr. King's math class?"

"No. It's not important. Just wanted to say hi."

"What are you doing now, Jen? Any children?"

"No, no children, but I do own a shop and am active in the community. You know . . ."

"Oh."

"And you?"

"I have five children. They keep me busy."

"I'm sure they do." A man appeared next to her with two drinks and handed one to her. She slurped it greedily, and said, "Do you remember Neil Henderson? We married right out of high school."

"Jen Palmer, I had such a crush on you." He said with a leer on his face. His balding head and stained tie told me what I needed to know.

"You did? That's flattering."

He eyed me up and down, "Yes, I did. But you were not available, as I remember."

"Really? I don't remember that." *And I don't remember you.*

Well, this was getting me nowhere.

I looked over to see Renee pointing across the room at a woman talking to a bald man wearing the white collar of a Catholic priest. I looked over and back to Renee and shrugged in question. She waved me over in their direction.

"Excuse me," I said.

I walked toward the couple and recognized the woman as Candy Crawford. She and Renee and I spent a lot of time together in our senior year, studying and being serious while the rest of the class smoked pot and ditched school.

"Candy?" I said. Her eyes widened in surprise and I received a warm hug. "Jen Palmer. How good to see you. I wonder every year if I'll see you, and every year I've been disappointed. Renee's kept me informed, though." Her voice dropped. "I'm so sorry about your husband." She squeezed my hand.

"Do you remember Adrien Shoemaker?" I turned to the priest and saw the picture on his name badge. I grew cold at the sight of his picture, then my eyes went to his face.

Hit with several impressions, I didn't quite know what to say, or what to think. Old, worn, calm, assured, fearful, and concerned all in one take. His eyes got me most. They showed his character, and it wasn't what I expected.

"Yes, of course. How are you, Adrien?" I extended my hand.

He cleared his throat and met my hand with a cold, clammy one.

I had met my enemy, and he was fearful.

"I'm fine, Jen. How are you? I gather you just lost your husband?"

"Yes, just this last December."

"I'm so sorry." He sounded so genuine, so caring, I wondered if this was the same person. All the things I wanted to say to him, every word I had practiced if I ever saw him again disappeared. Before me was a humble man, a man of the cloth. As much as I had extricated myself from the Catholic Church, I still respected the cloth and the dedication of a man who had devoted himself so completely. I found myself confused beyond measure.

"Thank you." I saw Renee staring in our direction. "Excuse me."

"Of course."

I went to the bar and ordered a vodka on ice. "Make it a double." The bartender smiled and poured.

"What was that about? You two looked so uncomfortable I thought maybe I had to come and do a song and dance."

"Uncomfortable? He's a priest now, for God's sake, Renee. What was I supposed to say?"

"The cloth still gets you, hunh?" She leered at me.

"That disgusting."

Renee stepped back. "Sorry. Didn't know I hit a nerve." Her sarcasm bit.

I put myself back together. "No, it's me. I'm just not ready for this. Too many bad memories."

"Well, he's off the market, anyway. All dreams smashed to hell."

"Believe me, he's the last person I'd want to hook up with." Renee shot me a look and kept her mouth shut.

I saw a few more old friends and spent some time with Candy and Renee. They were the only ones who I connected with, and we laughed a lot and caught ourselves up. All the others were just not clicking, and I was just as happy to stay out of circulation.

Adrien stayed in my head the entire time. I pretended I didn't see him look at me several times from across the room, a whiskey in his hand and a question in his eyes.

"I'm staying here tonight, so I can use another one of these," Candy said, raising her empty glass.

"I'll go with you." Renee jumped up and turned to me. "Jen?" I nodded and gathered my purse and scarf to go to the ladies' room.

"I thought they'd never leave you alone," Adrien said as he sat in Renee's chair.

Sweat dripped down his temples, and he tried a smile. The dimples that used to decimate me were still there, but deeper with age.

"Oh?" I sat back down.

"Jen . . ."

"Excuse me, just heading to the loo." I could feel his eyes on my back, and I exited the room into the hallway and found the Ladies'.

I leaned against the counter and breathed hard.

You have absolutely nothing to be guilty about. You have nothing to be guilty about.

Then why do I feel so awful?

"OK, what's going on?" Renee came in and locked the door behind her. She stood, feet planted shoulder width apart, arms crossed.

"What? I have to go to the bathroom."

"Then why aren't you in there?" She pointed to the stall.

"I'm just a little dizzy. Drank too much." I shook my head.

"Right. Then why did you run away from Adrien like he was the devil?"

"I didn't. I just really have to pee." I went into the stall.

"Have it your way." I heard the door unlock and open.

I refreshed my makeup, got a hold of myself and opened the door.

Adrien stood just outside, pacing.

"I don't know how to start this conversation," he said.

I looked around and determined we were alone. "What conversation?"

He looked crestfallen. "Don't pretend, Jen. Let's be honest. Finally."

"All right. You go first."

"Can we sit down? I need to sit."

I didn't want to give in to him, but he looked drained. I looked closer and saw his gray skin, the area surrounding his eyes light blue. This physical appearance made me queasy—gray, sad, used up. I found myself incredibly sad.

We found a small salon next door with one table and four chairs. We sat. I placed my purse and scarf on the table, crossed my legs and folded my hands in my lap.

And waited.

He leaned forward, elbows on knees, hands clasped. He looked up at me. "I remember that night."

I waited.

"I don't remember much of that decade, to be honest. Most of it's gone." He leaned back in his chair. "I was a drug addict, a criminal, and a lousy human being. But I do remember that night, and I consider it my worse offense."

"I'm flattered."

"Jen, please. Let me finish. I spent twenty years in jail for crimes that were so heinous I can't even believe them. I accept them as my doing, even though I don't remember committing some of the crimes. There was a list a mile long, and the lawyer made a plea deal if I would turn state's evidence. That tells you how much was on the table. My sentence was thirty years, but I got out in twenty." He shook his head. "I thought of you every single day. If there is once crime I wish I could take back, it's that one."

His eyes filled. "Please forgive me." It was a whisper. He hung his head. "God has forgiven me, and that should be enough, but I need your forgiveness, too."

All those years. To come face to face with a broken old man asking my forgiveness.

"I can't."

He shook his head. "I didn't think so."

I unfolded my arms, uncrossed my legs, and leaned in toward him. "Wish I could." I gathered my things and left him alone at the table.

Renee and Candy were at our table, and I downed my drink fast.

"Where were you?" Candy asked. "It's watered down now," she said, nodding to my drink.

"She was with Adrien." I looked over at Renee, who gave me a wan smile.

"Adrien? You mean Henry?"

"Henry?" Renee and I both said.

"Yes, he goes by Henry now. It's his first name. I think Adrien was a better choice as a child, don't you think?" She smiled.

"How do you know him so well?" Renee asked.

"He's my priest. He married me and baptized my children. Everybody loves Henry. He's done some marvelous, generous things over the years. He's not the same partier we knew in high school." She shook her head. "We're all praying for him."

"What do you mean?" Renee said.

"He made a real effort to get here tonight. He's dying."

I steeled myself against this news. I should have recognized the gray around his eyes. I'd seen it before.

After agreeing to meet for breakfast, Renee and I separated from Candy and went up to our rooms.

"What did Adrien want?" she said in the elevator.

I was quiet, trying to come up with something plausible while I stared at the buttons on the panel.

"I have a pretty good idea, have had for some time," she said, and put her hand up. "I'm not judging. Never have."

"See that you don't." I clicked my door open, glided in and let it slam behind me.

We had never discussed it. I don't know what my parents told her, but I know they had to say something.

Chapter Forty-Four

ONE TUESDAY MORNING WHILE IT UNCHARACTERISTICALLY POURED RAIN like a tropical storm, Robert seemed particularly on edge. He walked in quietly, barely paid attention to the conversation at the table and jumped at every sound. Then his phone rang. He answered it on the first ring and with a smile on his face, got up from his chair at the knitting table and went into the hall.

I grinned at the rest of the tribe. "Gee, I wonder who that could be?" I worked on the back of the dress, a simple column with no train, thankful that it would go much faster than the Zelda dress. Suzanne worked the front today.

Robert had told us about Bobby, his former love, who had moved to London to pursue an international investment banking career. Robert had been sulking and sad and had told us that communications had been short and less than exciting. He had been spending a lot of time with a man named Thomas, however, who we had met and liked.

"Bets, anyone?" said Iris. "I think Bobby would be crazy to leave him again. Such a nice boy."

"Whoa, we haven't even met this guy. We have no idea what he's like." Lupe said, a frown on her face.

"Is that important, dear?" said Iris innocently.

Robert came back into the room looking like the cat who just had excellent sashimi.

"Looks like I have a date for the engagement party," he said as he picked up his knitting. I noted his shaking hands and flushed face.

"Oh, someone nice, I hope? I like Thomas, but he is rather Sears/Roebucky if you know what I mean." Iris, her cobalt blue eyes looked innocently at Robert.

Iris was having an engagement party for Tricia and Carl. Helen snorted.

"Excuse me, what's wrong with Sears?" said Jade and Lupe in unison.

"Absolutely nothing . . . unless you're dealing with a Nordstrom, then there's a complete . . . what do you say today . . . disconnect?"

Robert smiled. "and what if I told you I happened to be in love with Thomas?"

"I would call you a prevaricator." She leaned toward Jade. "That means a liar, dear."

"Why? Thomas is a nice guy."

"Yes, Robert, I'm sure he is, but he doesn't light up your face like that phone call from Bobby did."

"How do you know it was Bobby?"

"How could I not know?" She put her knitting in her lap. "My dear, I may be older than Methuselah, but I'm not lacking in brain matter. When is the big arrival?"

"Next week."

"Oh, good. I can't wait to meet him."

"Now, Iris, behave yourself. None of your tricks." Robert smiled.

"Who, me? What tricks, dear?"

$$\times \quad \times \quad \times$$

The night of the party, cool and crisp, Iris's large house stood ready for guests, the entire house lit up, flowers everywhere, and a table set aside for gifts.

The thought of being trapped in a car with Maggie and listening to her complaints made me nauseated, so I drove myself.

I wore a bright turquoise jumpsuit of raw silk, a throwback to the '70s that had appealed to me. I made it in the kitchen of the shop during quiet hours, something very different from my usual attire, or what the others would be wearing. Where's the Oscar de la Renta? People will ask.

Well, let them. We used to laugh at people who made their own clothes.

I had arrived early to see if I could help—the good girl. Terence opened the door and escorted me into the living room and offered a glass of wine.

I took one and began to admire Iris's art collection. I heard Iris coming down the stairs and turned to greet her but stopped when I saw Jade behind her and didn't want to interrupt their conversation. I peeked around the corner.

Iris stopped in front of a large mirror in the foyer, and I saw her reflection through the doorway. She wore a long gown of fuchsia silk—and a tiara. "Why not?" she was saying. "If an eccentric old lady can't wear a tiara, who can? I think the last time I wore this was at Buckingham Palace after the coronation, or maybe it was at Jack's inauguration, I can't remember."

She adjusted her shoulders, her tiara, and her diamond pin that held a large ribbon going crossways from her shoulder down to her left hip, similar to pictures I'd seen of the Queen of England at official affairs. I stifled a giggle. "Oh, I hope this gets in the papers. You know your party is a smash when it turns up the very next morning in the newspaper."

Jade stared into the mirror behind Iris looking like a new woman. She wore a long dress of mustard colored silk and a pair of diamond drop earrings borrowed from Iris. Her hair held a severe style with gel, a finger wave in the front, slicked back and chic. The piercings had all but disappeared.

Iris's influence at work, no doubt. But what I found interesting was that Jade wore it so well, with such confidence. This was not a ragamuffin wearing a princess costume. She owned it.

"What do you think the highlight of the night will be?" Iris asked.

"What do you mean?"

"Andy and I used to predict who would make a pass a whom, or who would say something outrageous."

"I say Maggie makes a fool of herself," Jade said, with not a small degree of sarcasm.

"No fair stating the obvious. Look for something that would be a surprise," Iris said. "I'm betting Jen flirts a little. Maybe Bruce will escort her."

"Jen and Bruce? No way."

"Why not? He's a perfectly lovely man, and I bet he cleans up well."

"Jen and a contractor? Wasn't she married to a high-priced, influential lawyer?"

"Arthur was a doll, but that doesn't mean Bruce is not as valuable. Never judge a book by his cover, dear." She sighed. "Now. Let's get this party started. Oh, this reminds me so much of the many soirees we had . . . we usually got a write-up in the papers the next day, and I had scads of people hinting that they would just love to be invited to the next one . . . you always knew your party was a success when it appeared in the morning papers."

I hated to be talked about and was not happy that my non-existent love life was being discussed behind my back.

Their voices faded as I squared my shoulders and slid outside into the cool air of Iris's patio.

$$\times \quad \times \quad \times$$

As I moved through Iris's large house, I saw old friends, accepted their heartfelt sympathies gracefully at my loss (will this ever end?), and noticed the looks given at my appearance.

No wonder they looked shocked. My physical appearance had changed so much I saw some people couldn't place me. Fine with me.

My hair, no longer perfectly dyed and upswept, now short, spiky, and gray. I wore much more makeup; my expensive jewels were gone. I no longer wore four-inch spiked heels, but sequined Moroccan slippers, and I had gained about twenty pounds.

Carl and Trish accepted good wishes. Dave and Maggie's friends made up the bulk of the crowd, many of them I knew, but I discovered they shied away from me, the proverbial fifth wheel, the familiar stranger, as it were.

The Sticks Gang gathered around a table in the living room and we happily exchanged stories while Iris made sure everyone stayed comfortable. She had hobbled over to us as fast as she could using her cane and quietly said, "Holy Mother of God. Apparently, we got it all wrong."

"What are you talking about?"

"You'll see." That conspiratorial smile and laughing eyes told us one of her tricks might just explode. "It has nothing to do with me, I assure you," she said, reading our thoughts. "It's something I believe that has been a trick on us."

We looked at each other. "All will be revealed," she said. "All in good time."

"Now, I assume?" Helen said, nodding behind me.

I turned to find Robert in a pale yellow dinner jacket holding hands with a gorgeous woman. Tall, dark, with long chestnut hair falling gracefully around her bare shoulders, her dark brown eyes shining, she came toward us with Robert and extended her hand. "I've heard so much about you all," she said. "and I am thrilled to meet you."

"Please let me introduce Robert's good friend, Bobby," said Iris. "Isn't it coincidental that Bobby is short for Roberta? Robert and Roberta! How wonderful!"

I laughed and extended my hand. "I'm Jen Conrad, and I'm delighted to see you."

"But . . ." Helen said, looking around at us.

"Yes, Helen, she made it! All the way from London just to come to the party! Isn't it marvelous how easy travel is these days? In my day it took ten days, but oh, so glamorous!"

"But . . ." Helen apparently couldn't get the gist of it.

Jade gave Bobby a big hug. "Nice to finally meet you." She looked at Robert and said, "You rat."

"Whaaat." He looked at us. "This is Bobby!" He looked at us as and winked. "We have to run now, but we'll catch up with you later, kids!"

We stared at each other, nonplussed.

"Damn good transvestite." Helen frowned.

The rest of us burst into laughter.

Iris went to bed after drinking too much, Harold put Lupe in the car long before the rest of us left, Maggie and Dave were the focus of the party more than Trish and Carl, and I stayed until the bitter end.

Iris considered it a great success.

It was in all the papers.

Chapter Forty-Five

MAGGIE CAME BACK TO THE GROUP, I SUSPECT TO KEEP AN EYE ON THE dress.

"We have a new tenant," Suzanne announced as she came in one Tuesday morning. She sat with the group and exclaimed over all the work being done, and how fast it progressed.

"Yes, who, dear?"

"It's called Sandpaper, and it's a woodworking shop. This guy makes rocking horses for kids that look like other things. I saw one of a dinosaur that he calls Terantasaurus Rocks and a motorcycle with wooden spokes and handlebars with clutch pedals that actually work. He also does jewelry boxes, furniture and wooden toys. Not cheap, but excellent craftsmanship. He will also have woodworking classes."

Iris looked at Suzanne over her glasses. "I ask again, who?"

"Guess." Suzanne looked like the feline who had inhaled the proverbial canary. I half expected her to lick her lips.

"My dear, I couldn't possibly. Hello, Robert." Iris looked up and smiled as he plopped down on the green velvet chair.

"Bruce," said Helen into her knitting.

"How did you know? You should see these two rockers he made; they are fantastic. And he has a present for you, too." Suzanne looked at me.

"Me?"

"Well, the shop. You said you wanted a spinning room; he's making a spinner for you. It's beautiful, but he's having some trouble with the balance of it."

"I can relate," I said, grimacing. I had no idea Bruce was interested in joining our little art group, but it made sense. Now that the park started to get leased out and ready to go, he wasn't needed any more. Time to move on.

That theme keeps popping up.

But he hadn't told me. And I thought we were friends.

Iris wasn't about to let the elephant in the room go away. "So, Robert, would you like to explain yourself?"

"Why, whatever do you mean?" the grin on his face told me he wanted to play a little.

"Bobby?"

"What about her?"

"Oh, cut the crap, Robert. You're gay. At least be open about it," said Helen. Her face could have been a marble bust: gray and unmoving.

"I'm gay? Who said that?" he smiled at the entire group, but when he came to Helen he straightened up. "All right. I knew you made that assumption, and I allowed it to continue."

"But why?"

"Because believe it or not, being gay allows you to easily gather confidences and opens doors to people who think you will be discreet and understanding. I get more information, more inside information, and more access that I would if I were a straight man. It works."

"So you're pretending to be something you're not." Maggie's voice, lowered to a basso range, made me think of a parent catching a child in a lie.

Yeah, like she's real.

"No," he said, his face determined, "my personal life is my own. My professional life is whatever people think it is, and since this assumption was made long ago, I saw no need to correct it. Whether I am a homosexual or a heterosexual is no one's business, and I'm not going to discuss my sex life any more than you would," he said looking at each of us. "It just so happens that people's perceptions of me, while incorrect, allows me to be better at my job."

"I think it's ludicrous, allowing people to think you're gay." Maggie said.

"Why? Is there something wrong with being gay?" asked Iris innocently.

Maggie swallowed. I knew where she stood and wondered how she would handle this one.

"There is something wrong with giving the wrong impression."

"Like being perfect?" said Helen, her eyes bored into Maggie's.

Yowza.

"She shouldn't have told you," Bruce said as we stood in the shop. "I'm sorry. I wanted to tell you myself."

"Why the secrecy? I'm a little pissed."

He smiled. "Well, that says something."

I moved to the counter and started shoving things around. "Why didn't you tell me?"

"Because I thought you would think it was a move, a way to stay close to you, and that's not what this is about."

"What's it about, then? You don't want to stay close to me?"

He laughed and put his hands in the air, palms out. "No! I mean yes! Jen, you're making me crazy." His put his hands out to reach me and I backed off.

Stitches started to growl at him and lunged for his pant leg. He froze, and I screamed "Stitches!" which made the situation worse. I reached down to get her, and she snapped at me.

The girl doesn't like confrontation, and she's a protector. Sticks came ambling by, wondering what all the fuss was about and nosed Stitches away. She followed him.

"Well, that was weird," I said. "Are you all right?"

"Yes, she didn't get any skin. Can we talk?" We walked into the living room, and the babies followed us. Sticks first, followed by Stitches, nose on tail, as usual. "Hmm. Does that usually happen?" Bruce asked, pointing to them.

"The attack? No. Never."

"No, I mean the way they enter a room."

"I suppose so. Why?"

"That's what blind dogs do. They follow their mate and rely on them to lead them correctly. I wonder if she has issues with her eyes."

"Honestly, Bruce . . ."

"No. It makes perfect sense. She heard my voice rise and felt me moving toward you. It didn't bother Sticks at all, but she's all over it. She can't see, so she's reacting to something she perceived as a threat." He leaned down and put his hand out. "Stitches!" Sticks went right to him, but Stitches stayed where she was and looked around, her nose wiggling.

"Are you trying to change the subject?"

"No. I'm serious. I think you should take her in to get checked."

"I will, but can we address the situation at hand?"

He shrugged. "I've always wanted to market my woodwork. Suzanne talked me into it at the art party and I've been thinking on it ever since. The center is pretty much done, my being here on campus, as it were, is a plus. I can do what I love, maybe teach some kids or scouts a new skill, and be here on call for repairs and maintenance. I just have to get rid of that house to make it work. I'm honest enough to say that being able to see you every day is a bonus, but that, honestly, is not what made me make the commitment. It's what I want to do."

"Fair enough." I impulsively leaned forward and kissed him on the lips. He looked pleased. Before I moved back, I said, "And I promise to get Stitches checked out, but I'm sure you're overreacting." So why did I kiss him?

Stitches turned out to be losing her sight, a by-product of her early days and losing what nutrition came from her mother's milk. The vet said that Sticks may not suffer from the same malady, since we haven't seen it yet, but to keep an eye out. There was nothing to be done.

I had an imperfect girl child.

Chapter Forty-Six

BUSINESS HAD SLUMPED; IT APPEARED I JUMPED TOO SOON, AND THE shop wasn't going to make it. My sister was royally pissed, my mother didn't seem to care she was dying, I had a perfectly nice guy clearly interested in me, too young, too unsophisticated, and too early. My house felt like a mausoleum, Choyou had given her notice, and I had bills coming every day I couldn't pay. The phone rang incessantly, at first polite, wondering when I could pay "just a little to show good faith," and then a few fairly threatening.

The competition was eating me alive and I didn't know how to fight that. I admitted I was fairly sure Maggie had her hand in it, which made me even more sad. My own sister.

I became numb.

My grief seemed to be worse. I had no energy, no focus, and I had trouble getting up in the mornings. I felt so sad, so lacking in energy, and so beaten down I was ready to throw in the towel.

Not only did I feel of no value, I now was responsible for someone's paycheck and the success of a shop I had no business opening, and it wasn't going to be a success.

I skipped the knitting group one morning and lay in bed, engulfed in a physical pain I couldn't locate. I looked in the nightstand to see if I had any cigarettes left over and found a bottle of sleeping pills, given to me by the hospice doctor when I admitted I had trouble falling asleep. Now I had the opposite problem, and there were fifty pills right there.

There's my answer.

I shot up. I don't quit. I literally ran to the toilet and flushed the small white pills, and collapsed against the cool porcelain, sobbing. How could I get this low?

The phone rang. I let it go to voice mail.

"Mrs. Conrad? This is Lauren from the hospice. I was just doing our anniversary check in, wondering how you were doing and if you had any plans for tomorrow. We'd like to help you if we can. We have celebrations and tribute ideas if you feel you'd like to do something, or please share with us what you may be doing in Arthur's memory at this anniversary date. We like to pass on ideas to others who are struggling as well. I know it's a tough day. Please call me back if you'd like to talk. Remember we're always here if you need us."

Anniversary? Jesus. She's right. Tomorrow it's one year.

Great. Another thing to feel guilty about. I turned over and went to sleep.

I awoke to hear him mumbling in pain. My practiced hands drew the pink syrupy liquid into the syringe and ejected it under his tongue. I stroked his face, felt the soft whiskers and smelled the sickness. I filled the syringe again and plunged the liquid into his mouth. "There you go, honey. There you go." I did it one more time.

When his breathing became less labored, I lowered the aluminum bar and crawled in beside him. I draped my arm over his stomach and lay my head on his chest, mumbling to him that everything would be all right, that we had had a good run, that it was now time for him to leave. I could feel his slightly rattling breath moving my hair on the top of my head, in and out, in and out, like a butterfly that got caught in my hair and tried to escape.

I lay with him, quietly, eyes open. Some time later I heard him take a deep breath and let go. The butterfly had escaped. I held him closer and hoped wherever he was going it would be as wonderful as we imagined.

The old grandfather clock ticked loudly downstairs.

$$\times \quad \times \quad \times$$

I caved and made an appointment with a hospice counselor.

"Nathan, what I am going to tell you is confidential, correct?"

"Of course."

I took a deep breath and said the words that had formed in my head. "I am very angry with my husband. He betrayed me."

He leaned forward; hands clasped between his knees. "How?"

I sighed. Might as well tell him the whole story. I've never told anyone, and Arthur only knew half of it.

"When I was fourteen I went somewhere I wasn't supposed to be. My parents never knew I had slipped out of the house. After a few months, it became obvious I got pregnant. After a huge explosion my parents shipped me off across the country to have the baby. My parents are devout Roman Catholic, so this was a huge sin." I got up and paced. "I missed the last weeks of school and the summer. No one knew. It's what was done in those days." I took a breath, fidgeted with a paper napkin, and continued. "They knocked me out, I had the baby, and it was given up for adoption. My parents brought me home afterward, and they never failed to remind me what a sinner I had been, and how they would be ruined if anyone ever found out what I had done. They followed me everywhere I went and made sure I had no fun at all. They withheld all affection and continued to judge everything I did. I grew to hate both of them."

"Why do I think there's more to the story?"

"It wasn't consensual."

His pupils constricted. The silence became deafening. "You never told them the truth?"

"They wouldn't have believed me, and I was terrified of them. They both made life extremely difficult."

"Where are they now?"

"My mother is here in town. She has cancer. We don't discuss it. My father's in an Alzheimer's facility."

"Ouch." He actually winced.

"Arthur never understood my anger because I never told him about the baby. My father had convinced me I was ruined, and I thought that if I just erased it I would be ok, and Arthur would love me."

"Understandable."

Silence.

Nathan leaned in and whispered, "So where does the betrayal come in?"

I took a deep breath. "I just discovered Arthur had been paying for a place for that bastard to live and be taken care of, a very nice place."

My outrage began to show. "I thought he would be dead by now, and I have yet another obligation to fulfill."

Nathan rubbed his chin. "Arthur must have been one hell of a guy."

I stared at him.

"Sorry, it's not what you want to hear right now, but he had your back. That's pretty upstanding, even though he went against your wishes. He should have told you."

"You're damn right he should have told me!"

"What would you have done if he had told you?"

"I would have insisted he stop."

"And what would that have done to your marriage if he refused?"

I looked into his young face and saw where he was going. No doubt Arthur thought he did the right thing and didn't tell me in order to protect us, what we had. He had taken a huge risk.

But now I found myself angry that I had been played. *What she doesn't know won't hurt her.*

"How do you feel right now?" He asked quietly after a few moments of silence.

"Betrayed, angry, sad, and confused. What am I supposed to do now?"

"Damned if I know."

"There's something else." I swallowed hard.

"What's that?"

I took the biggest risk of my life. "I killed my husband." Tears ran down my cheeks.

He nodded. "Go on."

"I gave him far more painkiller than I should have. He was in such pain, moaning and clearly in distress. It had been days, and I couldn't stand it anymore."

He leaned over and put his hand on top of mine. "That's not murder."

"It's not?" I tried to laugh. "What would you call it?"

"Mercy."

I looked into his eyes. Nope, no judgment there, thank God.

We were quiet for a bit.

"Do you have to report that to anyone?"

"Probably should, but I'm not going to."

"Why not?"

He took a beat. "If I reported every instance of this I knew of, there would be more than a few doctors and nurses in trouble, much less husbands, wives, and children of people who were in terrible distress. I'm not going to be responsible for starting that stampede. I'm a coward." He gave me a small smile.

"Aren't you supposed to have all the answers?"

"No, ma'am. My job is to help you find yours. But now I know you have much more than your husband's death to deal with. Did you ever grieve for your child?"

"I've never thought of it as my child."

"Did you ever grieve for your childhood? Your innocence? The fact that you lost the biggest support network anyone can have, their parents?"

I stared at him. This was a whole new world, someone backing me up and seeing things I refused to see.

"What are you going to do about your father?"

"Clearly Arthur did it for a reason. I'm not sure my mother can afford such a huge monthly bill. I was shocked at how much an assisted living facility costs, and I doubt they had any long-term care insurance. I have to think about this."

"Maybe actually talk to your mother about something substantive?"

"Maybe," I said. The idea was so foreign to me I had trouble visualizing it.

He sat a few moments. "Here's your assignment," he said.

"What's that?"

"We all have different threads running through our lives. Most of those threads don't do anything but tangle things up. Go home and do something that ends a thread. Throw out something significant, burn something, or finish something. You'll know what it is when you see it."

✕ ✕ ✕

I opened Arthur's closet doors. I took his sunglasses in the monogrammed case, his keychain and his wallet and put them in a box. I put his special pen at my desk and his small notebook went in the shredder.

There. Clean as a whistle.

That wasn't so hard.

Now.

I toured my house. It felt so different from Bruce's warm and cozy house. I found myself resenting the designer touches and expensive fabrics. My living and dining rooms were empty and cold, the Persian rugs gone, silver centerpiece put away, and all the china and serving pieces I had used so lovingly and proudly for all those years packed in cabinets designed specifically for them.

What I spent on the redesign and redecorating of this house would pay the rent at Stitches for many, many years.

What a phenomenal waste. Why?

We had some great parties, fundraisers, and events at this house. But it was all about Arthur. His sense of humor, his way of putting people together, telling a story, making us feel we were the most important people in the world.

I was the machinery behind the engine named Arthur. I loved it, but it was gone.

I no longer needed this house, and I didn't want it any more. I wanted something small, like Bruce's, in the old neighborhood that had houses owned by generations of the same families. I wanted history. I wanted to make some more of that history. History that meant something, not just entertaining and putting on a pretty front.

I called Suzanne.

Maybe I couldn't have bicycles and skateboards, but I would have a home that was meant for me, and me alone.

Chapter Forty-Seven

"MY DEAR, I FEEL LIKE A TEENAGER AGAIN!" IRIS SAID ONE MORNING. "The girls keep me young. Their music is astoundingly loud, but good. I like the energy of the house, although I think Terrence is going to have a stroke."

I laughed. Lacey had moved to California, placing all her eggs in Tricia's care. Tricia had gotten her a job at her father's firm as the receptionist, giving them both time to study for the bar exam and saving Dave the cost of a receptionist. Iris had extended an invitation for Lacey to stay with her and Jade.

Iris had come to the shop earlier than anyone else. Jade had left to run to the post office and would be back shortly.

Iris's energy level was at an all-time high. "They cook, they sing, they dance, and they are extremely entertaining," she said. "I am so happy Lacey came to live with me. She insists on paying rent, which is ludicrous, but I suppose she needs to feel she contributes something. Money isn't important."

It is if you don't have any.

"Yes, I can't imagine Lacey taking advantage of anyone."

"But you have no idea how much she gives me just by being there. She is quite the individual. She is bringing Jade out of whatever world she inhabits, and they are getting along so well!"

"Tell me about Jade. We don't know much about her."

Iris looked down at her knitting. "My dear, I don't make a habit of telling others' stories. Let her tell you herself." She looked up. "But in her own time."

Iris rules.

"Are you sure you're not overtaxing yourself?" I was afraid to ask but felt somewhat responsible. At her age, I thought all the excitement might be too much. I should have known better.

"Nonsense, dear. I'm not cooking, cleaning, or doing their laundry. I'm just observing and having fun. It's good for me."

"Good, then do you have room for one more?" Lupe came in wearing sunglasses, and, given our history, I knew why. She took them off to show a big shiner. Lupe had gone home after only spending two nights at the shop.

"Son of a bitch," said Iris, her chin shaking. "Right now. Go home and get your things. You're moving in today. I will have no argument. Jade? Is that you?"

"Yes, ma'am, I'm here." Jade's voice came from around the corner.

"Good. Take Lupe to her house, gather everything you can and put her in the garden room at home. She's moving in with us."

Jade entered the parlor, looked at Lupe, and nodded. "Come," she said. "We have our orders. Welcome to the home for wayward girls." They turned and exited the front door.

Every nerve ending in my body vibrated on high alert. "Wayward girls," I whispered.

"What, dear?"

I shook my head to rattle the image of a home for wayward girls. "Nothing. Ah, Helen. Good morning."

"What the hell are those two doing? They look they are mercenaries on a mission." She pointed behind her shoulder.

"They are," Iris and I said at the same time.

"Well, I hope it's a good one. We need some excitement around here." We filled Helen in on the newest events and received a string of profanities that hung in the room like ugly party balloons. "I think it's time we did something."

"Now, Helen," said Iris, as she patted Helen's arm.

"Don't 'Now Helen' me. We are smart women. I say we make him understand how totally unacceptable this is."

"What are we talking about?" Robert came in with Tricia. "Who's in trouble with the Sticks Gang now?" he grinned.

"I'd like to run a stick right up his . . ."

"Helen!" Iris warned.

"Whoa!" Tricia said at the same time. The room turned quiet except for Helen's heavy breathing and I swear I heard that damn hair whistle.

Suzanne chose that moment to enter; clearly she knew something was up. She sat down quietly, crossed her arms over her chest and waited.

"Jade took Lupe home to get her things. They are moving her to my house immediately."

"Shit. He did it again. I knew he would." She mumbled. "It doesn't stop."

Tricia looked at Iris. "Good for you, Iris, and thank you. She had nowhere else to go, although I am sure any one of us would have taken her in," she said as an afterthought.

"Goddamn brute," said Robert. "Those guys shouldn't be allowed to live." He looked up at Suzanne. "My bad. Sorry. Bad choice of phrase, but those guys give the rest of us a bad name. What are we going to do? We can't let this stand. Let's call the cops, or better yet, form a lynch mob." He looked around the room. "Kidding."

"Please don't do anything," said Suzanne. Her eyes filled with tears. "Please. You can't."

"Of course we're not going to do anything," I said. "Emotions are running high. We all love Lupe and are having a knee-jerk reaction. We would never put you in jeopardy."

Suzanne shook her head. "It's not about me, although I thought joining a knitting group, especially consisting of women of a certain age, wouldn't trouble my probation officer," she smiled at us. "It's more concern for you. You have no idea the price you'll pay. I had to change my name and move to another state, learn a new trade, change my appearance, become a new person, and that even after being locked up for three years. You can't. You just can't. I wouldn't be able to survive without you all."

"Well," said Robert. "and I thought the gay community was highly emotional." We smiled and got back to business.

$\times$ $\times$ $\times$

Lupe came back in the early afternoon.

"We have come up with a plan," I said.

"A plan for what?"

"To make sure Harold is out of the picture entirely. It's risky, but it just might work."

"No."

"Why not?"

"I'll get a lawyer and get the police involved. I'll handle it."

"How's that worked for you in the past?" My thoughts were no longer being filtered through a society woman's brain.

Lupe closed her eyes for a moment and rubbed her now-protruding belly. "You're right. The legal system has let me down, and I don't want this child exposed to him for a second, so I'm willing listen. But no lynch mob."

"Okay, we entice him . . ."

"No. I don't want anyone else in on this."

"We're not doing anything illegal. Just listen. If he performs the way we think he will, he'll be the one in the wrong, not us. We'll be innocent victims. All we're doing is luring him in. If it doesn't work, it doesn't work, but if it does, you're home free."

"Who's involved?"

"Just you. And me as the owner of the shop. The others came up with the plan, well, all but Suzanne, but they'll be home waiting for news."

"Tell me."

So I did.

Chapter Forty-Eight

Harold,

I am leaving you. Please don't try to find me or come and get me. I won't go back to you. I have taken my things and have moved into the shop.

Please do not try to contact me.

Lupe

Chapter Forty-Nine

"*I* LEFT THE NOTE ON THE BED, WHERE HE WON'T FIND IT UNTIL HE GETS home."

We knew it wouldn't take long. After the last customer left, we bolted the door.

"Here we go," she said. We sat in the kitchen and picked at a pizza, drank iced tea and chattered quietly. At ten o'clock we turned off all the lights except for the bedroom light upstairs in the front of the house. We sat in the living room quietly, waiting. Lupe lay on the couch and I dozed in the chair a little, eyes snapping open at each sound. My small Bond Girl gun was in my lap. I had never had to use it but carried the concealed weapon license and kept the tiny gun oiled, ready, and in perfect shape for the last thirty-five years. It was small, easy to hide, but could carry a wallop if needed.

"Do you think he's really coming?" I whispered about one o'clock. "This could all be for nothing."

"He'll be here. If he doesn't come, that means either he's dead, drunk, or planning something worse."

Well, let's hope he does show up, then.

I reviewed the plan. Quiet. Check. Surprise. Check. Gun. Check. Innocence. Check.

Three hard knocks on the door startled us awake. Lupe's head popped up in the shadows and I heard her whimper. "Shhh," I whispered. "It's okay."

He tried again. He pounded the door. We ignored him in the dark living room.

When the glass shattered a few minutes later, I sat calmly with the gun in my lap. Lupe whimpered a little more but stayed where she was.

Moonlight coming from down the hall showed a black-gloved hand come through the broken glass pane. He turned the lock on the door. As the door slowly opened, creak by creak, I saw a body clothed entirely in black, including a ski mask, tiptoe into the shop, arms raised, elbows bent, carrying a pack.

He left the door open and took two steps in, quietly. I could see he was wound tight and crept like a cartoon character.

Might as well be wearing a black and white striped shirt, a beret, and a black eye mask.

"Stop. Or. I'll. Shoot" I spoke in a low monotone from the chair in the living room. He crept in further.

I pulled the trigger. Lupe yelped.

He went down, screaming in pain, clutching his left calf. Lupe ran to switch on the light.

"You bitch, you SHOT me!"

"Oh, dear, so I did." I said, with an exaggerated frown, standing over him, both hands on the gun.

"Call the police, Lupe, there's been an intruder." I said calmly. "and don't forget to change." She bumbled upstairs, tripping in her haste.

I stood over him as he bled onto the centuries-old wooden floor, cursing. I pointed the gun directly at his crotch.

"Harold, don't you dare move. Try and you will hurt a lot more," I said. I leaned over and upended the pack to find num-chuks, police batons, and brass knuckles. I scattered them around for effect.

Two minutes later Officer Martinez relieved me of my gun, took a good look at what was on the floor, and inspected the wound. He said, "You'll live," and ripped off his mask.

"Harold!" said Lupe, who had put on a short chenille robe and wound her dry hair into a towel. "What are you doing here?"

"You know this man, ma'am?"

"Yes, he's my husband."

Iris and Helen appeared in the doorway.

"My goodness," said Iris, placed her hand over her heart and leaned against Helen for support. Miss Marple again.

I said, "He's your *husband*? You mean your *estranged* husband?"

Officer Martinez looked from me to Lupe, back and forth several times. We stared at him quietly. He then looked at Iris and Helen, who looked back innocently.

He held up one finger and spoke into the mouthpiece on his shoulder. "Intruder shot by homeowner. Non-life threatening. Could use paramedics."

"What the fuck?" Harold shouted. "Why'd you shoot me?"

"Why did I shoot you? Why did I *shoot* you? Are you kidding me? You broke into my shop after hours, you had a mask on. What would you have me do, welcome you with tea and crumpets?" My nerves were showing.

"Wait." Officer Martinez turned to me. "Did he knock or ask for admittance in any way?"

"No, sir. I heard the glass break and went for my gun."

"Uh-huh. You have a gun. Do you have a license for that gun?"

"Yes, I do. I'm a widow now and I can't be too careful," I said, instinctively lowering my eyes as though I were ashamed of it.

"And you?" He turned to Iris and Helen, both of whom covered their mouths with their hands. "What are ladies of your seasoned age doing out in the dark at this time of night?"

"Do you think it's past curfew for people of 'a seasoned age,' officer?" Iris looked at him, those big blue eyes nothing but inquiring innocence. "Oh, we often take night strolls, good for the hips, you know. This is such a charming village, and very safe, don't you think, Helen? We saw that the lights were on in our favorite shop, and then we heard the gunshot. We were, of course, concerned." I saw Helen's car parked on the street.

"Uh-huh." The officer was clearly not convinced.

He looked at Lupe. "and why are you here, may I ask?" He looked at Lupe, beautiful Lupe, who had thought to make it look like she had just come out of the shower. As his investigative eyes roamed down to her slippers, he saw the bruises. Many, many bruises of many, many colors. His eyes came back up. He focused on her face and took in the yellowing around her left eye. I saw his eyes soften, then pinpoint as he got the picture.

"There's a room upstairs that I let Lupe use—she's the shop manager—when we work late," I said.

"Aha. I see." He stood in the middle of the room, looking once again from me to Lupe.

"Do you want to press charges?"

"I will press charges." I said, like a meek little lamb.

"And you, ma'am?" he said turning to look at Lupe.

Lupe took a deep breath, and said quietly, "I'm afraid of him. You should know there is a restraining order."

Almost there, babe.

Officer Martinez turned and looked down at Harold, who was whimpering and holding his leg.

"What was your intention here, sir?"

"I just wanted to see my wife. *Shit.*" He grimaced at the pain.

"Um hmm. At two A.M.? And why didn't you knock, ring the bell, announce your presence in some way?"

"I did," said Harold. "That bitch," and he pointed at me, "wouldn't let me in, didn't answer the door."

"That true, ma'am?"

Before I could answer, Harold said, "You know it is, bitch. She even knew who I was. Called me by name."

He looked at me and I shrugged. "I've never met this man before in my life." Which was the God's honest truth. "I've only ever seen him from a distance, but never met him." I was experienced in spinning a story for good.

"Okay, pal, you're under arrest for breaking and entering." He looked at all the weapons scattered on the floor. "We can add 'with intent to harm' to the breaking and entering charge."

I had managed to smash Harold's foot, so he landed, handcuffed, on a hospital bed for a week before he could be arraigned. Lupe and I went to the arraignment with Officer Martinez. Ron, as a favor to me, came along as well.

Mother always said it never hurts to have friends in high places.

Officer Martinez brought pictures of Lupe's bruises and a diary she had kept hidden documenting the abuse suffered over the past two years, including the reaction of the police and her fear of trying to report it again and again. The judge issued a stronger restraining order and threatened to up the ante to attempted murder of a fetus. Bail was denied.

We went to lunch.

"So, what are your plans now?" asked Officer Martinez.

Lupe contemplated this. "I don't know yet. I have a few decisions to make."

He shrugged. "Yes, I suppose you do. But remember they are your decisions, no one else's."

Chapter Fifty

"I THINK I'LL SELL THE HOUSE," LUPE SAID.

We had just gotten back and opened up the shop.

"Can you do that without his signature?"

"It's in my name. I inherited it from my grandmother." Lupe's house was paid off, and she received an income. My God, she was better off than I was.

"I think I'll talk to Suzanne on Tuesday."

"Mmmm . . . talk to Bruce. He has a nice house just two miles from here he's trying to sell."

"I can walk to work," she said, a smile coming across her face. It was good to see.

× × ×

After all the drama had been broadcast (the incident showed up on the front page of the paper, LOCAL SHOP OWNER FOILS ROBBERY. BRAVE WIDOW SHOOTS INTRUDER) in detail to everyone, the conversation took a turn and focused on Lupe.

"So, what now?" said Iris.

"Yes, what are your plans? Can you continue to live in the house? How soon will Harold get out? What do you need?"

Lupe looked from concerned face to concerned face and smiled.

"Honey, I have more money than sense, and if you need some to get you through, then just ask," said Iris. "I have oodles."

"I'll be all right now," said Lupe.

Suzanne was quiet, finishing up the back of the bride's dress. Her voice was quiet and shaking. "Are you going to be charged?" she asked me.

"No. I was defending the shop. He broke in and didn't stop when I asked him to. I did all the right things."

"How did you come to have a gun?"

"It's perfectly legal. I've carried a gun every day of my life since I could legally do it. I had a bad experience once and it's never going to happen again."

The group stared at me. "Nothing to share, just being cautious. It's registered, and I know how to use it."

"That's fairly evident," said Helen.

"Besides, I don't know what all the fuss is about. I only shot him in the arch."

Who knew you were a comedian?

Chapter Fifty-One

THE SHOP WAS PICKING UP. THE PUBLICITY THAT CAME FROM THE DRESS, the shooting, and Tricia's society wedding made a difference. With one house left to lease out, traffic had increased, and business grew substantially. The dresses were in the final phase of finishing, in plenty of time for Zelda to get mailed off, judged, and returned, and the Bride's dress would be ready for Tricia's wedding over the holidays.

I could take a breath and think about other things.

"Can you come over for dinner?" I had caught Renee one morning at her desk.

"Sure. Can I bring a date?" she whispered.

I laughed. "Sure. I'd love to see him."

It was an Indian Summer, a balmy, tropical night, so I set up the table in the outdoor kitchen. The salmon was waiting to be grilled and the salads were ready. I laughed when I thought that I could have done this for Maggie and Dave, but instead chose to serve them in the kitchen.

Served her right.

Renee showed up early and we chatted outside on the couch designed for outdoor living. She looked happy and relaxed. I commented on it.

"Why not? I'm a lame duck. This fall is the election and I'm finished with my political career. I can go do things I've always wanted to do."

"Like what?"

"I have absolutely no idea!" she laughed. I joined her.

Sticks and Stitches had greeted Renee when she came in. She sat in the family room and played with them, and they were particularly interested in her purse.

"Good sniffing, guys," she said as she pulled out a pouch of doggie treats. She gave them each one and put the pouch back in her purse.

We chatted happily until I heard one of them barking and recognized it as a snitch bark. The contents of Renee's purse were all over the champagne carpet, the pouch devoured, and Sticks was working his way through the leather handle. He was almost all the way through. Stitches either was tattling on him or wanted it for herself.

I used the tone Bruce had taught me. "Off!" I said. His jaws opened and he sat back, his sad little face stared back at me. Stitches sat, too.

How can you stay mad at that?

But Renee's purse was ruined. "I'll reimburse you."

"Nonsense. It's my fault. I should have thought about the treats and where I left them."

"Well, maybe I can find a purse you can transfer your things into in the meantime."

We went upstairs to my purse closet ("you have a closet for your purses?"), and I found myself embarrassed at the riches within those closet walls. Every designer, every color and every size displayed on shelves built specifically for these bags.

"Jesus, Jen, you must have $22,000 just in bags." She chose one and went downstairs.

Dingdingdingding.

Sell these babies and bring in some money. Maybe the shoes, too, and hats you'll never wear, the designer gowns . . . .

The doorbell rang as we hit the bottom step, and Ron, in all his splendor and heavy black, padded uniform, stood holding flowers and a bottle of wine.

Renee was a lucky gal.

We ate dinner outside, and I found myself happy to see the slight touching of hands and shy smiles. They were at what I hoped would be the beginning of a long relationship, and it tickled me to see her so happy and so infatuated.

We had talked about Iris for a bit, a little concerned about her slowing down, but recognized that she was in her nineties and that was to be expected. Ron reported he had been summoned for lunch one day last week.

"Iris always wants something," I said. "What did you talk about?"

"You know exactly what we talked about," he said, shaking his finger at me. I raised my eyebrows. "I know you're part of the anti-Ed Knowles committee."

"I admit it completely. I feel very strongly that someone should run against him. Someone who is well known, well liked, and well respected." I left it at that.

"Then in that case, since you got me into this, I will run for mayor only if you agree to become my Chief of Staff."

I stared at him and the pieces all fell into place. Renee watched both of us quietly.

"Let me think about it." Once again, I had no idea what I was getting myself into but jumped knowing Renee and Ron would be by my side. I had every confidence Lupe could run the shop without me.

But Chief of Staff?

$$ \times \ \times \ \times $$

I had gone to the dry cleaner's day after day after day. Nothing.

It had to be somewhere.

"I want to go back and look myself," I said on the seventh morning of my trips to the dry cleaners. "Maybe I can see what you can't."

"Ma'am . . ."

"I insist. This is too important."

He sighed. "Come this way."

I followed the owner back to where the work was being done and saw piles of clothes. How they kept it all separate and knew which pile was whose, I had no idea. I searched all around, but in that mess couldn't figure out where to start. The smell of the chemicals made me dizzy and nauseated.

"Show me the blocks you used to block the pieces," I said. He went outside and I followed. Piles of wood panels were thrown on top of one another.

"One or two of those," he said.

There were close to fifty of them, if I could estimate correctly. I sighed. We started back into the shop when something glittery from beneath a plank caught my eye.

A piece of gray yarn.

"Look!" I yelled. Like disaster relief workers, we started to pull away plank after plank until we found the one I wanted. We lifted it up, and, voila, the front of the dress appeared still pinned to the block.

When I arrived at the shop two hours later, I found the group sitting at the long table absorbed in the dress and other projects. I produced the four pieces of the Zelda dress, all in perfect condition and told the story. Someone had turned the planks to greet the steam coming from the wall unit, and someone else just thought they were blank planks and threw them out without looking at the back side.

Thank God there was no damage. They steamed them again and I left without paying the bill.

Chapter Fifty-Two

I HEARD THE FRONT DOOR OPEN AND LUPE JUMPED UP TO SEE HOW SHE could help. She had been gone quite a long time when I saw her motion to me from the dining room. I excused myself and entered the needlepoint room; and I stopped dead in my tracks.

A woman had her back to me, long brown curly hair down her shoulders. She wore white overalls with a navy-blue t-shirt under it. She was on the phone and laughed at something. That unmistakable laugh. Loud, boisterous, from the gut. Without her turning around I could see her mouth open as I had seen it many times on the big screen.

Julia Roberts stood in my shop.

She looked at the needlepoint supplies and described them to whomever sat on the other end of the phone. She clicked her phone closed and turned to us, both staring at her. "Good morning," she said, a huge smile on her face. "Something on my face?" She waved her hand in front of her face, grinning.

"I'm so sorry. I'm Jen Conrad, and I'm so happy to see you here. What are you looking for? Maybe I can point you in the right direction?" I felt like a star struck teenager.

"Ha!" That laugh again. "I can't seem to keep my hands still on a movie set. I finished the two sweaters I brought to the set—it's taking forever—and now I need to start another two sweaters for my twins. They grow so fast!" She talked fast and seemed completely bewildered by her own children. "They're into dinosaurs at the moment—do you have something like that?" Those bright eyes went from me to Lupe and around the shop. "This is such a nice shop!"

"Thank you. We just recently opened. Lupe, why don't you show her some yarn and I'll find a pattern. I think I have just the thing," and I went to my faithful old magazines and found exactly what I had in mind. When I walked into the living room to show her, she had plunked herself on one of the chairs at the table, and Sticks and Stitches were all over her. She ran her long fingers through their curly coats and cooed.

"I see you've met our special guest," I said, and I introduced everyone.

"Please, I'm not a special guest. I'm a customer who likes to knit. What are you making there?" as she pointed to the pieces of Zelda proudly displayed on the table.

"That is a dress we are going to enter into a contest." I showed her the sketch. She looked it over for a few minutes.

"This is awesome, and unusual. Almost from another time, sort of the jazz age, right?"

Tricia smiled. "Exactly. We're calling it Zelda."

"Oh, that's perfect!" Her head went back, and another loud guffaw came out. She looked at Suzanne's collection of baby hats she had knit for the hospital and asked for the pattern to contribute some, too. Suzanne gave her a copy of the pattern and yarn donated by the hospital.

Lupe had piled together some options on the front desk along with a copy of the dinosaur pattern I had found. She made her selections and we had the biggest sale ever.

"Bye, y'all," she said, and the movie star left the building. "I'll get some hats back to you soon."

We collapsed into hysterics. All except Helen. "Why such a fuss? She's just a woman."

Two weeks later, Julia came back with her co-star, the legendary Betty White. Julia brought in a dozen baby caps and gave them to Suzanne, and Betty brought dog treats for the babies. Apparently Julia had told her, and she came prepared and made friends immediately with them. She loved their names.

Betty looked at all the needlepoint supplies and told a story to the group: "When Alan came home from taping Password, we'd pour a drink and I'd work on my needlepoint every night while we chattered about our days before dinner. This went on for years." She waved a hand in the air. My heart fluttered remembering my own pre-dinner routine with Arthur.

"One night he came home, looked around the room at all the pillows, rugs, and hangings I had done and said, 'God we drink a lot!'" She smiled that special smile of hers, Julia guffawed, waved, and they left just as quickly as they came.

Women Who Mattered. At any age.

Chapter Fifty-Three

IT WAS FATHER'S BIRTHDAY, AND I HADN'T BEEN PART OF THE CELEBRATION for quite a few years, the two years before that I found Arthur's condition a good excuse not to attend. But this time I was stuck.

I didn't quite know what to do. Mother decreed that we would all gather at her place, another command performance, a catered event where, I knew, we were all expected to dress for dinner and celebrate the man who had given us what life we had. He would be brought in for the occasion.

I'd rather be drawn and quartered.

The good daughter put herself together, gathered wrapped gifts and went to La Jolla.

I walked in to find my father alone in his wheelchair in the living room.

"Hello, Father." His rheumy eyes looked up at me and he sneered. "Slut. Whore. Sinner. For-ni-ca-tor."

"What in the world?" Maggie stood in the doorway.

"Never mind. It happens every time."

"What happens, dear?" asked Mother as she followed Maggie into the living room carrying a silver tray with appetizers.

I didn't answer. I unloaded my bag of gifts and my tote and turned around.

"Daddy just announced I am a slut, a whore, a sinner and a fornicator. He certainly has accumulated a vocabulary at that place." I stepped over to the bar, grabbed a glass and poured some of Father's single malt scotch into it.

Mother's face had gone white and she started to sway.

"Mommy!" Maggie grabbed her arm and supported Mother to the silk couch.

"I'm all right. His decline is such a shock, though. I hate to see it. Maybe this was a mistake."

I shrugged off my sweater and laid it across an overstuffed chair. "It's not a mistake, Mother, and this is not about his decline. It's time we got all this out." I felt calmer than I should have. What had to be done would be distasteful to say the least, but it had to be done to release us all.

You go, girl. This is long overdue.

I took a slug and placed my glass on the end table. I placed my hands on the armrests on either side of his wheelchair and looked down at him. His neck failed to keep his head upright, but he could still hear me. I knew I had to say it, and I knew he had to hear it. I could see his scalp through the sparse hairs on the top of his head.

My anger showed up loud and clear.

"Listen, old man." I heard Maggie gasp. "It's time you and I had a little chat. I am sick and tired of being the victim here of your mean, painful, hurtful, spiteful remarks. I am not a slut, a whore, a sinner, or a for-ni-ca-tor. I am a woman. A grown woman who deserves some respect." I stood, and I know my words began to invade his psyche. I took a deep breath.

"I was raped. Do you hear me? Raped. It was not consensual, it was not expected, and it was not wanted. I screamed my head off, but no one heard me." I walked away from him and started pacing around the room, my resolve spitting out with my words. I spewed out everything I had held back for forty years.

"You never asked, so I never told. I believed you when you told me I was no good and would never amount to anything. I believed you. I believed you when you said I was broken and couldn't be fixed. I believed you when you said Jesus had to be disappointed in me. When I found Arthur, I was afraid I would lose him if he knew because I believed you when you told me no man would ever love me. The only secret I kept from him. I hate you for that."

I turned to Mother. "And you sat back and didn't do anything. You went along with it. You sent me off to God knows where and they 'took care' of me. My baby was given away. They tied my tubes so I could never have any more children. I never even looked at the baby. Was it a boy or a girl? I have no idea. Was it healthy? I never knew. And I was alone. You never came."

"But you were only a child." Mother's perfect facade crumbled. Her voice shook and I thought she might cry.

"Yes. A child. Who made a mistake. I sneaked out one summer night and suffered my own consequences. But you never let me forget it. And I can't forgive that. My innocence was taken, yes, as a consequence of my own stupidity, but you, Mother, you stole my adolescence and my identity. You stole my faith. You made me believe I was not good enough. You never even asked me what happened." I shook my head. "You believed I was a bad girl. You had no faith in me."

I took a breath. "My entire life all I wanted was your respect, yours and Father's. But I never got it. No matter what I did, I am still a sinner with a capital S. I always looked for a sign of forgiveness, but never got it. A good friend asked me if I forgave you." I shook my head and gathered my things. "It happened over forty years ago and it still comes between us."

As I picked up my things, I said to Father, "Christians forgive, Father. Christians are kind, loving, forgiving people. By no definition I know, do you even remotely fit into that mold."

I walked out of the room to find Tricia and Dave standing in the foyer, their faces in shock.

The secret was out. What they did with it would be on them.

I got in the car and turned the engine on. Before I could collect myself, my phone buzzed.

A distraction. Wonderful.

"Jen?" Lupe panting.

"Lupe? What's wrong?"

"I'm in labor. And it hurts so bad."

"Where are you?"

"At the shop."

"I'm half an hour away. Did you call Harold?"

What was I thinking?

"God, no."

"Okay, hang on."

I called Bruce, the only person who I knew could get there before I did. She sounded awful.

"Can you do a mission of mercy?"

"Sure—what?"

"Lupe's in labor. She's at the shop. Can you get her to the hospital?"

I heard him as he straightened up and the shock wore off. "On my way."

"I'll meet you there."

I called Robert, as per our telephone tree plan. "Operation Baby is in full swing," I said.

"Right. I'll pass the word."

By the time I got to the shop, Lupe and Bruce were long gone. I put the money away and hung a sign on the door: "Lupe's having her baby! Closed for the duration!" and left my cell number.

I broke all speed records and got to the hospital just as they spirited Lupe up to a labor room. Bruce looked like he had just come out of a horror movie: pale, shaky, and disbelieving.

Men.

"You can go now," I laughed. "The cavalry has arrived."

"I don't think so. I've gotten four messages. The group is on their way. Someone's got to sit with them, fetch coffee, and so forth." He smiled. "I consider myself the consigliere of this group."

"That so." Helen came in slowly. Today she used a cane to help her bad hip. "Perfectly capable of handling our own group, Mr. Miller, but if you care to keep us company, be glad to have you."

"I'll leave you all to straighten this out. I'm going to sit with Lupe for a bit." I laughed at them as they settled in.

"Good girl." Helen lowered herself slowly down to the chair with a grunt. "Iris and Jade are on their way. I suppose Margaret will be coming soon."

"Don't bet on it." Just then Trish entered, her scarf flying behind her. I was reminded of Nana Buford's expression: "We went so fast you could have played cards on our coattails." Trish came over and hugged me an extraordinarily long time. "You okay?"

"Yes. Finally." She looked me over and apparently decided I was fit to leave her arms.

"Mrs. Conrad?" a nurse looked at me. "She's asking for you."

I went into the labor room to see Lupe sitting up in a hospital gown with tubes coming out of her arms. She munched on ice chips. The TV played an old Dick Van Dyke episode, and she laughed out loud, then grimaced in pain.

"And how is your day going?" she asked.

"Don't ask. What you are about to do will more than make up for it." I smiled at her and recognized that one of the worst days of your life can turn on a dime.

"You know you're my best friend in the world."

"Give you some good drugs, did they?"

"I mean it. You have been so good to me. You and Arthur. Without both of you, I'd just be a statistic." Her face turned into a spasmodic display of real pain. "Apparently not enough drugs," she said.

The nurse came in, did some measurements, looked at the stock paper coming off the machine on Lupe's bedside, said, "Looks like it's time for you to go to work," and went out into the corridor.

Lupe's face contorted again. "What, this isn't work?" she mumbled.

A young intern came in, wearing blue scrubs and bags under his eyes, followed by a more seasoned doctor who seemed bored and uninterested.

"Now, look below and tell me what you see," the older man said, without greeting either one of us. The intern, on the other hand, nodded to us.

Lupe looked at me and I looked at Lupe. We both started laughing. "Is this a joke?" she asked.

The intern smiled. The seasoned doctor did not.

No sense of humor. Not good.

"Look," then Lupe got hit with another contraction, grimaced, breathed, and continued. "I don't care if you're in training. Just get this thing out of me. It's starting to get annoying."

"All in good time. God knows what's right," said the older doctor. "It's in His hands now." The fact that the father was not here apparently gave him license to lecture.

"Lupe, is this your regular doctor?" I asked her. She shook her head.

"Then can you find Doctor . . . ?" I looked at Lupe.

"Henderson," she gasped.

"Henderson? I'm sure she would be much more comfortable with her own doctor." I put on my good girl-please-if-you-don't-mind-too-awfully-much smile.

"But you," Lupe pointed to the intern and took a deep breath, "can stay."

"This is highly irregular." The man I dubbed Dr. Christ's silver mustache quivered in indignation.

I didn't give a rat's ass.

"Yes, I'm sure it is, but your comments are offensive." The doc stared at me. "Look. Her husband deserted her after abusing the living daylights out of her. She is now on her own and she needs to be as comfortable as possible. I'm sure you understand." The good girl I'm-sure-I've-convinced-you-now smile didn't work, either.

"But I am the doctor on call." He was actually whining.

Good girl gone bad. I stood up. "I don't give a goddamn who is on call. You will find Dr. Henderson and get him over here so he can deliver the baby he's been watching for the past eight months." His eyes opened wide. "NOW GO." He literally backed out the door. Maybe he was afraid I would bring out my ninja knives.

Lupe laughed. The intern smiled. "I'm going into OB/GYN if this is the theater experience I get."

"Excuse me. I've had one hell of a day," I said.

Lupe was on her phone calling Dr. Henderson. "This might be faster."

Lupe delivered a beautiful baby girl after only two hours of labor. I stayed with her all through the process and found myself completely enraptured.

The miracle that presented itself to me had thick dark hair, ten perfect fingers and ten perfect toes.

When Lupe fell asleep in her room, I left to find some coffee and found the entire group in the waiting room. Iris, Helen, Jade, Suzanne, Robert, and Tricia all had projects in front of them. I had to laugh and told them the good news. We all hugged each other many, many times.

Helen, surprisingly, unearthed a bottle of Dom Perignon and six flutes.

"To Catherine," she said. "May she be as strong as her mother."

One of the nurses came over and said, "I'm so sorry, that's not allowed in the lobby. You can have that in the room, but not in the lobby."

Iris and Helen said, in unison, "Don't care." Jade and I looked at each other and laughed. Suzanne had her hand over her mouth, raised her class to the center of our group and we all clinked glasses again.

The nurse spun on her heel and left.

Some rules are made to shatter.

Chapter Fifty-Four

I HAD TAKEN ZELDA TO THE DRESSMAKERS ALONG WITH THE FABRIC TO GO underneath, and, for once in the project, the end result was fabulous. The seams were nonexistent: she had matched up the lace pattern so there was no disruption. The under dress showed through beautifully, and I couldn't wait to see it on Tricia.

I pulled out my sewing dummy and adjusted it to Tricia's measurements. I carefully put the dress on her and stepped back.

My anticipation of the pleasure I would take in this masterpiece was replaced by severe disappointment and a sharp temperature spike.

Something's not right. Unbelievably, it's too plain. It needs something to perk it up.

Shit. It's not good enough. Not perfect.

The phone rang. Irritated, I picked it up.

"Can we talk? Mommy is very upset."

"Maggie, you're sixty-two years old. It's time you stopped calling her Mommy."

Silence.

"What's going on with you? You're a different person." Maggie's voice became smaller, quieter.

"Stronger?"

"Let's just say . . . more forceful."

I laughed. "Yes, I suppose so. I'm tired of all the bullshit. All the hiding. All the polite chatter."

"I've never heard you swear before."

"Hmm. Well . . . Maggie, what do you want?" I felt so tired I might just fall over, and I had no patience for niceties. Tell me what you want and let me either deal with it or not.

"Did you really have a baby?"

"Now, why would I lie about that?"

"Look, if you're not going to talk about it, I'll let you go, then."

"Maggie, it's been forty-two years. There's not much to talk about. You know about as much as I do. Those are the facts. There's nothing else."

"But Daddy . . ."

"Daddy can go to hell." My voice remained calm, my breathing quiet, if it had been shown on a hospital screen, completely flat. No change. I meant it, finally.

There was a definite click in my ear.

Just a short time ago that would have dismembered me, someone cutting me off and disrespecting me and my feelings. Today I just didn't care.

It was her choice, and I could live with it.

I got back to the Problem of Zelda.

Tricia, Carl, and Ray sat around Carl's dining room table for an update. It had been months since they communicated about the project and when Ray had called for a meeting, they knew they might have something.

Ray drew three file folders on the table and handed them each one.

"You were right, but there is more."

"More?"

"Much, much more . . . I'm at 90 percent, so I am sure, but I want to be at 100 percent, and I am waiting for a few documents, three affidavits and two depositions."

They stared at him, dumbfounded. "You want affidavits and depositions?"

"Of course." He looked at them. "That's what you wanted, right?"

"Well . . ."

"Look, I said if I do this, I go all the way. No guesswork. I want backup. It's my reputation on the line, but it's your family's firm. It needs to be solid.

I wasn't about to just look at the books and make a calculated, educated conclusion."

Tricia started to shake. "What's involved?"

"Are you sure you want to know?"

She nodded.

"It runs from one instance of attempting to influence a judge to outright fraud, plus my predecessor was harassed."

"How much is the exposure?"

"For clients? You can probably compensate them easily. What's involved there is simply a misrepresentation of settlement amounts; they were told one settlement amount, but the firm was paid a higher amount. I'm not sure where the extra went—it didn't go into the firm's books."

"Dad?"

"I don't know, but it went somewhere. I'm waiting for copies of emails and phone call transcripts to back up the judicial influence, and Richardson had some evidence he took with him. He's handing that over, hoping to get Dave in jail. We had a very long conversation; he really hates the guy."

Tricia had her hands in her hair again, rubbing her face. "What's the exposure?"

"It's in the file." Ray nodded to the purple folder in front of her. "You might want to have a drink first. It's brutal."

Carl looked at the bottom line and gasped. "He's right. Let's have a drink."

"How did Dad even think about going to the judge and trying to influence his decision?"

Ray took a slug. "It wasn't your dad."

"Oh God." Tricia put her head in her hands.

"Fortunately, the judge knew who he was dealing with and didn't make a big deal of it. He called Dave and told him what his wife had done and admonished him to 'get his lady in line' and let it go at that. Dave was lucky, but it did happen, and he's sending over a testimonial to that effect."

"Fraud?"

He shrugged. "Nothing really big, but it's there, and it adds up. So far no one has discovered it but me, I think, but be prepared to hear if any of this gets out."

"And Richardson?"

"Mrs. Putnam threatened him; I'm not sure with what, but he quit toot suite. She must have had something on him."

"We handle this quietly . . ." Tricia mumbled. "Shit."

"That's what you wanted, right? Save your Dad, save the firm, and make things right if what we thought was correct?" Carl asked.

"Can I ask how this got started? What got you thinking this might be a problem?" Ray asked.

Tricia took a slug of her drink, and said, "I interned a few summers ago and went to trials to observe. I remember one in particular. The defendant was really cute," she looked over at Carl, "sorry, but he was, and I remembered they settled in court for $12,000. I remember it so distinctly. I kept notes, even. When I ran across the file that summer, I pulled it out, and lo and behold it said $10,000, which I thought was weird, but I didn't question it. I went back and looked at my notes and verified it should have said twelve. It stuck with me." Tricia shrugged. "I was a stupid first-year legal student and didn't question it."

Carl jumped in. "I saw a few things, too, things that didn't sit right. Billable hours knocked up, services that weren't done being billed, etc., and I didn't feel right about it, so I asked Dave and didn't like how *he* handled it. He said he'd have accounting look at it and not to worry—that mistakes were made and soon corrected. Tricia and I talked once about it and began to check some things . . ."

"Okay," Ray said, and sighed. "Look the file over and let me know if you have any questions. Don't do anything until I have the last piece in place."

"What's your advice?"

He rubbed his hands together, looked up, and said, "Sell the firm. Lock, stock and barrel. That beautiful office, all its furnishings, along with the current cases and employees. Someone will scoop it up easily because it's not a huge business anymore, but they can rename it and start over. You can open up your own firm in a much more economic space and do what you want. That way you can make reparations and make things right."

"And Dad?"

"You can retire him, I think, and save him jail time or bar removal. Just let him go quietly, but he'll have to sell some assets as well to contribute to the reparations. That's IF you can contain it, which will be a miracle."

"And Mom?"

"I don't know that she has any liability except for the judge thing, and it's hard to think that was the only one, knowing the extent of it; she had to have done it earlier." He saw Tricia's face. "I'm sorry, but I believe this is not the first, nor the last time she's done something like this."

Tricia nodded. "Probably not," she whispered.

"Remember, you wanted the truth."

Chapter Fifty-Five

We WERE IN THE HOME STRETCH.

Zelda had been completed and I had found some lightweight crystals to stitch onto the opening down the front, which finished it off easily. As an afterthought, I put one on each point of the wrist as well.

Very Zelda. I sent it off to Elan by the due date and hoped for the best. They promised to return it after one week of judging. I enclosed a prepaid, special delivery overnight label just to be sure.

The Bride's dress, however, was proving to be more stressful. It had been finished, blocked and stitched together, with the blush fabric under it, and it was gorgeous—until I hung it on the dummy. Again, a problem.

The bottom rolled up onto itself. We needed a little weight. I sewed pearls around the bottom, thinking it would add more weight.

Nope, just made it flare out and ripple awkwardly.

Shit.

Back to the steamer.

I had no choice but to hem it, hiding the over steamed edge and adding pearls to it for weight.

Again with the stiff flare.

Shit. It's not perfect.

I crumpled into the chair in my sewing room and stared at the catastrophe. I wandered into the living room and poured a vodka, my hand stopped mid-pour.

Hold on. It's beautiful. Who says it has to be perfect? It's made with love. Its imperfections only make it better, give it more character.

Right. I put the drink down, went into my office and wrote the letter I had been composing in my head ever since the reunion.

$$\times\ \times\ \times$$

A week later my phone rang, and my world changed once again.

"Mother?"

Silence.

"Mother? Are you all right?"

A quiet voice came over the phone. "I'm all right, dear, but your father has died."

Boom.

I didn't know what to say. Butterflies ran through my head tickling what little sensation I had, and my fingers grew cold over the receiver.

"Okay, okay," I said quietly, as though talking to a child with an ouchie. "What would you like me to do?"

She took a quick, gasping breath and said, "You'll have to start telephoning everyone. Start with your sister."

"Maggie doesn't know?"

"No." Silence.

It occurred to me to ask about her state of mind. "Are you all right?"

Silence.

"I am somewhat weak, and in considerable pain. You'll have to handle this."

"What about the arrangements?"

"Talk to Father Brennan; it's all arranged. I just can't right now." She took another breath. "I would prefer you wait until three o'clock to start telephoning. I have to make myself presentable for the visitors who will appear over the next few days."

She hung up.

The phone was still in my hand.

Father was dead.

I wanted to feel some sense of relief, some sense of freedom, like a lasso around my body finally coming loose, but felt nothing but an ache that was so familiar I bent over and collapsed against the bed. Sticks and Stitches

265

bounded in and stopped short when they saw the tears and heard my howls. Sticks lay across my legs and Stitches licked the tears away with a warm tongue.

It was over. And I had made no move to fix it, probably made it worse, but it was what it was.

The ache was replaced quickly with resentment. I had just done this for my own husband. She couldn't make a few phone calls? Surely arrangements must have already been made.

Is this some kind of sick punishment?

An hour later, I stood at the front door of my mother's house, key in hand, determined to find out why she was doing this.

I rang the bell. No answer. Knocked. No answer.

At the hairdresser, no doubt.

I had never used my key before. Invading her home was not acceptable. I only had it for emergencies.

Well, if this wasn't one, I didn't know what was. I turned the key and entered.

Mother lay in her bed, eyes closed, breathing shallowly, with a guttural exhale that made me nervous.

"Mother?"

"Mother?" Louder.

"Mother?" I shook her shoulder.

Nothing.

I tried a few more times, then called nine-one-one.

The paramedics arrived and took her to the hospital, and I followed in my car.

Is it possible I lose both parents in one day?

I waited for my pulse to drop and get a grip. I accepted a cup of coffee from a volunteer and pulled out the notebook I carried with me everywhere and started to list things I had to do both for Father and for Mother.

The list was long. My brain was firing on all cylinders now, one item led to another, and I had my list.

I called Lupe and told her she would be handling things for the next few days. Then I called Dave.

"I'm sorry, he's in a meeting and can't be disturbed."

"This is Mrs. Conrad. Tell him it's a family emergency." Let him try to get out of that.

"Jen?"

"Dave. Mother's in the hospital. I went by her place and she won't wake up."

"Is she okay?"

"Dave, I just told you, she won't wake up."

"Yes, of course. Sorry. What do you want me to do?"

"You can tell Maggie. I have too much to do here. Sorry, it's going to be a bad conversation."

"Why?"

"Because Father died this morning."

"Oh, shit."

"You'll have to break it to Maggie, I'm afraid. I'm stuck here with Mother and I have to get Father taken care of. I don't have time to deal with her."

"Tell you what. Why don't you come by at lunch and we can both tell her."

I took a deep breath.

"Dave, go home right now, and be with your wife. She's going to need you."

I hung up.

Coward.

Chapter Fifty-Six

Mother had been moved up to a private room. I sat with her as she slept quietly. I was knitting and adjusting my list when Dr. Kelsey came in, which gave me a jolt.

Dr. Kelsey was Arthur's oncologist, and I hadn't seen him in quite some time. He looked just as surprised to see me. We shook hands and he gave me an update on Mother.

"The cancer has progressed rapidly. I gave her some pain killers earlier to help her get through the day, but she overdid it. No damage done, but we'll have to adjust the dosage and keep an eye on it." He looked at me over his glasses. "But I believe it's time to call in hospice."

I had heard those words before from his very mouth, and it all came back in a rush. The nurses, the volunteers, the chaplains, the social workers, the home healthcare workers. The team that had worked with such precision and caring and had made my life as simple as it could be so I could focus on Arthur.

Those angels.

"I had no idea it had progressed this fast. She's good at hiding it." I shook my head. "Yes, if you think it's time for hospice, then let's bring them in."

"Is there anything else I can do?" He said as he held my hand in both of his. "This can't be easy for you, having just lost your husband."

"You have no idea. My father died this morning." I wished I could have taken the words back. Now he's going to think Mom tried to off herself and assign a psychologist to the case.

With a shock, I realized that just may be the case.

"She's awfully weak, so we'll have to build up her strength," he said. "I'll make a list with some suggestions but be sure to rely on those hospice people. They can work miracles." He turned and walked toward the door, then turned around.

"It was lovely to see you again, Mrs. Conrad. I wish I could be of more help."

"Thank you."

I sat again and wondered if I should stay.

"I heard every word of that," Mother's distinctive high-pitched voice came from the bed. The heavily starched pillowcase crinkled as she turned her head to me. "Hospice. Not yet."

"Mother . . ."

"Nonsense. I can deal with this. I just got a little overanxious this morning and wanted to get control over my body. There's a lot to do."

Mother was back.

$$\times \quad \times \quad \times$$

The good girl in full swing. Mother was home and steady, Father's casket had been picked out, the church was booked, limousines ordered, Father Brennan stood by, Maggie was sorted out, the telephone tree activated, and I felt better than I had for some time.

I was strong. I could do this. Confident. Marge in charge.

Renee sat with me in the front of the church. "Oh dear God," I heard her mutter as Maggie came up the aisle, leaning on Dave's arm, with a pristine white handkerchief handing from her fingers as she dabbed at her eyes under black netting. A full theater production. All eyes were on Maggie, the poor daughter in such distress.

Maggie crawled over us and sat next to me. I grabbed her hand, but she pulled it away.

"Gladiolas? What in the world were you thinking? He hated gladiolas," she whispered.

I didn't respond.

"And you know that." Renee said out of the side of her mouth. "What else did you do?"

I leaned over and whispered into her ear. "Just little things. The casket is a level below the one I picked out for Arthur."

She cocked an eyebrow at me and lowered her chin. "No itching powder?"

I leaned in. "Damn, should have thought of that. Maybe some devil horns."

She smiled and leaned to my ear. "He'd be immediately accepted. No questions asked."

I started to giggle. "Some *Playboy* or *Hustler* magazines."

"Better yet, boy on boy action. Or maybe nun on nun action."

I guffawed and turned it into a cough. Mother shot me a look. Renee was trying to get a hold of herself, but kept making odd noises in her throat, which made me continue to clear my throat as though I was trying to get through my grief.

The truth was, earlier that day I had gone to the funeral parlor and put my teddy bear, the one I carried with me to New Hampshire, in with him, so he would never forget what he did to me.

That gave me more satisfaction than anything. The gladiolas were just an afterthought.

Mother handled herself well through the reception at her house, but she excused herself early, and Maggie escorted her upstairs. I knew they both had to be drained.

Once again, I stood at the door, welcomed people and watched them go, accepting condolences, gifts, cards, flowers, and casseroles.

I wore the same gray dress, but this time I remembered the pearls. I wondered how soon I would be doing this yet again.

Mother rallied a few days later, but she was clearly maimed.

Choyou came to the shop one day with a small burlap bag.

"You boil in water, give to Missy Palmer." She circled her fingers like a witch stirring a special brew. "Make Mama-san healthy. Have energy. Then when she strong, bring her to shop. Auntie has special powers."

"Excellent. Thank you, Choyou. How are things going over at your shop?"

"Go good. $30, please." Her hand was out.

"Oh. Of course." She doesn't work for me anymore. She's a business-woman who expects payment.

How could I be so stupid? Old habits die hard, and people don't just give you things anymore. You have to pay for them.

"Woo-woo stuff," Lupe said when she left.

"I'll try anything," I said. "Besides, we have to support our shops." I sighed. "If it works, I'll do a testimonial."

Lupe opened up the bag and smelled the dried product. Her head jerked back, and she made a scrunched-up disgusted face.

It smelled like feet.

$$\times \quad \times \quad \times$$

"Mother, I'm coming over in a while. Do you need anything?"

"Yes, dear, if you don't mind, a new prescription is ready at my pharmacy. Would you mind picking it up on your way over?"

"Of course I will. See you in about an hour."

We had picked up where we left off before the scene at Father's birthday.

I had made some butternut squash soup that I thought might tempt her. The good girl. I pulled it out of the refrigerator when I thought about the dried herbs. "Why not?" I said to the puppies as they watched me in the kitchen.

I put a pot of water on to boil and emptied the bag into the water. Leaves and twigs floated on top as the water began to bubble. I ran upstairs, puppies behind me, to change and get ready for the trip across town.

I pulled on some jeans, ran my fingers through my hair, and was just throwing on a sweatshirt when the doorbell rang. We all ran downstairs, wondering who it was, puppies barking and thinking there was a game afoot.

But the smell hit me halfway down the stairs. A god-awful, stinky smell permeated the entire house.

I threw open the door to find Matthew from the car towing place, Big Bessie's new owner, grinning at me.

"Just wanted you to see what I did with her," he said, and pointed to the street.

Big Bessie was there, in all her glory, shiny and new, but with red and yellow flames painted down her sides like a car in a cartoon.

"What is that smell?" His face scrunched up. "You have a dead animal in there?"

I laughed. "Come on in. It's an Asian tea I'm about to take to my mother. Some witch doctor gave it to me as a gift. She's in such pain, I'll try anything." I closed the door behind him.

"Pain from what?"

"Cancer."

"Your *mother* is dying now?"

"Yes," I said, leading him into the kitchen.

"Bummer."

"You can say that again." I took a spoon and dipped it in the pot for a small sip of the hot tea and grimaced. "That is absolutely the worst stuff I've ever tasted."

He grabbed a spoon from the counter and tasted it himself. "That shit'll kill her." He dropped the spoon into the sink. "Hang on." He dashed outside to his car and came back in with a baggie.

"Don't call the cops on me, but this is some good stuff and will help with the pain and will bring her appetite back." He handed it to me.

"Is this what I think it is?" The good girl.

"If you think it's grass, it is. High grade."

I handed it back to him. "No, thanks."

He didn't take it. "It's a gift. If you don't want to smoke it, then grind it up and put it in brownies or something. I promise you it will make her feel better." He drew out a packet of what I knew were rolling papers and left it on the counter next to the baggie.

"Bye." And he was gone.

"Wait. How much of this can go into a brownie mix? All of it?"

"Try half of it, then if that doesn't do the trick, call me and I'll get you some more." He grinned and flew out the door.

Holy shit. Could I do this?

"Mother, I'm going to be another hour. Can you hang on that long?"

"Yes, dear. I look forward to seeing you."

I opened Mother's door with my key, balancing the soup, the tea, and a plate of special brownies.

Mother sat on her chair in the living room, dressed properly with makeup on.

I poured the tea from my thermos into a proper teacup and handed it to her. "Choyou's concoction."

She sniffed it and reared her head back. "Those Asians know what they are doing." She took a small sip and grimaced. "It's really not that bad," she said.

I laughed. "It smells like dirty socks."

"It certainly does." For the first time, we laughed together.

I found the soup excellent, if I did say so myself, but Mother pushed hers away after just one slurp, her salad untouched and the soft baguette pieces ignored. I finished all mine.

"Now for dessert."

"Dessert? We never have dessert."

"I made the most incredible brownies. You have to have one. Maybe it will settle your tummy." I arranged them on a plate, made some English tea, and brought it all in on a tray.

I poured the tea, placed a brownie on the saucer, and handed it to her.

I held my breath as she took a bite. "Very good," she said, and sipped her tea.

"Why don't we watch some television?" I asked. "Let our dinner settle."

"Good idea." We moved to her sitting room and turned on the TV.

Mother ate two brownies in the space of fifteen minutes. I didn't dare have one, not knowing how it would affect my driving.

"I believe I'm ready for some of that soup, dear. It smells delicious. And maybe some of that bread."

"Of course. Let me get it for you." I smiled my way into the kitchen.

Mother fell asleep after eating a bowl of soup, two pieces of bread, and another brownie. I woke her up after I had washed the dishes and walked her to her room.

"Yes, those Asians really know what they are doing. That tea made me feel so much better. I can't tell you."

I snuck a brownie into my purse and drove home, feeling like an outlaw and thinking about the loose pot and rolling papers hidden in a tea tin.

Bye-bye good girl.

Chapter Fifty-Seven

"Are you going to the rehearsal dinner at Maggie's?" I asked Renee.

"My invitation must have gotten lost in the mail."

"You weren't invited? To the wedding, either?"

"Negatory."

"I'm sorry."

"Don't be. Although I will probably miss a few of Maggie's episodes. Give me a report, will you? And give Tricia my best. I've sent a gift. A set of boxing gloves. Kidding."

I heard the click of another call coming in and signed off with Renee.

"Hello?"

"Jen? It's Lupe."

"Hi! Everything OK?"

"Well, it was, but I'm going to be out for a few days. My house just burned down."

"What?"

"My house burned down. They are saying it's arson."

"Arson? You mean deliberately set?"

"Seems that way."

"You mean . . ."

"I mean Harold did it. He was sent to jail just this morning. They caught him; the neighbor videotaped it and called the fire department." She laughed.

"Are you hysterical?" I asked.

She calmed down. "No. Just happy. This is the best thing that could have happened. The insurance guy says they will pay to rebuild, and I had a rider on it to pay for housing. We'll be fine, and he's going to jail for a very long time."

"How long is very long?"

"Well." She laughed. "Arson is taken seriously enough, but we were in the house. They're going to charge him with attempted murder. I'm free, Jen."

"I'm sorry about your house."

"I'm not. I hated that old thing. This way I can rebuild, and with all the money I've put away from the firm paying my salary for the past year, I can even make it better for us."

Rebuilding.

$$\times \quad \times \quad \times$$

After the scene at Mother's, I suspected Maggie would not be well, but I also was certain Mother wouldn't miss tonight or the wedding of her only grandchild. I wasn't about to miss it, either, or make another scene on Tricia's special day. I just hoped my sister felt the same way.

I drove to Maggie and Dave's house the night before the wedding a half hour before the rest of the guests were to arrive for the rehearsal dinner. Terence, borrowed for the evening, admitted me to the living room where I found Maggie with her head in her hands, Dave comforting her, a hand on her shaking shoulder.

Honestly the amount of drama surrounding this family was unbelievable.

I turned left and raised my eyebrows to Carl, standing helpless in the dining room; he lifted his hands and shrugged his shoulders. He looked neither happy nor unhappy. Caterers ran hot and cold, placing platters around and making sure everything got wiped down and perfect, ignoring the missus having a breakdown. No gravy spots or stray pieces of fruit showing on Maggie's highly polished silver trays.

Tricia floated down the stairs in the Zelda dress that had come back just yesterday looking very Zelda like. She wore it better than I imagined. Maggie looked up when she saw her daughter and howled.

Problem identified. Trish had taken over.

Tricia rolled her eyes and hugged me. Lacey came up right behind her in a pair of dark green palazzos and a silk shirt, her ragged hair a bit longer now, softer. She wore makeup, tasteful jewelry, and high heels.

I would not have recognized her.

"When in Rome," she said. I felt like a schlub, she was so glamorous.

"Wowza," said Carl. Trish went to him, grabbed both his hands, and planted a kiss on his lips.

That's when the doorbell rang, and life as the Putnams knew it would never be the same.

Chapter Fifty-Eight

*L*ACEY TURNED TO LOOK AT HER FRIEND, GRINNED, AND RUSHED TO THE door. She opened it to a tall, tanned man, with thin silver hair that brushed his shoulders, wearing white linen trousers. A high-necked white linen shirt hung loosely around his thin frame. Lacey jumped into his arms. He smiled and put her down. "My God, girl, is that you?" in a low baritone. I stole a glance at Tricia, who looked as though she had been shot.

He held Lacey at arm's length and took a good long look. He smiled, yellowing imperfect teeth in a smile that disappeared in an instant. I heard him say quietly, "Where is she?" Lacey stepped aside and swept her arm toward Tricia, who stood shock still. Her face matched the dress. I saw the crystals jump on her chest and guessed this was a surprise manipulated by Lacey.

"Nice dress," he said as he gazed at the shocked woman standing before him.

She screamed, flew into his arms and held on tightly. Maggie and Dave appeared at my side.

"What the hell is this?" roared Dave.

"Mr. Putnam, This. Is Adam," said Lacey.

Maggie looked like she wanted to strangle someone.

"Adam . . . is Tricia's love," said Carl, smiling.

Maggie leaned against Dave and put her head in her hands. He turned her around, back into the living room.

Not knowing what else to do, I stayed where I was. Tricia's footsteps were firm and deliberate as she disengaged herself from Adam and moved to Carl, noses two inches apart. Carl's smirk surprised me.

"A deal is a deal," Tricia said into Carl's face. "This is the plan, and it doesn't change."

Carl took two steps back. "And deals are made to be broken. It's why we're lawyers." I heard Adam snort in an attempt to stifle a chuckle—or was it a grimace?

What the hell?

They stood, face to face, eyes blazing. Lacey turned to me.

"Mrs. Conrad, this is Adam Petchek," said Lacey.

Petchek. Ah, the artist's signature on the sketch.

Adam put out his hand to me. "Nice to meet you. I hear you're the designer of the dress."

"It's Jen, and if I'm not mistaken, you are actually the designer," I said slowly as I started to put two and two together. "It is for her wedding to you, wasn't it?" Yup, my filters were gone. Six months ago I would have kept that information to myself.

"It was. And it is." I gathered from looking closely at his skin and his hairline he was not much younger than I. "I'm here to steal her away." He smiled and turned back to Trish. Maggie moaned.

We were in the middle of a soap opera.

Carl swept his arm over to Trish and took a step back. He was giving her up. Tricia's eyes welled up and she put her head in her hands. "I can't."

The room stood shock still, like a freeze frame in a movie. I heard Maggie's deep labored breathing and Dave's calming voice coming from the other room. No one moved.

If this had been a stage play, I'd have been on the edge of my seat, heart pounding. What's going to happen next? No one could have written this script.

"I'm very confused," I said. "This is none of my business." I turned to Tricia. "If you love Carl, marry him. If you love Adam, marry *him*. Don't marry anybody. I don't really care as long as you do it for the right reason with the person you absolutely positively can't live without for the rest of your life." Then a thought occurred to me. "Or his," I said in a lower voice. "It's that simple."

"But there's so much more involved," Tricia said between sobs.

"It's. That. Simple." I repeated and retreated back to the living room. I spied Dave and again raised my eyebrows. Maggie sobbed. Her hysterics seemed a bit overboard to me, but then again it's Maggie, and the night before her only child's wedding. The hoi polloi were expected any minute. I helped myself to a drink.

Nerves stood on the surface, but I wondered how she would cope on such an emotional night. The subject of Eric would undoubtedly be brought up, and tomorrow Maggie would lose her little girl—and control.

I shrugged and walked out into the back yard. Lacey followed me shortly.

"Is anybody going to tell me what's going on?"

Lacey sighed. "You know those rumors Robert kept alluding to? They were about Dave. Carl has for some time now suspected Dave of unethical, much less illegal, things at the firm. Carl and the new CFO have dug up evidence that the bar would be interested in. Tricia didn't want the bar involved just yet, not until it all unraveled. We now are fairly sure that Dave has not been a good boy in the legal world. He has been telling clients that settlement amounts were far less than the actual settlement amount and pocketing the difference. We think that Maggie has been doing some things as well. We know she tried to intimidate a witness on one of Dave's cases."

"What?"

"Tricia still wants to protect her parents," continued Lacey, "she's kept things under wraps and is negotiating quietly so that they will be corrected, and her father will not lose his license or be disbarred. Every one of the corrupted clients thinks they are the only one this 'error' happened to, and they are, of course, thrilled that the firm has been honest in discovering and returning the funds." She stopped. "I think Dave is going to be retired tonight."

"What? How?" I had a tough time catching up.

"Apparently when the firm was built out and went uptown, Arthur put more money up than Dave and had an additional ten shares issued to him, making him the majority stockholder. He gave them to Tricia."

So that's what was in the envelope.

The light bulb went off. "and you're going to join them."

"Yes."

"But what about Adam? How does he fit in?"

Lacey laughed. "Trish tried to forget about him, but he's the love of her life. He's an artist and can live anywhere. I've filled him in on what we are doing here, and he finally came out, thank God, to reclaim her."

"But what about Carl? Won't he be crushed?"

Lacey shook her head. "Carl only wants what's best for Tricia. Because he loves her." She looked into my eyes in the twilight of the evening in San Diego. "You don't know, do you? Carl loved Eric. Really loved him. They were going to run the firm together, that was the original plan, but when Dave and Maggie found out Eric was gay, they became extremely angry and it got ugly. They cut Eric off completely, although they never knew it was Carl." She crossed her arms over her chest. "Tricia told me Eric did not die in a skateboard accident. He killed himself with some of Maggie's medications. That was the beginning of Tricia's withdrawal from her family, although you wouldn't know it. She's planned all this meticulously. I just found out about it myself."

I hung my head hard and felt a flush of acknowledgment. I knew something felt wrong with that story. Maggie and Dave had been too severe, too strong, too upright when Eric died as a result of the "accident." Now I understood, and I hated my sister for not loving her own child enough.

How could this be? A sham marriage, to save her parents' reputation and get control of a law firm? Tricia? And Carl would go along with it. And Lacey.

Not so much Adam, I'm positive.

This was going to be an interesting night.

Robert arrived with his camera and entourage to write up the big event for the social papers. I wondered exactly what his report would be.

"What a night, huh?" he said in passing.

"You have no idea," at which he looked at me funny.

Carl and Tricia emerged from the family room, followed by Adam, to a full house. They greeted guests as they came in, quite a few of them bodies I hadn't seen in years. Most of them didn't recognize me unless my name was used. I saw a few people turn their heads, look me up and down, and then turn back, unamused.

Adam drifted to my side and brought me a flute of champagne. "So, how's this workin' for ya?" he asked with a smile, pointing to all the well-dressed, highly proper people gathered around.

I couldn't help but like the guy. I took a gulp, clinked my glass with his, and said, "Boffo. You?"

He put his head back and roared, a deep, real, thunderous laugh that became infectious. I laughed along with him, with gusto. No more ladylike chuckles. This was a gut laugh, and one I needed and could not stop. Dave had gotten up to make a speech, and the entire yard turned to look at us. "Sorry," Adam said to the crowd, "But this lady is hilarious!"

I thought Maggie would faint. Lacey had her hand over her mouth and Carl grinned and winked at me. Tricia was in shock. My mother was nowhere to be seen.

"My, this is a happy occasion, isn't it?" said Dave. "Thank you all for coming. My little girl is going to be married tomorrow. I couldn't have picked a better guy."

"Oh, but *she* did," said Adam under his breath. I turned to him, but he pointed his nose back to Dave.

Tricia stood by Dave. "A toast—to Carl and Tricia."

I stifled a fit of giggles because this situation had become so incongruous. I didn't know what to do, and I didn't care.

"How in the hell is this going to end?" I asked out of the side of my mouth.

"Happily ever after?" he raised his glass to mine. We each took a slug.

Carl came over to us. "Adam?"

"Carl?"

They laughed and shook hands. Carl's phone dinged. He read the message and looked around. "Excuse me," he said and grabbed Tricia, who stood behind him and showed her his phone. Her eyes grew wide. "Tonight? It has to be tonight?" Carl grabbed her and they went inside.

"Ah, more intrigue," Adam smiled lopsidedly and gulped down more champagne.

"That looked suspiciously like a covert action. Is the world ending?" I asked.

"Dave's is, I'm guessing."

"What? You mean he's a spy and his cover's blown?" I continued the game.

"Something like that, I gather. Lacey filled me in on some drama."

"Oh? Is this a murder mystery? Aren't they passé?"

Adam smiled. "I'm afraid this is real. Hang on, this is going to get bumpy."

So I suspect.

"Tricia, we have guests. We can't just disappear," Maggie said as she entered the family room, where one of the caterers directed us at Tricia's request. Dave stood behind Maggie and said, "Sit down, Maggie. This is not like Tricia, so it must be important." She looked at Adam. "Why are you here?" She said it like Adam was a homeless person, or maybe a trash collector. I couldn't resist. "He's my date," I said. Tricia looked at me and frowned. I crossed my eyes at her.

"This looks like a family matter. Shall we?" Adam extended his elbow to me, and I took it. He started to skip into the living room, and I skipped, too. And laughed. I introduced him to people I knew as 'Tricia's friend'. He was comfortable with everyone and eased into the party as though he had been coming here for years. I had secret names for people that described them perfectly: names I had kept to myself like the Terminator, Ladykiller, Twinkletoes, God's Gift, and Humble Pie. I whispered them to him knowing he would get the meaning immediately.

This was a night to remember, and it hadn't even started yet.

About half an hour later Trish, Carl and Dave came out of the family room. All but Maggie. Dave looked at me and cocked his head back to the family room. I followed directions and went in.

"Nice party, Maggie," I said.

"And you've ruined it."

"Exactly how did I do that?"

"The dress, putting ideas in her head about defying me . . ."

"Oh, I think Tricia can think for herself."

" . . . this sham of a marriage," she continued.

"Sham of a marriage? Aren't you calling the kettle black?" I wasn't sure which marriage she alluded to yet. She stared at me. "Come off it, Maggie. I know yours is not a marriage made in heaven. You married Dave because you couldn't have Arthur. You've loved him all these years, haven't you?"

"And you stole him from me." Her voice was raised, venomous, spitting.

"No, Maggie. I didn't." I kept my voice quiet and reserved. "He made a choice. When I asked him home for Christmas that year, you met. He was nice enough to introduce you to Dave, and Dave fell for you hook, line, and sinker. Arthur would not have made you happy."

"And I suppose your marriage was made in heaven?" she sneered.

"Maybe. Or as close as you can get. I was happy with him, with our life together. But, Maggie, we never had children." I tried to smile but I'm afraid it came out a grimace. I was trying to show her how she had won that one. "But now that's over, and if it's possible, I am just as happy, but maybe in a different way."

"With the handyman?" she sneered.

I didn't need to tell her he was actually an architect with a Masters' Degree in Environmental Design. It was none of her business. "Yes, maybe," I smiled, "with the handyman."

"Good God, have you no standards anymore?"

"Yes, but they are my own, not yours, not Mother's, not Arthur's. I do what I want." I smiled at her, for the first time feeling sorry for her and her empty shell of a life. The words flew out, and they were true. "What about you, Maggie? What are you going to do?"

"Do? About what?"

It was no use. I knew with everything I had that she could no longer live the life she once had. My buyout would lower their income, and Tricia's manipulations had decimated their upwardly-mobile direction. There would be no more social events at which she ruled as top dog, and certainly no campaign for District Attorney.

Me neither, for that matter, but that was my choice. Maggie didn't make choices. She apparently never had, except to bully her way into outcomes that would make her the winner.

Maggie looked out the window at all their friends in her award-winning garden, her happy daughter, and her husband, the father of the bride, with his jacket off and his tie loosened, a beer in his hand. "This is the worst day of my life."

Really? Losing your son isn't right up there?

With nothing left to add, I decided to go join them, and apparently she followed me. Two minutes later she was at my side at the back of the crowd.

"Speech! Speech!" The crowd wanted to hear from Tricia and Carl. Tricia took the mic. "Carl, you know I love you. I've always loved you. I've known you since you and Eric became friends. You became a member of this family long before we started to get together." The crowd chuckled. "Tomorrow is a big day, and as my Aunt Jen just advised me, marriage should be for one reason only. You marry only the person you cannot live without for the rest of your life." A heavy sigh and some groans wafted overhead.

"But." She turned to Carl, who graciously held out his arms to the crowd and nodded. "Go ahead," he shouted. "You won't hurt my feelings."

The crowd roared.

"But . . . it's not you." Carl put on a sad clown face, his lower lip extending down his chin. There was not a whisper heard. The crowd froze.

"The love of my life is here. Adam, where are you?"

"Here, Zelda!" Adam bounced forward to Tricia who embraced him and gave him a big kiss. "Everyone, meet Adam, who tomorrow will be Mr. Tricia Putnam."

Maggie folded flat on the grass. I had seen it so many times in the movies that it seemed comical. Mother appeared at my side in an instant. "Leave her alone," she whispered to me. "She'll wake up any moment and be embarrassed by complete strangers. It's best if we just pretend we didn't see it and focus on something else. Let her get her composure." We moved a few feet to our left and turned our bodies away. Mother escorted me further down the yard. "One more display for attention and I'd have to do something. That girl has had way too many people catering to her, and I'm one of them. It's about time she looked after herself."

"Mother, this has been a rough night for her. I'm not sure I could have withstood everything she has."

She stopped and turned to me. "Look what *you* have withstood. What your father and I did, what Maggie's done, Dave doing nefarious things, and Tricia skulking around like Mata Hari trying to respect everyone and almost screwing up the entire deal."

"You knew?"

"Of course I knew. I watched it all unfold. It was I who put the idea in Arthur's head to leave her the ten shares and a few notes of things that Arthur suspected. Arthur knew something was wrong but couldn't put his finger on it, and he was too ill to pursue it. He knew I had no respect for Dave, so I wouldn't defend him. I did my own snooping and came up with a few nuggets I fed back to him, which gave him the bigger picture. I suspect he passed it all on to Tricia along with the shares, and I believe she did exactly what he expected her to." She looked at me. "Even Choyou helped. She tracked down some papers Arthur had hidden in the trunk of that jalopy of his."

"Why not me?"

"Because Maggie is your sister, and you're too nice." She looked at me thoroughly. At my hair my body, my clothes, and my feet. "At least you were. Now you're strong. You can do anything you set your mind to. I'm proud of you."

"Thank you. Can I ask you something else?"

"You may." Some things never change.

"Why was Arthur paying for La Jolla Haven?"

"He wasn't."

"I saw the payments, Mother. He paid it every month."

"Yes, he did. Because he managed to get a long-term insurance policy for him as his father-in-law under the firm plan. He paid the bill and I reimbursed him."

"Oh."

"Anything else?" Her eyes challenged me.

"Yes. Was a boy or a girl?"

Mother's lips trembled. "I don't know. I didn't ask." She threaded her arm through mine and started to walk. "Arthur thought it was a girl. I don't know if your father told him that or if he just imagined it. He told me that one day after he'd had a lot of scotch and you were upstairs crying when Maggie told us she was pregnant."

Electrical shocks wound through my body. "He knew?"

She bowed her head. "It was not one of your father's finest moments." She lowered herself onto a white wooden bench under the avocado tree and sighed.

"Arthur came to the house before he asked you to marry him and asked for our blessing. Your father proceeded to tell him about your past, or his version of it. Arthur, to his credit, listened quietly, stood up, and walked out. We thought that was the end of it. An hour later you called to tell us you were engaged."

"So he knew all along."

All that time wasted worrying and keeping secrets. He loved me no matter what.

"Now," she stood and linked her arm through mine. "Maggie's going to need you once I'm gone. You are the Executor of my estate, and you can deliver the funds any way you like. You can help them or not, your choice. Frankly, I think Tricia is being overly generous. I wouldn't have. She got the niceness from you, I think." She winked at me. "You'll do the right thing."

The day had been long, the night even longer.

And tomorrow was the wedding.

Chapter Fifty-Nine

I DROVE STRAIGHT TO BRUCE'S AND FILLED HIM IN ON CURRENT EVENTS. I told him about the baby, about Arthur, about everything. He listened quietly and absorbed every word. On my third glass of Sauvignon Blanc I found myself reacting, coming out of what I knew was a bit of shock. He had let me tell the story, his hands clasped between his knees, his head down, paying attention to every word.

"And then my mother tells me she's proud of me! Can you believe it? Why did I have to wait fifty-eight years and go through hell to get it?"

He looked up for the first time. His face turned to mine in the twilight, his voice low. "Maybe because you're finally showing your true colors." He sat up and took a gulp of his beer. "Look, I don't know who you were all these years, but I like the woman you've become. You're real. I know you. I'm not sure I would have known the Jen Conrad everyone talks about. Hell, I'm not sure I would have liked her." He grimaced. "Sorry, but I have to be honest here. I don't like your sister because she's only interested in impressing people. She's complete veneer."

"Whoa," I said as I held my hand up.

"I know she's your sister. I'm well aware of that. But I don't like her. She's crass, she's patronizing, and she's rude. I can't stand her, and I'd prefer not to have anything to do with her. That's my choice. But you don't have that choice. I understand that." He looked over at the big window and his back yard, which he continued to maintain meticulously. "But if we are going to have a relationship, and I mean a real man/woman relationship, I have to be clear. I don't have time to spend with people I don't understand and don't appreciate. Time is expensive real estate. I choose only to spend time with people I connect with."

"Time is expensive real estate," I repeated. "That's fairly passionate."

"I am passionate. My experience with my own father taught me that. I don't have time to waste with someone who consistently disapproves and is disappointed in me for the choices I have made." He smiled.

I had been listening while gazing into my glass. I looked up to find him staring at me. His face turned ruddy and blotchy. He had tried hard to send a message. But he hadn't finished.

"If you haven't figured it out yet I'm crazy about you. I am prepared to wait as long as you need to. Just to see you every day is enough for now. Work out what you need to work out and know that I am always here. But I want the real you, not some fabrication made by your mother and a sister who is competing with you."

"Competing?"

"Yes, love, competing." He smiled at me. "Think about it."

We sat in silence for a bit. "My mother is dying," I said.

"Jesus. And the hits just keep on coming."

"Not really." I smiled. "Life is a process, and she's nearing the end of hers. She's handling it gracefully and has arranged everything so that it's easy and dignified. I'm thinking of ways to help. Apparently I'm in charge."

"I'm sure you are." He pulled another beer out of the refrigerator and came back. "What can I do?"

I put my hand on his cheek. "You are so dear. Give me some more time."

"Of course."

"Come with me to the wedding tomorrow."

"Wouldn't miss it. It should be quite a show." He turned my hand over and kissed my palm.

I smiled. "Some day will you tell me about your father?" Something clicked. "Wait. Miller. You mean your father is Frederick Miller? Who built the Sports Arena, Symphony Towers, and the airport?"

"The one and only."

"Jesus."

"Yeah."

The wedding was to be at sunset at Heritage Park. I had the morning free. Lupe had the store covered. She had Catie in her little basket, and I wanted to gather a few more things to sell. So far I had made a small fortune selling my bags, shoes, and hats. Now I was on to the gowns and other clothing I knew I would never wear.

I was knee deep in textiles and memories when I heard the doorbell ring. I opened the door to find Dave standing on the bricks, starched white shirt open at the collar and khaki pants, holding a large manila envelope. "Can I come in?" he asked.

I stepped aside and opened the door. Dave looked at my empty living room and back at me. "Changes."

I pointed toward the family room, and he went in.

"Can I get you anything?"

He shook his head. "I have a confession to make. Several, in fact."

"Go on."

"It seems my daughter is brilliant. I didn't give her enough credit." He shook his head and looked up at me.

I stayed silent. I wanted to scream at him for Arthur's sake, but, honestly, what was the point?

"I wanted you to know Arthur was out of this. It didn't start until after he was really ill."

I continued to stare at him, afraid to speak and break whatever relationship we had. I had already risked too much. I finally managed to say, "I'm not sure what you are talking about."

He handed me the envelope. "The audit has not been completed, but this is a down payment on what you are going to be owed. I wanted this done on my watch; the only decent thing I could think of to do. As of tomorrow, Tricia owns what is now to be called Putnam and Associates, and I'm out. I couldn't let you wait any longer once I found out that Maggie had engineered having the audit postponed."

"Maggie?"

"Yes. And she apparently tried to bribe a judge. She needs help, Jen."

I looked at him and didn't respond. The man I thought I knew was far gone.

"That's all I wanted to say. Maggie and I will work things out. She's stopped seeing her therapist, you know, so I have my work cut out for me." He smiled and started to walk toward the front door.

"You know, I could be disbarred, even jailed if any of this came to light, but my daughter has saved me. And for that, I credit you. Your goodness and sense of honor has rubbed off on her, despite her parents." He looked at me from under his bushy brows. "And for that I thank you." He turned and left.

I poured myself a vodka. Another chapter closed.

I opened the envelope to find a transaction report telling me that a huge mountain of money had been poured into my personal account.

Jade had gone on ahead with Lacey and Trish to the art park to make sure the site was ready for the wedding. I volunteered to go get Iris.

Terrence opened the door. "Hello, Terrence. We're off to a wedding. Is Mrs. Anderson ready?"

"I'll just go and check." Terence was in an Oahu shirt, cargo shorts and flip flops. Iris loved that. She called him Ohana Jeeves.

I walked into the parlor to wait, admiring the artwork and framed photographs. A few minutes later, Terrence came into the parlor, back straight, gait steady. His face had turned white. "Please . . . um . . . come with me." He slowly ascended the curved staircase and opened the door to Iris's bedroom. He stepped aside to let me enter.

Her room was a study in mint green with crisp white accents and fresh flowers. Her scent permeated the room. The curtains were open, allowing the sunlight in. Iris lay on the bed under a fluffy white eiderdown, a biography propped open face down on her chest as though resting between pages. Her breakfast tray lay to the side.

Her blue eyes were open.

I approached the bed and touched her arm. She was cold. I hung my head.

"Okay," I said. "Okay." I closed her eyes, giving her cheek a quick brush. "Okay."

I waited a moment. "Terrence, it appears we have to make a few calls."

"Yes."

I turned to find a tear running down his cheek.

"It was a good death."

"Yes."

"No pain."

"No."

"No fuss."

"No."

"Just gone." My voice squeaked, and I cleared my throat.

He turned and left the room.

I called the paramedics, who came within ten minutes and took her away. I did not allow them to put her in a body bag while still in her own house, giving her a last piece of dignity. I don't know why that was important.

Terrence appeared by my side and handed me an envelope. Iris had made her own arrangements and had given the instructions to her staff, along with generous checks and permission to stay in the house as long as they needed.

Iris was gone.

Chapter Sixty

"THOUGHT YOU WERE BRINGING IRIS?" SAID HELEN AS SHE SPOTTED ME looking for Bruce, waiting for the guests to arrive.

"She decided to stay home and rest. I sat with her for a while; she insisted I leave her. She's really very tired."

"Expect the hourglass is running out." Helen said.

Silence.

"I should go to her," said Jade.

"No. No, you stay. It's what she wants." I said, palm out.

"If you're sure."

"I'm sure. Terrence is with her and she is well taken care of."

Bruce sidled up to me, all prettied up in a suit and festive tie. If I wasn't so shaken up, I would have been impressed. "Buy me a drink, sailor?" I said as I started toward the bar. I heard the others laugh and even heard a wolf whistle.

"What's wrong?" Bruce read my mood through the humor.

"I went to pick up Iris, and Bruce, she's dead." My eyes filled.

He took my arm and we went for a walk. There were too many people around. "Does anybody know?"

"No, Iris would hate to have the day ruined because of her. She got such a kick out of last night. She loved Adam and approved highly." My breath caught as I tried to control my emotions. "She was just . . . laying there with a smile."

"That's Iris," he said.

"I closed her eyes." I collapsed against his chest.

"God, Jen." We swayed back and forth a few minutes.

"It seems sort of insulting to be sad, doesn't it?" His voice vibrated through my body, and I liked it.

I took a deep breath. "You're right. Iris would hate that this wedding could be turned into a wake. Let's make it a celebration, shall we?"

Bruce leaned in to kiss me. "Yes."

I liked that, too.

We sat behind Dave and Maggie on the covered aluminum chairs arranged at Heritage Park on a beautiful afternoon. Tricia had made specific arrangements to suit her new groom, and I saw Maggie's huge expensive hat shake. She did not speak to me or nod to me, but I noticed she plastered on a smile for everyone else. She sat next to Mother, who grinned broadly coming up the aisle on the arm of a very handsome groomsman. She had feathers coming off her hat that blew in the slight wind of an early November day.

She looked happier than Maggie.

Lacey came up the aisle in the gray dress, and it looked fabulous on her, even though she wore combat boots. I stole a look at Maggie; her lipstick disappeared between her lips clamped so tight I thought maybe she had lost her teeth. Lacey looked so happy for her friend I wondered if she thought she were the bride. Then I saw her look at the new CFO, Ray something, who stood as a groomsman next to Carl, who, awkward as it might seem, acted as Adam's best man. Lacey and Ray both blushed and looked at the floor.

Aha. Iris would have picked up on this last night.

This isn't your normal wedding.

I thought Maggie might faint when Tricia came up the aisle with Adam on her arm. They both grinned and laughed out loud all the way down the aisle. She looked beautiful in the Barbie dress with the long pointed sleeves and the mandarin collar. Instead of the tiara and veil Maggie had ordered, she wore a ring of fresh flowers around her head with pastel ribbons flowing down her back.

She and Adam wore no shoes, which was perfect because we had lost two inches at the hem with my steaming and maneuvering; the flaw I had worried over did not exist. I had to laugh out loud. Maggie threw daggers at me, and Mother smiled politely, but her eyes gleamed.

Carpe Diem.

Tricia and Adam had created not a traditional ceremony but a more eclectic one with poems and music that were decidedly not traditional. Maggie grew smaller and smaller in her seat. I knew she wanted to fade away into the grass like Alice in Wonderland. When the priest asked the crowd to sing along, she refused. Dave, however, gave it a go and got into the spirit of the occasion. Maggie sat like a stone statue and refused to take part in such an undignified process.

They danced back up the aisle after the pronouncement, and the crowd clapped and shouted their joy and started to follow the bride and groom, emptying into the aisles together, dancing along behind.

Maggie, the honored Mother of the Bride, was the last one in the procession.

A steel drum band had started calypso music from the back of the large lawn, and guests moved to the other side where they found large tables loaded with food and small tables set up for groups of four, six, or eight.

I knew that Maggie had planned for a head table to be elevated above the crowd, a table for the cake, and an order of toasts and speeches as in a traditional wedding. We found a much more casual set up.

"But where do we *sit*?" I heard Maggie whining to Tricia as I approached to give the new couple a hearty hug.

"Anywhere you like," said Tricia, opening her arms to the crowd of tables. "Sit with friends, sit with strangers, sit anywhere you like. This is very casual. Have fun!"

Adam held two shots of tequila and gave one to Tricia.

Maggie looked like she had been shot.

"Oh, go on, Margaret, loosen up. It's your daughter's wedding." Mother stood at our side now and turned imperiously to the waiter. "Bring us ten more of those," as she pointed to the shot glasses that were, at the moment, upside down. "Better yet, bring an entire bottle and a dozen glasses. Keep them coming."

He grinned. "Yes, ma'am."

Tricia and Adam turned to greet others behind them. Boisterous laughter eclipsed what Mother said to Maggie.

I heard Dave's laughter from far away. He collapsed against someone who had told him something and three other men laughed along with him. Dave took off his jacket and put it on a chair.

"Look, even Dave is having fun," Mother said to me.

He would, I thought. He just dodged a huge bullet, thanks to his daughter.

Maggie collapsed into a chair and put her head in her hands. Mother looked at her a moment and said, "I think we'll just go on and have our own fun." The waiter approached with a full bottle and a tray of shot glasses. "Now, that's the ticket! Tricia?" She waved Tricia and Adam over. "Pour, please, um . . . " she stooped to look at his name badge, "Juan. And keep it coming. We have a lot of people to loosen up." Juan grinned and expertly lined up all the shot glasses and poured at one swipe.

"To life," said Mother, raising her glass, "and to Tricia and Adam. May you live long, happily, and passionately. Welcome to this crazy family." She nodded to Adam, downed the shot, turned the glass upside down and slammed it on the table.

Bruce and I looked at each other, clicked glasses, and threw our heads back, the warmth dripped all the way down and we grinned at each other. To life.

To Iris.

Juan poured another round and I kicked off my shoes.

Mother never ceases to amaze me.

The Sticks Gang took a table to ourselves, and, along with Lupe's Catie, who wore a hand-knit dress made of the same yarn as the bride's dress, enjoyed ourselves immensely in the twilight. Adam spent some time with us; he and Robert traded one-liners and seemed to enjoy each other, and Adam kissed hands and bowed to the entranced Helen, Choyou, and Suzanne. He thanked them for turning his design into a reality, no matter who wore it. Jade spent most of her time dancing on the grass and meeting people her own age.

I felt Iris with us at every laugh, every story, and already missed her.

The sun started to set, the most important people to Tricia hung in at the party, and the third-tier guests had gone. Dave got Maggie off her chair and tried to dance with her, but her heels kept getting stuck in the grass. "Take 'em off, Mom," yelled Tricia, and her friends joined in. She had no choice but to take her shoes off and dance with her husband. She looked like a rag doll.

Bruce had me in a clinch and I felt happier than I had in a long time. I really connected with this man. He understood me, flaws and all, and still accepted me, even loved me. I smiled at him, and he smiled back. "Want to sell me your house?" I asked.

He threw his head back and roared in laughter. "If that's what you're offering up today, yes." He laughed again. "I was rather hoping for a bit more of a sale, if you know what I mean, but I'll take it."

I looked around at my new friends, my new life, my new mother, and what was left of my sister. I saw the group laughing, relaxed, and making notes to tell Iris about the party. I made a note to find out more about Jade, who, for some reason, never disclosed anything about herself. Now that Iris was gone, I wondered what her next step would be. And Renee? What's her next chapter? I'd have to wait and find out on both counts.

Acknowledgments

Many, many thanks go to a team around me who made this possible:

To my husband, who unfailingly supported me through the process and cheered me on; the Mavens, who stood behind me and enthusiastically followed the process; Lois Gordon for her common sense, proofing and editing skills, and invaluable questions; Shayla Raquel for her inventive and creative marketing efforts; and Melinda Martin for her perfection and professionalism in the art of actually producing a book.

My thanks are immeasurable.

ABOUT THE AUTHOR

Kathy Weyer

KATHY WEYER IS AN AUTHOR, ARTIST, AND ADVOCATE. AFTER RETIRING AS a human resources executive in Corporate America, she committed her time to helping others through volunteer efforts, including animal and children's welfare, literary advocacy with Palm Springs Library and Read San Diego, and business coaching for women entrepreneurs.

Through her work as a grief and bereavement counselor, Kathy has interviewed hospice patients to record their life stories and is a court-appointed special advocate for children in the foster system. She was awarded first prize (twice) by the Palm Springs Writers Guild for fiction and memoir contests and has been published in several magazines. She is on the board of directors for the Friends of the Palm Springs Library and the Palm Springs Writers Guild.

Despite her busy life, she de-stresses by getting creative with paint, fabric, yarn, paper, and whatever is handy. She lives in Palm Springs with her husband of forty years and their rescued pets. She is the author of *Stitches* and the forthcoming sequels, *Canvas* and *Pages*.

Made in the USA
Las Vegas, NV
03 April 2021